NOBODY'S DARLIN'

DEAD PALMS MC, 1

SARAH BLUE

Cover design - @maldodesigns

Editing - geeky good edits

Chapter art - @brielyasmin

Dead Palms MC

Tallahassee Original

Prez (Kurt) (Alpha)
Dread VP (Alpha)
Smiley (Beta)
Davidson (Beta)
Pipes (Alpha)
Boomerang (Alpha)
Heath (Alpha)
Maverick (Beta)
Ambien (Leon) (Alpha)
Mickey (Alpha)
Jay (Alpha)
Torn (Alpha)
Tank (Alpha)
Blaze (Beta)
Hugh (Beta)

Sweet Butts

Shelby (Beta)
Cora (Beta)
Kim (Beta)
Tammy (Beta)

Newly Patched

Tate (Alpha)
Axel (Beta)
Cash (Alpha)
Atlas (Alpha)
Ink (Alpha)
Doc (Alpha)
Sasquatch (Alpha)
Taz (Beta)
Dutch (Beta)
Tex (Alpha)
Deek (Beta)

Family

Teresa (Omega) - Pack Omega to Prez and Dread - mother to Ambien and Lily

Lily (Omega) - Stepdaughter to Prez and Dread. Biological daughter to Teresa and sister to Ambien. Stepsister to Tate

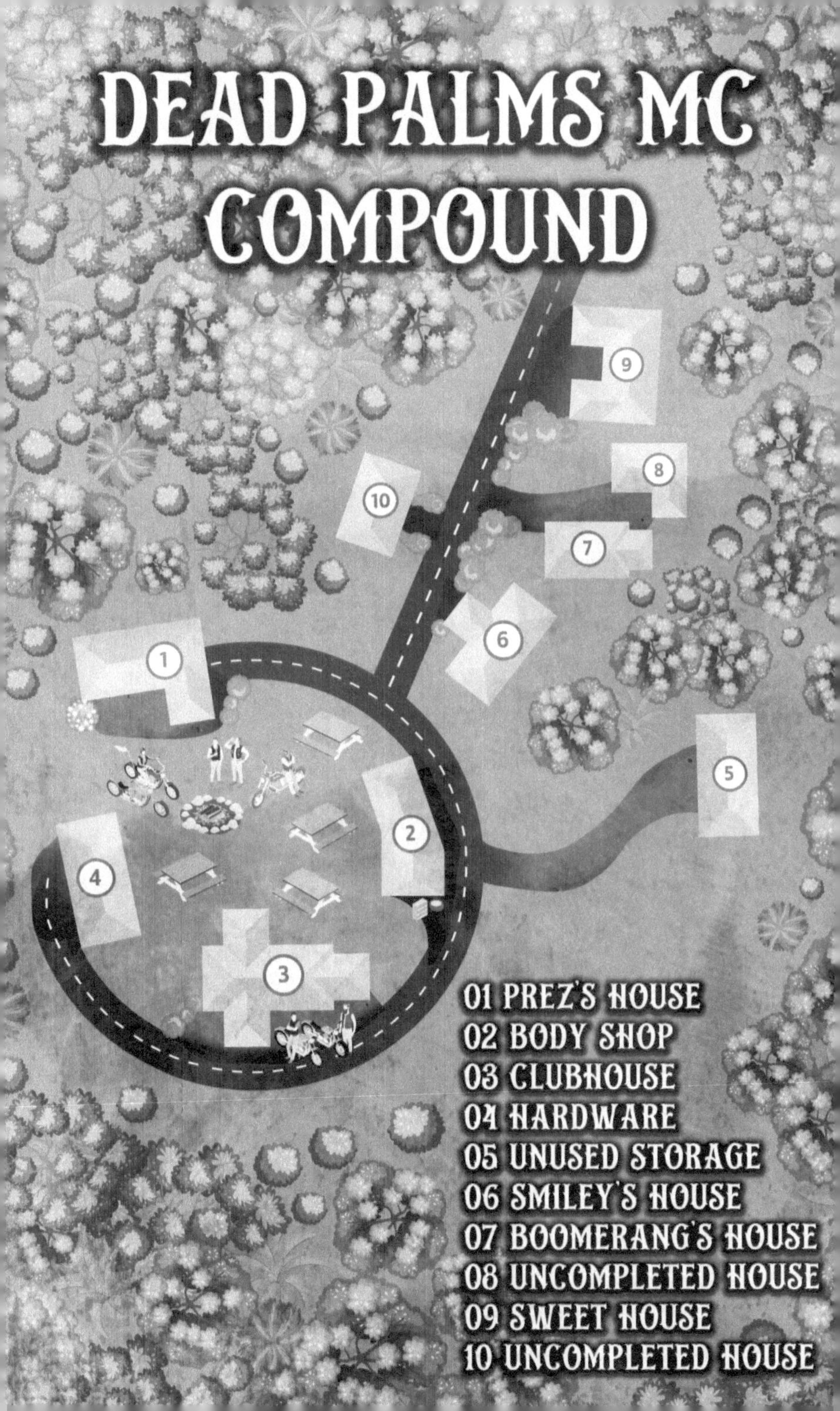

DEAD PALMS MC
COMPOUND
1
2
3
4
5
6
7
8
9
10
01 PREZ'S HOUSE
02 BODY SHOP
03 CLUBHOUSE
04 HARDWARE
05 UNUSED STORAGE
06 SMILEY'S HOUSE
07 BOOMERANG'S HOUSE
08 UNCOMPLETED HOUSE
09 SWEET HOUSE
10 UNCOMPLETED HOUSE

SPOTIFY PLAYLIST

Summertime Sadness – Lana Del Ray
Softcore – The Neighbourhood
Marry The Night – Lady Gaga
Ride – Lana Del Ray
Delicate – Taylor Swift
Howlin' for You – The Black Keys
Ride – Twenty One Pilots
My Oh My – Camila Cabello, DaBaby
The Hills – The Weeknd
Oh Darlin' What Have I Done – The White Buffalo
I WANNA BE YOUR SLAVE – Måneskin
Aerials – System Of A Down
Animal I Have Become – Three Days Grace
Make You Mine – PUBLIC
Bad Things – Machine Gun Kelly, Camila Cabello
I Feel Like I'm Drowning – Two Feet
Your Needs, My Needs – Noah Kahan

Glycerine – Bush
Coming Undone – Korn
Dark Paradise – Lana Del Ray
Nothing's Gonna Hurt You Baby – Cigarettes After Sex
Dollhouse – Melanie Martinez
Do I Wanna Know? – Arctic Monkeys
WASTE – Kxllswxtch
Mount Everest – Labrinth
Baby – Bishop Briggs
The Pinterest Board for Nobody's Darlin'

WHAT IS AN OMEGAVERSE?

An Omegaverse is an alternate universe where humans have a specific designation in a hierarchy based on their biology——**in my series they are not shifters**. You are either an Alpha, Beta or an Omega. Your designation determines specific traits of your physiology and personality.

Alphas tend to be aggressive, they're generally more dominant and hold positions of authority. Many Alphas form packs which increase their wealth and dominance. Alphas have a history of taking advantage of and abusing Omegas. Alphas who are assigned male at birth have a fleshy ring near the base of their penis that swells during intercourse called a knot. It allows them to "lock" into place with an Omega. While Omegas are the most physiologically compatible when it comes to taking an Alpha's knot, Betas (or even Alphas) can take a knot with practice. Female Alphas have a lock that clenches around the penis and holds it inside, female Alphas and male Omegas are a great fit for this. Female Alphas can lock with other designations.

Betas are the closest to everyday humans. Their scent and sense of smell are not as strong as an Alpha or Omegas. They tend to be the most level-headed out of the designations.

Omegas tend to be the softest and most gentle of the designations. Generally, they do not hold positions of power, are homemakers or have positions in lower standing. Their scents are extremely arousing to Alphas. Out of all the designations, Omegas are the most likely to be abused or treated poorly. Alphas have the most opportunity to reproduce with Omegas.

Omegas go through **heat cycles** during which they are the most fertile. At this time they're sensitive to light, noise, and scents. They require the comfort of a nest full of soft fabrics and textures. Their body requires a large amount of sexual stimulation during a heat cycle, and it can last for several days. If the Omega is with an Alpha, their Alpha or Alphas will do everything in their power to make sure they are cared for and comfortable during their heat. Going through a heat cycle as an unbonded Omega can be unsafe for their physical health and sometimes their safety.

CONTENT

Welcome to the Dead Palms MC universe. This is a why choose omegaverse romance. If you haven't read an omegaverse before, I suggest going back and visiting my **What is an Omegaverse page.**

Please note that this is the darkest omegaverse (not dark romance) I have written and to heed the content warnings, which can be found here on my website. wwww.authorsarah blue.com/content-warnings/

To twenty-one-year-old me who hopped on the back of a guy's bike and had the funniest night of your life. You're so lucky you didn't die, you stupid bitch.

ONE
MARIELLI'S MASS

LILY

THE SUDS WASH my sins down the shower drain. The pinkish bubbles swirl in a perfect circle and disappear before my eyes.

It would be like any normal shower if I didn't have a few hundred subscribers watching. I can't hear the dinging of likes, or read the comments over the loud flow of the water, not that the people watching care. They're only here to watch my online personality, Marielli, not me.

I have a few rules when it comes to my lucrative online business. First and foremost, I don't show my face. It's not that I'm ashamed of what I'm doing for money, it's more about my safety. The last thing I need is one of these subscribers trying to find me in real life. In all honesty, it would probably get them killed in the process. This leads me to my other reason for never showing my face. If my family—blood or otherwise—found my channel, I can't even imagine how badly everything would blow up.

My second rule is no personal attachments. I hardly answer messages, and for whatever reason, that seems to make some of my followers even more rabid. It must be the allure of the chase, of what they can't have. Either way, responding to a ton of messages is a lot of work and time that I don't plan on putting into this online persona.

Number three, I'll stop once I meet my quota. Do I have a set number? Not particularly, but I think around a hundred grand is the goal, and I'm just about there. I need a nest egg—no pun intended. While I'm so ready for a nest and pack of my own, this secret bank account is a security blanket that I need to truly commit to a packed lifestyle. I refuse to end up like my mother, not her current life, but the one she had before we found our home with the Dead Palms MC.

I sigh just thinking about it and finish scrubbing up, careful to not bend over or, if I do, I use my long dark hair to cover my face. I cut the water off and grab a towel, standing in front of the camera so they can get a good glance at my wet breasts. They're small by most people's standards, but my followers seem to enjoy my cute little tits well enough.

The phone chimes with tips coming in, and I smile to myself. Every dollar is another step closer to the life I dream about having for myself—which is equally as complicated.

It's not that camming was my only route for income, but it's pretty close. I'm kept close to home at nearly all times, and it's the only way I can make the kind of money I need in such a short amount of time. Plus, why the fuck wouldn't I try to monetize being an Omega before I'm locked down with a pack for the rest of my life?

"Thank y'all so much. Thank you User26738 and AbbyLicks69," I say sweetly off to the side of the camera. I always make my voice a little more wispy when performing. "Mark your calendars for two weeks from now. It's what you've all been waiting for. Make sure you're subscribed to Marielli's Mass," I remind. More hearts pop up on the screen, and I quickly close the stream, putting my phone face down on the counter as I look in the mirror.

I love myself; I love my body, my face, who I am as a person, so I have no problem looking in the mirror. I appreciate this body that is affording me my future life. It's the only way I'll be able to move forward. Not that I have packs lining up for me... well, I would, if it weren't for my stepdad laying down the law that I'm off limits.

I roll my eyes every time I think about it. I use the towel to dry myself off and wrap up my hair before I go into my bedroom to get dressed for the day. It's the club's annual summer bash. They hold it on a different day every year, so they aren't predictable. But this year should be more exciting than others because the nomads are coming.

The Jacksonville chapter got busted and a mix of their old members and other nomads are looking for a new home. It's not like they're a viable option for me, at least not in my parents' eyes. But damn, I could use some more eye candy around here. If they're going to force me to hang around the compound most of the time, the least they could do is initiate some hotter club members.

I choose to dress in a light blue sundress that has spaghetti straps and flares out at the waist. I don't even bother with a bra and just stick with some biker shorts underneath because I know I'll be sweating my fucking soul out. Plus, I need to tamper down my scent slightly around all these feral men.

I constantly have dreams about not hiding my scent and letting them all run a train on me over a picnic table. But that's a complete fantasy. They all abide by the no-touching rule. That is everyone except for one very hot and wild Beta that I know will be here today. I may or may not take extra care when applying my makeup with him in mind. I can't help myself when I decide to shoot him a text. I know I'm not supposed to utilize the guys' phone numbers unless it's an emergency, but I don't care. He's the one person I look forward to seeing at any club event.

Are you coming tonight?

AXEL

You make it really hard to be a gentleman. Yes,
I'll be there tonight.

I bite my lip and smile, I need to find a way to get him alone. We don't text often, but when we do there's always a flirty undertone. Every time we're at a club event together it's like we're two magnets, unable to stay away from each other. Who would have thought out of a club with primarily Alphas the Beta would be the one I was hopelessly pining after?

Knowing how hot it's supposed to be, I keep my makeup simple with just some winged eyeliner, mascara, and a red lip tint. I don't bother with blow drying my hair; I just use a wet brush, knowing that my hair will dry quickly in the summer heat.

Before I leave my room, I take my suppressants by the sink, rub some deodorizer on my body, and slap a hair tie on my wrist. I leave my phone in my room and make my way downstairs.

I can't help the smile that takes over my face when I see my mom on my stepdad's—well, one of my stepdad's—lap. Kurt is the head Alpha of her pack and the Prez of the Dead Palms MC. He's gripping her hip tightly as he kisses the scarred part of her face. Watching him do that small action is like having a fist gripping my heart and squeezing.

It's sweet that he loves her no matter what, but remembering where she got those scars always makes my heart sink. My mother used to be the most beautiful Omega I had ever seen, which is not to say that she's no longer beautiful. But the burn marks on the left side of her face are usually the first thing people notice. Her eyes are still brilliant blue and her blonde hair flows down her back.

Every day I wish I looked like her and not so much like my sperm donor. Luckily for me, my mom doesn't see me that way.

"Hey, sweetie, we're just about to take the food out," she says.

"Oh, is that what we were about to do?" Kurt teases, kissing her face multiple more times.

"Kurt, stop or we'll never make your party," she chastises.

"Tell me how I'm supposed to go to the party when I've got my beautiful Omega on my lap?" Kurt jokes. I smile, not only because my stepdad loves my mom so much, but because only we get to see this side of Kurt. Outside these walls? In front of his club? He's a different man, but with his family, he is so loving and tender.

My Mom's other Alpha, Dread (I still don't know the man's real name), tugs her off Kurt's lap and wraps his arms around her chest.

"There, now you can go," he says, making my mom giggle.

"You sure you still want to be with this asshole, T? I could still kill him," Kurt jokes.

"All bark, no bite," my mom retorts, and Kurt nuzzles her neck with no care in the world that Dread's face is right there.

"I'll show you fuckin' bite, Teresa, don't push me," he taunts, rubbing his nose along the scar tissue on the side of her face.

"Gross, you three," I tease as I pour a cup of coffee for myself, which is more creamer than coffee.

"You'll understand one day," my mom sighs with a beaming smile in my direction.

I want to say something sassy about how the fuck am I supposed to understand when no one in this house will let me go out and explore or find the pack of my dreams? I already know how Kurt feels about it. He's made it clear. But maybe I just need to push harder.

"Lily, hun, can you help me with this?" Kurt asks. I put my coffee down and follow him into the living room. I love this house. It's so cozy and sweet; you can tell Kurt decorated it with my mom in mind. It's more reminiscent of a high-end cabin in the woods than any home I've seen in Florida.

"What's up, Pop?" I ask him. He smiles at me, his sun-worn skin crinkling at the edges of his eyes, which are a deep shade of brown. He's wearing a hat—he always does, now that he's gone bald—but his black and gray speckled beard is still going strong.

"I need you to stay close to the girls at the party," he says.

"You don't trust your guys?"

"There's going to be a lot of new blood tonight. Men that I don't trust enough around my daughter." My heart beats rapidly in my chest. It's hard for me to defy Kurt, the streaming has been my only major defiance ever. How can I be hurtful to someone who raised me as his own and loved me deeper than my biological father ever did? My sense of loyalty runs deep when it comes to Kurt and the club.

"What about the patched guys?" I ask. Kurt gives me a stern look and then nods.

"Fine. Your brother will be there, anyway." I smile even bigger at hearing that. Leon has been gone for weeks on club business. I've missed him. While being with my mom and her pack brings me comfort, Leon is my true home. Sometimes Leon can feel more like a second father than a brother to me, but I wouldn't change it. I just selfishly wish he was around more, but his responsibilities over the last year have taken him away from the compound more often than not.

Kurt holds out his arms and gives me the much needed hug I'm itching for. It's not even in the realm of the same way he touches my mother. It's just like any dad hugging his daughter, only I need affection to survive. Maybe that's dramatic, but it feels like it's getting worse lately.

Kurt inhales, clearing his throat before taking a step back. "After the party, I think we need to have some serious discussions about finding you a pack."

When I roll my eyes, he grabs my chin. "Don't you go

rolling your fuckin' eyes at me. You're turning twenty-one in a few weeks. We should have started lookin' before now, but shit's been busy."

"There are dozens of guys outside that would make a fine pack," I say, reiterating how I've always felt.

Axel is truly the only one I have in mind when I say that. Part of me wishes I didn't have such an immense crush on him, but I can't help myself. Maybe it's because we're forbidden to be together and the Beta doesn't seem to give a shit, flirting with me at every opportunity. But I want him... no, I need him.

I'm open to other guys in the MC as well, especially since there are about to be some new patched members. I'm not meant for some rich, boring-ass pack. Listen, don't get me wrong, I love money, nice things, being doted on, but more than anything, I want some adventure. I want to actually live. I don't want to be tucked away in a big house with my only purpose being to pop out babies and keep the house clean. That's not me and it never will be.

"I want better for you, Lily. I want you to have the world," he says. And I know he isn't trying to be a dick. My stepdad genuinely thinks this place isn't good enough for me.

"What about my mom? Is she not good enough to leave this place?" I ask, knowing I'm being a petulant brat.

"You know damn fuckin' well your mom is too good for this place, but she's mine, and there's no changin' that now. You have a chance, Lily. A real fuckin' chance to have whatever you want in this world. I promise, things are calming down with the club. We'll make finding you a pack a priority," he vows.

"Okay."

He flicks my chin, and I scoff at him. "Go help your mom, yeah?"

"Yeah," I reply before walking away, feeling nowhere closer to getting what I want. Maybe I have to take things into my own hands like I did when I started Marielli's Mass. I'm just not sure how to make that happen with a Beta; it would be so much easier if I already had Alphas who were a part of the club in mind. I smirk to myself as I go back to the kitchen. My mom and Dread grab handfuls of food, and I do the same. Dread walks in between us as we enter the square.

The square is what we call the vacant area between the body shop, the clubhouse, and Dead Palms Hardware. The two businesses are owned and run completely by the club. And I'm sure they all launder a fuck-ton of money; significantly more than what they bring in because they're not even open half the time. I'm not an idiot, I know the club does some very illegal things, but being the Prez's stepdaughter doesn't make me privy to that information. Hell, even as an ol' lady and a bonded Omega, my mother isn't allowed to know anything about club business.

The gates are closed for non-members today, but during the week they're periodically open to where people can come and go to the businesses. But most people don't come, unless they have some affiliation to the club, or have been local for a long time. It's the way the club likes it.

The prospects and a few of the younger, patched-in guys are helping out by setting up the tents. The sweet butts are also contributing by dropping off food on the long rectangular tables, and I smile at each of them. They are the only friends I have; I'm not sure how tv shows depict club life, but in reality, we're a family. Sure, there's always drama with a smaller group like ours, but we all depend on and love each other.

Dread kisses my mom's head and whispers in her ear. She smiles to herself and shakes her head. Dread is different from Kurt, what you see is what you get. His only soft spot is for my mother. I know that he only cares for me because I'm a piece of her, and I'm okay with that. I don't have the same relationship with him and that's okay. To be honest, the man still scares the shit out of me. He's a huge Alpha, and well... he didn't get the road name Dread without reason.

"You want me to fix you a plate?" my mom asks, and I

politely shake my head. "You need to be eating more, sweetie. You're too thin," she comments.

I'm not too thin; I'm just extremely toned because running is one of the few things I'm allowed to do around here. And lately, I've felt the need to expel more energy than usual.

"Where's Leon?" she asks.

"You mean, Ambien?" I scoff. My brother getting the road name Ambien has been the highlight of my whole life, and it takes everything in me to not laugh whenever I hear it.

She smacks me lightly with the dish towel she's holding. "You leave your brother alone. He's proud of his name."

"They named him after a drug that helps you sleep," I deadpan.

"Well, he doesn't sleep. They're lucky to have him work so much at night," she responds, giving me the scolding mom look.

I hold up my hands in mock surrender, and she rolls her eyes as she continues to get the barbecue set up.

The purr of multiple engines alerts us to some of the guys arriving. My brother is one of the first headed towards us. He's wearing a black t-shirt, his black cut, and jeans. Once he parks his ride, he automatically wraps his arms around my mom, making her grin from ear to ear before he kisses the scarred side of her face.

"Hey, Ma."

"Hey, baby," she greets, turning around to get a good look at him. Her hand cups his face, and he grimaces. "Leon, have you been sleeping at all?"

My brother removes her hand and gives her a look that says 'don't baby me in front of the club'. She scoffs and shakes her head.

"What?! No hello for me?" I jest.

My brother just rolls his eyes, wraps me up in his arms, and lifts me off my feet in a tight hug. He nearly takes away my breath with how tight the hug is, and I smile against his shoulder. I hold onto him just as tight, inhaling the leather of his cut and his comforting Alpha scent. It's not gross like you would think, it's just comforting. Leon is five years older than me and has always taken care of me in any way I needed. His designation wasn't surprising, and it only made him even more overbearing.

"How've you been, Lil?" he asks. Dread calls my mother's name, and she gives us a soft smile before walking away.

"Bored out of my fucking mind," I tell him plainly.

He kicks at the patch of sandy grass beneath us and exhales. "Well, that should be changin' soon, right?"

"What do you mean?"

"Kurt said he'd be findin' you a pack soon," he replies.

"I can find my own pack. Fuck you, very much."

He holds his hands up in mock surrender. "Listen, Lily, it's your life. I just want you to be happy."

"Just as long as this club isn't a part of my life, right?"

"It's dangerous. You need to get out of here, Lily. I mean it," he says, making me want to smack him across the back of the head, but I shove down the instinct. There's no point in arguing.

"Okay, but what about you?" I ask him, wiggling my eyebrows. "Any special person caught your eye lately?"

"There's always a special person, if you know what I mean," he replies with a wink.

"You're gross." I grimace.

"You started it. But there really might be someone special."

"Are they here or in Georgia?" I ask, wondering if a girl is why he's been gone longer than usual this time.

"Like I'd tell you, if it works out, you'll be the first to know."

"You're so boring. If you're going to come back home you should at least come back with some good gossip," I tease, making him laugh.

"Oh, so not happy to see me, huh? You just want the gossip?"

"Hell yes I do, it gets boring in my ivory tower."

He rolls his eyes but taps his chin. "I did hear a rumor that I have a present for you," he says, and my smile widens as he takes the handful of peach taffy out of his pocket. I hold out my hands as he pours the candy into them.

"Thank you. I love these," I groan, glad that my dress has pockets as I stash the sticky goodness away to eat for later.

"Kurt's been stressed lately?" Leon asks, grabbing some food off the table and shoving it in his mouth.

"I guess a little about the club growing, Who all's coming, anyway?" I ask, wondering if he will give me more insight than Kurt did.

"About fifteen of em' comin'. Ever since the Jacksonville chapter went down, there's a lot of men needin' a new club. We need to impress them," he answers quietly so that only I can hear. "Where the fuck is the keg?" he questions, looking around. The two prospects sitting at the picnic table opposite of us stand up quickly.

Two prospects I don't know the names of look at my brother wide-eyed. "On it, Ambien," they say, and I do my best not to laugh. I'm proud to report that I succeed.

"You waiting for me to stick a finger in your ass or some-thing? Hurry the fuck up," my brother barks at them, and I smile to myself. I love seeing how much the club respects him. My brother kisses the side of my head and abandons me to help the two idiots with the keg.

Bored, I place a few pieces of watermelon, cheese, and a handful of pretzels on my plate. The sun is scorching, and thank fuck, they put out multiple tents this year. I'm sweating and praying for a light breeze when I pop a piece of watermelon into my mouth. The juices drip down my forearm, and I quickly lick them up.

"Hey, Lily," a familiar voice says. I look up and sure enough, it's my favorite Beta and long-time crush, Axel.

My perfume automatically pours out of me, and a smirk takes over his face. I'm starting to wonder if he's torturing me on purpose without any true intentions of moving past flirting. If he made an actual move, I'd pounce on him in a heartbeat. It's hard to tell with him, if he flirts because it's fun or if he wants more. I desperately want more.

"Hey, Axel."

He grabs the rest of the watermelon in my hand and pops it into his mouth. I swear I nearly watch it melt on his tongue before he swallows. He gives me a grin as he leans down on the table with his knuckles pressing against the wood. He has the prettiest blue eyes, and they glisten with mischief as he winks at me.

God, I want him. I've been pining over him for an embarrassingly long time, watching as he comes and goes from the compound. He gives me little tiny crumbs of attention, and I devour them whole. If he were to make a stand against the club and decide to be with me, I'd do whatever he wanted.

Maybe it's pathetic, but if you had a second of Axel's attention, you'd understand. He makes me feel like the most desirable woman on the planet, and that says a lot seeing as we haven't kissed, barely touched, and I have thousands of people who watch me online for money.

"Fucking delicious," he whispers.

There's a loose piece of dirty blond hair blowing in his face and every inch of me is itching to tuck it behind his ear. Damn, I want to be able to openly touch him so bad.

"Do you want another piece?" I ask softly.

"Yeah, I think I do," he says.

I watch as he looks around the picnic, just waiting for one of his brothers to come over here and ruin the moment—they always do, and it's usually my brother. Axel is a Beta, and I suppose to most of the club that means he's less of a threat to me, but his reputation in the club probably makes him the most dangerous person for me to be around.

Axel didn't seem to give a fuck when my stepdad declared I was off limits and instead should be seen as an expensive jewel the club needs to protect. While Axel has definitely done his fair share of Omega-sitting duty, he's the only one in the club who flirts with me. His defiance against my stepfather only makes me want him more.

It doesn't hurt that he's one of the younger guys in the club too. He's beautiful, wild, and devastatingly fun. I know there will never be a dull moment with him around, and I desperately need some adventure in my life.

I smile as I pick a piece off my plate, taking a bite before holding the rest of the fruit to his lips. He purposely licks my fingers as he sucks and draws the watermelon into his mouth. He's intentionally slow as he leans away from my hand.

The things I would let him do to me with that mouth. He knows the power he holds over me as he licks his lips while pulling back.

I'm about to open my mouth and say something flirty when my brother interrupts the moment, grabbing Axel by the cut and pulling him away. Axel just smiles in my brother's face, listening to him rant about how I'm off limits or some shit.

Axel and my brother are close in age and are tight, so I know when we flirt it pisses Leon off. I don't really care, though. Leon can date whomever he wants, so can anyone else in this club. It's unfair that the one person I want for my own is someone I can't have.

It's involuntary when my eyes roll to the back of my head. It's so stupid that they want me out of the life. I love being here; I *belong* here. Wouldn't it be better for me to bond with people my stepdad already trusts instead of ending up with an outsider who might have less than great intentions?

My attention shifts from my brother and Axel as I note a presence to my left. Before I turn, I already know who it is by her scent alone. She might be a Beta, but Shelby always wears the same perfume meant to emulate an Omega's scent. I don't blame her. Designations aside, women have got to do whatever they can to get ahead in life. I'm actually pretty fond of the flirty Beta.

"Hey, Shelby."

"Did you hear about the nomads?" she asks but doesn't pause long enough for me to answer. "It's about time we got some new dick around here. Some girls are getting bored," she says.

Shelby and a lot of the guys in the club refer to her as a sweet butt. She enjoys hanging around the club and keeping the club members happy. She also gets protection, affection, and the lifestyle she wants. Plus, as far as clubs go, she could have done much worse; Dead Palms isn't a bad choice. They treat their women right and do their best to take care of those they love.

"Do you know anyone who might want to patch in?"

"Hopefully, some of the younger guys," she replies, and I nod in agreement.

"We could definitely use some more eye candy around here," I sigh.

"Oh, is sweet little Axel not doing it for you anymore?" she asks.

"I don't watch Axel," I lie.

"You were literally staring at his ass in those jeans when I came to sit down."

"No, I just wanted to know what he and my brother were talking about," I deflect.

"You and I both know they're talking about you not being an option and for him to keep his grease-riddled hands to himself."

I rest my elbows on the table and press my fists against my cheeks. "I don't want him to keep his hands to himself."

"Well, find a way to get him alone. He seems like he'd be willing to break club law for you," she says, laughing, and I shove her arm.

But, truly, I'd do just about anything he said if he was willing to break the rules for me. To have a man willing to do anything to be with me would be the romantic gesture I've been craving. I want someone to be desperately all in when it comes to me, and I want them to be in this club.

"You're bad. Who are you hanging around with these days?" I ask her.

She's on a bit of a rotation. She's also painted a lovely image of quite a few club members' penises with all her escapades in the club. It's information I've stored for a later date. Axel's is, fortunately, not one of the said penises she has described in detail to me.

"Ambien," she winces.

I smack her arm with my elbow. "Well, I definitely don't want those details. You can absolutely keep that to yourself."

She laughs and shakes her head. "I think…"

"What?" I ask, her pretty blonde hair falling to the side as she tucks it behind her ear.

"I think I want more with him," she admits.

"You want to be my brother's ol' lady?" I ask

"Yeah, I think I do."

"Well, if you want my blessing, you have it. I don't know if he's ready for a commitment though," I warn, knowing how much my brother likes to play the field.

"It's worth a shot, though, right?" she asks, and I'm about to answer when a cacophony of engines purring loudly distracts me. I watch as the possible new members of the MC arrive.

"Yeah, Shelby, it's worth a shot," I breathe out as I watch the line of motorcycles park in front of the clubhouse and the riders dismount. Most of them don't even bother with helmets. So I recognize them immediately.

Sure enough, my favorite nomad is lighting a cigarette as he walks this way. It's been years and maybe it's the Omega designation I now hold, but damn, my stepbrother is looking good.

TWO
THE PRODIGAL SON
TATE

I DON'T WANNA FUCKIN' be here.

The Dead Palms Tallahassee Chapter was the last place I thought I'd find myself—again. I turn off my bike, running my hands through my windswept hair before lighting a cigarette. The cold burn of the nicotine makes its way down my throat as I scan the place where I grew up.

Things haven't changed much. Sure, a few things have been updated, but the layout is still the same. I've parked my bike in front of the clubhouse along the rows of other members, who are riding in for the party. Well, they're riding in for a fuckin' hell of a lot more than that. But today is supposed to be a celebration before we get down to real business.

The other chapters have all fucked up in one way or another, and they're all migrating here for salvation. I guess I'm a part of it as well. I've been a nomad for nearly eight years now, traveling between each chapter. I spent the most time in Miami, for obvious reasons.

But Tallahassee? I haven't been here in at least four years, and there's a reason for that. I stay seated on my baby, pulling another cigarette from my pocket as I contemplate my next move. Maybe I should cut my losses, burn off or cover my tattoos, toss my cut in a bonfire, and start all over.

I inhale the smoke deeply and sigh. As much as I don't want to fuckin' be here, there's no other club for me. I was made to be in this club. Fuck, I was born to lead this club one day.

Another bike pulls up beside me, and I nearly crack a smile when I see who's next to me. A fellow nomad I've done multiple runs with named Cash.

The man doesn't talk much, and I suppose he doesn't have to. He's fuckin' huge, even towering over me. As he gets off his bike, he gives me a look.

"You coming?" he asks.

"Workin' on it," I reply.

He shakes his head at me. He's probably the man I'm the closest to at this fuckin' party. I know he'll have my back. You would think from his sheer size that he would be an enforcer of some sort, but the fact is, his brain is even bigger than his muscles. Cash got his road name because he's so good with money. He's good at moving it, hiding it, and earning it.

He doesn't leave, though; he waits for me to stop being a little bitch. I toss the butt into the sand and promptly get off my bike before heading towards the square. Cash doesn't ask me questions while we walk over to the picnic tables, and I'm grateful for it. Everyone knows who my dad is, but most of them don't know why I left, why I would rather be a nomad than stay here and pine after my father's gavel.

I note some of the familiar faces as I walk around and stall the interaction I've been dreading. Speaking of Dread, the old man claps a hand on my shoulder and squeezes. Isn't it funny how the person who isn't your biological father can be more paternal than the man you share actual blood with?

"Missed your ugly fuckin' mug around here, son," he says by way of a greeting.

"Well, if you're lucky, you'll be seeing it all the time, old man." He claps my shoulder one more time before walking off.

Dread is another man of few words. He still looks good for being in his late fifties. Still has the same short dark hair and mustache to match. The scar along his eye used to freak me out as a kid, but as I got older, I understood that he had seen some shit and made it out on the other side.

I'm too busy watching him walk away when a soft hand grips my arm. By her scent alone, I already know it's Teresa, my father's Omega. When I look down at her, she gives me a sheepish smile. Teresa never had anything to do with the issues between my father and me; shit, by the time they bonded we were already too far gone. Yet, it still unsettles me every time I see her. She looks so much like my late mother it's uncanny.

"Thomas, honey, you look great," she compliments.

"Tate," I remind her, and she shakes her head.

"I'm sorry. Tate. Can I get you a plate? A beer?" she asks.

"A beer would be great," I tell her. She gives me a smile, the burned side of her face crinkling as she turns and walks away.

I bring my hand to the back of my neck and squeeze, trying to calm myself. Seeing Dread and Teresa back-to-back means that the inevitable is going to happen sooner rather than later. I'm looking around the large outdoor space, but I don't see him. I'm hoping that he greets me now, so this pit in my stomach will go away.

Teresa hands me the cold beer and looks up at me with a soft expression. Even if I could muster up any hatred over how much my father loves her instead of me, I couldn't. Teresa is the epitome of an endearing Omega. There's not an ounce of me that can blame her for this shit, though I'm truly not sure what she sees in that old bastard.

"It's so good to see you. How was the ride over?"

"Not too long. I was in Jacksonville. Place hasn't changed much," I reply.

"Sometimes things might seem the same at first glance. But there's been a lot of change around here," she says, and I can't tell if she's trying to be coy with her meaning.

"Yeah, I'll believe it when I see it."

Suddenly a force is crashing into my side and wrapping their arms around my middle. An incredibly sweet-smelling force. She smells like coconuts and jasmine. I'm wondering why this Omega is latched around me like a koala bear when she finally pulls back. Deep pools of brown blink up at me.

"Lily?" I ask.

"Of course it's me. It's been so long since you've been home," she gushes. It sure as fuck has. I didn't even know she designated as an Omega, let alone that she looks like... this. Her dark hair is slightly wavy around her face, and her skin is a perfect golden shade, probably from spending her summer in the sun. It's a fucked-up thought, but I can't help thinking she's the most beautiful woman I've ever seen.

Ain't that some shit? My cock is finally stirring after months and it's over my goddamn stepsister. Not that I truly view her or even consider her my family. She is *his* family, however.

"You, um.... grew up," I say stupidly.

"Yes, well, that's usually what people do. I didn't know if you were coming. Are you thinking about patching over?" she asks, and I swear her expression is hopeful. I look over at Teresa and she's giving me the same big, doe-eyed look. I need to get the hell away from these two, immediately.

"Maybe. I'm not sure what I want to do just yet," I lie and take a step away from the two Omegas.

Lily smiles at me, and I take a heavy swig of my beer. Maybe I should leave. I could never join another club, but that doesn't mean I couldn't still ride. Maybe I could live a simple life, settle down, get a normal job. The fantasy feels like flames burning in my chest, and I shake the thought away. I was born and bred for this life. There's no turning back now.

"Is the Prez around?" I ask them both, refusing to say his name or call him my dad.

Lily's brows furrow, and she crosses her arms over her chest. "He's in the house," she answers, tossing her thumb over her shoulder and pointing to a house I'm more than familiar with. As much as I might have major issues with my old man, I can admit that his tenure of being the Prez of the club is incredibly impressive. He's held this place together for nearly two decades, and he's now the last chapter standing. It makes me wonder how the fuck he does it, I shouldn't start off by being a cynic, but something doesn't sit right.

I want to smoke another cigarette—fuck, maybe a whole pack—but I make my way to the house instead. The grass is sandy and uneven as I begrudgingly walk up the front steps of the porch. The sigh that leaves me is tragic as I tap my knuckles against the front door.

"Comin'!" he hollers from inside the house. His voice startles me, not having heard it for nearly four years.

It's not like the man beat the shit out of me. He did yell at me more often than not, but we just never saw eye to eye. He treated me more like an annoying prospect than he ever did a child. As I grew up and rebelled, things only got worse. Resentment grew even deeper and this need to prove myself outside of my birthright became crucial to me. I'm not completely sure if I've failed or succeeded in that respect, but I'm here now, and how this first conversation goes could dictate how I live the rest of my life.

The door swings open, and I realize for the first time in my life that I'm taller than my father, broader too. He looks mostly the same, besides some extra wrinkles on his face and less hair on the top of his head.

His face is blank, giving nothing away as he looks me up and down.

"You lookin' to patch in?" he asks. No hello, no I miss you or how are you? Right to the fuckin' point.

"Yeah, I'm looking to settle down with the club."

"Then enjoy the picnic. Get familiar with your brothers, enjoy some pussy. We'll bring it to a vote next week," he states dryly, not touching me as he walks past me towards his Omega.

I shake my head at the encounter, not sure what I was expecting. I mean, I didn't expect a warm hug; if anything, I expected a fist to the face and a stern talking to. But all I got was casual indifference, and I think I would have preferred if he had hit me.

I'VE HAD TOO much to drink.

But it feels so good not to feel anything right now. To have this moment where I'm just a member of a club enjoying the company of my brothers, their families, and the pretty Betas who love to hang around.

I'm nearly on my way to being completely sloshed when a flash of light blue piques my attention, along with an asshole who has his arm pinned above her head against the wall of the hardware store.

I finish my beer, tossing the cup in the trash can as I leisurely walk over. I realize that it's Atlas crowding Lily's space. He's trying to patch over from the failed Jacksonville chapter.

"I think I'm going to like it here just fine," he says to Lily as his hand slides down the skin of her arm.

"You fuckin' lost?" I ask him.

He doesn't drop his hand and just looks over his shoulder at me. "Nope, I'll see you inside," he dismisses, shrugging me off as he turns back to Lily.

"You know, considerin' your fuckin' name is Atlas, you should know when you're in the wrong place," I snark. Atlas rolls his eyes and removes his hand from the wall, turning to face me.

He holds up his arm and points to the table where other guys have women on their laps. "There are plenty of other girls here, man. I'm sure you can fucking manage," he sneers.

I smile wickedly at him. The alcohol is running thick in my

veins, and I pull my fist back, punching him in his stomach. A whoosh of air leaves his lips as he buckles over. Lily doesn't gasp or make any noise; she just looks pissed as I grab his cut.

"She's the Prez's stepdaughter, you dumb fuck. Go inside."

"Shit," he wheezes, holding his stomach as he stumbles toward the clubhouse.

I straighten up, dust myself off, and look over at Lily, who is glaring at me.

"What the fuck was that?" she demands.

"It was me welcoming him to the club," I reply, leaning up against the wall beside her.

"I don't need another fucking guard dog," she sasses.

"Mmm. Lookin' like you sure as fuck do, darlin'."

She huffs and plants herself further against the wall next to me. I do my best not to suck in her scent, look at her long exposed legs, or peer down the front of her dress at her small, perky tits.

I need a lobotomy.

"I'm so over all the men of this club thinking they know what's best for me. I'm not some dumb, helpless girl. I'm a woman now; I'm an Omega now, and I have needs. Needs no one seems to take into consideration while constantly cunt blocking me around here," she seethes.

"Cunt blocking?" I ask with a laugh.

"Yeah, Kurt wants me to find a pack outside of the club. Has laid down the gavel that I'm untouchable in all ways to anyone with a Dead Palm symbol on them. Patched in or not."

"He's right," I say, the agreement with my father feeling foreign coming out of my mouth.

She glares at me before walking away. I grab her by her arm and pull her back into the shadows between the two buildings. "Why would you want to stay here?" I ask her.

Her eyes narrow at me. The realization that she's not the sweet little girl I met on a few rare occasions sinks in the moment she speaks. "Because this is my home, and that means something to me," she states. Tugging free of my grasp, she walks towards the house I grew up in, her dress swishing in the late-night breeze.

I'm not sure what I thought I would find when I came home, but a half-hard dick over my stepsister and a near-complete dismissal from my father wasn't it.

THREE

MY BROTHER'S KEEPER

TATE

IT'S LATE, and the party is still going on strong, though most of it has moved into the clubhouse. The one place I'm not allowed unless accompanied by Kurt or my brother.

It's fucking annoying. I'm just so tired of being treated like a child or like I'm a complete idiot around here. I'm far from naïve, I know more of the club's secrets than I should. Part of that has to do with how much of a night owl I am and how much I hear when I open my bedroom window.

My room is on the second floor and it overlooks the square. Sometimes I feel like a princess in a tower waiting for someone to ride in on a motorcycle and save me from this life. It's not even the lifestyle but my current life that I need saving from. I'm so goddamn bored, I want to scream.

I thought maybe with Tate coming home and seeing how different I am, maybe he would see me as the adult woman I've become. But he didn't. He sees me just like Kurt does. Like I'm on some ridiculous pedestal and if I stay here, the club will tarnish me. I desperately want to be dirtied up.

I'm sitting on the nook Dread built below the window as I look out into the square. There are a few pairs of people fooling around outside, and a lone figure smoking on top of a picnic table. I slowly crack the window open so I can hear and see if I know who it is.

They're just sitting there alone for a moment until someone else approaches them. Based on their size, I have a few guesses on who it might be, but then the man who is sitting speaks, and I immediately know it's my brother.

"Fuck off, Mick. I'm not in the mood tonight," he says.

"I see how it is. You've got that sweet piece and now you don't want me anymore. Is that how it is?" he replies. I'm shocked by this information, not because I didn't know Leon's preferences, which is anyone who's attractive, but because I would have never guessed that he's been fooling around with Mickey. I guess he didn't tell me about Shelby, either. My brother keeping so many secrets from me has me feeling like he's pushing me further away from the family.

"Go bother someone else tonight, Mickey," my brother sighs softly.

"It's Mickey now? Go fuck yourself, Leon," Mickey snarls before storming off. I watch as my brother takes a deep inhale of whatever he's smoking before lifting his head to the sky to blow out the smoke.

I'm about to close my window, maybe read or listen to something to help me fall asleep when I notice the first crack in my brother's armor as he crumbles before me. His hands dive into his hair and his elbows fall onto his thighs as he sits there, clearly upset. I'm on my feet and headed downstairs before I can even think. Just as I open the door, I look down at myself. My pajamas are presentable enough, so I pad across the square in bare feet.

"Seat taken?" I ask him, his head popping up from his hands. He forces a smile and shakes his head no. "What you got there?" I ask. Instead of giving me an answer, he hands it over to me. I bring the vape to my mouth and let the sticky tang of weed travel down my throat. I cough a few times before handing it back to him. "Is everything alright, Leon?"

"Nothin' you need to worry about," he replies.

"You're my brother. I'll always worry about you," I remind him.

"It's club business. I don't want to talk about it." He isn't as shitty with me as he was with Mickey a few moments ago, but he's still being standoffish.

Instead of dwelling on his attitude, I change the topic. "What do you think about all the guys who want to patch over?" I ask him.

"It'll be nice having more young guys around here, that's for sure. But it's definitely going to be an adjustment."

"Ten new guys is a lot," I say, doing the math in my head. If they all patch in then that means the club will have twenty-six members, which isn't massive when you think about some of the clubs out there, but for one chapter, it's pretty significant.

"We're gonna have to expand on the compound to fit all of 'em."

"Are any of them packed up or bringing their ol' lady?"

Leon looks over at me skeptically and shakes his head. "Not that I know of. But we only have four available rooms at the clubhouse. So it's gonna be tight for a bit."

"I could help," I offer, hating how everyone here treats me like I'm incapable of lifting a finger.

"Nah, Lil, you've got other important shit you need to worry about," he states.

"Like what?" I question with attitude.

"Like finding a pack and getting the fuck out of here," he responds sternly.

"Why does everyone in this fucking place want me out so bad? Am I that much of an inconvenience?" I grumble, getting up off the picnic table, fully ready to storm away. Leon grabs my arm and forces me to park my ass back on the bench seat.

"Don't be a fuckin' brat, Lily. You know it's not like that."

"It feels like that," I admit shyly, wrapping my arms around myself. "Sometimes it feels like everyone here just wants to hand me off and let me be someone else's problem."

"You're not a problem," he reassures softly, his hand now rubbing where he grabbed my arm. "This place is no good for you. We're not good fuckin' men, Lily. You've got to know that."

"I never said I wanted good men," I point out, and Leon groans, taking another hit of his pen.

"For fuck's sake. Why would you want to stay here? Do you want to end up like mom? Huh? A scarred face and two kids she can't take care of? Is that what you want? 'Cause if you stay here, that's what's going to happen."

I stand up and turn to face my brother. I really, truly look at him. He's exhausted and miserable, but I'm not sure why.

"You know I'd never end up like Mom. And if Kurt thought for a second that any of the guys here were capable of hurting me like Mom was hurt then they wouldn't be a part of the club," I declare.

He shakes his head, inhales deeply, and puffs the smoke out of the side of his mouth. "Then you're even stupider than I thought," he scoffs before standing up and going to walk away. I grip him by his cut and spin him to face me. I force him to look at me while trying to hold back the tears that are threatening to spill over.

"Whatever you're going through doesn't mean you can hurt me, Leon."

"Well, maybe I need to do it more often to knock some fuckin' sense into your goddamn head, Lily. No one wants you here. You don't belong here. Now go the fuck to bed," he sneers, and my tears fall, trailing down my face. He gives me a regretful, tender look before completely closing off his expression and walking off toward the clubhouse.

My brother can be a dick, that's no secret, but he's never talked to me like this before. He's never been so pessimistic either. I don't know what's going on with him. Maybe it's the

Shelby and Mickey drama. But that's no excuse for him to talk to me like that. I'm too upset to go back home, knowing that if I do, all I'll do is lie in my bed and cry like some poor wounded animal.

Instead, I go to one of my favorite places on the compound; the old twisted oak tree that sits between our house and the hardware store. I've loved this tree since we first moved here, when Kurt and Dread brought us back to the compound. I wasn't allowed outside much when we were with the Wraiths, and as soon as I saw this massive tree, I fell in love. It became my secret little hideout. It's probably pathetic that I'm turning twenty-one and I still like to climb trees to think, but I don't really care at the moment.

It's dark out and I use my phone's flashlight so I don't trip over anything. As soon as I see the flared-out branches, I feel some peace settle inside of me and forget all about Leon's harsh words. I'm careful as I climb up the lowest hanging branch, tugging myself up into the little nook where one large trunk splits in half.

I close my eyes as I lean back and let the humid air hit my face. The cicadas and frogs are loud, but they help drown out the lingering party that's still taking place in the clubhouse.

A yearning feeling floods my stomach. I want to be *in* the clubhouse. I want to be perched on an Alpha's or Beta's lap while they joke around with the other guys. I've grown up in this lifestyle. I know how these guys talk, think, and treat their women. I can't imagine being with someone who is considered normal. It feels hopeless if I'm being honest.

I just know Kurt and my brother are going to force me into a pack that isn't right for me. I close my eyes and try to think about anything else.

I land on thinking about how in a few weeks I'm going to finally masturbate on Marielli's Mass. I've been building up to it, making my viewers wait, and they're eager for it. At least I'll have a big payout then. I'll finally have the money stored in my account and no matter who I end up bonded to, I always have a backup plan.

Leon throwing Mom's history in my face was a low blow. I'll do anything to not repeat history, but I know if I packed up with guys in the Dead Palms, that would never happen. I can never see any of them raising a hand to me, ever.

If anything, trying to set me up with a bunch of strangers is a bigger risk. Someone can put on the sweetest facade on the outside but can be absolutely evil on the inside.

A crunch has my eyes popping open, and I have to wait a moment as they readjust to the darkness. I can't see whoever is approaching me, but as soon as I hear their voice, I know who it is.

"You want some company, darlin'?"

Axel.

"Sure," I reply quietly.

He takes no time at all climbing the tree. He stands on the lower branch and holds on to another with an outreached arm. His face is beneath mine, but his smile is contagious and welcomed as he looks up at me.

"Didn't think you hid in here anymore," he says softly.

"It's been a while," I reply.

"Have anything to do with the foul mood Ambien is in?"

I wipe my face, making sure there are no signs of my previous tears, and sigh. "He said some hurtful things," I tell him. Not wanting to throw Leon under the bus or tell Axel all of his business.

"Do you wanna talk about it?"

I wrap my arms around myself, feeling a little more self-conscious over what I'm wearing. "They want me to find a pack outside of the club."

"And you don't want that?" he questions, and I swear I could cry all over again. No one seems to be asking me what I want, only telling me what I should be doing.

"No, I want to stay here."

He nods and looks at me with compassion. "I want you to stay here too." His smile is tilted towards the left side of his face, and it gets me every fucking time. I can't help but smile back.

"Because I'm a part of this family?" I ask, goading him into telling me what I want to hear.

"You know damn well what I think of you, Lily," he playfully chastises.

"I don't. I need you to tell me," I taunt, leaning down further so our faces are close together.

"You should be my girl. I want you on the back of my bike, in my bed. I know you have needs, and I can't keep you all to myself, but you should be mine. You and I both know it," he states.

"I know," I whisper. His hand kneads the flesh of my thigh, making me perfume immediately. The summer night air is overtaken with coconut and jasmine. His touch grows firmer, and I clench my thighs, squeezing his fingers between my legs.

"Tell me you want this too and I'll work on making it happen," he says, his thumb rubbing the top of my thigh.

"You won't be able to change Kurt's mind," I sigh.

"Baby, I didn't say shit about the Prez. Tell me you want me too, and I'll work on makin' it happen."

I blink at him and his confidence. Axel has to be one of the most attractive Betas I've ever met. He doesn't need a scent to turn me on or draw me toward him. Just his personality and looks is all I need because *he* does it for me. I know he would take care of me, cherish me, and indulge my every whim.

"I want you too," I confess softly. His smile widens, and he kisses my bare leg with a groan.

"Let's get you inside," he says plainly.

"What?"

"It's late. I don't know some of these new guys. I don't like you out here by yourself."

That makes me smile even wider, and I agree to get down.

He holds out an arm and I glide down his front to stand on the same branch he's on. He's taller than me, but not to the point of towering over me.

He's gentle with his touch as he pushes my hair from my face and cradles my neck. I'm hopeful that he's going to kiss me, but he doesn't. He leans down to whisper in my ear. "You have no fuckin' idea about all the messy, nasty things I want to do to you, darlin'. But I know as soon as I have you like that, I'll be obsessed. Unless you want me to kidnap you right now and we run off together, you need to go to bed." He squeezes my neck for good measure, making me whimper. "I'm gonna be hearin' that noise in my fuckin' sleep," he rasps before wrapping his arms around me in a hug.

We stand there for a while, his arms wrapped around me tightly and mine wrapped around his trim waist. He doesn't have an overbearing scent, but he smells like hints of oil and soap from working at the shop.

The thing that breaks our hug is my name being shouted loudly in the square. "Lily! Get your ass back in here, goddamnit."

Axel's arms leave my body, and I already miss his touch. His bruised knuckles glide across my cheekbones.

I want to live in this tree I decide. This small bubble where Axel and I never have to worry about the outside world ever again.

"Lily!" Kurt shouts.

"You better go," Axel says softly, his eyes looking between my eyes and lips. I'm bold as I touch my fingers to my lips and then to his.

"Night," I breathe before jogging to the back door. I don't look back at Axel, but I know his watchful eyes are making sure I get home safe.

Kurt looks pissed, standing on the back porch with his arms over his chest.

"And where the fuck have you been?" he demands as I walk past him inside the house.

"Just needed some night air."

"You can't be roaming around outside like that. And sure as fuck not when these assholes have been drinkin' all night."

"I'll work on it."

"Goddamnit, Lily—" I cut him off before he can lecture me.

"It's late. Can you yell at me tomorrow?" He pinches the bridge of his nose and sighs.

"Fine, good-fuckin'-night," he replies gruffly.

I smile and shake my head as I go upstairs and crawl into bed. I'm too excited and giddy from my encounter to sleep, so instead I just lie there and plot.

What if Axel isn't the only member of the Dead Palms that might help sway the tide in my favor?

FOUR
OUTLAWS AND DAYDREAMS

AXEL

THE PARTY last night was a little out of hand, and it's clear that some guys drank more than their fair share. But work needs to be done, and if these guys want to patch in, they need to earn it.

We all woke up late as hell. The sun is already setting as we ride down to the warehouse to get what we need for tonight. Tate, Cash, and I are riding our bikes while Ambien and the prospect, Kyle, are driving the cage behind us.

It's about time we saw some fuckin' action around here. We've been lying low for way too long. Rival clubs are getting a big head, and they absolutely need to be put in their fuckin' place. It doesn't hurt that I suddenly seem to have more motivation lately. Motivation in the form of a tiny, dark-haired Omega who also wants me.

I get why the Prez and her brother want to keep her safe, but the fact is no one can keep that biker princess more safe than I can. It doesn't hurt that the club stands firm on how we treat women, especially Omegas. I don't have a full-blown plan on how I intend to make this all work, but I'll be damned if I let the Prez ship her off to some fuckin' stuck-up group of rich pricks.

The warehouse is a decent ride away, and it gives me some

time to think. It would be one thing if I could just bond with her. There would be no disputing that she was mine. What I need, regrettably, are some Alphas that can help me keep Lily right where she belongs, at the club, with me.

The clubhouse is safe, and I'll always protect her. Plus, we keep everything near the clubhouse on the up and up besides a little laundering here and there. Nothing big enough to cause a stir or get the feds up our ass. We store all the goods or illegals offsite and off the beaten path.

The warehouse is technically Heath's sister's place. She's a nurse and completely off any law enforcement radar. She barely even spends any time at the club. Until we came along, she was using the house as a rental property, and I guess she still does… it's just the club that's renting from her now.

Tate rides beside me, and I can't help but wonder what his deal is. I wasn't part of the club when he left. I know he's the Prez's son, but I'm wondering how similar they are. Prez likes his rules to be followed to a fuckin' T, and sometimes that shit pisses me off. *Well, maybe it's just the specific rule about his step-daughter being off-limits.*

God, the things I want to fuckin' do to that girl.

I will eventually, now that I know full-and-damn-well that she wants me as much as I want her. I've just got to find a way to keep her, make her mine forever. Because the thought of her leaving and joining another pack makes me murderous. And I'm not above killing someone to keep her. All I want is for her to be mine, to make her feel good, to give her the world. I thought nothing could be more impor-tant to me than the club, but I think Lily could easily become the one thing that tops it; she'll be my entire world.

I'll never be able to be a law-abiding citizen with the white picket fence and all that shit. But for Lily, there's a lot of fuckin' lengths I find myself willing to go to so she'll be happy. I just have to be cautious and smart, especially because I keep having thoughts of kidnapping her, which I can't act on. At least, not for now… it's option C, for sure.

We'll figure this out. *She'll be mine soon enough.* I keep chanting this in my head so I can focus on the task at hand.

The sun is nearly completely set and even though it's still humid, it feels nice not to have the sun blazing at my back. We all shut our engines off and hop off our bikes. Cash is the only one who wears a helmet, and after he tucks it on his seat, we head into the stowaway house.

"How big is the warehouse?" Tate asks.

"At least three thousand square feet," I reply as I grab a pistol and a bag of weed.

Tate is digging around the materials we have like they aren't a fuckin' explosion hazard.

"You wanna be a little more careful there, pal?" I joke, and he glares at me. *Definitely see a resemblance to the Prez in that glare.*

"How big of a message are we sending?" Tate asks.

"A really fuckin' big one," I answer, and Cash nods his head. He's grabbing another handgun and so does the prospect. Ambien is in another room, gathering more shit.

"How many guards do you think they have right now?" Tate asks.

"I'm guessin' they sent their prospects to stand guard. It's their annual seafood thing."

"Seafood thing?" Tate parrots.

"I can't fuckin' remember what it's called, but they do it every year, same day in July," I explain, trying to remember what the fuck the event is called. Not that it truly matters.

Cash just shrugs his shoulders. He's quiet, and it makes me curious about him. He was a fully patched member in Jacksonville but became a nomad shortly before that chapter got busted. It's enough to make me suspicious and to be more cautious around him.

Tate has the prospect load up the SUV, and we lock up the house before making the drive down to Panama City.

Fuck, nothing beats riding my bike on a late summer night. I've tied my hair back, so it's not in my face, and I have my night glasses on since Florida fuckin' mandated it. The humid air hits my skin, and I feel so fuckin' alive.

Joining the club has been the best thing I've done in my life. While jail still isn't off the table for me, I'm honestly shocked my record isn't longer than it is. Without the club, I know I would have done something absolutely reckless and got myself locked up by now.

The club gives me purpose and direction. It's my whole life. I live and breathe for the Dead Palms, it's who I am.

So it's baffling to me that Lily can have such an effect on the thing I hold closest to me. The club is my life, but I'm ready to mess it all up and make her my fuckin' everything.

I spend the whole ride daydreaming about Lily's small tits and sucking them into my mouth... till we finally arrive just outside of Bottlenose Outlaws MC. Stupid fuckin' club name, if you ask me. Like we get it, there's fuckin' dolphins. It honestly makes them sound like a bunch of bitches to me.

"Dumb fuckin' name," Tate growls, and it makes me smile.

Maybe he's not so bad after all.

Cash pulls out a pair of night vision binoculars that I'm apparently not allowed to carry. You lose one fuckin' thing and suddenly you're not allowed to carry anything cool. It was one rifle. The serial number was scratched off, but you would have thought I lost a fuckin' baby or somethin'.

"Three," Cash states softly.

"Dead or Alive?" Tate asks.

I sigh regrettably. "Alive."

Tate just shrugs his shoulders and pulls out what looks to be a tranq gun.

"When the fuck did we get a tranq gun?" I question.

Tate grins widely, to the point where I can see all his teeth. "Brought it along with me, thought it might come in handy."

"How long will it knock them out for?"

"Let's just say they're definitely goin' to get a good night's sleep," he replies.

The prospects for the Outlaws clearly aren't taking their job seriously, considering the fact that they are all standing together and drinkin' while they're supposed to be guarding and patrolling the warehouse.

"Go a quarter mile to the left, we need to separate them. Make some noise and let's hope one of them goes to investigate," Tate instructs.

I take up a light jog until I'm a good distance away from Tate and the guys while still being close enough to the warehouse so these stupid motherfuckers will hear me.

"Uhhh, yeah!" I yell.

"You hear that?" dumbass number one says.

"I didn't hear nothin'," dumbass number two replies.

"I'm goin' to go check it out."

Dumbass number one decides to walk around the warehouse, his eyes squinting into the distance. These stupid pricks have such big spotlights on their warehouse that it's almost like they put out a neon sign that says 'we have illegal shit here'.

Tate is quick and efficient, hitting both guys by the front door with the tranquilizer. As cool as it looked to shoot them with that, I have plans of my own. I wait in the shadows as the Outlaws prospect gets closer and closer to the darker side of the property. He sighs heavily when he reaches the edge and scratches the back of his neck. I can see a heavy sheen of sweat on his pale skin. No fuckin' way this dude gets patched in. *Then again, this club is full of a bunch of pussies anyway.*

He turns to walk back to the warehouse, and that's when I jump on his back. My arm locks around his throat as I hold him in a chokehold.

"Go night-night, bitch," I whisper in his ear as he struggles against my hold.

I might be a Beta—hell, my feet are nearly off the ground holding onto this Alpha's neck—but I'm not weak or small. I work hard to have the body I do, and I plan on using it at every opportunity. He drops his gun and gasps for air, but it doesn't do him much good as I squeeze his windpipe harder, eventually bringing him to his knees.

He still resists passing out, so I just squeeze harder, until he finally gives out. His large body collapses to the ground, making me grin.

I tug down my zipper and pull out my dick, pissing on his back. I try to write my name, but I'm not sure it translates. My piss splatters against the leather of his blank cut, and I smile to myself.

"You done?" Ambien asks as I tuck my dick away.

"Lookin' like it," I reply, and he shakes his head with a smile. We've been friends for a while now, even if I want to marry and fuck the shit out of his sister. He's been going on solo runs for a few weeks now, so it's nice to have him back for this job.

He takes one arm and I take the other as we drag his limp body over to his buddies, who are also taking a little nap. Tate looks down at the man and back at me before shrugging his shoulders.

"Looks like we won't need the bolt cutters after all," Tate comments as he pushes the door open. The place is like a massive barn, but instead of cute little animals, it's filled with growing pot plants.

Ambien is in charge of taking the plants that matter while Tate, Cash, the prospect, and I take whatever else looks valuable. Having more time to steal shit would have been nice, but then again, we don't exactly want them knowing who set their warehouse on fire. Though they'll probably have an idea anyway.

It doesn't hurt that the Outlaws have plenty more enemies that they've pissed off.

We haul out a few of the already processed and packaged bags, along with a few bags of soil that Blaze requested. I'm taking the goods back to the car with the prospect as Tate gets the explosives set up around the warehouse. He's quick with it, just setting up M-100s in each corner of the room, placing two on top of bags of fertilizer before taking out his lighter and setting each row of plants on fire.

"You sure that'll be enough?" Ambien asks. Tate doesn't reply, just rushes us back toward our bikes and the SUV. We all walk back quickly, but I can tell we're all skeptical. That is until the first major explosion… well, explodes, ripping the roof off the left-hand side of the building.

"Holy fuck," I chuckle in amazement as I throw my leg over my bike and start the engine. When I look over at Tate, he's laughing wildly with enthusiasm. It's contagious, and we're all riddled with excitement as we ride away with the blazing building at our backs.

Maybe the new guys aren't so bad after all.

FIVE
FUCKIN' EYELASHES

LILY

IT'S EMBARRASSING how much I've thought about Axel since the other night. I haven't gotten a chance to see him or talk more about our plans. But for the first time in a long time, I actually feel hopeful. It's nice to finally have someone on my side when it comes to my future.

My excitement is short-lived because Kurt walks into the kitchen while I'm drinking my morning tea.

"You've got a date tonight," he informs me. He wasn't asking me if I wanted to go on a date. He's telling me with no room for arguing that he's set something up for me.

I know I can go about this a few ways, but no matter which way I choose, it'll end up with me going on this stupid fucking date.

"With who?" I ask, taking the path of least resistance. I take a sip of the lukewarm beverage and look up at him from the mug.

"Two Alphas, Yonis and Greg. They own a ton of commercial properties in the area, and they'd take good care of you," he says while he digs in the fridge for something to eat.

"And if I don't like them?" I question, wondering how far he plans on taking this mission of controlling my life.

"Then I'll set up another date. All I ask is that you give them a try," he pleads, his voice and face softening to reveal the old man that's strictly saved for me. At least, that's the way it feels sometimes. I know Kurt's reputation around town isn't the best, and I trust him to an extent. But when it comes to the rest of my life, I can only trust myself.

"I'll give them a chance," I tell him.

He smiles before kissing the top of my head and walking away. I probably should have asked for more details, like... how old are these Alphas? What are they interested in? However, as soon as he said that they own commercial properties, I knew they're going to be boring. But I'll go on this date, buying myself some time for Axel and me to come up with a plan.

I'm anxious because I haven't seen him in a few days. He texted me that he was lying low for a while and he'd see me when he got back. It wasn't as good of a reassurance as I would like from him, but it has to be enough for now. I shake my head and decide to put some effort into this date, at least for appearance's sake.

Grabbing my purse, I make my way outside, through the square, and down the dirt road that leads to the rest of the housing for the club. It's still a work in progress, but it's home and what I'm used to. The houses are specifically for packed members or in one case, there's the sweet house. I'm not a huge fan of the term sweet butt, but the girls don't seem to mind.

Besides my house, I spend most of my time there. Not just because Shelby does my lashes and Cora does my hair, but because I love it there. The girls just get it; they understand the life, and I feel like they understand me more than anyone else in this sandy compound.

I'm almost to the light gray house with the pink door when the rumble of a bike pulls up next to me.

"Where you headed?" Tate asks, and I have to refrain from rolling my eyes.

"To see Shelby. Do I need a hall pass or written permission to see her?" I sass.

"Why the fuck are you hangin' out with the sweet butts?"

"Don't call them that; they're my friends. Plus, Shelby is a lash tech."

"A what now?" he questions, his dark brows furrowing as he looks at me, confused.

"They're eyelash extensions. They make your eyes pop," I tell him.

"Your eyes look pretty to me as they are," he says.

"Well, that's great and all, but I like them. So if you'll excuse me," I reply, walking away. He just uses his feet to roll on his bike alongside me, and I turn to glare at him. "Is there anything else you need?"

"I'll just be beside you till you get to the house," he answers smugly.

I halt immediately and cross my arms over my chest, glaring at him even harder. "I'm fully capable of walking to a house on my own. I don't need a babysitter. Especially not one I barely know. You up and left, Tate. You've been gone a long time. Our parents might be bonded, but that doesn't make us family, and it definitely doesn't make me your responsibility."

Wrong fucking thing to say.

He's up off his bike quicker than I've ever seen anyone dismount before. He makes sure his Road King is stable and standing straight before he grabs my chin roughly. I'm tough, and I don't back down as he stares into my eyes while the tips of his fingers dig into my chin. He isn't hurting me, but I wouldn't call it a gentle touch either. His fingers are warm, besides the cool press of his two rings against my face.

"As long as your pretty little ass lives here, on this fuckin' compound, you're my fuckin' business. You understand?" He squeezes tighter with his last words. I don't respond immediately, just continuing to stare at him.

"Well, lucky for you, that might not be for much longer."

"What the fuck does that mean?" he asks, his hand softening against my face. His flesh is warm against mine, and I definitely shouldn't be taking in a deep inhale of his rich, musky scent. He smells like leather, pine, and salt of the earth. I enjoy it far more than I should. He's not only a soon-to-be club member I'm meant to avoid, but also my stepfather's son.

"What does that mean?" he asks again softly, making me realize I've gotten completely swept up in his rich scent.

"Kurt, your dad, he um… set up a date for me tonight," I stammer, far less sassy than I was only moments ago. It's hard to have an attitude when you're trying to wrap your head around being extremely attracted to your stepbrother's scent.

"And that's what you want?" he asks, his hand dropping away from my face. I miss his touch instantly.

I shake my head and turn to walk toward the sweet house. Of course, I'm not lucky enough for him to leave me alone. He catches up with me quickly, not touching me this time as he walks beside me.

"Kurt has a way of making everything about what he wants and not thinking about what other people may want or how the two might differ," he states plainly.

I won't deny that my curiosity is piqued when it comes to their relationship. I never truly understood why they didn't get along, but just Tate saying that leads me to believe he was pushed to be someone he wasn't. Or at least, Kurt tried to make him into someone he didn't want to be.

"Well, I'm almost out of time… I'll figure it out," I brush his concern off without looking at him. He grabs my arm, spinning me around, and I have to do everything in my power to not sigh or swoon over the touch.

"Don't go then. Don't let him tell you what to do, how to live your life."

"You wouldn't understand, Tate. I'm an Omega. The world isn't my oyster and time isn't on my side. If I don't find a pack soon, the…" I shake my head and stop talking. I don't know why I'm even explaining myself to him right now. "I need to get to Shelby. I was supposed to meet her at ten."

His hand drops from my arm, but his eyes continue to explore mine questioningly. I wonder what he sees in my expression because when I look at him, I can't help but see an ally. Sure, he told Atlas to fuck off and keep his hands to himself. And yes, he probably wants me to leave the club like Kurt does, but I can also see that he wants me to have a choice and that Kurt shouldn't be the one making all the plans for my future.

"How much is it?" he asks, nodding his head towards the sweet house.

"She gives me a discount, so one hundred."

"And that's the fuckin' discount? For fuckin' eyelashes?" he questions dumbfoundedly.

"Yes," I reply sharply as I turn around and attempt to get as far away from this encounter as quickly as possible.

"Here," he says, placing a crisp hundred-dollar bill over my shoulder.

I look over at the money before turning back around with a grin. "What about a tip?" I reply, and he shakes his head, smirking at me. I know that smirk is going to be replaying in my mind for the rest of the day.

"What time will you be done?"

"It will probably take an hour and a half, and then I'll probably hang out with the girls for a bit."

"They're your friends?" he asks, his brows furrowed.

"Yes, they're my friends, and I'm late. Thanks for paying, step-bro," I say, seeing him repulsed by the title I threw his way.

"Don't fuckin' call me that. And I'll see you at dinner tonight," he responds.

"No, you won't. Date, remember?"

"Right… see ya round, Lily," he says.

I watch him light a cigarette and walk back to his bike. When I get to the front steps, I take a risk and turn back to take one last look at him. He's casually sitting on his bike, watching me, just like I'm watching him. His dark, loose hair is pushed back and a cigarette hangs from the side of his lips. He should be the poster child for bad-boys-you-should-keep-away-from-your daughters. He's also every temptation I should stay far, far away from.

And I will… I have Axel, and we'll be coming up with a plan soon. A plan that doesn't involve my broody yet sweet stepbrother. I groan at myself for even thinking about it and turn, knocking on the door.

Cora is the one to answer, and she wraps me in a hug.

"Hey, Cora."

"Hey, Lily. Shelby's running a little behind. Do you want something to drink?"

"Water would be great."

"You got it," she replies.

The bangles around her wrist clink as she walks to the kitchen. Cora is the epitome of an awesome biker bitch if I ever saw one. If I needed someone to have my back, Cora is who I'd call. She's not that much older than me, but she's a nurturer just as much as she is a badass.

I tuck the money Tate gave me into my purse as I sit patiently in the living room. I love the sweet house. While a lot of the compound is all black, broody, and manly, the sweet house is feminine, clean, and gentle. Currently, four women live here. Shelby, Cora, Tammy, and Kim. Tammy's been here for God only knows how long. Honestly, I don't think she even fucks any of the guys anymore. Mostly because I'm not even sure Smiley or Pipes can even get it up still. The thought alone makes me want to gag.

Kim, on the other hand, is new, and I'm not sure if she's going to last. She seems to really want that ol' lady title and so far, no bites. It's only been a few months, but I'm not sure if she's going to work out or not.

Cora comes back with the glass of water and a smile. I know

she's close to Maverick, a younger Beta. I could definitely see them being in it for the long haul, and I sure hope so.

A woman I'm not familiar with walks down the hall with a smile, her lashes looking immaculate as Shelby gives her a hug and escorts her outside.

She looks a little flustered as she waves me back to her room.

"So sorry, I'm running late today. She had way more lashes than I thought. You can never tell when they have light lashes what you're going to be in for."

"You're totally fine. I'm in no rush."

"Let me just put a new table cover on really quick," she says as she takes the sheet off the table bed and replaces it with a new one.

I lie down as Shelby switches on some meditative music from the country station that was playing moments ago. I always let her pick the music during my time because even though we always start off talking and catching up, it quickly turns into me taking a nap.

"Have you seen your brother around lately?" she asks.

"I was just about to ask you the same thing," I reply. "I haven't seen him since the BBQ. He was kind of a dick, actually," I comment.

"Yeah," she sighs.

"He isn't being an asshole to you, is he?" I ask her, wishing I could open my eyes to look at her and see if she's being honest.

"Nothing like that. I just feel like he's being distant. Maybe I'm imagining it. He just hasn't been by for the last couple of days," she tells me, sounding sad about the fact.

"I'm sure he's just busy doing club stuff. I haven't seen Axel around either."

"You've gotta hit that before you're out of here for good," she encourages me.

My forehead must crinkle because she straightens it out with her soft fingers. It's probably pathetic how much I loved to be touched, even by my girlfriends. It gives me so much joy. I love getting cosmetic stuff done as much as possible because it means someone is usually touching my face or playing with my hair.

"What if I want him forever and don't want to get out of here?" I ask quietly.

"Then we better start scheming, because the Prez and your brother seem pretty dead set on you getting your cute Omega-ass out of here and settling down with a ridiculously wealthy pack," she warns as she continues working on my lashes. Her ability to work and talk always amazes me.

"Well, if you come up with any ideas, let me know."

"I mean, the quickest route is to get one of these guys to bite you. Can't ship you off if you're bonded," she points out.

"That's the problem. Right now, Axel is the only one I'm interested in."

"What about Mick?" she asks, and I grimace. Knowing that he and my brother hook up is enough to put me off for life. "Okay, so not Mick. There are a lot of new guys," she suggests. I keep my brother's secret about Mick even if it makes me feel like a shitty friend to Shelby.

"Bonding with someone can't be a hasty decision," I tell her, just as much as I'm telling myself. No matter who I bond with, I need to get it right on the first try. I don't think I'd survive bonding with someone and them not being the right choice.

Shelby pets my face slightly before responding. "You're right, it's the most important decision in your life. I didn't mean to make a joke about it."

"You didn't, Shelby. It's honestly the quickest way to stay here. But I need a pack that's perfect for me, not just perfect for this moment."

"That you do. You deserve the best, you know that?" she says.

"Shelby, you better stop being so sweet or I'll cry, and then you'll get pissed at me for ruining your hard work."

"You're right. Take your little nap and let me finish," she says, ending the conversation.

Maybe it's an Omega thing or my ability to sleep anywhere, but Shelby's gentle touches and the soothing music lull me into the perfect nap.

SIX

OMEGA MATH

I PUT MORE effort into my appearance than I should, considering this isn't a date I want to go on. But it's still a date, and if Kurt thinks I'm actively sabotaging his matchmaking—or whatever the fuck this is supposed to be—there will be hell to pay.

I'm on my phone, and I have about fifty messages on Marielli's Mass asking me where I've been and when I plan on going live again.

Is it wrong that since Axel said he's interested in me, I feel like I can't stream anymore? I know I don't show my face, and it's all a part of my plan to make money before I settle down, but something about it doesn't feel right.

I swallow that down. It's a means to an end. Once I reach my goal, I'll be able to stop and move on with my life.

It's not that I have shame when it comes to streaming or showing my body. I just worry about what Axel would think. If he found out, would he change his mind? Would he think I'm not as sweet and desirable anymore?

I'm shaken from my thoughts as Tate walks through the front door. He's got on a white t-shirt, his cut, and dark denim jeans. His hair looks slightly wet as he pushes it back and sits at the dining room table with me.

His hand rests on the table, his signet ring for the club on one finger and another ring I'm not sure of the meaning rests on another. *Why do I want them to touch my face again so badly?* I look away from him, and he must notice because he speaks.

"You cancel your little date?" he asks.

Before I can answer, Kurt is walking into the kitchen and speaking for me. "No." He looks away from Tate and over to me. "You ready to go, hun?"

Tate looks between Kurt and me like Kurt is speaking a foreign language. I suppose Tate didn't get this fatherly side of Kurt, not that I would know. This is truly the first time I've seen them interact, and it doesn't seem like Kurt even cares Tate is here.

"I thought we were havin' dinner?" Tate asks Kurt. I can tell he's trying not to come off as petulant.

"We are. Teresa will be getting started on it soon. I've just got to drop off Lily first," Kurt tells him.

"I can take her," Tate suggests and Kurt laughs.

"No chance. Let's go, Lily," he instructs, and I furrow my brows, wondering if Kurt doesn't trust Tate around me or if he's just being an asshole.

Tate gives me an irritated look, but I just give him a weak smile before grabbing my purse and following Kurt to his pickup truck. Honestly, the amount of vehicles we have as a whole on the compound is insane.

Considering how many bikes are here, it's depressing how long it's been since I've ridden. No one will let me get my license and ride on my own, so I'm stuck hitching a ride with whoever will let me. Which as of late has been no one, not even Kurt or my brother.

Kurt is quiet for most of the ride until we're parked in front of some fancy Italian restaurant.

"Call me if you want to be picked up," he tells me.

"Okay. You've met them already?" I ask, wondering why he feels so comfortable just dropping me off.

"Yeah, they're good people. You enjoy yourself."

"I don't even know what they look like," I point out, feeling even more uncomfortable about this date as it approaches.

"They're in the lobby, you can't miss them," he says.

There's a part of me that wants to get out of this car and run away instead of going on this date and maybe take my chances in the real world. But self-preservation kicks in as I clutch my purse and get out of the truck.

Kurt rolls down the window. "They'll drop you off afterwards," he says before rolling up the window and driving away.

I'm left standing in the parking lot gaping at his truck as he drives away. Not only did he not walk me inside, but he's just okay with complete strangers driving me home. The realization of Kurt's callousness is enough to almost make me cry, but I suck it up and take a deep breath. I do my best to not let his carelessness affect me so harshly.

But there is this nagging in the back of my brain that makes me feel like a burden. Like I'm this annoying little thing that he wants to get rid of. He'll have my mother's complete focus once I'm gone; I won't be in his house anymore either.

I breathe in and out. *No, I can't get upset over this.*

I could still leave, now that he's driven off, but that would leave me stranded here, and I know he would find out if I didn't go. I'm not sure what the consequences would be. It's not that I'm afraid of Kurt. Well, I'm not afraid of him physically hurting me. I'm not a complete idiot. I know Kurt does bad things and there will always be a level of fear when it comes to going against what he wants.

He could have presented me to a pack and told me that was my only option. Though, I'm not sure how this is much better.

I huff out a breath and fiddle with the end of my braid as I walk into the lobby.

No. There's no fucking way Kurt did this to me.

The two men waiting in the lobby are the absolute opposite of what I'm attracted to. Sure, they're Alphas, and they're clean and dressed nicely.

But they're very clearly in their forties. One man looks like he does equations for fun and the other looks like his idea of a party is sitting around a table and eating nachos while we watch a movie.

Not that there's anything wrong with that. But it's so wrong for me.

I want to just spin on my heel and walk out. What's the point in wasting everyone's time? That's when the nerdier of the two spots me.

"Lily?" he asks.

I plaster a smile on my face and nod as I grab his outreached hand. "I'm Greg, and this is Yonis." He puts his hand on the other Alpha's shoulder, who is clearly extremely shy and nervous. Yonis is the more attractive of the two, with short buzzed hair, glowing brown skin, and deep brown eyes. Greg has curly amber hair, green eyes, and is only a few inches taller than me.

"So nice to meet you," I lie, beautifully.

"Let's go take a seat," Greg suggests politely as we walk through the restaurant's waiting area. Yonis is considerate as he pulls my chair out for me when we sit down.

The server gets us water and Greg awkwardly orders a bottle of wine. The waiter looks at me and back at the guys before walking away.

"That's right, you aren't twenty-one yet. I'm so sorry," Greg says.

"Two weeks," I reply, and he gives me a soft smile.

I have no qualms about dating older guys, but I think my limit has to be late thirties. Even just sitting here at the same table with them, I feel like a child. Our lives are so completely different. What the fuck could these two possibly have in common with a sheltered twenty-year-old?

"My stepdad says you two sell commercial properties?" I ask. Yonis smiles before he speaks.

"We own them and rent out the commercial spaces to business owners. What about you, do you have any hobbies or are you working on an advanced degree?" he asks.

"High school was more than enough for me. I like running, reading, and I like making bath products sometimes," I reply.

"That's cute," Greg states, and I can't help but take it for the dig that it is.

Asshole.

"So you two are looking for an Omega?" I ask, not knowing what else to say, really. I just want the date to be over with, and we haven't even ordered yet.

"Yes. Yonis and I have been partners for a while now and feel like we have the time and lifestyle now to take care of an Omega," Greg says.

I'm pretty sure I'm not controlling my face well as I watch his cheeks heat and he takes an awkward sip of water. The way he just spoke about Omegas like we're fucking pets and not human beings, who are fully capable of living our daily lives without assistance, pisses me off.

"Gotcha," I say, and I'm more than relieved when the server pours the wine and gives me a glass. When the server turns away, I snag it before Greg can and nearly down half of it before he can take the glass from me.

"I didn't mean that Omegas can't take care of themselves. Just… you know what I mean?" he asks.

"No, I don't. Please tell me, help me understand, Greg," I taunt.

Greg looks over at Yonis, who looks like he would rather die than sit in this restaurant for another minute.

We're quiet as the server takes our order, and we wait.

"What is it like living with the Dead Palms?" Yonis asks, really speaking up for the first time all night. When I look back at him to see if he's being snarky, I can tell he's genuinely curious.

"I actually really love it. I love riding bikes, the sense of family, and all the people there," I explain, giving him a soft smile.

"A sense of community and belonging is invaluable," Yonis agrees, and I nod my head. Some of the animosity I felt toward Greg slips away.

"It really is. Do y'all have a group of friends you regularly hang out with?" I ask. Greg looks slightly repulsed, but Yonis smiles and answers.

"We have some friends we've been close to for a few years, but nothing like what you have with the Dead Palms."

Yonis and I mostly hold the conversation the rest of the night. Greg will chime in from time to time, but he seems out of his depths when it comes to speaking with me. While I'm still not attracted to either of them, I enjoyed speaking with Yonis, but only as a friend.

I'm nervous when the date ends and Yonis opens the backseat for me. I slide in, staying alert the entire time Greg drives to the compound. I have to put in the code at the entry gate and Greg drives through, pulling up in front of the body shop.

"This is where I should be dropping you off?" he asked with some concern on his face.

"Yeah, this is perfect. Thank you for dinner," I say.

"You're welcome. We'll let Kurt know we appreciated your time, but that we won't be going on another date," Greg states almost snidely. Yonis pinches the bridge of his nose and exhales dramatically.

"Right, can't start a pack if the spark isn't there," I agree, knowing that I full well didn't want another date with them. So then why does my little Omega heart want to fucking throw a fit over not measuring up to their standards?

"Exactly! When there's no scent or physical attraction, it

won't work," Greg continues to over-explain, even though I have already agreed with him. I step out of the car and slam the door harder than I should.

"Lily–" Yonis says softly.

"Goodnight," I cut him off petulantly as I walk into the body shop. Maybe Axel is working, he could make this all better.

Realization hits me before I can even put my finger on the feeling.

Rejection.

I've never really dealt with rejection before. It's even more confusing to me because I very clearly wanted nothing to do with Greg or Yonis in a relationship sense. So why does Greg telling me I'm not pretty and that my scent sucks have me crying right now?

I should not be crying over mediocre Alphas in their forties not thinking I'm pretty. It's pathetic, and all I want to do is scream and punch Greg in the face. I'm wiping away my tears with the back of my hand when I walk into a wall of a man.

A man that smells like vetiver and lavender. It's the sexiest combination of a masculine, earthy scent mixed with a touch of sweetness. His hands are gentle as they wrap around my upper arms. The warmth of his skin makes my body hum in approval, and I can't help but lean into his touch.

My eyes travel along his broad chest, which is covered in a tight black t-shirt, leaving little to the imagination when it comes to his physique. When I finally reach his face, my lips part. I've seen him from afar, and I know his name thanks to a major rundown of all the guys by my girlfriends, but seeing him up close? They were totally right; he is the hottest possible new patch in. His skin is a rich brown, and he has a short trimmed beard that frames his face nicely. His eyes are hooded and framed with amber-hued irises while his head is adorned with black and gray tattoos instead of hair.

He should be terrifying, both because of his size and all the tattoos that cover his body. When I look at the arm that is still outstretched and holding onto me, all I find is more tattoos.

Cash.

I'm not sure how he got that name or how it fits with the larger-than-life man in front of me, but his scent and his looks have me wanting to find out.

I'm so lost in his presence that I don't realize how long we've been standing here or what I was even upset about.

"You alright, sweetheart?" he asks. The timber of his voice is deep and delicious.

"What?" I blink at him like an idiot.

"You're walking around here late at night, and you're crying," he points out.

I wipe my face and let out a self-loathing laugh. "I was having a bit of a dramatic moment," I tell him, but that's apparently not good enough.

"No, you got dropped off by a vehicle that isn't permitted into the compound, and whoever was in it left you crying. Why?" he demands gently. The way he speaks is different from the other guys. Maybe he's not from the South originally, but it's more than his dialect. I just can't put my finger on it.

"It's stupid," I deflect, realizing his hands are still on me. He must realize it at the same moment as I do because his hands fall away from my skin.

"I'm sure it's not," he counters. His tone is nothing like Greg's was tonight. No, it's sweet and assuring. He doesn't think my feelings are irrational or un-based in logic.

"Take a seat," he says, pointing his chin towards the desk beside us. I take a seat and look around. He wasn't working on a bike. His hands are extremely clean, too.

"What were you working on?" I ask curiously, trying to take some of the attention off of myself.

"I'll tell you what I was working on if you tell me why you were crying," he barters. I arch an eyebrow at him but nod. My nosiness outweighs my dramatics any day. "Been working through some financials for this place and the club. I don't know who did this before, but it's a complete fucking disaster."

"Calvin used to do it, but he died like five years ago?" I inform, and Cash nods.

"That makes sense. That seems to be when everything went to shit."

He moves some papers and piles them up before taking the seat in front of the desk. "You going to tell me what happened?"

"Do I have to?" I joke, watching in amazement as a dimple forms on his left cheek when he gives me a closed-lip smile.

"You don't have to, but you would be breaking a promise," he teases, and I return the same smile.

"Well, I certainly can't go breaking promises."

SEVEN
TO ANARCHY

CASH

I PROBABLY SHOULDN'T BE TALKING to the Prez's daughter, finding her endearing, or giving a shit about why she's crying. But I can't help it.

Even if she wasn't an Omega, I wouldn't have been able to let my curiosity slide. Now that she's dried all of her tears and is joking with me, I'd feel better if she walked away and went back to her house. That doesn't mean I want her to, though. I haven't spoken much since I stepped foot on this compound, and I've been torn about my next decision.

Patch in, stay nomad, or leave completely. I already know some guys are suspicious of me. It's not a good look when you go nomad two weeks before your club gets raided and most of your chapter ends up doing time.

But I more than warned them about what was coming. Do all the illegal shit you want, just do it in a way that won't get you caught. The Prez of the Jacksonville chapter thought he was untouchable, not to mention a real fucking prick.

I'm not sure what I think of this Prez. I haven't been here long enough. But I know Tate and the fact that he hates his father isn't making me want to stay, and neither is this financial mess I'd be digging this club out of.

But it is nice to be needed by a club, appreciated. Probably not as good as it would feel to be needed by an Omega. But the one sitting on the table in front of me definitely isn't an option.

Prez let all of us know that she's completely off limits and you're risking your hands if you touch her. But I'm not even thinking of her in that way right now. I just want to make sure she's safe and okay. Maybe it's because I know she's attached to the club or the fact I can't stand seeing an upset Omega. Either way, this is completely platonic, and that's okay.

She takes a deep breath after she says she doesn't want to go around breaking promises. She wipes her face and squishes her hands between her thighs before speaking. "I had a date tonight," she announces.

"Did they try anything? Did they hurt you?" I ask, ready to hop on my bike and kick their ass. They didn't even make sure she got home safely. What kind of man does that?

She shakes her head and sighs. "No, nothing like that. It's stupid really."

"Tell me," I urge her, still ready to beat the shit out of them.

An embarrassed noise slips from her throat, and she tries to cover it up with a cough. "I didn't like them. I knew I wouldn't before the date even started. But when they dropped me off, the one guy all but said they didn't find me attractive and they weren't drawn to my scent... It's so stupid, I didn't even like them. So I'm not really sure why I'm having this big of a reaction," she confesses softly.

"Surely you don't need those assholes telling you that you're pretty, sweetheart. Come on, now," I say.

She gets off the table and goes to walk away. "See, I told you. I was just being dramatic." She's waving me off like she's embarrassed. I step in front of her, but she just stares at my chest. I tilt her chin up with a finger and find her eyes are glassy.

"Sweetheart, you know damn well you're gorgeous. You don't need those weak-ass Alphas who dropped you off thinking so. The fact is, they know they could never have an Omega like you. Nothing's more fragile than a weak man's ego."

"You think so?" she asks, her big brown eyes pleading for confirmation, and I shouldn't like it. I shouldn't want to wrap this small Omega up and show her just how precious she is. She's off limits, too young, and I don't even know if I'm staying.

"I know so. It has nothing to do with you being pretty or smelling like a tropical fucking paradise. It has everything to do with them trying to hide their own rejection. Motherfuckers didn't even walk you to the door. Doubt they'd even know what to do with you if they were lucky enough to have a chance."

She finally looks like she's calmed down, and I wonder why she doesn't have a pack already. It's clear she's close to her heat. I try to tamper my concern. *It's none of my fucking business.*

"You're right," she sighs, rubbing the back of her neck. "I hate feeling like this, though."

"It will get better once you have a pack," I tell her.

"How do you know?" she asks. She's not trying to question me, but I think she wants to know if I'm just someone telling her what she wants to hear or if I actually have a fucking clue what she's going through.

"Obviously, I don't know what you're going through, but my little sister is an Omega. She had a lot of really big emotions before her first heat. Things changed for her once she bonded," I explain.

"Is she happy?" she asks.

I don't have the fucking heart to tell her the truth, so I lie through my teeth. "Yeah, she's happy."

That makes her smile. I shouldn't like putting a smile on her face, but I do.

"Let's get you home," I tell her. She doesn't fight me as we walk side by side in the night to the main house.

"Are you living in the clubhouse?" she asks.

"Yeah, for now."

"You don't want to stay?" she questions.

Fuck, how does she read me so well?

"I haven't decided one way or another, yet."

She nods as she walks up the two steps of the front porch, making us the same height. "Goodnight, Lily," I say, making her smile again.

"Goodnight," she replies, and I go to walk away when she calls my name. "Cash?"

"Yeah?"

"If there's anything I can do to help make you stay, let me know," she offers, and I can't help but feel like she's flirting with me and that I like it more than I should. I just give her a nod before I sulk back to the body shop.

I'M knee-deep in paperwork at the body shop, my mind half on a dark-haired Omega I shouldn't be thinking about and the other half is wondering where some of this money is coming from.

You can't expect people who do illegal business to hold a paper trail or have any information about their illegal activities, but in general, there's some way to write about what's coming in and what's going out.

And the numbers aren't adding up.

Unless there's something I'm missing, there seems to be a lot more money coming in than what's being spent. I mean, it's not the worst problem to be having, but it's still odd. When this Calvin guy was around, he wrote everything down on paper, green highlighter was weed money—how original—yellow was guns, and pink was the proper businesses the club has like the body shop and the stores.

It could be tossed quickly in a pinch, but gave the club

enough information on how much money was liquid, and what was coming in and out. When I look back at his files from about five years ago, there are numbers listed, but they aren't highlighted. *Where is this money coming from?*

A clang and the smell of smoke breaks my focus and Tate rolls into the body shop, looking like he's had more than his fair share of a few beers. He plops down on the worn, black leather sofa next to the desk and inhales his cigarette like it's a lifeline.

We're silent for a long while, me looking through the old files trying to find a connection and who knows what's rolling through Tate's head.

"I think I'm stayin'," he declares. I'm not sure if he's saying it out loud for himself or for my benefit.

"Okay," I reply plainly.

"Patch in with me. I need you to have my back, man."

I sigh as I hold up the coded files. "This place is a fucking mess."

"So let's change it. My dad... these old, out-of-touch assholes have been runnin' shit for too long."

"You want to overthrow your dad?" I ask, this being news to me.

"No, not necessarily, but we need to do shit different. We can't end up like the other chapters. We need to change this place from the inside out," he says.

I hold up the papers and toss him the folder from last year.

"Any idea what they could be selling or doing to make the money that's coming in?" I ask. Tate scans the documents but looks just as confused as ever.

"I'm not sure what I'm lookin' at."

"The un-highlighted amounts. They don't have an identifier saying where the money is coming from," I explain.

Tate's brows furrow as he flips through the files. "Let's keep this between me and you, yeah?"

"Yeah," I agree easily. The last thing I want to do is seem like I'm looking too close into things when I just got here. I already know there's some suspicion on me with the way I left Jacksonville. I'm no fucking rat, but I'm not an idiot either.

"Patch in with me. Help me fix this shit."

"Do you even have a plan, man?"

"No, but I'm workin' on it. So many of the other guys are tired of the way Kurt runs shit with a dictator-style gavel. The whole point of joining a club like this is to live freely. Fuck the government, the state of Florida, and fuck my dad for thinking he can control the way we all live," he rants.

"This sounds more personal than anything," I point out, not wanting to find myself in the middle of some serious family drama.

"It is to a degree, but hell, maybe we could patch in and then start our own chapter if that's what it takes. Aren't you tired of the same shit with each chapter? The best part of being a nomad was the freedom, but it came at the cost of not feeling like you're a part of somethin' real. Don't you want that?"

I wish Tate wasn't making so much sense. I wish I didn't get what he was saying, but I do. I joined a club to live the way I see fit, not to do so by anyone else's standards.

"Alright, Tate. I'll patch in. But if shit starts looking dicey, I'm out of this motherfucker."

He grins at me and pulls out a bottle of Jameson. He flicks the cap off, sending it across the room.

"To anarchy," he cheers, taking a deep swig and handing me the bottle.

"To anarchy," I repeat, wondering if this will be the worst decision of my life. The whiskey burns as it travels down my throat, and I find myself more than willing to make some reckless decisions.

EIGHT
REBELLION RISING

AXEL

IT'S BEEN A SHIT WEEK. Not only because I had to stay back and see what type of retaliation we would be lookin' at from the Outlaws, but because I haven't been able to communicate with Lily.

Lucky for us, they have too many enemies and none of their pathetic little prospects got a good enough look at any of us, which means I get to drive home today.

It's crazy that there's nowhere I'd rather be. Not just because my girl is here, probably wondering where the fuck I've been or why we haven't talked since that night, but because I'm gaining more brothers tonight. We're voting on who gets patched in.

As soon as these fuckers get their new patches and the booze is flowing, I'll be sneaking out to find Lily.

I should be concerned about the way she floods my thoughts. It's obsessive and destructive, but I don't really give a fuck. Without an outlet for my attention, I implode. I can't help but feel like Lily would always keep me centered.

The room is the fullest it's ever been. The oldest and longest-standing members sit around the long wooden table while the rest of us stand, except for the prospects who are waiting out in the main area of the clubhouse.

Prez is front and center, his fist wrapped around his gavel as he bangs it against the table.

"Alright, settle down. The quicker we get this shit over with, the quicker the lot of you can get your dicks wet. Now, if you're here and you ain't lookin' to patch in, walk your ass out that door now. No hard feelings. But if you stay, you're one of us. You'll wear your Dead Palms patch with the Tallahassee Original emblem. You'll be a part of this family, something bigger than yourself, and the men around you will become your brothers. It's unprecedented to have so many members patch over at the same time, but this club is moving forward and growing." Prez shakes his head and sighs. "Enough with the bullshit. Everyone who's still here is patching in, yeah?"

There's a rumble of yes and some soft bangs on the table in agreement.

"If anyone has any concerns about any of these fuckers patchin' in, now's the time to state your piece," he says.

No one utters a word, and he bangs the gavel one more time. "Welcome to the club, boys."

There's slapping on each other's backs, along with a ruckus as the doors open and we're released from Church. Probably the quickest patch over I've ever seen, but I'm definitely not mad about it.

I'm keeping to myself, mostly just sipping my beer at the bar when Tate sits next to me. Haven't spoken to him since our little trip down to Panama Beach. Cora gives him a smile from the bar and hands him a beer before walkin' away.

"Sup, man?" I ask him, and he nods his head in greeting. "Welcome to the club, I guess."

"Was pretty uneventful, wasn't it?" he asks, and we laugh.

"Suppose he already patched you before, didn't need to make a big deal of it again."

"Suppose not," Tate says. "You got a minute?"

"Sure," I say, taking the opportunity to at least sneak out of the clubhouse, which is part of my plan, anyway. I follow Tate to the body shop, wondering if he needs me to look at his bike or what's goin' on. When we're finally inside, he directs me towards the back office where we sit on the piece-of-shit couch that Ambien and I picked off the side of the road on collection day.

"How do you feel about makin' some extra money?" he asks, making my brow furrow.

"I'm always down for a job. What is it?" I ask, not even asking if it's club-sanctioned.

"I got some intel that the Wraiths are transporting some cargo over the next few weeks. I think we need to make sure that shipment doesn't get to where it's supposed to be goin'."

"You know Prez signed a truce with them?" I ask him, wondering if he doesn't know or if he's trying to stir the pot.

"That's odd, isn't it? The club that abused his Omega, the one that killed one of his best friends is the one we have a truce with," Tate questions.

"I assumed it was a matter of self-preservation. They're the biggest club in the south by far," I reply.

"It doesn't make you curious?" Tate asks, and I take a moment to really think about it. I guess I never really gave much thought to it before. I patched in, was told we had beef with this other club, but it was squashed now, and that the Wraiths were off-limits.

"Listen, man, I know you have shit with your dad. Is this really the way you want to go about it?" I ask him.

"Forget I mentioned it," he says, and I tilt my head at him.

"You know going after the Wraiths could rip this club in half right?" I ask.

"Well, maybe it's about time someone did. I've been here less than a week, and I can see every vulnerability of this place, and what has my father done? I'm here to set shit right, go back to being an actual fuckin' club where every voice matters. Aren't you sick of him controlling everything, controlling you?" Tate asks.

Lily is the first thing that comes to my mind. If the Prez is out of the picture, there's nothing holding us back. It's an extremely fucked up thought, and I feel like shit for it even crossing my mind. But if I take this job with Tate, I might at least get some serious coin out of the deal, enough to start over with Lily.

But if the Prez wasn't standing in my way at all, I could have everything I wanted. The girl, the club, the freedom.

"I'm in," I tell him, not taking another second to debate over it in my mind.

"I'm trustin' you," Tate warns.

"Yeah, and I'm trustin' you to not get us killed and destroy this club in the process," I counter.

"That's not what I want. I want this club to be run differently. I want everyone's voice to matter. You can't tell me you think the way shit is runnin' right now is fair," he poses.

"I'm ridin' with you, man. I've got my own motives," I reply.

"As long as you got my back, I've got yours. Things are goin' to be different around here," he promises.

"You'll let me know when the shipment is?"

"As soon as I know more, I'll let you know."

"Who else is in on it?" I ask.

"Me, you, and Cash right now. Anyone else we should trust?" Tate asks me, and I think carefully about who might be disgruntled around here.

"Maybe Mickey, Maverick, or Atlas, but other than that, I'm not sure they wouldn't tell Prez."

Tate nods, and I take it for the dismissal it is. So much for a simple patch ceremony. Shit just got ten times more complicated.

When I leave the body shop, I don't go back to the tumultuous laughter from the clubhouse. Instead, I make my way over to Lily's tree. When I see she's not there, I climb the Prez's roof. He'd probably shoot me in the ass and leave me in the grass if he caught me doing this, but I don't care. I need to see her.

The slope of the roof is easy enough to climb up, and I spot her window right away. She's wearing latex gloves and pouring a concoction into some sort of mold. I knock lightly on the glass, startling her as she turns around. Her face starts off confused but quickly turns to elation when she sees that it's me.

She takes off the gloves and walks over, pushing up the window for me.

"Hey, darlin'," I say, expecting a warm greeting.

"Where have you been?" she asks.

"Had to spend a few days in Panama Beach," I tell her. She doesn't offer for me to come into her room, and I don't push my luck. "You know, I wanted to get back as soon as possible. Nothin' changed from the last time we spoke."

"Maybe for you. Did you know I went on a date two nights ago?"

"You did what now?" I ask, my temper rising.

"Kurt set me up on a blind date."

"And how did this date go?" I ask dryly, trying to temper down my need to kill somebody.

"Terrible, I hated it. If we want to be together, we need to come up with a plan sooner rather than later," she stresses. I can see the panic in her eyes.

"I'm workin' on somethin', darlin'," I tell her.

"Care to share?" I grin at her and shake my head.

"As soon as I have more news, you'll be the first to know."

"I didn't want to go on the date," she says, and I believe her. "I have a feeling he's going to make me go on another one soon. Lately, it seems like he wants me gone as soon as possible."

My brows furrow, and I tilt my head at her in confusion.

She sighs and reaches out to touch my wrist. She seems more content once we have some physical form of contact. "I don't think he wants to risk me going into heat and being here.

The sooner I'm packed up, the sooner he has one less problem on his hands."

"You're not a fuckin' problem," I correct her. She smiles softly at me and shakes her head.

"I don't know what to do, Axel. I'm scared."

I push my way into her window, and she steps back to give me space. "Hey," I say, cupping her face. "I'm goin' to fix this. I'm figurin' it all out. We'll run away if we have to," I vow.

"You'd do that? You'd leave the club behind for me? Axel, we hardly even know each other," she says. Sure, she's using logic because she's smart and perfect, but I don't give a fuck.

"When you know, you know. I know I can't be your everything, Lily. But I want you to be mine."

"Are you sure I'm really worth all this trouble?" she questions. "What if you go through all of this and we find out we aren't compatible, or you resent me for needing a pack, or what if I ruin it all?"

"You won't. I'm gonna take care of everything. I'm gonna take care of you."

"I can't let you risk anything with the club. I like it here. I want to stay," she pleads.

"That's my plan too, darlin'. You just let me worry about figurin' this out and you play nice with the Prez."

"Even if that means going on other dates?" she asks.

My nostrils flare, but I nod my head. "If they so much as try to touch you, I'll kill em'. Just know that, alright, baby?"

She nods her head and blinks at me.

"You know, you sure talk a big game for someone who hasn't even kissed me yet." She's trying to push me into kissing her, and I love knowing that this attraction isn't one-sided. I take some peace in knowing that it's not pheromones. She likes me for me.

I shake my head, rubbing my thumbs against the soft skin of her jaw, and lean down to whisper in her ear. "Only because I know you'll fuckin' own me as soon as I taste you. Be patient for me. Can you do that, darlin'?"

She bites her lip and nods. She leans against me, and I hold her head against my chest. This is where she belongs.

This obsession with Lily started long ago. Longer than I'd like to admit, longer than I've been hyper-fixated on anything in my life. I don't know when Lily decided I was worth anything, let alone the privilege of pursuing her, but I'm going to do anything and everything I can to keep her here with me where she belongs.

I had almost given up hope that anything could happen between us, with the Prez making her untouchable and how few opportunities I had to be around her. But I can't deny this connection we've been toeing around for years. The small flirtations, the stolen glances, it might mainly be physical, especially on her part, but I plan on showing her the type of man I can be, the type of man I'm willing to become to be worthy of her.

She makes me feel unlike anything in my life ever has. I never hated being a Beta. Even joining a club like the Dead Palms, I never felt less than when compared to my Alpha brothers. But holding Lily right now fills me with more purpose than anything I've felt in my life. It's as exhilarating as it is terrifying.

I don't know if I made the right decision aligning myself with Tate, but I know it's truly my only option if I want to be with Lily, especially with the sand of time drifting away faster than I'd like.

NINE

FUCK THE IRS

I'M STREAMING for Marielli's Mass, and you'd be surprised how many people will tune in to watch you make soap topless. Might as well get paid to do both. For making the soap, and for letting people look at my tits while doing so.

I have two bars I need to get shipped out today, not that making soap puts a dent toward my nest egg. I almost thought about telling Axel about it last night, how I have nearly sixty-thousand dollars saved up. But I didn't, and I don't know why.

As much as I'm drawn to Axel, as much as I love the idea of starting a pack together, I'm not sure I can fully trust him when it comes to this. I don't think I can trust anyone but myself.

I wish I wasn't so jaded. But how can I not be? I barely remember most of my childhood. I looked it up online and apparently, it's your brain's way of protecting you from trauma, which tracks. To be honest, I don't remember most of my time from when we lived with the Wraiths, and considering that entails the first decade of my life, it's a pretty significant amount of time.

What I do know is that my mother is traumatized. The scars she wears on her face, the way she flinches at loud noises, or how she breaks down when someone raises their voice at her. I know I don't want that to be me; I don't want to be afraid to live life, but I also don't want to get trapped with a pack who would ever even consider hurting me.

She survived living with them for nearly two decades. She doesn't talk about it—any of it, really. And I know she's happy here with Dread and Kurt, but I just can't end up like her; trapped with a pack that uses and abuses me with no way out. My mom had nothing, and they used it against her, ripped her off the street when she perfumed at sixteen. She had my brother after her first heat, trapping both of them there. I don't know how she prevented getting pregnant after that, but she did. Until she had me. The details of how the Dead Palms found us are still blurry, but I know they saved our lives. If we had stayed there and I perfumed, my fate would be a generational curse.

My brother is just as lucky, getting out before he designated or he would have been completely indoctrinated into their club.

The Dead Palms saved my family's lives, and I can't help but feel like I'm deceiving them. When it comes to what I'm doing for money, the bank account itself, and the way I feel like I'm manipulating Axel into keeping me here. I guess it wouldn't be considered manipulation if we both want the same thing. It still feels like a lie.

I close out of the stream. Two thousand dollars isn't so bad for sitting there and making soap. I toss on a shirt, and I'm cleaning up my supplies when there's a light knock at the door.

"Come in," I say. I'm happy when it's my mom walking through the door with a stack of mail.

She hands it to me and looks around the room. "It smells like a brothel in here," she comments, scrunching up her nose.

"Yes, well, people pay a lot of money to buy soaps that help them smell like an Omega," I retort. She gives me a warm smile and sits on my bed.

"How did your date go the other night?" she asks, and I grimace.

"Not great, and I'd rather not talk about it."

My mom winces. "Then it's probably not a good time to tell you Kurt set up another date for tomorrow night?"

"Tomorrow?" I ask, the deep sinking feeling of betrayal running down my spine. *Just how fucking bad does he want me off this compound?*

"If it helps, these guys are younger, still in their late twenties," my mom states, trying to be enticing.

"That helps. But you know that's not what I want," I try to plead with her.

"Please, Lily. Don't make this more difficult. Kurt knows best. He's just trying to take care of you. We should have tried to find you a pack a long time ago. And for that, I'm sorry."

"Shouldn't I get a choice?" I protest.

"You are getting a choice. No one is forcing you to bond with anyone," she counters.

"But I'm also not allowed to pursue anyone in the club."

My mother stands and looks at me with compassion but also a bit of irritation. "We want more for you. Can you please just do your best to be pleasant on this date?"

"I'll do my best," I concede. She sighs, but says nothing else, accepting this as the win it is.

I sit on my bed and sort through my mail, nothing standing out except the last envelope.

"The IRS?" I say out loud to myself. When I open the paper, my heart sinks into my stomach, and I feel like I'm going to throw up.

It's vain and stupid, but my first thought is that Omegas shouldn't have to worry about shit like taxes. Some of the verbiage in the letter is confusing and scares the absolute shit out of me.

I'm panicking, my stomach hurts, and I want to cry. *Why wasn't this something I even thought about?*

I obviously can't go to my family with this or they'll wonder where all the money came from and where I'm keeping it. I could go to Axel, but as much as I care for him and adore him, I'm not sure he's ever paid taxes before in his life. I'm tugging on the ends of my hair when a person who I know is good with numbers pops into my head.

I slide on my sandals and fold up the paper before heading out the door. Only to realize that I don't know where to find Cash. Maybe I'll get lucky and he'll still be working in the office at the body shop.

Honestly, I'm being very brave right now, not spiraling into a fit of tears as I make my way through the shop where the guys are working. Most of them ignore me. Though Axel gives me a curious look. I give him the best smile I can manage until I make it to the office. To my sweet fucking relief, he's there.

It's stupid. I know it's dumb, but I burst into tears as soon as he says my name. "Lily? What's wrong?"

"Fuck, I've got to stop crying around you," I joke as I try to compose myself. He seems sympathetic to my breakdown, and I wonder if he thinks I'm insane. *Probably.*

"Sit down," he urges, and I do, taking a seat on the shitty couch next to his desk. He hands me a bottle of water, and I take it. "What's wrong?" he asks again. We both look down at the paper fisted in my hands. With a dejected groan, I hand it over to him.

After he reads it, he looks back over at me. "Lily, how… okay, this is what we're going to do—"

"You're going to help me?" I ask hopefully.

"Yeah, I'm going to help you. Because the IRS coming after you could lead to them coming after the club."

"Oh my God, I didn't even think about the club. I'm so stupid," I chastise myself.

His palm on my chin is tight as he forces me to look at him. "Don't say bad shit about yourself again. We're going to fix it. It's going to be simple. You gonna tell me how you made this money, sweetheart?"

"I'd really rather not," I say.

"Is it legal?"

"Yes. Obviously, if the IRS wants a cut." He gives me a look, and I swallow down the sass.

"Fuck the IRS," he grumbles. "You don't have to tell me how you got the money. Can you just promise me that you're safe?" he asks.

It makes me want to cry again. All this emotion is fucking bullshit, and I hate it. I hate feeling like this, and I hate knowing what it means.

I'm running out of time.

My eyes must water again, and Cash leans down and kisses my forehead before sitting down at the desk. The action was so out of left field and endearing for a man who looks like he could rip a car in half.

"You know what's bullshit. The IRS knows exactly how much money you owe, yet they expect Americans to figure this shit out on their own. You're not alone, and you're not in trouble. We just need to pay the Federal tax from what you made last year and it will be fine. You're going to be okay," he reassures.

"Okay," I reply softly. "Can we keep this between us? No one knows about this account."

"Why doesn't anyone know?" he asks skeptically. I don't know what it is about Cash, but I just feel comfortable around him. The moment I ran into him that first night, he made me feel safe, and right now I feel precious and taken care of. He's helping me out massively, not only by calming me down but helping me with my problem.

"You've seen my mom?" I ask him, and he nods. "Her first pack did that to her. I wanted… I wanted a guarantee that I would always be safe, always have a backup plan."

He looks at me with what I would call affection as he replies. "That's smart, Lily. Your secret is safe with me."

"Thank you. For helping and for not telling anybody. I just…" I shake my head as I trail off.

"You just what?" he asks.

"It's nothing. How bad is the damage?" I ask him as he logs into the site that the letter from the IRS directed us to. I have to get off the couch and lean over him slightly to put some information in. When I see the amounts, I want to scream and cry all over again, but I hold it together.

It doesn't hurt when Cash's strong hand rubs up and down my back. "Just breathe. Do you have enough to cover it? Do you need help?" he asks.

I'm shocked when I look over at him. "You'd do that?"

"You're a part of this club, we'd all do it," he answers, and I nod my head, understanding that it's an offer as an extension of this club, not something personal between the two of us.

"Do you know your checking and routing number?" he asks.

"My what?"

"Do you have a banking app on your phone?" he asks. I nod and pull it up. I watch his eyes widen when he looks at the amount. "First off, as soon as we pay this, you're opening a savings account and transferring all of this over." I don't mention how I, in fact, thought all this money was already going into a savings account. "If you wanted, you could invest some of it, but that's more of a gamble."

"No, I just need it as a backup, just in case."

He types out a few more things and asks me for my email, which sends a digital copy of the receipt showing I'm now a law-abiding citizen.

"So… that's it?"

"That's it. It's all taken care of. When you need to file next year, I'll help you get it all sorted."

I can't help it. I wrap my arms around the large Alpha's neck and squeeze. I probably shouldn't be hugging him so hard or taking deep inhales of his scent, but I do. He also wraps his arms around me and doesn't let go. The hug feels more than just two friends sharing an embrace, but I don't let myself get the wrong idea. Cash is simply a good fucking guy, who clearly has a soft spot for trainwreck Omegas.

But I swear his scent is getting thicker…

The door to the office opens, and it's Axel's voice that brings us back to reality. "Darlin' you all good in here?" he asks. I step back from Cash, and he hands me the papers from the IRS.

"Yeah, Cash was helping me with something," I respond, giving Cash a nod. My hand grazes past Axel's as I leave, and when the door shuts behind me, I wince, wondering if Axel is going to get pissed.

GET ON THE FUCKIN' BIKE

IT'S ONLY BEEN one day since I thought the government was going to cart me away for tax evasion and I was going to get thrown in some high-security Omega prison. But having to go on a date with more Alphas is making me think an orange jumpsuit might be better than having to keep up this charade.

I'm wearing a floral mini dress when I see Axel walk across the square, headed toward his bike. He looks pissed as I get into Kurt's truck.

"What crawled up that boy's ass?" he asks, also noticing Axel's mood. I just shrug my shoulders while I internally scream. *Why can't all this be easier? Why can't Kurt just let me stay with the club?* Guilt makes my stomach churn, and I wonder how I'm supposed to eat knowing that Axel is upset? All while there's nothing I can do about it.

I don't even bother listening to what Kurt says as he drops me off at the front doors of the restaurant. At least this one is more casual, plus Mexican food is my favorite.

Three large men stand in the lobby. They're attractive enough. Maybe I just need to have an open mind? When the broad, blond one speaks, I know I'm doomed.

"Come on, Omega. Let's go sit at our table," he orders.

He's large but in an Alpha-finance-bro kind of way. Nothing like the guys in the club who put time and effort into their bodies. This guy is simply big because of his genetics, not because he ever does manual labor.

"My name is Lily," I introduce myself while trying to swallow down any attitude. I really can't afford to have another crying session after another date.

Just play nice, and get this over with.

The one with the beard tilts his head as he listens to my voice. "Right, we're Paul, Dave, and Phil."

"Right," I parrot, hating this whole situation.

I'm not sure which name belongs to whom since he just said them all rapidly and didn't point to anyone in particular.

We sit at the table, the blond one and the one with the beard flanking me, while the quiet one with longer, light brown hair sits across from me. He also looks like he doesn't want to be here, and I wish I knew why.

It's the same awkward small talk from the first date, but this time the server brings all of them beers and me a virgin daiquiri. I hate it; the date, not the drink. The sweet taste of strawberry cooling my throat is the only thing I like about this date.

"So, Kurt tells us that you like to make soap?" the bearded one says.

"Yes, I have an online store where I sell them. I like having something to do," I tell him.

"We have a spare room in the house that would be perfect for any projects you'd like to do," he states as if it's a done deal. It's extremely presumptive, but semi-sweet, so I let it slide.

"Where do y'all live?" I ask them.

"We live right on Lake Jackson," the quiet one sitting across from me answers. I whistle in my head, knowing how expensive properties on the lakes can be. But also how ridiculous it is to buy property on a lake in Florida when it might just get gobbled up by a sinkhole.

"That must be nice," I comment, keeping my tone polite.

"It is, but we've been looking for that missing piece," bearded Alpha says.

"And for you, that would be an Omega?" I ask, and bearded guy nods his head, narrowing his eyes at me.

I'm not sure why he looks at me so attentively when I speak, but it makes me a little uncomfortable. He's checked me out more times than someone should when first meeting. The only thing worse than his uncouth behavior are the words that spill out of the blond one's mouth.

"Right, we're ready for kids and settling down," he says.

"Well, I turn twenty-one next week. I'm not ready for kids yet." To be honest, I'm not even sure if I'm mentally ready to bond yet. At least not with any of the assholes I keep going on dates with. I think about if Axel were an Alpha, would I let him bite me? *I think I would…*

"Things change when you're bonded," the blond one counters.

I just ignore his comment and thank the server when he brings our chips and salsa.

The bearded one snaps his fingers. "I thought your voice sounded familiar," he exclaims, his eyes going wide.

"Sorry?" I ask.

"Can't you hear it, Paul?" the bearded one asks, so I at least know the dickhead blond one's name is Paul.

"What the fuck are you talking about, Dave?" Paul asks him.

"Can you say *thank you for the tip user26738?*" Dave asks, and my heart sinks. I'm placing my napkin on the table and standing up to leave the restaurant before he can even finish voicing his request. I have my phone out, making my way out of the building, and ready to call Kurt to pick me up. *But what if they tell Kurt everything?*

Oh my God. This is so bad. There's no leaving this date unscathed. Unless maybe I can convince these assholes to keep their mouths shut? I'm leaning against the side of the restaurant facing the parking lot, attempting not to have a panic attack. *Fuck, why does every emotion I feel have to be elevated right now?* I want to crawl out of my skin instead of feeling like this. It's like the world is crushing me slowly, and I'd rather be sucked in than have to bear the weight of my circumstances.

A hand wraps around my wrist way too tightly, jarring me from my thoughts. It's not gentle at all, and I know he's going to leave a bruise. I'm used to roughness, but this borders toward hurt. This man wants to hurt me and show his dominance for no other reason than that he can.

"Get your ass back inside," Paul demands. His grip tightens, making me wince as I try to tug myself away, which only makes the pain radiate up my arm.

"I think this date is over," I say, even though I hear the wobble in my voice. I hate feeling so weak.

"And I say it's not. You have no problem letting strangers pay to look at your tits or that bare little pussy of yours online. I think you can handle us paying for your meal," Paul sneers.

I've never felt lower than I do when this man speaks to me. It's like I'm not a person, but a thing created to please Alphas and men alike. What I do for money has nothing to do with my value as a person, nor does my designation. Tears well in my eyes, but I try to stay strong. Deep down I know I'm strong, maybe not physically so, but I'm not letting this Alpha take me anywhere without a fight. I'll kick, scratch, bite, whatever I have to do to get away.

"Get your hands off of me," I yell at him. He doesn't relent, tugging my wrist to get me to go back into the restaurant.

Dave has joined us outside, and I have some hope he will talk some sense into his pack mate. Sure, he realized who I was, but he was the most polite throughout the date, even if he gave me the creeps.

"Oh, come on, *Marielli*," he sneers my pseudonym.

I want to throw up knowing they know my true identity. I'm not sure it can get worse than this. Not only has this date gone to hell, but more than likely he's going to tell Kurt. I haven't thought about the ramifications of him finding out the truth about what I've been doing. Maybe that will push him to do something drastic, more drastic than these ridiculous dates. What if this is the last straw, and he ships me off to some pack without my say? What if I never get to step foot on the compound again or see all the people I love and care about? No matter what happens tonight, I know there will be consequences, ones I certainly don't want to face.

Paul's hand is still tight around my wrist and Dave brings his hand up to grab the nape of my neck. "Come on, Omega. We've already seen it online. Might as well give us our money's worth. Especially with the price Kurt put on you," he taunts. I tilt my head, trying to absorb his words.

"Price seems a little steep for a biker whore, if you ask me," Paul complains.

My eyes sting, my wrist hurts, and I'm trying to not shut down. I could do it, I think. Let my brain shut off and let my body pay the price. The thought has bile rising in my throat. I can't, I won't. I need a way out of this.

"Please let go of me," I plead.

"Oh, look at that. She has manners," Paul spits.

Tears spill over and stain my cheeks as I hear the voice of an absolute angel.

"She said to let her go," Axel commands calmly, leaning against his bike with a lit cigarette hanging from his mouth. He looks fucking deadly, like a demon raised from Hell to ride in and be my savior.

"Mind your own goddamn business," Paul snarls, dismissing Axel.

Axel laughs and blows a trail of smoke into the air before tossing the rest of the cigarette out on the concrete. He steps away from the bike and looks to the right of his ride, where he picks up a steel pipe.

He drags it against the pavement, creating a menacing

sound. "I said, let. Her. Go," he repeats. Dave and Paul's hands drop from my skin and the relief is instant. "Lily, get on the fuckin' bike," he orders. I must be in shock because I don't move. Axel's eyes meet mine, and while there's anger on the surface, I see the softness he reserves for me. "Baby, get on the bike," he commands.

I slowly walk away from Dave and Paul, but I don't get on the back, knowing he needs to get on first. But I wait as close as I can to his VRSC.

"Listen, man, things got out of hand," Paul starts backtracking while holding his hands up.

"Oh, is that what happened?" Axel asks with a laugh, a smile taking over his face as he swirls the pipe in a circle.

"Yeah, man. You just take her home. We can part ways amicably," Dave tries to negotiate.

"You're right. You'll go your way and we'll go ours," Axel agrees, and the guys both take a breath of relief. "Except you left a bruise on my girl. I think you owe her an apology," Axel demands.

"Listen, man, it was a—" Paul doesn't get another word out because Axel swings the pipe and hits him in the stomach.

"I said, apologize," Axel yells in his face. The smile he had before is gone, and he nudges Paul's stomach with the end of the pipe.

Paul sputters and coughs as he holds his stomach while leaning against the wall. "I'm… I'm sorry," Paul slurs.

Axel points the pipe at Dave, who holds his hands up in surrender. "What about you, asshole?"

"I'm sorry," he whimpers, looking at Axel, who takes two steps forward.

The end of the pipe pushes against Dave's stomach, making him take a few steps back until he's trapped. The wall of the restaurant at his back and the force that is Axel in front of him.

"To her, you dumb fuckin' cunt," he growls, nodding his head in my direction.

"I'm sorry. I'm so sorry," he whines in my direction.

It's hard to get the words out, but I somehow find them trapped in my throat. "They can't tell Kurt what they know," I whisper.

Axel furrows his brows but doesn't question it. He immediately takes my side and seems to be putting the pipe down to reason with these guys.

Paul and Dave seem relieved, but that quickly fades away when Axel pulls the pipe back and whacks Dave right in his thigh. I swear I hear something crunch; it makes me wince as the Alpha falls to his knees.

"You come around Lily again, I'll fuckin' kill you. You tell anybody about tonight, and I mean *anything* about tonight, I'll find you and I'll do more than fuckin' kill you."

"Fuck, we won't say anything. We're sorry," Dave pleads.

Axel lifts his leg and kicks him in the same spot where he hit him with the pipe, making him cry out.

"We said we're sorry!" Dave snivels trying and failing to hold back tears.

"I know. But you're not forgiven, and I sure as fuck ain't forgettin' this anytime soon. You feel me?"

"I feel you," Dave cries out in pain again.

That's when the last guy, Phil, comes rolling outside. As soon as he sees his two pack mates on the ground, his eyes go wide and he backs up.

"He touch you, darlin'?" Axel asks.

"No... he didn't do anything," I tell him, but Axel points the pipe at him, anyway.

"Pick up your pack mates and get the fuck out of here. I see any one of you anywhere you're dead fuckin' men," Axel threatens, tossing the pipe a considerable distance away from us.

He isn't wearing a helmet and doesn't have one attached to his bike. He tosses his leg over and tilts his head for me to get on.

I take one last look at the men crumpled on the ground and the man on the bike in front of me. I know the show of violence shouldn't do so much for me, but it does. Now that I'm protected, I feel bold as I give my failed dates the middle finger and jump on the back of Axel's bike.

My arms wrap around his middle, holding him tight as his engine purrs and we leave the chaos we created behind us in the dust.

No one ever lets me ride without a helmet, and my hair is whipping wildly in the wind as he drives through the night. He's cautious with me on the back, but he doesn't hold back on the turns or slow down his speed too much. I appreciate him even more for not treating me like porcelain.

I thought he might take us back to the compound, but he's headed in the opposite direction. I bask in the ride, my face pressed against the cool leather of his cut, and I take in his natural scent. It soothes me, calming down my nerves from the earlier altercation.

If Axel hadn't shown up, I have no clue what would have happened. How far would have things gone? And what the fuck did they mean about the price Kurt is asking for me?

I press my head even harder against Axel's back, seeking his comfort. His left hand leaves the handlebar, and he uses it to knead the flesh of my thigh, letting me know that he's got me. We might be going too fast with no helmets in the middle of the night, but I feel safer on this bike than I did at the restaurant. I'm not sure what it says about me that I feel more comfortable on the back of a bike with a criminal than I do with what society would consider good men, but I do.

I hold his cut like a lifeline and thank God that he was there to protect me. As always, the reality of my situation hits me like a slap to my face.

I need protection; I need a pack; I need Axel.

Things are only going to get harder for me. My emotional state has been all over the place. My sexual desires are running rampant. I know that after my birthday I won't have much time before my heat.

Running away with Axel won't be enough, as much as I wish it was. Even if he were an Alpha, it wouldn't be enough for me. As safe as I feel in this moment with my front pressed against his back, all I feel is complete fucking hopelessness.

ELEVEN
GOOD

AXEL

LILY'S HOLDING on for dear fuckin' life around my waist as we drive through back roads. I know I should have taken her back home. That's probably where she wants me to take her.

I couldn't get a good enough read on her at the restaurant, didn't help that I was close to killin' those fuckin' guys. *Who do they think they are putting their filthy fuckin' hands on a woman — my woman.*

Honestly, I don't give a fuck if Lily is scared after seeing how far I'll go to protect what's mine. If anything, it's better that she sees this side of me sooner rather than later. Sure, she knows we can get rough, she undoubtedly knows we do illegal shit, but we keep the violence away from the compound. The clubhouse is our sanctuary, where we can let shit go.

But out in the real world? All bets are off, and when it comes to somethin' I consider mine? It's fuckin' game over.

Her small fingers grip the leather of my cut and the press of her cheek against my back brings me back to reality.

What if I wasn't there?

What if I wasn't so fuckin' jealous and pissed off that she was goin' on a date that I stayed home? What would they have done to her then?

My anger is bubbling towards the surface, and I do everything I can to tame it. I can't let my temper spill out on her. That's one thing I'll never do.

She didn't want to go on the date in the first place; she's just following her stepfather's rules. The same man I find myself being led by, and the same man I'm beginning to resent as the days go on. Tate's plan is sounding more and more solid each and every day.

I drove off with no destination in mind, but it seems my inner child or some shit led the way. I slow down as we near the lake. Solar lights illuminate the path down to the pier, and I park by the bench.

We both just stay how we are for a moment, neither of us eager to stop touching each other or talk about what just happened.

If she's scared, I'll just have to promise it'll never happen again, even if it makes me a liar. I'm probably a piece of shit for thinking of ways to keep her, but I don't care. I never claimed I wasn't selfish.

"Axel," she sighs against my back.

"Yeah, baby?"

"Where are we?" she asks, her question throwing me for a loop. I thought her next words would be to take her home.

"My granddad's lake house," I tell her.

She squeezes me from behind again before getting off the bike and standing next to it. Her dark hair is wild and tangled from the ride over, and I can't help but find it sexy.

"The club knows about this place?" she asks.

"Nope," I reply, and she smiles.

Seeing her light up at me has my chest deflating with relief.

She takes a step closer to the bike, one of her hands gripping my shirt while the other is flat on my chest. "Thank you for being there tonight. I don't know what would've—"

"Darlin', if you start talkin' about what those motherfuckers could've done to you I'll turn around and shove that pipe so far up that blond jerk-off's ass it'll be coming out of his mouth," I snarl.

"Okay," she says, her hands not leaving my chest as she looks around at the back of the house and the dock by the lake. "I didn't take you for a lakehouse kind of guy," she teases.

"It was my granddad's dream. I don't use the place much," I admit, feeling a bit like a fuckin' sap, and missing the old man.

"Show me around?" she asks.

I nod my head, and as much as I don't want her hands to leave my chest, they have to in order for me to get off the bike. Once I know the bike is upright, I hold out my hand to her, and she takes it. It's a warm summer night, the kind where it feels like the air is drenching your skin. It makes Lily's feminine scent even richer. While I don't spiral over her scent like an Alpha would, just knowing that it's her signature gets me hard.

The frogs are bellowing and the bugs are fuckin' everywhere, including lightin' bugs that dance around as we make our way to the dock. The music of the night is the only thing we hear along with our footsteps as we walk to the end of the dock. She slides her sandals off, sitting down on the edge and I follow suit.

I haven't felt a moment this quiet in a long time. When I look over at Lily, a dark piece of untamed hair is sticking to the side of her pretty face. I let this moment sink in, committing every detail to memory. It's a blink-of-an-eye type of memory, but somehow I know I'll cherish it forever. Just a man and a woman sitting together, taking in the summer night.

I never thought I could feel like this, like I would crave a softness in my life, but it's clearer than ever that I need it. I need Lily's soft smile, touch, and heart in my life like I need to fuckin' breathe. The idea of her being taken away from me, bonding with some trust fund pieces of shit… it makes me sick.

I know she can't just be mine, and I've been wrapping my small fuckin' brain around that fact. But right now, on this dock? We're the only two people in the world that exist, and I can live with that.

"What are you thinking about?" she asks softly, her legs swinging above the water freely.

"Too much," I respond, instead of spewing my fuckin' heart out.

I can't. I can't give her everything until I know she's mine to keep. I've gotta work with Tate, to either get rid of the Prez or have someone else at the gavel, making the club less of a dictatorship. At the very least, I need to help Lily find other possible packmates so we can stand beside one another.

Lily and I alone can't change her fate. I'm not naïve.

"I'm thinking about how nice this is," she admits. "This is the kind of date I would have liked to have."

"Watchin' me beat the piss out of some guys?" I question teasingly, and she laughs.

"I enjoyed that more than I probably should have. But no, just this… no fancy dinner with stupid small talk, no trying to impress someone you don't even like. Just existing beside someone else and loving every moment, even the quiet ones," she says. I can't look away from her. The moon shines against her skin, and all I want to do is scoop her up, savoring these quiet private moments with her forever.

"You said it way more fuckin' eloquently than I ever could," I joke, feeling out of my depths.

She bumps her small shoulder against mine, and I lean in as we both stare out at the soft moving water, the moon's reflection glinting against the lake.

"What if we never went back?" she whispers. It's so soft I almost think I imagined her saying it.

"You really want that?" I ask her seriously.

She sighs and shakes her head. "No, I love living at the compound. I love my family and the people. I think we both know that we belong there," she states, and I nod my head.

"Are we being crazy? We hardly know each other, but I can't help this tug I feel towards you."

"No, we're not crazy. It's the rest of the world that needs to get with the program. You shouldn't have to consider anyone else's opinion but your own when it comes to buildin' your pack."

"Thank you," she says, and I shake my head.

"You don't need to thank me. That's just common fuckin' respect."

"You don't think I'm stupid for wanting to stay with the MC?"

"No, it's all you know. Why wouldn't that be what you want?" When I look back at her, her big brown eyes are glassy, and I wonder if the night is catching up to her. "Baby, I didn't mean to upset you," I try to soothe.

She shakes her head. "You didn't." She makes an adorable, irritated growling noise. "My hormones are all over the place. I wasn't sad, I just… finally felt understood," she mumbles.

"I'd like to understand you a bit more," I coax quietly like some asshole is hiding behind a tree watching me be vulnerable or some shit.

"I'd like that too," she agrees, but it's then that her stomach rumbles, making her cheeks heat.

"They didn't even fuckin' feed you on the date?" I ask, and she shakes her head. "You got anything against Ramen?"

A wide smile takes over her face as she shakes her head. I stand up first and hold out a hand to her to help her up. She pushes her dress down and slides on her sandals as we pad our way to the lake house.

I don't come here often, but I do come here enough to keep it stocked up with non-perishables. This place is my Hail Mary if shit ever hits the fan. Her hand is warm and pliant in my own, and I'm hit with an overwhelming feeling of rightness.

We've only had short-lived moments on the compound that always seem to get interrupted. This is the first time I'm alone with her where we don't have to look over our shoulders and can actually be ourselves. It's just the truth slapping me harder in the face. We're supposed to be together.

I enter the code to the door, not caring if Lily is paying attention or not. I do my best to keep the place clean and updated, but it's clearly not lived in. I flick on lights as we walk through the house. Lily takes in all the family photos and old portraits of landscapes my granddad loved.

Once we're in the kitchen, I open the pantry and rub the back of my neck. "I don't have much," I warn her. She just politely smiles and walks in beside me, grabbing multiple things and bringing them to the cooktop. "I didn't mean for you to make us somethin'," I mutter.

"It's fine."

"I can take you somewhere to eat," I offer.

"I want to stay here for as long as we can get away with it," she says with a smirk.

I wanna fuckin' lock her in here and keep her prisoner, but I know that won't do shit for either of us.

The noodles she makes aren't anything to write home about, but it's also the best meal I've ever had.

We eat and we just talk. It's so confusing how simple this connection is, yet everything around us seems so fuckin' complicated.

"How are the new guys working out?" she asks.

"Haven't got to know all of em'. Tate, Cash, Doc, and Atlas seem cool enough," I tell her.

"What about Sasquatch?" she jokes, and I shake my head, wondering how in the fuck he earned that road name. I mean, he's a big dude, but it's not like he's a hairy freak or anything.

"Jury is still out on that one. How have things been at home with the Prez?" I ask her.

I know that he loves Lily. He loves her mother more than anything. But the dates he's setting her up on are shit, she needs a real man—men. I can honestly understand him wanting her out of the club. She's sweet and perfect, and I know my dirty hands are going to soil her up. On the other hand, she wants me too, and I'm gonna give her everything she wants. But the blatant disregard of her free will? Yeah, that shit ain't sittin' right at all. I hadn't thought about him treating the club the same, but ever since Tate asked me to join him, I've been doing a hell of a lot of thinking about how much of a dictatorship this club has become.

"Fine, I guess. Kurt doesn't seem stressed or anything. Well, at least, not with the club."

"You need to tell him those assholes put their hands on you," I urge her.

"I can't," she whines.

"Does this have to do with what you didn't want them to tell Prez?" She nods, and I click my tongue. I don't like secrets between us, yet I hold so fuckin' many. If this is something she needs for her own peace, I'll leave it… for now. "Just tell me you're not in any danger, and I'll drop it."

She licks her lips, and she looks me in the eye fiercely, letting me know that she's being nothin' but honest. "I'm not in any danger."

"Okay, then your secret's safe with me," I promise, and she stands while I stay seated.

Her dress hits her calves, but the way she saunters over to me… she might as well be wearing next to nothing as she wedges herself between my legs.

"I think I'd like to keep some more secrets tonight," she flirts, her hands going to my shoulders and shifting to the back of my neck where her nails drag against my scalp.

My hands immediately wrap around the back of her thighs. They're toned from running; I probably shouldn't plan my day around when I know she's going for a run, but sometimes that's the only chance I get to see her.

"What'd you have in mind, darlin'?"

"I want to feel good," she begs me, not mincing words, or

asking me something stupid like *what I want to do to her*. I want to do everything to her. I want her in every single depraved way my mind can come up with, and then some. But I know myself. I know how obsessed I'm going to become as soon as we take the next step.

I try to talk myself out of it and fail. I already followed her on her date. I'm already hooked.

My forehead presses against her shoulder as I inhale her scent. Her nails scratch my scalp seductively, and all I can think about is her tugging on my hair while I fuck her into oblivion.

"As soon as I touch you, it's over for me, darlin'."

"What do you mean?" she breathes.

My hands glide further up her legs till I'm just barely touching her ass. I want to consume her. I want to be her only thought; I want her to need me; I want her to risk every single fuckin' thing for this feeling.

I lift my head from her neck and look into her needy brown eyes. She bites her lip as she looks down at me. A true fuckin' queen if I've ever seen one.

"There's *no how we're goin' to make this shit happen*; if I touch you, it's happenin'. You're mine, and there's no goin' back. If I have to kidnap your ass, kill somebody, take down the club, I'll do it."

She swallows audibly, taking in my vow.

"Then touch me, show me what I've been missing," she whispers.

I should be a stronger man, I should hold back and tell her not yet, that she doesn't understand that I'm truly serious. That if there's a single threat of her being taken away from me, everything is forfeit. The club has been my refuge, the thing that made me a man. But Lily? She's the woman worth risking it all for.

I grab the hem of her dress, pushing it up so my hands are touching the skin of her thighs, and she sighs at the touch. It's never been like this for me, never this intense or meaningful.

Her skin is warm and soft under my touch, and I can't imagine this ever being taken away from me.

"You're gonna fuckin' ruin me, darlin'."

"Good."

She tugs on my hair slightly, forcing me to look up at her. "I want you to ruin me too," she murmurs. "Kiss me," she requests.

My hands ache as I remove them from her legs and stand. She looks up at me with hooded eyes as I use one hand to cup the back of her head and the other to tilt her chin.

And when our lips meet, I know that my fate has just been sealed forever.

TWELVE
NO ONE ELSE CAN GIVE YOU THIS

LILY

AXEL'S KISS IS SOFT. Nothing like the man who beat up two Alphas in my honor with a pipe a few hours earlier. No, this is the sweet man who took me to his granddad's lake house and just sat in comfortable silence with me to make *me* feel better.

It's a powerful feeling knowing that it's me that makes him softer, gentler. I have a power over him not because of our designations or pheromones, but because we're meant to be. I don't care if the rest of the world doesn't believe in soul mates.

That's bullshit, and this kiss proves it.

Axel was right about us, as soon as our lips touched, I was done for. I'm not an inexperienced virgin, my Florida public school education was worth something, but this? This is what people mean when they talk about intimacy. I didn't know what I was missing out on until this moment. Sure, I love being touched, kissed… everything. But this kiss? This kiss has me feeling weak in the knees. It has me forgetting all about the outside world and the problems that are waiting for me. There are no designations, pressure, or other people to worry about. It's just Axel and me and nothing else is of importance.

His fingers tighten in my hair as his lips part and our

tongues meet. He makes a noise of satisfied male pleasure, and my knees go weak. The hand he was using to hold my chin wraps around my middle as he tugs me closer.

The hard length of his cock presses against my stomach, and I already know I'm soaking wet. Coconut and jasmine are the only notable scents in the space.

Axel must notice because his kiss turns more aggressive like he can't get enough of me. I'm addicted to this feeling, and I never want to let it go.

He shocks me, his hand dropping from my body to wrap around the back of my thighs. He hefts me on top of the table without his lips ever leaving mine. He has my dress pushed up toward the top of my thighs, and I gasp when his hands grip my flesh. His club ring is cold compared to the rest of his hand.

Axel is slow with his hand movements, his fingertips getting closer to my core as he kisses me. I can't help when I shimmy myself closer to him, to his hand. He laughs against my mouth, which makes me smile against his lips.

"Tell me, darlin'. What do you need?" he asks, wanting me to beg for it. And God, do I want to fucking beg for it.

"Touch me," I tell him.

"I am touchin' you," he replies.

"Touch my pussy," I correct. His breathing stills and his eyes meet mine. We keep eye contact as he drags his knuckle along the seam of my panties.

"Like that?"

"More," I breathe, begging shamelessly.

He uses the same knuckle to rub a soft circle around my clit. "Like that?" he teases. I let out a soft whine, and I watch his pupils dilate. "Does my baby need to be full?"

"Please, Axel," I whimper.

He grabs the fabric of my panties and rolls them down my legs, pocketing the material instead of letting them hit the floor. His hands are gentle as he pushes my dress up toward my waist, my bare ass now pressed against the table.

I widen my legs for him, and he groans. He takes a moment to just stare at where I'm undoubtedly wet and ready for him. It should be uncomfortable, awkward even, but it's not. I feel reverent and wholly cared for. Once he's done staring, he takes a step closer to me, grabbing me roughly by the neck and bringing our lips together in a show of desperate need.

He's still kissing me as his hand slides down my body. He teases me with his touch, not touching me where I've begged him to. Suddenly, his fingers glide through my obscene wetness.

"Fuck, baby," he moans between kisses. His fingers explore more, until one slides inside of me, a second one quickly following suit.

"More," I whine.

"Does my Omega need this sweet cunt filled up?"

"Please."

"Fuck, you're so beautiful," he says, our gazes meet when our faces part. He just watches me as he works me over, adding a third finger inside me and his thumb to my clit.

My hips involuntarily tilt towards his hand, my body craving more. It's been so long since someone else touched me like this, let alone set my whole body on fire the way Axel does.

"You feelin' greedy, darlin'?" he teases.

"Always," I reply, sticking to the truth, which makes him smile.

"I need you to cum before I finally give you my cock. That's what you want, isn't it?"

His forehead presses against mine, and I wrap my arms around his shoulders, the chill of his cut cooling my warm skin.

He presses his lips against my ear before he speaks next. "You want me to fuck you so bad, don't you, baby?" I nod my head, and he nips my earlobe in response. "Then you better make a fuckin' mess for me."

He pushes all of his fingers except his thumb inside of me, and it's exactly what I need; that full feeling of taking a knot.

His fingers don't fully get me there, but his thumb rubbing small circles around my clit does.

"No one else can give you this. Can they, baby? You need me to take care of this perfect pussy, don't you?" he asks.

His words completely shatter me. His free arm circles my back, holding me up as I break apart. My thighs are trembling, and I can feel the gush of wetness around my thighs. I'm not even sure what words leave my mouth. I only know that Axel likes them by the noises he's making.

I swear my hearing even goes out for a second. The only thing bringing me back to reality is the slow glide of Axel's fingers leaving my body. The whine that rips out of my throat is desperate and needy, but Axel doesn't mind as he kisses the side of my head.

"You're so fuckin' perfect. You did so good," he praises. I tighten my arms around his shoulders and hold him close.

"Thank you," I say, and I swear he shivers. I pull back to look at his pretty blue eyes. "I believe I was made some hefty promises," I joke.

He smirks and grips his belt with his slick free hand. I'm biting my lip with the excitement of seeing and feeling his dick when his phone rings.

He groans but digs it out of his back pocket. When he looks down at the name and his face falls, I know our precious stolen moment has come to an end. He gives me a look of apology before bringing the phone to his ear.

"What?" he barks out.

He holds up his slick-covered hand and my cheeks heat, he slides them into his mouth while the other person on the phone speaks. Even him using his tongue to clean his fingers isn't enough for the mess I made of him.

I hop off the table and grab some paper towels, wetting a few to clean off his hands while he listens.

"You've gotta be fuckin' kiddin' me. No one else can help?" he barks over the phone.

He gives me a soft smile as I clean him up, even though he's irritated with whomever he's speaking to.

He looks at the ceiling with annoyance, saying, "I'll be back in a half hour," over the phone while nodding along to the rest of the conversation.

Once he hangs up, his hands quickly return to my thighs. I love how easily the affection between us has progressed. I've always wanted more with him, always admired him from afar or flirted when I got the chance. I thought that's all we could have, small moments kept between us. But after tonight? I know we're going to be so much more. Between the two of us, we'll figure something out.

"Sorry. We have to go back," he sighs.

"Is everything okay?"

"Yeah, it's all good," he dismisses, not giving me any more details. "I'm makin' you mine, Lily Rose," he vows, and I grin at the use of my middle name, nodding my head.

"I need more moments like this," I plead, and he leans down to kiss me again.

"I'll figure it out, baby," he promises, and I have no other option but to believe him.

AXEL IS smart about parking near the side of the compound. His plan is to sneak me home before he makes his way to whoever he's meeting at the body shop.

Riding the whole way home without panties was… interesting. I made sure my dress was tucked safely for the whole ride.

Axel holds my hand as we saunter through the night to get me home. I know as soon as his hand leaves mine I'm going to be devastated, so I hold on as tightly as possible while I can.

We're rounding the space between my house and the body

shop when I get yanked to the left by Axel, who is currently being accosted by my stepbrother, Tate.

"What the fuck is this?" Tate spits. He takes a moment, looking between the two of us when his nostrils flare, clearly smelling my scent all over Axel. I should be embarrassed that he's smelling my scent, but all I'm truly worried about is him snitching on us. "You've got to be fuckin' kiddin' me. Is she why you said yes?" Tate demands.

My brows furrow, but I smartly keep my mouth firmly shut.

"Yes, and what does it fuckin' matter to you?" Axel counters, releasing my hand and pushing Tate off of him.

"You got a fuckin' death wish?" Tate asks him.

"It's none of your goddamn business," Axel responds.

Tate shoves Axel's shoulder, pushing him against the wall, and I wrap my arms around myself, not wanting to get in the middle. I know how these guys work, and my stepping between the two of them is only going to make things worse instead of better.

"I'm with you. That's all that fuckin' matters. Now, let me get Lily home."

I look between the two of them in confusion, wondering if both of them want what's best for me in their own way. While it's irritating to constantly have people—men—always telling me what to do, it is comforting knowing so many people care about my well-being.

Tate looks back at me, and I can't read his expression at all. I wonder if he still has the same mindset as the night he came home or if my words from a few days ago stuck with him.

"This what you want… *who* you want, Lily?" Tate asks me. His voice is demanding, letting me know he needs a straight answer.

I will not cry over him asking me what I want, I refuse.

"He's who I want," I confirm.

"You know you're not enough for her?" Tate spits at Axel, which is rude and a dig he didn't need to throw out there. But my confident Beta shocks me by shrugging his shoulders, the insult rolling off his back easily.

"I know that," Axel agrees before grabbing my hand. "Doesn't mean she isn't mine," he declares, pointing at Tate. Axel is so confident; he has complete faith in me, in our connection, and it makes me feel safer than I ever have in my life.

I wish I could read Tate, but I can't tell if he's pissed, contemplative, or what. He sighs and rakes his fingers through his dark hair.

"Fine. Then we're bringin' her along," Tate says.

I don't care what this is about, I'm just excited to actually be a part of club business.

"Like hell we are," Axel growls, and I want to roll my eyes.

He just put in all that work to make me swoon and now he's being over protective. I mean, it's part of why I'm so drawn to the club, but I'm also not weak, and I'm dead set on proving it.

I want to be protected, cherished, but I also don't want to be tucked away some place where I don't get to actually live. The thought is bitter as I think of my mom. She doesn't seem to mind never leaving the compound, but that's not me. I love it here. It's home. These people are home, but fuck, there's so much world out there.

"I want to go," I say softly, squeezing Axel's hand.

"You don't even know what we're doin'," he scoffs. Which, fair enough. But the possibility of going out with some of the guys for an adventure or a job? I'm not letting it pass me by.

"She's coming with us," Cash reiterates, popping out of nowhere, making me jump and scaring the shit out of me. "Sorry, sweetheart," he whispers quietly to me.

"She can't go home right now," Tate says.

"Why the fuck not?" Axel argues.

"For one, she smells like she just got…" Tate shakes his head and scratches his beard. "It's not a good time for her to go home. Trust me," Tate says.

I want to ask more, but I don't, because I also want to be

included. Plus, the idea of going home after that failed date and what those assholes said… I'm not sure I'm ready to face Kurt. I need a better plan for when I go home. What am I going to say when he asks about the date? How can I figure out what they meant when they said *the price Kurt has set for me*?

"We wouldn't let her come along for anything high-risk. One of us will stick with her the whole time," Cash reassures, the left corner of his lip tilting up. I can't help but smile back at him.

I was already attracted to him, but his insisting that I tag along has me ready to climb up his tall body and offer to give him whatever he wants. Damn, he looks fucking good tonight. I take note that neither Tate nor Cash are wearing their cuts, just simple dark clothes. The way Cash's black t-shirt clings to his broad chest should be illegal, or should only be worn around me. The idea of other women ogling this massive man doesn't sit right with me. He might not be mine, but he also feels like he is. I can't stop staring at him until loud clearings of throats break my attention.

My cheeks flush when I realize it's because of my scent. No panties, heat any day now, and being as turned on as I am has me assaulting them with coconut and jasmine.

Thankfully, everyone is polite, and no one calls me out on my embarrassing display of being turned on by Cash's words alone.

"Are we going?" I ask, breaking the silence and redirecting the conversation.

Axel scrubs his face with the palm of his hand, dragging his skin down. "Yeah, we're fuckin' goin'," he mutters with a groan.

THIRTEEN
WE'RE ALL COMPLETELY FUCKED

TATE

I'M gonna wring that blond-headed fuck's neck.

I'm not sure why I'm feeling extra murderous. I don't care that he smelled like Lily's sweet scent or that he was holding her hand. I'm just pissed because now we've got a tag-along, and it's her… and she smells like… that. Like some summer wet dream that is completely off the menu. A menu I want her to be on, and don't know how to handle that fact.

Axel doesn't even know the world of shit he just stepped in. Or that he's dragging Cash and I along, because with her being her, it's makin' this shit ten times more complicated.

I know what my father is doing when it comes to the club, and I know his reign needs to end. I'm feeling the pressure of being the one to make that happen. There's a deep feeling of needing to right my father's wrongs, or maybe I just need to prove to myself that I'm a better man than him.

The way he's kept me at an arm's length since I've gotten here doesn't sit right with me. There's only one reason he would do that, and it's because he has something to hide. I know he's hiding something big, and I'm not sure who I can truly trust with this information. That's why Cash and Axel are the only other members I'm trusting right now with the raid on the Wraiths. *Thank fuck that wasn't tonight.*

Tonight is minimal, nothing that could harm Lily, but what she and Axel are doing? This could absolutely be the downfall of all of us.

My father loves Lily, I can tell that much since coming home. He loves her more than he ever loved me, his biological son. It should bother me that he cares more for her than he does me. But it's Lily, I would feel the same way, and I'm not sure how to come to terms with that fact.

She's an Omega; she's sweet. She's nothing fuckin' like me, and maybe that's her greatest appeal. Even if she wasn't my father's stepdaughter, or even associated with the club, I would still feel this way about her.

This—against my own fuckin' will—need to protect her, to make sure she's alright is fuckin' with me, and it has everything to do with her designation and personality. It has nothing to do with her looks or her scent that seems to be caught in my throat... *the fuckin' lies I tell myself are ridiculous, I've never found someone more beautiful.*

We're going for incognito as we take one of the SUVs to the trailer park. Axel took off his cut, and he and Lily sit in the backseat while Cash drives and I ride shotgun. No one is saying a goddamn thing, but I just know this motherfucker is gonna smell like coconuts for weeks. I'm going to have to air it out or I'm going to risk nuttin' my fuckin' self like some lanky teenager every time I get in the car. I don't know what's worse, her scent affecting me like this, or knowing damn fuckin' well that if two other dudes weren't in the car I would be taking care of my hard dick.

This is so completely fucked.

"Where are we going?" her soft voice asks.

I can't even be mad at her as much as I want to be.

Cash answers for us, saying, "Learned about some illegal dog fighting."

"You've got to be fuckin' kiddin' me. You thought it was alright to bring her to a fuckin' blood sport, are you fuckin' braindead?" Axel scolds.

I roll my eyes, and Cash glares at him in the rearview mirror.

"We're going tonight because we know those pricks aren't going to be there. We're going to go in, get the dogs, and leave," he informs us.

"What's stopping them from just getting more dogs?" Lily questions.

"We'll be handling that when you're not around, sweetheart," he tells her, giving her a smile in the mirror.

Great. Fuckin' awesome. Not only is Axel walking around smelling like he spent all night under Lily's skirt, but now Cash is giving her a pet name and soft smiles.

We're all completely fucked.

"Plus, Lily will stay in the car with me," Cash points out.

"So let me get this fuckin' straight. You two assholes interrupted my night when this is only a two-man job?" Axel seethes.

I grin against my fist, kinda liking that I ruined his night. He might smell like her, but with that bit of information, I know it didn't get too far.

Serves the prick right.

"Would have been better with three," I chime in, and I feel the hard press of a knee in the back of my seat.

"What's your fuckin' problem, man?" Axel snaps at me.

I spin around to point at him in the backseat. "You. You're my fuckin' problem."

He grins at me, and I watch with irritation as his hand lands right on Lily's thigh, squeezing her flesh hard. A thick outpour of coconut and jasmine fills the car as her cheeks flush. A low growl involuntarily leaves my chest as I glare at him.

"Now I get it," he says, a smile breaking out across his face before he leans over to kiss the side of Lily's head.

"Go fuck yourself," I sneer, and he laughs.

"Well, if you two didn't interrupt my night, I'd be fuckin' Lily, which sounds a hell of a lot more pleasant," he boasts pridefully. Her cheeks redden further, and she squirms, pressing her thighs together.

Nope, fuck no.

I turn around to force myself to stop noticing all her small movements. I feel a little sickened with myself, with how much I'm noticing every time she shifts and the effect it's having on me. I cannot be looking at my stepsister in that light.

Thankfully, we're almost at our destination. Cash kills the headlights as we drive to the back lot. I know we're in the right place when we see a line of abandoned dog cages.

"This is it," Cash announces.

I get out of the SUV and Axel follows, leaving Cash and Lily in the car alone. My boots crunch against the gravel as I go to the trunk. We grab the bolt cutters and leashes, and each of us slides on a pair of leather gloves. I check my weapon before tucking it in the back of my pants, and Axel does the same.

"You're lucky I love dogs or I'd kill you for ruinin' my night, dickhead," he grumbles as we walk over to the cages.

"You're lucky Lily likes you, or I'd shoot you and shove you *in* one of these cages," I joke. We both let out a soft bout of laughter as I cut through the first cage, which is empty.

"How many dogs are we lookin' for?" Axel asks.

"From what we heard, this prick, William, just went through a string of losses. But he recently bought a pregnant pit bull off Marketplace. Let's get home as many dogs as we can. I figure we'd come back in a day or two and finish the job," I tell him.

"Should beat him to death," Axel comments.

"Sounds like a plan to me," I agree, already having had the same thought. This piece of shit deserves a brutal punishment for the pain he's caused. Especially to innocent animals.

I'm not a good man, never claimed to be, but I do my best to leave the innocent out of club business. Kids, animals, and Omegas are some of the things I consider off-limits. So, the asshole who put these dogs through this deserves every bit of fuckin' pain I plan to give him.

The cages on the outside seem like a maze, and I'm cutting through every chain linking them together, but we still haven't found anything. It's only when we get to the center of the cage, where there's a small dog house, do I hear a small whimper.

I cut the wire holding the cage shut, and Axel immediately gets down on his haunches.

"Hey old girl, you doin' okay?" he asks. I bend down too and see the large gray and white pit bull nursing what looks to be about six puppies.

Her short stubby ears pin down, and she gives us wide concerned eyes. Axel shows no fear as he lets her sniff his hand. I have the dark thought that the dog is smelling Lily's scent, but if anything, that should work in our favor.

The dog submits, letting Axel pet her large head.

"How are we doin' this?" he asks me.

"I'll carry as many puppies as I can, if you can take the mama and two pups?" I ask him. He nods his head, cooing sweetly at the protective mother.

"It's okay, mama, we're gonna get you and your pups somewhere safe."

The puppies are pretty large, and I'm wondering how the fuck I'm supposed to carry four of the adorable fuckers when there's a loud click behind us.

"You fuckin' lost?" the seething voice taunts from behind us.

Axel and I slowly rise to our feet as we turn around.

"Nope, not lost," I tell him confidently. He has a shotgun pointed right at my chest.

"You better get the fuck out of here unless you wanna die tonight, son," he threatens. I take a good look at the man. He looks like shit, his pupils dilated to hell. He's wearing a stained white tank top and plaid boxer shorts. I'd say he's malnourished, but I think he's just on a steady diet of meth based on the current shape and color of his teeth. "I ain't gonna tell you motherfuckers again." The shotgun is already loaded, or at least he makes it seem that way as his finger lingers over the trigger.

"You sellin'?" Axel asks, his stance relaxed as he looks at the man with the shotgun.

The man snorts a wad of snot and rubs his chin on his shoulder before lookin' at Axel.

"Sellin' what?" he asks.

"Been hearin' you have the best crystal in town," Axel says, turning on the charm and lying easily to the man.

"Is that so?" the man asks, his gaze flicking between Axel and me. "If you were lookin' to buy, why the fuck are you around my dogs?"

"Love dogs, man. I don't know what else to say," Axel states nonchalantly.

The man narrows his eyes at us, his shoulders tensing. And I know we need to act soon. There's a quick horn honking that breaks his attention, giving me the opportunity to smack the shotgun up towards the air. It goes off, but I grip the barrel in my hands as Axel tackles the man to the ground.

As soon as Axel is on top of him, he just starts wailing on him, his fists connecting with the man's face. The writhing man gets a few hits of his own in before I join in, kicking him in the stomach and tossing the shotgun to the side.

"William?" I ask and the man sputters.

"Fuck," he groans.

I don't need another word said or any other reason besides knowing he's an absolute piece of shit. I pull my handgun out of my pants and aim between his eyes, not even blinking before I pull the trigger. The shot is clean, and he lies there limp.

"Well, he deserved worse," Axel grumbles, whipping away a smear of blood from the corner of his lip.

"He did, but we need to get the fuck out of here, and after him seein' us, we didn't have a choice," I reason.

"Nah, man, you're right. I'm with you," he says.

"You with me because you want to be? Or because you want to be with Lily?" I question.

He looks down at William's dead body before looking at the doghouse. "Both," he says plainly.

I might have questioned his motives and wanted to kill him before we got here. But after tonight, I can tell we're on the same team and that he's someone I can count on. In this life, that's invaluable.

The poor female dog looks startled, but she lets me pick up her pups, even if she's frightened. Axel has to sweet-talk her to get her out of the kennel, but she eventually does, allowing him to loop the leash around her neck.

She's stalky, but sweet as she stares at us, likely making sure none of her pups are left behind. I have to leash half of them and the others I carry in my arms. Axel has another two as we make our way out of the chain-link fence we came through.

"This took longer than I thought it would," I say and Axel nods, both of us worried about leaving Cash and Lily behind.

But that's all for naught as we walk toward the SUV with arms and hands full of puppies to find Lily sitting on Cash's lap in the driver's seat.

"Guess we know where that honk came from." Axel laughs, shaking his head.

"Aren't you jealous?" I ask him.

"No, man… are you?" he asks, leaving me dead in my tracks as he taps on the trunk.

There's no fuckin' way I can be jealous when it comes to Lily. *No fuckin' way.*

FOURTEEN
BABY GIRL

CASH

AS SOON AS Axel and Tate leave the SUV, Lily is climbing over the middle console and making herself comfortable in the passenger seat.

"How long do you think they'll be?" she asks.

"Hopefully not long," I reply, glancing over at her. Her cheeks are pink, her hair is wild, and she looks so fucking perfect just sitting there. I shouldn't be this drawn to her. She's over a decade younger than me, and she's the Prez's stepdaughter. I suppose if Axel, a Beta, is man enough to make a move, maybe I should be too.

"What?" she asks, pushing a piece of hair behind her ear nervously, and it makes me realize I've been staring at her this whole time.

"Ain't I allowed to look at you?" I jest, and her blush deepens.

"Only if you want this car to smell like me for weeks on end," she jokes back.

"I think I like the sound of that," I tell her.

"You do?"

"Why wouldn't I?"

"I just didn't think you found my scent appealing or that... never mind," she says shaking her head.

"Baby girl, if you need me to show you how I feel about you, all you've got to do is come over here and sit on my lap," I taunt her. What I don't expect is for her to actually do it. She's an Omega, so she's on the smaller side, especially compared to my size. But she's quick as she climbs over the center console and makes herself as comfortable as she can on my lap.

My hands wrap around her waist, and I sit her down on my lap, where there's no doubt she can feel how attracted I am to her.

"Oh," she gasps.

Her body is warm, soft, and having her so close has my brain blanking out on any and all other thoughts. All I can think about right now is sinking my cock in her and marking up her pretty little neck. I shake my head.

Fuck.

I clear my throat, and she stirs in my lap. "I can go back over there," she offers softly, dipping her head to the passenger seat.

"I don't want you to," I respond.

She leans forward, and I'm drowning in her scent as she seductively whispers in my ear. "What do you want, then?" she asks.

I'm like a man unhinged as I grab the back of her head and bring her mouth to mine. Her lips are soft, but her movements aren't. She's just as demanding as I am while we kiss. Lily has one hand wrapped tenderly around my neck as the other braces against my chest for balance. I can't help myself as one hand slides up her thigh to her hip, and I note she doesn't have any panties on.

"No panties?" I ask her.

"Mmm," she mumbles back.

"You're driving me fucking wild," I warn her.

She smiles before leaning down and kissing me again. Has a kiss ever felt all-consuming like this? I've been with Omegas before and enjoyed every second of it. But with Lily, in this moment, I feel consumed. I never wanted to bite any of the other Omegas before, but with Lily, I feel feral, like I should put my mark on her immediately so my claim is clear. I pride myself on being controlled because I know if I'm not, there's no telling what I could be capable of.

She wiggles on my lap from my words, her ass accidentally hitting the horn and making her giggle.

"Sorry," she whispers, her hair creating a curtain on the one side of her face.

She's biting my lower lip when we hear a loud crack. She jerks upright in my lap, and her eyes are wide when mine meet hers.

"What was that?" she asks, and I place a hand over her mouth.

She doesn't fight it as I crack the window and listen for a sign of another gunshot or anything else. We just sit there for a few moments, but when there's another shot, tears start to flow from Lily's eyes, and I press my hand tighter against her face, needing for her to be quiet.

"That was two different guns," I explain.

The first sounded more like a crack, while the second had more of a pop sound, like a handgun. Tears continue to fall down her eyes, and I contemplate getting out of the car to see what's happening with Tate and Axel. But if I do that, I'd be leaving Lily here unprotected.

There's nothing but silence after the two pops, and all we can do is wait. My hand drops from her mouth as I cradle her face.

"I'm sure they're fine. They can handle themselves," I assure her, but she shakes her head back and forth as if trying to expel the horrible what-ifs from her mind.

"We should go out there and make sure they're okay," she tries to reason, and then I'm mirroring her, shaking my head in disagreement.

"No, we're staying right here. We will give them a couple of minutes. If they aren't back soon, then I'll go in while you'll stay here."

"No," she argues, tears still running down her face.

She goes to grab the door handle and open the door, but I have no clue what the fuck is going on out there. All I know for damn sure is that I won't let her leave this car until it's safe. I grab her wrist, and she tugs against my hold to grab the door handle.

"We need to go make sure they're okay."

"Listen, you've got me all sorts of fucked up right now. But I will use my Alpha bark on you if for even a fucking second you think you're getting out of this fucking car," I warn her. She stiffens and blinks at me. "Sorry… just give them some time to get back. If they don't come back in a few minutes I'll go check on them," I promise.

My hands run up and down her arms, trying to calm her when there's a tap against the trunk, right before it opens and Axel lifts a dog into the back. The sigh of relief that leaves Lily is palpable, and I can't help but feel the lingering fear rattling through her.

"I'm going to fucking kill them," she mutters, glaring between the trunk and the other side of the car where Tate is standing with a handful of puppies.

I grab her chin and force her to look at me. "You want to be a part of this, to prove you can handle it?" I ask her. Her brown eyes fill with fury but she nods her head. "Then don't go out there swinging and cursing and showing how much you were affected. If you run out there, tears streaming down your face and throwing frustrated curses at them, they won't ever let you tag along again," I state.

"Well, I don't think I ever want to come along again anyway," she sasses and tries to climb over to the passenger seat, but I don't let her.

"What happened tonight isn't over. We're gonna talk about

this later," I tell her. She huffs out a breath but nods her head, and I let her climb into the seat. The guys are quick with getting the dogs loaded, and I'm grateful as they jump in the backseat so we can drive off.

"You okay, baby?" Axel asks, throwing his hand over her headrest and touching her shoulder.

"Yeah, just tired," she deflects, taking my advice. "What are you going to do about the puppies?" she asks.

"I know a guy who helps transport animals to a rescue. I'll give him a call," Tate chimes in.

"Are you going to tell us what happened?" Lily asks them, trying to keep her composure, but she's failing.

"No. Now, let's get home," Tate replies sharply.

Lily crosses her arms over her chest but stays silent the whole way home.

The ride is tense, and I'm just as fucking curious as to what went down tonight, but it's club business. If Lily wants to stay here and be a part of the club, then she needs to understand her place. Because if she knew everything we did, she would get the fuck out of here and never look back.

We should all want that for her, but I want her back on my lap more than I want to be a decent human.

I park the SUV by the side of the body shop that doesn't have cameras, and we all get out, going to the trunk where each of us takes at least one dog. We set the mom up in the office, and I make a note to go to the pet store first thing in the morning for all the supplies they may need while they're here.

Axel and Tate are talking around the corner when Lily grabs the smallest one that looks more blue than gray. She holds it against her chest as she cuddles up on the shitty couch.

"You good, sweetheart?" I ask her.

"No, but I will be," she sighs dreamily before passing out.

When Tate and Axel come back to the office and see her sleeping, there's a moment of awe before they tell me every-thing that happened tonight.

"Should we just leave the body there?" Axel asks.

Tate shrugs, and I nod my head. "He's a known criminal. There are so many people who'd have a reason to take him out. Plus, that part of the trailer park was pretty remote. With the heat coming in, he'll rot faster if we just leave him be," I say, and they both agree with my assessment.

"She shouldn't have come tonight," Axel chastises, looking pissed at the both of us.

As much as I agree with him, I can't regret bringing her along.

"We won't make that mistake again," Tate growls. "Whatever it is the two of you have goin' on with her, end it now."

"Like fuck," Axel seethes.

Tate's right. I know he's right. I just don't care. My desire for Lily outweighs whatever good intentions he has.

"Not happening," I say, standing my ground.

"Great, so then this whole thing is completely fucked," Tate complains, storming off and leaving the body shop.

"Damn, didn't know he was such a drama queen," Axel comments, and I can't help but laugh. It has Lily stirring on the couch, and Axel clicks his tongue. "She's gotta get home," he sighs.

"How you planning on doing that?"

"Her window," he answers quickly.

"I don't want to know how you know that," I reply.

He shrugs, getting down on his haunches, and brushes her hair out of her face. I don't know the Beta well, but his devotion towards Lily and the way he was able to leave fucking her for club business, tells me everything I need to know. I wouldn't hate it if he was in my pack.

"Darlin' you gotta wake up," he tells her softly.

"No, go away," she mumbles, and I can't hide my smile.

"I'd have this big fucker over here pick you up, but it's nearly three in the mornin'. You're gonna have to go home through your window," he tells her.

Her brown eyes blink open and she groans, tugging the puppy closer to her chest. "I want this one," she states. He looks over at me like I'm going to tell her no, and I just shrug my shoulders.

"We'll see what we can do. But can you get up? We need to get you home so the Prez doesn't fuckin' kill us all," Axel tries to reason with her.

"Fine," she grumbles before kissing the puppy's head and placing it down with its siblings and mother.

Axel takes her hand, and I follow them outside where we quickly approach the side of the Prez's house.

It's a good five feet between the ground and the roof, so I grab Lily by the waist. She yelps but quickly stifles it as she clings on to the side. Axel follows suit, jumping and pulling himself up to make sure she gets home safe.

He scales ahead, and Lily turns around to look down at me.

"Goodnight, Cash."

"Night, baby girl."

She gives me a beaming smile, and just like that, I've completely sealed my spot alongside Tate and Axel. No matter what we do, the impact we leave on the club is going to be irreversible.

FIFTEEN

WHY HAVEN'T WE EVOLVED?

LILY

I HARDLY SLEEP.

I wasn't actually asleep on the couch last night at the body shop; I heard everything.

I should be terrified. I should ask Kurt to set me up on more dates with respectable men who don't casually kill people. But I don't… and I won't.

I'm not going into this with rose-colored glasses. Last night taught me as much. It taught me I cared more for Axel and Tate than I realized. It felt like my heart dropped out of my ass when I heard gunshots and didn't know if they were in the line of fire. It has me wondering how much I truly want to know about club business and if I can handle them constantly being in danger.

While I don't need to know every detail of what they do for the club, I refuse to be treated like blown glass. It's the only reason I took Cash's advice, and I appreciated it. Now that I've had time to think about it, he's right. If I would have cursed at them, told them how scared I was, they wouldn't ever take me anywhere or tell me shit again.

Which leads me back to Cash and that kiss.

How could one night be as life changing and chaotic as last

night was? It's like in a matter of twenty-four hours, the entire trajectory of my life has changed. It's been nearly too much to process. So despite my headache and the pit in my stomach, I begrudgingly get out of bed and get dressed for a run.

I always do my best thinking while running, and I desperately need some clarity. Not about how I feel per se, but how the hell we're going to make this work. My feelings for Cash, which he seemed to eagerly return, changes things in a good way. It's not just Axel and I against the world or club anymore. Three members is what you need to make a pack... though, it won't be enough.

I feel like such a greedy bitch saying that, but it wouldn't. I need another Alpha. An Alpha who is notably *not* my stepbrother... although my pheromones and mind don't seem to catch on to that fact. Why does he have to be so handsome, broody, and smell so goddamn good? I swear it's like the universe is slapping me in the face.

Why couldn't he just not be Kurt's son? I almost feel like if they didn't have such a complicated relationship maybe it would be easier. Maybe I wouldn't feel this way if we all had a closer relationship. However, nothing can take away how beautiful he is.

He respected my wishes, killed an animal abuser, and the way he looked at me last night? *Ugh, I've got to stop thinking about it.* I shake my head as I tie my shoes and ramble downstairs.

Thankfully, no one is up yet, and I take a deep breath of relief before leaving the house and jogging my usual route around the compound. I run through the grass, passing the reservoir, and looping around the hardware store like I normally do.

My heart rate is up, my breathing is labored, and there's a sheen of sweat on my forehead when a cramp, so debilitating it feels like every nerve ending is firing off, crashes into me. My stomach was upset all last night, but I chalked it up to nerves.

But now I groan in distaste, realizing my period is here or is about to be. I finish my circuit even though it's painful.

As soon as I get home, I turn the shower on and let the warm water hit my head as I sit on the floor.

The pain is more intense than any of my periods have ever been, and I groan. My body is getting ready for my fucking heat, making the perfect little nest in my uterus to house a baby.

"Fucking traitorous body," I seethe at myself as I wash up.

This couldn't have come at a worse time, either. I was supposed to finally go all the way tomorrow on Marielli's Mass. That certainly won't be happening now. They're going to be so disappointed.

I try to not let my distaste of disappointing people linger for long, taking care of myself and drying off. The cramps only get worse, and I find myself in the fetal position on my bed whimpering in pain.

It feels like hours pass by, the pain so intense I don't even have the energy to turn on the tv or an audiobook; I just lie there and suffer.

Why the fuck haven't we evolved yet? Why do I still need my period to rip me to shreds every fucking month?

There's a soft knock on my door, and I groan. The hinges creak and there's a hefty weight added to the end of my bed.

"Everything okay, hun?" Kurt asks.

"I'll be fine."

"How was last night's date?" he asks, and I swallow. Tears prickle my eyes from the pain, the memory, and the fear of what I don't want my stepfather to know about.

"It's not a match," I say weakly, keeping it simple and honest.

"I was hoping to set you up with another date tonight," he offers encouragingly.

"I really don't feel good, Pop. Please..." I trail off, and he shushes me, his large hand squeezing my shoulder.

"It's fine, hun. You don't have to go tonight. Do you need

anything?" he asks sweetly. The glimpse of the stepfather I've always known shines through. Maybe Dave and Paul were fucking with me, or I misunderstood? "Do you want the heatin' pad, some Tylenol?" he asks, and I nod my head, sniffling a confused sob. "I'll be right back," he says, squeezing my shoulder one more time.

I curl up and hold my knees to my stomach, willing the pain to go away. All I hear are footsteps as he returns, but he doesn't enter my room right away. After a short pause, muffled voices filter through my door.

"What are you doin' here?" Kurt demands, his voice not soft. He sounds more irritated than anything.

"I wanted to talk to you," the voice responds. It's obnoxious that I immediately know it's Tate speaking

"Nothin' to talk about," Kurt dismisses.

"I come home after a decade and you really don't want to talk about it?" Tate asks.

"You left. You didn't want to be a part of this—now that there's no other options for you is when you grace this club with your fuckin' presence. What? You expect me to be fuckin' happy to see you again?" Kurt snarls, and I wince at his tone, along with the cramp rolling through my abdomen.

"I was hopin' we could start over, try to mend this," Tate reasons.

"You're patched in, you're a part of the club, that's all you're gonna get from me," Kurt states coldly, and my heart breaks for Tate.

"If that's all that you want, fine," Tate says, but through the door I can't see his expression. There's a silence as the handle of my doorknob turns. "Is she okay?" Tate asks, his voice a little louder now. Kurt must have the door partially open. I'm curled up facing the window so I can't see them.

"It's none of your business. She's my family, not yours," Kurt sneers. There's silence as he walks through and then shuts the door behind him. I take a shuddering breath, having heard their conversation that was clearly not meant for my ears.

Kurt plugs in the heating pad and hands me the Tylenol. Maybe in my current state, he's more willing to answer my questions. "What happened between you two?" I ask, and Kurt sighs. His hand rubbing up and down on my back.

"Nothin' for you to worry about, hun. We'll figure our shit out," he says, in lieu of answering the question.

"It sounded like you don't want to figure it out," I reply. His hand pauses on my back, and he looks down at me contemplatively.

"I guess… maybe, I'm still hurt by the past," he admits.

"Giving him the cold shoulder isn't going to help," I tell him honestly.

How in the world does he expect to have a relationship with his son when he talks to him the way he does? I barely remember Tate being around when I was growing up. He left the compound not long after Kurt bonded my mom, and I only saw him every now and then. Tate was always kind and generous to me, but always kept me at an arm's length. I guess I was too young to read the tension between him and Kurt. But now, I'm just wondering how we got here. To the point they can hardly share a few words.

"I'll work on it, hun," he says softly. He goes to stand up, and I turn onto my other side.

"Kurt?"

"Yeah?"

"Would it be okay if I set up my own dates?" I ask, feeling bold. I'm not telling him who my planned dates are, but I can totally lie about it later.

He scratches his beard and looks down at me. "The last two dates were that bad?" he asks, his brow furrowing as he looks at me.

"Yeah, they really were."

"We can try it your way, but I need to know the details.

You've got to be safe," he urges. I nod my head, but remember how un-fucking-safe I felt on the last two dates he set up for me.

"Alright then, feel better," he says, leaving my room. I turn on my side, enjoying the small victory, which is shortly lived by another round of blinding pain.

I'M NOT sure how much time has passed, but I note that it's dark in my room. I pick up my phone and groan as I see one am flash across the screen.

My stomach rolls, and it's then a tap on the window catches my attention. It must have been what woke me up in the first place. I feel too gross and in pain to even get up and get it. I just groan, knowing that the window is unlocked. If it's Axel, he'll just let himself in.

The window opens and shuts softly; I clench my eyes tightly closed and breathe as the presence comes to sit by me on the bed. With their weight and scent, the person who snuck into my bedroom takes me by surprise.

I say nothing, just lying there as let his leather and earthy scent wash over me. It soothes the pain more than pain medication or a heating pad ever could. I'm not sure how to handle that realization, so I just continue to be silent and take whatever relief I can get.

When his hand lands on the center of my back, I nearly shiver at the comforting touch. I shouldn't crave it, it shouldn't be him who brings me comfort. How can it feel so right and so wrong at the same time?

"Fuck," he mumbles before standing up. I whine like a needy little bitch when his touch leaves me, and he sighs. "Just give me a second," he whispers. I listen and swallow down the desperate noise that's trying to escape my throat.

I hear the sound of boots being slid off and something else

hitting the floor before he lifts my blanket and crawls into bed with me. His body isn't close to mine as he just lies there, breathing but otherwise quiet.

A cramp hits me so hard I feel like I'm going to throw up, and I curl in on myself, taking a deep inhale through my nose. Tate's scent floods my system, giving me a sense of peace I've never felt before.

Without speaking, he wraps his body around mine, while still keeping his hands safely to himself.

"Is it always this bad?" he whispers in my ear.

I shake my head no, instead of opening my mouth. I know the second I speak I'll break down into tears and, to be honest, my ego can't take that hit. I don't want Tate to see me as some fragile little girl. I'm not sure how I want him to see me, or if I'm just disassociating from what I want from him because the reality of what I want from Tate is too forbidden for me to wrap my head around.

His hand finally touches my skin, his palm resting against the clammy skin of my forehead.

"What do you need?" he asks. His tone is probably the softest I've ever heard it, a gentle whisper just for me. A tear leaks out, and I wipe it away quickly with the back of my wrist.

How do I tell him that his scent and presence are the only relief I've felt all day? I can't. It would be like opening Pandora's box to dissect what's between us. We're not dumb or blind. Clearly, we both find each other physically attractive to some degree. I've caught the way he looks at me, and there's no doubt he's caught the way I respond to his scent.

But having feelings for Tate? It would make his relationship with Kurt even worse than it already is. To be honest, I wouldn't care about any other public outrage than Kurt's and my mother's. I think Tate might even feel the same way when it comes to not giving a shit what people think. But the two people's opinions I care about most wouldn't approve.

Hell, Kurt wants me far away from the club; he definitely

doesn't want me with his son whom he holds extreme resentment towards. With that decided, I need to tell Tate to leave.

But then something happens… something I've never experienced before.

Tate's chest rumbles and a purr emanates from his chest. He doesn't stop it, and it vibrates against my back. I feel like I'm finally able to breathe without pain radiating throughout every nerve of my body. He doesn't speak as his hand slides across my side, holding my lower abdomen.

"Just go to sleep, darlin'," he murmurs against my hair. His voice is deep and husky, and his purr gets even louder.

He just lies there, bringing me the comfort of an Alpha that I desperately need. The true reality of why my period is so bad slaps me in the face. My birthday is nearly here; I'll be twenty-one soon and every fiber of my being knows I need a pack to take care of me.

What I can't wrap my head around is how badly my body seems to want Tate to be a part of said pack.

I shake my anxieties away and just let myself have this moment because I know I'll never have it again. If this is the only time Tate holds me like this, then I need to take advantage of every single second.

"It's okay, darlin'. I've got you," is the first phrase I hear in my dreams, and it helps me fall into a peaceful slumber.

SIXTEEN
CLAIMED

LILY

I SPEND the next few days lounging around the house. Tate has wordlessly climbed through my window every night. He takes off his boots, cut, and jeans before lying down next to me, all without saying a word every time.

He leaves after I fall asleep, and all I'm left with is his scent haunting my room like a ghost.

I swear I've almost gaslit myself into thinking it's a figment of my imagination, and that he truly hasn't come in to visit me every night. But when I wake up to his scent, I know it's real, and I don't know how to deal with this information.

How am I supposed to grapple with the fact that I'm attracted to my stepbrother, that he cares for me when I'm in pain, and that I'm never going to wash my sheets again? I need his scent like I need to breathe, and I'm not sure how to look past that. Will I always have this ache and need for a man that I can't have?

I haven't had a chance to see Cash and Axel yet, but I need to see them badly. I need to know that they're still all in. Even if it now brings me some pain knowing I won't be complete with just the two of them. If we make a pack without Tate, is this longing going to follow me around forever, or is it something I can get over?

I'm sitting on the porch, enjoying the sun for the first time in a few days, when Axel walks up, looking like some sort of model. *How did I forget how beautiful he is?*

He grins at me and sits down on the step; he keeps plenty of room for Jesus between us, and I groan in disapproval.

"I'm workin' on it, darlin'," he reassures me.

I rest my head on my knee and look at him. I'm still not feeling great, and I'm not sure how to manage all my feelings. This is the shit no one tells you about when you designate as an Omega, all these pesky emotions. Emotions that sometimes make absolutely no sense.

I logically know we're on the compound and Axel can't be affectionate to me right now, but with the distance between us, all I want to do is cry because I feel rejected. This is all so incredibly fucked. I just want to feel like me again, and I'm not sure if that will ever happen. *Will I feel better after my heat, after I bond?* Even thinking about it makes me anxious because both factors are so unknown, and all I want is to be me again.

"The dog guy is comin' soon. You want to say goodbye to the puppies?" he asks, and I nod my head. He looks at me like he wants to take my hand and lead me over to the body shop, but he doesn't, much to my distaste.

The sun is beaming hot, but welcomed on my skin as we walk over to the shop. His hand grabs my wrist as he tugs me into a tower of tires. His hands cradle my jaw gently as he looks into my eyes.

"I miss you," he says softly.

Nope, I will not cry. You're a bad biker bitch, not some weepy Omega.

"I miss you too," I reply weakly.

"You feelin' alright?" he asks, pushing my hair out of my face and feeling the temperature of my skin.

I curl my lips between my teeth, holding back all the word

vomit that wants to come out; about how I don't feel alright, that my stomach and head hurt, that the only comfort I've found lately is in the arms of my stepbrother, and I don't know how to handle that. Or that I feel like he and Cash are going to see me as more trouble than I'm worth.

I don't spew it all over the place, but he must pick up on something written on my face. "Hey, baby. It's okay," he reassures, using the knuckle to tip my chin up so I'm looking at him. "You're my girl. I'm gonna take care of you. When I said I was workin' on it, I really meant it."

"Are you going to tell me about your plans?" I whisper back.

"Not yet, but I meant what I said before. There's no goin' back. You're mine, and I take care of what's mine. You got me?" he asks, his lips leaning down and touching mine. It's a sweet, gentle kiss that leaves me feeling dizzy. That soft brush of his lips is enough to calm my nerves and remove the illogical sting of rejection.

"I got you," I reply softly, and he kisses me again, his calloused fingers rubbing against the skin of my face. "You know I've been doing some plotting of my own," I admit proudly.

"Oh, yeah. Whatcha got?" he asks with a grin. God, I love it when he smiles. It's always laced with a mischievous promise that I can't get enough of.

"I asked Kurt if I could set up my own dates, and he agreed," I tell him. His smile drops, and I shake my head. "The date is going to be you, dumbass," I tease him, and he shakes his head, his smile returning. "I set up a dating profile, but it's fake. I'll tell Kurt about the guys I'm meeting, giving him all their information, and have him drop me off, but really I'll be meeting you and Cash," I explain.

"Pretty and devious. I'm so lucky," he jokes, kissing me again before leading me out between the tires and up to Cash's office in the body shop.

The relief on Cash's face when he sees me sends a thrill through me. The fact that I have such an effect on the large and logical Alpha makes me feel powerful. Cash stands and holds out his arms, which I easily step into. His scent has the same soothing effect as Tate's, and I just stand there and let him hold me. I press my arms and the side of my face against his chest. When he leans down, his cheek pressing against the top of my head, I think I about die from satisfaction.

"You been okay?" he asks, and I nod against his chest. "We were worried our night out scared you," he confesses.

It's then I realize Tate has kept our nights together a complete secret. *Why does that make it feel more wrong?*

My cheeks flush as I back away from him. "No, I just haven't been feeling well," I say, feeling embarrassed and not wanting to share that I've been bleeding so much I'm unsure how I'm still fucking alive.

"Do you need anything?" Cash asks.

"Just some time with you and the puppies before they leave," I state, and he grabs my wrist, sitting down on the couch before perching me on his lap.

Cash's lap is quickly becoming my favorite place to sit as Axel grabs my favorite puppy. She's precious, with blue/gray fur, and a white stripe on her chest, snout, and paws. Her eyes are a soft blue, and she licks my face as soon as Axel places her on my lap.

"Prez ain't big on having a dog in his house, but she can live in the shop while we get everything sorted," Cash offers as he rubs circles on my back.

I gasp and look between the two of them. "Seriously, I get to keep her?" I ask.

"Seriously. What are you gonna name her?" Axel asks from where he sits on the ground, petting the mama's head while the other puppies playfully bite at his pants and shoes. He doesn't care as he smiles and pets their large, cute heads.

"Winnie," I say softly, pulling from one of my favorite movies, *Tuck Everlasting*.

"Winnie it is," Axel states.

The door to the office swings open, and I nearly jump out of Cash's lap. I relax when I realize it's Tate. He doesn't make eye contact with me as he speaks. "Rescue guy is here," he announces.

Axel pets the mama dog's head one more time before gathering her leash, as well as the other puppies'. He hands me a purple one to clip onto Winnie's collar, and I take it as we head outside.

"How the fuck do people live here? It's hotter than Satan's fucking asshole," I hear the heavily tattooed Beta complain to his two companions. One of them is a blond Alpha, who competes in size against Cash, and the other is probably the prettiest woman I've ever seen.

"Don't worry, we'll be on a plane back to Connecticut before you know it," the woman reassures. She smiles widely at the Beta and kisses his cheek.

Her Alpha holds her wrist tightly like she's on some Omega leash. It makes me smile while also trying to hold back a laugh. Knowing what the club looks like, he's probably terrified to let her out of his sight. I swear he relaxes his grip some when he sees me walk out alongside the guys with the puppies.

"Oh my God, they're so cute," the woman exclaims, getting down on her knees to pet the puppies Tate has on a leash.

Suddenly, music blasts from the square, and Tate curses under his breath. "Club is havin' a party tonight. I've got to take care of some things," he says, handing the Beta the two leashes he was holding. "Thank's for comin' so quickly man. It was unexpected," Tate tells him.

"Liv was next to me when you called. She's the one who had us drop everything to get here as soon as possible," he says, looking affectionately at the Omega sitting in the sandy grass.

"Either way, man, thanks. We'll catch up soon. Good seein'

you, River," Tate says, giving the man a slap on the shoulder before walking away.

I don't know why I feel drawn to the Omega kissing the puppies, but I do. Truly, the only other Omega I've spent time with has been my mother. I want to know more about Liv and possibly having someone else to confide in is an opportunity I can't turn down. I love the girls on the compound with my whole heart, but I don't always feel like I fit in.

I get down on the ground with Winnie, and Liv smiles up at me. It's a true smile too, not a fake friendly one.

"Are you keeping one?" she asks me.

"Yes, this is Winnie," I tell her.

"Ah, I love that. It's going to take everything in me not to bring one of these babies home," she sighs.

"Not unless you want Dean to have a stroke," River jokes with her.

"Who's Dean?" I ask her.

"He's my other Alpha, he couldn't come. He's in the middle of opening up a new restaurant," she explains excitedly.

I look around at all the men standing around us, blatantly staring. I want to ask Liv questions I haven't been able to ask another Omega before, but I'm sure as fuck not going to do that with them all eavesdropping.

"Do you guys want some food and drinks before you go?" I ask politely, hoping to have more of a chance to talk to Liv.

She smiles widely at me, picking a puppy up under her arm. "That would be wonderful, thank you," she replies.

"Sweetheart, I don't know…" her big Alpha, whom I still don't know the name of, says.

"Grayson, it will be fine. Let's go," she commands.

The big man sighs but reluctantly nods. He keeps Liv in arm's reach as we head to the square. It's early so everyone is clothed and on their best behavior as we sit down at a picnic table with the dogs.

"River, will you get me a drink?"

"Sure, angel," he tells her, kissing her hair. I look between them and use the same tactic.

"Axel, do you mind?" I ask.

"Sure thing, darlin'," he says.

That just leaves Cash and Grayson. Liv sighs heavily and looks at the two of them. "Can you two sit at that picnic table right there so I can speak to... my new friend for a moment," Liv asks.

"Lily," I whisper quickly.

"So I can speak with Lily," she reiterates.

Her Alpha looks at the both of us and agrees. Cash isn't so quick, but when he looks at Grayson, he changes his mind.

"Thanks," I whisper, and Liv smiles at me.

"Do you leave here much?" she asks, looking around the compound.

"Not much, but I love it here," I tell her.

"I could see that," she says, not being snide, but truly getting it. "You're unbonded?" she asks, but it feels more like a statement.

All that word vomit I couldn't tell Axel comes out of me now. "Does it get better after you bond? After your heat? Will I always feel this terrible?" I ask her. She reaches out and gently touches my wrist.

"Before your first heat is the worst. I promise it gets better, and it looks like you already know who you want anyway," she says.

"You could tell all of that just from one small encounter?" I ask her in disbelief.

She shrugs. "It's a gift. So why haven't you bonded them?" she asks.

"My stepdad is the President of the club, and he wants me out. He would probably kill them if he knew," I tell her plainly.

She gives me a soft smile, something in her soft blue eyes telling me she understands to some degree of what I'm going through.

She's about to speak when I narrow my eyes at Tate, who is talking to a group of women that I don't know. With all the newly patched in members, it seems they needed to ship in some new girls for the party. A tall, pretty Beta with long blonde hair touches his arm as she laughs, and I want to throw up. My stomach ripples in pain, and it takes everything in me to not march over there and break her wrist.

Liv turns in her seat, following my gaze to who I'm glaring at, and she clears her throat.

"What's his deal?" she asks softly.

"He's my stepbrother."

"Wow, this place is seriously like a soap opera," she deadpans, and I give her a little glare. She laughs it off and shakes her head. "I think you need to let her know he's off the market," she teases.

"He's not," I respond, hating the truth spilling out of my mouth.

Liv pinches the underskin of my arm hard, making me shout. "What the fuck?" I ask her, but she just grins at me. I blink at the madwoman in front of me as Axel, Cash… and Tate all immediately start heading in my direction.

Liv leans forward and whispers in my ear, "You seem pretty fucking claimed to me."

"You're kinda crazy, you know that?" I tell her, and she just smiles wider.

"It's part of my charm," Liv replies.

"You alright?" Axel asks quickly.

"Yeah, I'm fine, just banged my elbow on the table," I lie. He arches an eyebrow at me, looks over at Tate, and shakes his head with a smile. He puts down my drink and walks away.

Tate's eyebrows furrow as he looks at me and then back down at the ground before walking away as well.

Liv pulls out her phone and hands it to me. "Put your number in. I need to know how this all plays out," she snickers. Her pack mates look completely unphased by her behavior, and

I quickly put in my number, feeling totally confused but in awe by our encounter.

"Liv, sweetheart, it's time to go," her Alpha Grayson says. Liv rolls her eyes.

"I swear if he could microchip me he would," she tells me, and I smile at that.

"Thanks for helping the dogs, their situation was terrible," I tell her.

"Of course, I just wish we could have stayed longer," she says.

"Liv, we've got to get on the road," Grayson urges, putting a hand on her shoulder.

"Calm down, Daddy. Damn," she grumbles, just casually tossing that word out there.

She grabs my wrist gently and smiles at me. "If you need anyone to talk to, you have my number. It was nice meeting you, Lily," she says, standing up, her Alpha two steps behind her, not letting her stray far. I wave at her and smile. Something about our small chat eased my anxiety.

I think I just found myself an Omega mentor to help me get the fuck out of this mess.

SEVENTEEN

I CAN'T

LILY

"WHAT ARE YOU UP TO?" my brother asks, leaning over my shoulder. I look up at him, and I note that he looks like complete shit. The dark circles under his eyes are deep, and I swear his hand trembles slightly as he holds his coffee cup.

"Dating app," I snark, still not over our last conversation.

"Why do you need a fuckin' datin' app?" he asks.

"Hmm, let's see." I hold up my middle finger at him. "For one, you and Kurt seem hell-bent on me finding a pack not in the club, and the last two dates I had were horrific. So I took matters into my own hands," I answer, still giving him the finger. He pushes the finger down when he sits at the table with me.

"Did they try anything on this date? You know I'll handle it," he reminds me.

I want to tell him that Axel already handled it, and then me after, but I keep my mouth shut.

"It's fine. I can handle myself," I state.

Leon takes a long sip of his coffee before placing it on the table and looking at me intently.

"I'm sorry for the night of the BBQ," he apologizes.

"Water under the bridge," I lie, still feeling bitter about it all

—about how Leon is keeping so many secrets and the way he's pushing me out of the club.

"The sweet butts and a few of the guys are ridin' out to Madison Blue today. You wanna come?" he asks.

I try not to jump out of my seat with excitement. "Who all is gonna go?" I ask, which is the only appropriate response. I'm sure I would have a fine time without the men I sure as fuck hope are going to be there, but it would make things a lot more enjoyable.

"Shelby, Cora, Axel, Maverick, and a few others," he lists.

"I'm in. Let me go get dressed," I tell him.

"Shorts, Lily. Wear fuckin' shorts," he begs of me.

I roll my eyes but run upstairs and praise God that my period is finally over. I grab a small olive green bikini, putting it on first before throwing on a pair of jean shorts and a Dead Palms T-shirt. I put together a small bag of essentials and toss it over my shoulder.

Leon gives me a small smirk and shakes his head before opening the back door and ushering me out.

"Thanks for inviting me," I tell him softly.

"I think we all need a little fun," he says.

We walk over to the clubhouse where far more members and girls than I thought are waiting to get on the road. Axel is there, giving me a tight smile. I sadly don't see Cash, but Tate is here and not even looking in my direction.

"Lily, you can ride with me," Axel offers and my brother scoffs.

"Like fuck she is," my brother dismisses, looking around at who else is available. It's obvious he wants Shelby on the back of his bike. He whistles, grabbing Tate's attention. "Lily's gonna ride with you," he tells Tate, not leaving any window for argument.

Tate looks around and just nods his head. I suppose we're acting like last week didn't happen. *Okay, then. That's fine, it's totally fine...* except I'm about to spend an hour on the back of his bike with my thighs wrapped around his body.

I can totally play this cool. He's my stepbrother, he loves me in a platonic caring way, there's nothing else there. I can ride on the back of his bike, no problem. I've ridden on the back of Leon and Kurt's bikes multiple times. It's not a big deal.

"You better get a fuckin' brain bucket before we leave your ass here," my brother says with a smirk.

Shelby is a sweetheart and hands me one, giving me a grateful smile. She knows if I told my brother I was uncomfortable, he would have booted her to ride with someone else. I would have felt like a completely shitty friend doing that to her. I can handle an hour on the back of Tate's bike.

I pull my hair into a low ponytail and situate my sunglasses before putting the helmet on.

"You're with me," Tate repeats, not looking at me.

"If that's okay?" I ask, feeling insecure.

He just nods, tucks my belongings into his saddlebag, and swings his leg over on the bike, waiting for me to get on. I take a deep breath and look over at Axel, who is glaring daggers in our direction. I huff out a breath but get on the back of Tate's bike.

My grip is light on his sides, and he lets out a frustrated noise in the back of his throat. "Hold on," he demands. I grip his cut a little tighter, and he jerks the bike forward, forcing my front against his back as I squeeze around his body. "There you go," he teases.

Fuck, he smells good. I need us to get on the road so that the wind might clear the fog from my head, or at least rattle some of my brain cells so that my focus isn't solely on how our bodies are touching.

I don't have to wait long before we're all on the road. Butterflies are flapping their wings rampantly in my stomach, and I do my best to ignore them and just enjoy this. Being surrounded by other bikes as we ride together as a group, it's what I love the most about the club. These people are my family. This feeling of freedom with them is something I could never leave behind. This is where I belong.

I must be getting sentimental, and so I squeeze Tate harder. His hand grabs my knee, squeezing lightly, a reassuring gesture that he's got me.

It shouldn't feel so good being this close to him, but it does, and I know I don't want it to stop. When his hand leaves my knee it feels like a substantial loss, and I selfishly think of ways to get him to touch me again.

THE PARK IS BEAUTIFUL, but I really don't want to get off the bike. I know as soon as I do it will all feel like it didn't happen, just like those nights in my bedroom. All I'll have is the lingering haunt of his scent and a memory of what was.

He drags his fingers through his dark hair and puts his glasses on the top of his head before squeezing my thigh.

"Ride's over, darlin'," he says.

I swear this motherfucker knows what he's doing to me.

Two can play that game.

I take off the helmet, holding it with my left hand as I grab his shoulder to whisper in his ear. "Thanks for the ride, Tate."

He stiffens, and I might touch his back longer than I need to before hopping off. I hand him the helmet, and he sets it on the seat before getting off himself.

All the girls who came waste no time at all taking off their clothes and stripping down to their bathing suits. I do the same, but I stare at Tate as I undress, his eyes never leaving my body as I pull my shirt over my head or shimmy my shorts down my legs.

"Can I leave these on your bike?" I ask him sweetly.

He nods his head dumbly, and I place my clothes in a pile on the seat before I walk away, adding extra sway with each one of my steps.

I swear I hear him curse behind me, but I don't think too much of it as I reach the rest of the group. Most of the guys stay clothed. Honestly, the idea of seeing them in bathing suits is borderline humorous to me. I doubt most of them even own a bathing suit.

"Come, jump with me!" Shelby exclaims, and I divert my attention to her.

She looks amazing in her all-white bikini, which my brother seems to appreciate. I smile back at her and walk over to the platform.

"Did they drive out here just to ogle all the girls in their bikinis?" I ask, making her laugh.

"Just wait till the prospects get here with the beer," she giggles.

"I thought beer wasn't allowed in the park," I reply, and Shelby laughs again.

"Oh, sweet Lily. Are we jumping or what?" she asks, and I nod my head, looking over the edge.

I'm a little nervous, but there's no way I'm going to chicken out. When I look to my right, I can't help but notice two men who seem a little on edge with me standing on this platform. Tate is chain-smoking cigarettes like his life depends on it, and Axel looks like he wants to hit someone.

"Let's do it," I tell Shelby.

We take each other's hands as we take a running start before leaping off the edge. I can't help the small yelp that leaves me as we go over and before we hit the water. It takes a few moments for me to get my bearings, but when I do, I swim up to the surface with a huge smile on my face.

"Wasn't so bad," Shelby pants with a smile, her blonde hair wet and sticking to her back, but her eyelashes still look amazing.

"That was so much fun," I reply with a smile of my own.

"Now to get our guys to jump in with us," she schemes.

"Guys?" I ask puzzled.

"Ambien and Axel," she says, and I take a relieved breath. "Unless there is someone else you had in mind… like, I don't know… a broody, hot stepbrother, perhaps?" she jokes, and I splash her with the water that's too warm for this summer heat. "I fucking knew it," she squeals, splashing me back.

"I'm not going to do anything about it," I tell her sternly.

"I mean, if you're going to disobey the Prez you might as well go balls to the fucking wall and fuck his son too," she teases, and I swim over to her and dunk her head under the water. She swims back to the surface, laughing her ass off as we swim over to the stairs.

The steps are slippery, and I hold the railing as I walk up. Though, I still somehow manage to slightly slip, hitting my knee on the concrete edge. The large hand that wraps around my forearm is a familiar one, with two shiny metal rings.

"You got a fuckin' towel or somethin'?" Tate drawls at me.

"Yeah, in my bag," I tell him. He holds my arm, not letting go as he grabs my bag and drags me behind some old-looking building to sit at a worn-down table. He has me sit on the top as he blots my knee with the towel. It's hardly bleeding, but he acts like I've just been told I need an amputation to survive.

"Tate, I'm fine," I tell him.

"I know," he grumbles, holding the towel on my knee and not looking at my face.

"Are we going to talk about this?" I question him.

"About what?" he asks, still not looking up at me.

"Tate," I sigh his name, and he stands to his full height, dropping the towel.

He looks at me like he either wants to bend me over this table and fuck me or like he wants to rip his hair out.

"I can't. I can't fuckin' do this with you. No, we aren't gonna talk about it, because there's nothin' to fuckin' talk about," he blurts.

"It didn't feel like nothing when you were sneaking into my room every night last week, or the way you look at me," I reply, feeling frustrated.

I hate the way he's acting, like there's nothing between us, like I'm imagining it all.

"It was a mistake. I overstepped. It won't happen again. You're my stepsister and that's it. I care about you, but not in any other way besides that," he says.

"Why are you denying this? It's not like you even care what Kurt thinks," I snark, not knowing why I'm arguing with him. I agree that nothing can happen, but I still want him, even though I know I shouldn't.

"No, darlin' I don't. But you sure as fuck do, so unless that changes, you need to stay the fuck away from me, do you understand?" he asks.

I repress a whine, the underlying feelings of rejection bubbling up to the surface. It takes everything in me to shove it down. We're both lying to each other and ourselves by saying we're on the same page. I take some solace in knowing that he isn't unaffected by me; he is attracted to me, but he knows we can't be together. That reasoning is the only thing that holds me together and prevents me from making a blubbering fool of myself.

As if I need proof that Tate is attracted to me in order to calm my brain down, I cross my arms over my chest, and I can't help but smirk when he looks down at my breasts. He groans in frustration.

"Find another ride, I'm leavin'," he announces before he storms off.

I sit at the table for a long time until I hear my name being yelled. I sigh with defeat and walk back to the group, wondering to myself if Tate gave in, would I as well? The scary thing is... I think I already know the answer.

The party goes on without Tate. Sometimes it feels like no

one notices him. I mean I definitely do, but he won't let me in. I don't think Tate lets anyone in, and it makes my heart ache.

Shelby has a chocolate cake set out on the picnic table, and she cuts me a slice before sliding it over to me. She's nearly perched on my brother's lap, and I can admit that I kind of like them together. Leon needs someone who will call him out on his bullshit, and Shelby needs someone who can reign in her crazy moments.

Shelby scoops up a piece of cake and puts it in my brother's mouth before leaning in and giving him a kiss. I don't think I've seen Leon this happy in a really long time.

"Take a picture, it'll last longer," Leon jokes, grabbing his own fork and shoveling cake into his mouth.

"Har-Har. Can't I enjoy seeing my brother happy?" I reply back, and he covers a smile with a fork full of cake.

I expect him to go on a full-on tirade of how I need to leave and find a pack, the same old shit, but he doesn't and it makes my smile even wilder.

"I am happy, ain't I?" he says, grabbing Shelby by the hips and peppering kisses all along her neck and tickling her sides.

"Stop!" she shouts while still laughing, clutching at his shoulders. He finally relents and smiles at her before kissing her again. She pinches his side, and he winces.

"Fuck. You're stronger than you look, you know that, sugar?" he says to her, and she beams.

"That's right, so you better stay in line," she jests, pointing at him.

"I haven't been on the receiving end of Shelby's violence, but I can absolutely attest to the fact you don't want to get on her bad side," I tell my brother. I'll never forget that time she kicked that girl's ass in the middle of the square. Three guys had to pull Shelby off the woman before she killed her.

"It's part of her charm," Leon retorts with a twinkle in his eye.

"So… you gonna make her your ol' lady or what?" I ask, being a complete menace.

Shelby looks at me like I just asked the million-dollar question. But my brother looks over at me like he'd like to stab me with his fork. I shovel cake into my mouth and act completely innocent.

Leon pushes her damp hair off her shoulder and really looks at her. He looks at Shelby the way Axel looks at me. Like no matter what fucked-up shit is happening with the club, no matter any of his personal shit, he wants Shelby to come first.

"That what you want, sugar?" he asks her and she nods her head. "You know I'm on the road a lot more than the other guys, and I can't bring you?" he reminds her, but she nods again anyway.

"That's what I want. I want you," Shelby declares, and my brother wraps her in his arms.

From the corner of my eye, I swear I see Mickey glaring. I wince when I think about what I heard not that long ago. I honestly like Mickey, but I don't see how he and my brother would ever work. But the jealousy is clear in his gaze.

"I'll get you a Property of Ambien jacket when I can," he says, and I can't help but burst out laughing. Shelby throws a piece of cake at me with a glare, and I laugh even harder.

"Come on, you've got to admit it's a little fucking funny," I say, but they both shake their heads as they kiss acting like no one else fucking exists. I envy it, but I'm happy for them more than anything.

This is the lightest I've seen Leon in a long time, and it makes me so happy. My brother deserves happiness more than anyone I know. He's a great protector, and I make a note to let Shelby know she's lucky, though I think she already knows.

Leon always made sure I was taken care of when my mom wasn't able to, and I don't think I've ever truly thanked him for that. A lot of my childhood is a blur, but Leon is the one shiny bit in a pile of shit. He taught me how to read, color, and shoot a gun. I smile at the memories.

They part from their kiss, Shelby leaving her arms wrapped around his neck. The smile on her face is radiant as she mouths a thank you to me.

I wince at the information I have to tell them. "Tate left, I need a new ride home," I sigh.

Leon exhales through his nose and looks at Shelby with a look of irritation. "Look, I know the rules. But there's no reason Axel can't drive me home. We're riding as a pack, it's not like he's gonna do anything bad with you right there," I try to reason.

Leon looks back at Shelby, resting his head against her breasts. It's honestly incredible that they haven't started fucking right here on this table.

"Fine, but he stays in formation. He might be my brother, my friend, but if he gets out of line I'll tug him off his bike by his fuckin' man bun."

"I have better blonde hair for you to tug," Shelby attempts to whisper, but it's heard clear as day.

"Fuck," my brother moans, and I back away from the inevitable makeout sesh. I shake my head and go to wait by Axel's bike.

A huge grin spreads across his face as he struts towards me. I wish he would have taken his clothes off when we swam. But he looks just as good in his jeans, black shirt, and Dead Palms cut.

"You waitin' for your ride?" he asks, pushing some hair from his face.

"You're my ride," I tell him with a grin.

"How the fuck did you manage that?" he questions looking around.

"Leon made Shelby his ol' lady. They're about to fuck on the table over there," I state, using my thumb to point over to where they are heavily making out.

Axel laughs and shakes his head. "About fuckin' time. You know if I could—"

I cut him off, shaking my head. "Axel, I know that if it were up to you we would have been together a long time ago," I softly reassure him, meaning it with every fiber of my being.

I've known most of these guys for years, including Axel, but it was always different with him. Each conversation was laced with a flirtatious undertone, he was never known to be with any of the sweet butts, and he's just so ridiculously good-looking.

"Sometimes it feels like a lot of time lost," he sighs, not getting close to me. Both of us are facing the water so no one can tell what our conversation is about.

"We're making up for it now, right?" I look back at Leon and Shelby, wishing I could have the same open romance as they have. I sigh, truly so happy for both of them, but jealousy does still rear its ugly head.

"That's right. You want to get the fuck out of here?" he asks.

"Part of the deal was staying in formation," I tell him, and he groans.

"At least I'll get to have you touchin' me for an hour," he flirts and I smile.

Besides my confrontation with Tate, I can't imagine a better day.

I'M a little irritated I have to share this small amount of time I have with Lily with Cash, but she is the one who plotted a way to get off the compound, so I'll take what I can get.

Cash and I look like we're on our own fuckin' date because she hasn't gotten here yet.

"How are we going about this?" Cash asks, taking a sip of his beer.

This place definitely wasn't my first choice, but it was what Lily wanted. I take a sip of my own beer. I have my own plans in play, but with Cash on board, it definitely helps give me more options when it comes to making Lily mine.

"I've got a few ideas…" I trail off, not telling him that my plans involve things like kidnapping or running away.

"We're not running away," Cash states as if reading my mind.

"Runnin' away is the last option," I reply.

"I don't know Prez well enough to know how he will react if we just take a stand. I could bond with her. What could he do in response?" he throws out.

I smile against the lip of my beer, quite liking this newly-patched Alpha. At first I thought he was all strength, then I thought he was too smart for his own good. But now? I'm happy he's on my fuckin' side of things.

"He will lose his shit. There'll be violence. Besides the club, the only thing that man cares about is his Omega and Lily," I tell him, hoping he can read between the lines. Simply put, I wouldn't put the Prez above murdering someone when it comes to Lily. "Even if she pleads her case for us, we wouldn't have a spot left in the club. He banged his gavel, statin' Lily was off limits. We'll have broken club law," I explain.

"Fuck club law. I see why Tate hates the prick," Cash comments.

"You know until y'all rolled up and switched shit up I never really thought twice about how club business is being handled," I tell him honestly.

"As soon as this Wraiths raid is done, if she wants it, I'm going to bond her," he says confidently.

"Are you gonna ask her permission, or just bend her over a table and take what you want?" I spit defensively. He glares at me, a completely unamused expression on his face.

"Of course, I will ask her what she wants. It's fucking fast, but she doesn't have much time. You want some other assholes taking care of her during her heat? Or her getting shipped off by the Prez to bond with some stale-ass, cookie-cutter douchebags?"

"No, I don't want any of that shit. But I do want to live," I argue.

Cash puts his beer down, leans forward, and speaks in an even and calm voice. "I'll kill the man myself if I have to," he vows before sitting back in his seat.

"And here I thought you were a cute little fuckin' bookworm," I tease, and he cracks a half smile while shaking his head.

"Maybe I'll kill you too," he jokes, and I grin at him.

"That would make Lily terribly fuckin' sad. Hate to break it to you, but you better get used to my handsome fuckin' face," I jest.

"Unfortunately," he sighs.

I'm saved from this awful date night conversation when a smiling Lily grabs the chair between us and sits down. She looks fuckin' gorgeous wearing a white sundress with her hair in a high ponytail.

"Thanks for coming. I thought Kurt was going to follow me in here for a second," she says, her cheeks turning a cute shade of pink.

"No worries, darlin'," I reply. Both Cash and I throw an arm on the back of her chair. Cash glares at me, so I drop my hand onto her thigh. I clearly win this round.

"I guessed your shoe size," Cash says, handing her the hideous fuckin' bowlin' shoes.

"Thanks," she shyly replies with a blush.

Cash and I are not wearing the bowlin' shoes, and I dare a motherfucker to come over here and tell us to put them on. We're both fully wearing our cuts and staying local. All these assholes know who we are and what we're about.

Cash inputs our names into the computer, with Lily going first. She smiles as she grabs a seven-pound ball that's sparkly and pink.

"It's almost as smooth as your head," I tease Cash, who glares at me. *Man, riling him up is so much fuckin' fun.*

"Go ahead, baby," Cash encourages.

"Should we get bumpers?" she asks while holding the ball against her chest.

"Darlin' there isn't much I wouldn't do for you, but I'm not bowlin' with bumpers," I deadpan, and she rolls her eyes at me, turning away and standing straight in our lane.

She takes a few steps and flings the ball pretty straight, but it's hard to watch where the ball is going, 'cause when she bends over all I notice are the tight black shorts she has on under her dress.

It seems like I'm not the only one looking either. Cash I can deal with, I'm wrapping my mind around the asshole becoming my pack mate, but the greasy fuck who sprays the stink-away spray in the bowlin' shoes? Ain't no fuckin' way.

"You tryin' to lose an eyeball today, asshole?" I ask him, his forehead furrows as he looks at me with his beady eyes.

"I was just watchin' everyone bowl," he replies.

Lily waves at us from the alley, and I give her a quick wave before I stand up and walk to the next table, leaning down to get in his face.

"Look at my girl again. Go on, do it," I taunt him. He doesn't listen, so I grab the back of his neck and force him to look at where Lily's standing. "I said take a fuckin' look."

The man sputters, but with my hand on his neck, he follows directions.

"Girls like that don't look twice at a piece of shit like you, do they?"

"N-n-no," he stutters, a sheen of sweat coating his skin, and it makes me wonder if I can get him to piss his pants.

"Didn't think so. I get it, big man. She's hard not to look at. But I promise you, if you look up my girl's skirt again, I'll scoop your fuckin' eyes out and shove them up your dick hole. You feel me?"

He swallows and shifts in his seat. "I feel you," he confirms.

"Good boy. Now, fuck off," I growl, slapping the back of his neck harder than necessary.

I go back and sit at the table. Lily's cheeks are pink, obviously having heard the tail end of the conversation.

"It's your turn," she squeaks.

"Thanks, darlin'."

I take my turn, and to my dismay, when I look at the scoreboard I realize Lily knocked down two more pins than me.

"It's not too late to get bumpers, ya know?" she teases as I take my seat back. Cash laughs at her joke, and I grab the bottom of her chair, dragging her over to me.

"You think you're funny, darlin'?"

"Yeah, I think I am," she sasses with the cutest fuckin' smirk I've ever seen.

I lean forward and give her a chaste kiss against her lips. Satisfaction courses through me when her scent fills my nose. It's heady, knowing I can get her so turned on by a single kiss. It makes me want to do more in this shitty bowlin' alley. But that scent was for me, and I don't plan on letting any of the local jerkoffs catch a whiff.

Cash clears his throat, his pupils blown as he takes in Lily's scent.

"It's your turn, baby," he says to her. She pops up out of her seat, and I make extra sure no one is looking at her ass or up her dress as she bowls.

The rounds go by quickly. Cash and I are a few pitchers in, while Lily sticks to Dr Pepper.

"You want a glass?" I ask her, holding the beer up.

She scrunches her nose and shakes her head.

"I could get you one of those girly drinks," I offer, and she gives me a small smile.

"They don't have cocktails or wine here."

"No, but they have those things. What the fuck are they called?" I ask, lookin' at Cash.

"Seltzers?" he asks, lookin' at me like I'm fuckin' stupid.

"That's okay. I don't really like those either. Plus, it's only two more days until my birthday," she points out.

"Anything you were hopin' for on your birthday?" I ask. Her face falls a little, but she shakes her head.

"I'm going to run to the bathroom real quick," she says.

"I'll go with you."

She points at the bathroom, which is less than forty feet away. "It's right there. I think I can manage," she says with a smile. She leans down and kisses my cheek before kissing Cash's.

"I didn't realize her birthday was in two days," he comments like I was the one keeping this big secret from him.

"Yeah, twenty-one," I tell him, and he winces at the number. "I guess you're robbin' the cradle pretty fuckin' hard," I taunt, and he gives me the finger.

"I'm thirty-two."

"Practically ancient," I joke.

He sips his beer and tilts his head at me. "Do you mind if I have a moment with her before we go home?" He asks the question in such a pleasant tone that it lets me know that I've kinda taken over the date.

I have a tendency to do that shit. As much as this idea of sharing eats away at me, sometimes I put it on the back burner for her.

This man has all but said he would bond and bite her if she wanted it to keep her here. I needed something like that to turn the tides, giving me at least some hope that we can stay with the Dead Palms and get the girl.

"Yeah, man. I can hang here, or meet you back at the compound," I suggest.

"Appreciate it."

We sit in silence until Lily comes back, but she isn't as happy as she was when she first left us. Her face is downtrodden, and she's holding her arm.

"Everythin' okay?" I ask her.

"Yeah, I'm ready to go," she deflects, looking down at the ground.

"Let me see your arm," I demand.

Her big brown eyes search mine as she bites on her lip.

"Axel, it's not a big deal. I just want to go," she begs.

"Show me your arm and we can leave."

She removes her hand, and I see a red splotchy mark on her arm. It won't leave a bruise, but clearly, someone grabbed her hard enough to disturb her skin.

"Who touched you?" Cash asks her in a tone that's so

nearing on an Alpha bark, that it even has me going quiet for a moment.

"The guy in the red polo," she sighs.

"And what did he say?" I ask as calmly as possible.

"He said it was a misunderstanding, and he asked me not to come back here with you two," she blurts out.

I give her a smile and rub down her arm. "Cash is gonna take you home on his bike. I'll see you tomorrow, yeah?"

"Axel," she breathes my name out like a plea.

"I'm just gonna settle the tab. I'll be home later."

"I know you're not just settling the tab."

"And that's why this is gonna work, darlin'. I'm not nice to anyone but you. I warned that fucker to not look at you. Guess I didn't specify about touchin', but it doesn't take a rocket scientist to know that was off the table, too. He's gonna get a lesson in manners and how to treat a lady while Cash takes you somewhere to enjoy the rest of our date night," I tell her as calmly as possible.

"You can't get in trouble," she reminds me. I smile at her, giving her a quick kiss.

"It would be worth it," I whisper against her face, kissing her cheek one last time before giving Cash a quick nod. He looks pissed and torn.

Like he can't decide what's more important, time alone with Lily or ripping this asshole to shreds. Apparently, the rage written on my face is enough to let him know I got this covered as he leaves the bowlin' alley with my girl.

If I wasn't simmering with anger I would think about how mature I am for letting them go off together and how I have no doubt in Cash's ability to take care of Lily.

But right now, I have other business to handle, so thinking about all that shit is gonna have to wait. I pull out my phone, look at the time, and groan. If Cash didn't need to get Lily out of here, it would have been an easy two-man job. I have no doubt that I could beat the shit out of this fucker by myself, but I'm feeling creative.

I make the call and he answers on the third ring.

"What?"

"I need you at Dino's bowlin' alley in thirty minutes," I state calmly.

"Why the fuck do you need me at the bowlin' alley? It's almost ten," he complains.

"This man at the counter grabbed Lily, and I was thinkin' I would teach him a lesson. But if you're not in, I can handle it on my own," I reply, knowing I'm going to get my way.

"I'll be there in twenty," he replies, hanging up the phone.

I sip my beer and just wait. The announcements let everyone know they are closing for the night, but I just continue to wait for him to get here.

He strolls into the bowlin' alley with a furious look on his face, and I grin at him.

"Where's Lily?" Tate demands.

"Cash took her home," I answer.

"Why do you need me?" he asks, looking irritated that I took him away from no doubt some boring shit he was doing back at the clubhouse.

"He grabbed Lily's arm, left a mark, and was lookin' up her skirt," I remind him. Tate looks around like he will know immediately who committed the crime. "He's the dude spraying the shoes. He works here so he can bowl for free."

"What did you have in mind?"

"He's a bowler. Let's hit him where it hurts," I suggest, nudging my head to the lane. "He's gonna have to stay till clean up, meaning we'll wait in the bathroom until he's here alone."

Tate seems irritated with the plan but goes with it anyway.

We sit in the bathroom for what feels like forever until I decide the timing is right.

He has music playing on the speakers as he bowls a round

with all the patrons gone, so he doesn't even notice us approaching. Tate makes the first move by wrapping his arm around the guy's neck and dragging him to the ball return machine.

Tate is easily twice the man's size, so it's no hard feat to get the guy bent over the machine and hold him there.

"Heard you like puttin' your hands on Omegas that don't fuckin' belong to you," Tate seethes in his ear.

"I didn't mean anything by it. I just didn't want her comin' back here," the man sputters.

"Why? Cause you can't keep your eyes or hands to yourself?" I ask, picking up a bowling ball with each hand.

Tate goes to put his right hand in the hole that spits out the balls, and I tsk. "He was bowlin' with his left," I say, and Tate groans, having to readjust the asshole to get his left hand and arm into the return.

"No, please. It was a mistake. I won't do anything like it again. I promise," he begs. Tate grins down at the man, and I toss one ball down the lane and quickly toss the other.

"Do we need a third?" I ask Tate in a weirdly sweet voice.

"Yes," he says, forcing the man's body to hold still along with his arm.

"You're so right. You know, three is the perfect number," I joke, winkin' at Tate.

He doesn't even appreciate my joke as I toss the third ball down the lane. We don't have to wait long as the balls attempt to come back to the front of the lane.

The man cries and begs, but Tate holds him down. I join him as the balls return to us, the machine whirling and the man screaming as we listen to his fingers and wrist breaking. He goes limp against the machine and cries as we step away. He holds his arm pathetically as he looks up at us.

"Fuck with the Dead Palms again and we take more than just your hand," Tate warns, spitting on the man before we both turn away and leave the establishment.

We stay silent until we're both on our bikes, and I cut the tension.

"Thanks for comin' so fast."

"I came because he disrespected Lily," he replies.

"Right… the S.Y.W.T.F."

"What the fuck does that stand for?"

I grin at him and start my engine before I yell out the acronym. "The stepsister you want to fuck." I feel his glare burning into me as I ride home, wondering if by any chance I'll be able to catch Lily for a quick kiss—or more—before she goes to bed.

NINETEEN
NOT READY

AS BADLY AS I want to be back inside that bowling alley giving that dumbass the beating of his life. I know Axel has it covered, and I don't want Lily around for that shit.

She's not dumb. She knows the things we do, why guys walk around the compound with black eyes and bloody knuckles. But it's one thing to know something and another to see it. For me, I don't want my Omega to deal with that shit.

Maybe it's a double standard, but I don't really give a fuck. I want her protected and only to be involved in club business when it's necessary or safe enough. I think our night at the trailer park taught me a lot about Lily.

She isn't scared of the danger or the lifestyle. She just wants us to be safe, and I can't imagine asking for much more than that.

I had to modify my bike so she could ride with me, seeing as I've never had anyone on the back of my bike before.

"Are you sure we should leave him in there alone?" Lily asks me as I usher her through the side door toward my bike.

"I'm pretty sure that deranged psycho can handle himself better than most Alphas," I reply, and I don't miss her smile at my comment. I'm not sure how much she would smile if she actually saw the violence happening in there, but she clearly isn't upset over it. "He'll be more than fine."

"You're right," she sighs. "Where are we going?"

"I was thinking we could sneak into the body shop so you could spend some time with Winnie," I suggest, and her face lights up.

"That sounds perfect."

I grab the helmet I specifically brought for her; she reaches out to take it, but I shake my head, placing it on her head and buckling the chin strap myself.

"You don't have to do things for me," she says softly.

"I know. I do them because I want to."

Her cheeks are flushed as I get on the bike first and she hops on the back. When her arms and scent wrap around me, I think I might die. At the very least, the drive home is going to fucking suck with a hard-on.

I toss my helmet on, and she speaks before I start my engine.

"Not a lot of the guys wear helmets," she comments.

"Yeah, and a lot of them are fucking stupid too," I respond, making her laugh as she tightens her hold on me.

I'm not sure why it feels so good with Lily, but it does. Something about her scent calls to me like no one else's has. Maybe it's the fact that I'm forbidden from being with her, or how badly I want to take care of her.

I know it would be the same with any Omega. My instincts automatically default to caretaker, but with Lily, it feels like more. It's more than just taking care of her when it comes to her heat or being a protector. I find myself wanting to do things for her that I've never wanted to do for anyone else, like let her ride on the back of my bike, keep a fucking puppy in my office, and make sure she's taking care of herself.

Her hands rub up and down my abdomen, as she holds on tight. I'm driving far more cautiously than I usually do, but it feels nice. Nicer than I ever imagined, it's an intimacy I've never experienced before, and I know it's something I want more of. I know a lot of the guys will toss whoever needs a ride on the back of their bike, but for me, it seemed too sacred to just let anyone on my bike.

The ride is uneventful, yet peaceful, as we reach the compound. I know where Prez's cameras are, and I also know where my cameras are. It's a tidbit I've only shared with Tate. After these past few days, I think I'm ready to share it with Axel too, but not yet.

The cameras on the compound aren't club knowledge. The Prez is the only one with access and that didn't sit right with me, so I added my own.

I avoid all the cameras I know of and park just outside of the body shop. Lily pops off first, removing her helmet and hair tie, letting her long, dark hair flow down her back. I follow suit and place a hand on her lower back to guide her to the office in the back.

"So, you know where all of my stepdad's cameras are," she states, and I smirk to myself. I like that she's relatively street-smart. She might be naïve in some regards, or rather sheltered, but she grew up around a bunch of criminals. When that happens, you have to be observant. She clicks her tongue before saying, "That's how you knew about the car when those assholes dropped me off."

"Something like that," I reply, and she rolls her eyes.

As soon as we open the door, Winnie is bounding towards Lily who gets on her knees to give the dog some love.

"She's a good dog," I tell her. Lily smiles at the compliment.

"She is, isn't she?"

"Hasn't hardly pissed on anything and doesn't seem to bite much."

"I wish I could be with her all the time," she says longingly while scooping the dog up and sitting her on her lap once she takes a seat on the couch. I take the spot next to her and pet the little fucker's head.

"About that—" I start, trying to figure out how to segue into this conversation.

"Kurt likes dogs, just not at his house," she interrupts- and I wonder if she's concerned about me not being able to handle the dog.

"Are you ready to be on your own? Well, to have a pack and be away from your mom and the Prez?" I ask.

She shrugs, and I abort my mission to tactfully enter this conversation, choosing instead to just blurt out what I'm thinking. "We could bond. Prez wouldn't be able to say shit with my bite mark on you." I drag my fingertip along her collarbone, making her shiver.

She takes a moment to let my words sink in, all while looking down at the dog petting her. "Would you hate me if I said I wasn't ready?"

"Baby girl, I could never hate you. I know it's soon, we haven't even had much time to get to know each other. But your scent does something to me that I can't explain, and I know you're running out of time."

She sighs and pets Winnie's fur. "I know, and my hesitation has nothing to do with you. I just need a few more days until I can get settled," she says.

"Is this about the money?" I ask her, thinking back to how much was in her account and how she didn't want to bond until she knew she was safe. I could tell her how safe she would be with me, but I don't think it would matter. She needs this money in order to *feel* safe in a relationship, and I can respect that.

"I'm so sorry, Cash. It probably seems so stupid to you. I know that you and Axel could take care of me. I don't want you to feel like I'm saying you can't provide." Her voice is timid, and I can tell she's more worried about hurting my feelings than anything else.

"Hey, shhhh," I soothe, sliding closer and grabbing the back of her neck. "This money will make you feel safe? Make you feel complete? Ready?" She nods her head. "Then we'll wait till then, okay?"

"Thank you for being understanding. It's just… I don't want to end up like so many other Omegas, with no options, no safety net. It's not even a matter of worrying about if you would hurt me like my mom's old pack…" she trails off.

"Do you want to talk about what happened?" I ask her.

"I don't really remember much," she admits, and my brows pinch together.

"You don't remember what, exactly?"

"Most of my childhood, really." She shrugs and continues petting the dog. Alarm bells go off in my head, but I keep it to myself. You don't repress your childhood unless you really need to. "Most of my memories are with the Dead Palms, and maybe that's why I'm so adamant about staying here. But I also don't want to be cooped up either."

"You want adventure?" I ask her with a smile that she returns.

"I don't expect lavish vacations or anything like that. But going out on the road? Visiting all the states? It's kind of a dream of mine."

"I want to make it happen," I tell her confidently.

"Why?" she asks, her deep brown eyes meeting mine.

"Because I've never wanted someone in the way that I want you. It's never been like this for me, where I've been drawn to someone so quickly and easily. I want to make you my Omega and in doing so I want to give you the fucking world."

She swallows. "What about the club?"

"I love the club, and I'm still finding my footing with this chapter, but I'd give it all up to be with you. I would walk away."

Her mouth gapes open. "You'd leave… for me?"

"I don't want to leave, but if it came down to it… yeah, I would. Me and some of the other guys could start our own chapter or some shit. I couldn't leave the life fully, but if being with you meant leaving Tallahassee, it's an easy choice."

Lily picks up the dog that's fallen asleep and places her on the dog bed on the floor before scooting closer to me. She cups my face and looks up at me with a mix of hope and awe.

"I'd leave Tallahassee for you… Axel too," she promises.

It feels like barbed wire wraps itself around my chest at that promise. She climbs on top of my lap, and my hands automatically go to her exposed thighs as her hands wrap softly around my neck. Her thumbs rub small patterns against my skin, and I shiver slightly at the touch.

She grinds against my hardening cock, and I groan as I look at her face.

"I know I said no bonding, and I'll work on getting ready—I promise—but if you could help me take away some of this ache…"

"Why didn't you say you were hurting?" I ask, rubbing the skin on her smooth, toned thighs.

"I've gotten so used to handling it myself, but lately… I need more," she admits.

"How much more?"

My heartbeat thunders against my ribcage as she leans in, her modest chest pressing against mine as one of her hands holds the back of my head and the other rests on my collarbone.

"I need what only an Alpha can give me," she whispers in my ear.

It flips a switch in me; I'm no longer the controlled man I aim to be. I'm a man driven by his needs and baser instincts. My hands grip her ass roughly as I push her pussy against my clothing-covered length, and she moans in my ear.

The room fills with the combination of our scents, and I remind myself that she said no to bonding. Above all, I need to be an honorable Alpha to her—no one else.

I grip her hair and wrap it in my fist, pulling her head back to look at her. "I just need you to know I'm going to control myself, no matter fucking what. But the minute you tell me to bond you, baby girl? I don't care if you're in heat, or if it's in front of the whole fucking compound, I'm putting my mark on you."

I don't know if she takes my words for the absolute truth that they are, but truer words have never been spoken. I want her to be mine, and as soon as she gives me the green light, she will be.

She moans and crashes her lips to mine. It's a kiss laced with need and desperation for one another. She tastes even better than I remember, and I swear to fuck if we get interrupted this time, someone is going to fucking die.

Her hips rock back and forth on my lap, begging for friction. I let her, enjoying the slow torture of her scent filling the room and just waiting for her slick to dampen through the spandex shorts she has on under her dress.

She bites my bottom lip before pulling back. Her pupils are huge, and her cheeks are pink as she looks at me, her hips never stopping their movement. Her small hand wraps around my chin, and I revel at the power she holds over me even though she's half my size.

"Pants off," she demands.

"You first," I retort. She doesn't hesitate, quickly getting off my lap and sliding her shorts and panties down her thighs. I swallow down the masculine pride of how wet she is when the fabric slaps against the floor. "Your dress too. Show me those cute tits."

She bites her lip but follows suit, not a single ounce of shyness left on her features.

Lily stands before me completely naked, and my breath hitches. "You're fucking perfect," I breathe. That comment is what makes her blush, but she doesn't cover herself. She just stands there confidently, waiting for me to get undressed as well.

My eyes don't leave her body as I undo my belt, sliding my

pants and underwear down before kicking one leg free. Her perfume thickens as she looks down at my hard cock and legs.

"You're really covered in tattoos," she breathes out.

"Come here."

She takes her place back on my lap, her wet pussy pressed against my aching length.

"Shirt too," she says. I clear my throat, and her eyes meet mine. "Is everything okay?"

"Just don't freak out," I tell her softly.

Her eyes widen a fraction, but she nods.

When I pull my shirt off from the back of my neck, I watch as she takes in the scarred marks across my chest. She doesn't look disgusted or like she pities me, but concern is written in her bright eyes.

"Does it hurt?" she asks, her fingers gently grazing over the scar tissue.

"No, I'm fine," I answer, wishing I took off my shirt before we got to this point because I sure as fuck don't want to go through my sordid history, how I got these marks, or how it was all for naught.

She surprises me by leaning forward and placing a gentle kiss on my deepest mark, which stretches along my collarbone. It sends a shiver down my spine, causing me to inhale dramatically. The softness she offers me isn't something I thought I would be craving, but now that I have it there's no way I can let it go.

Lily doesn't push me any further, so I sweep her hair off her shoulder and just admire her for a few moments. I don't know how I'm able to ignore my aching cock or how her scent is driving me fucking wild, but I do, because she's special, and she's going to be mine come hell or high fucking water.

CASH LOOKS at me like I'm special. It's addictive the way he makes me feel; safe, cherished, and protected.

He would bond with me in a second, he's that sure of me, and I don't know how to handle someone that confident. Sure, Axel is extremely self-assured, and I have no doubts about his intentions, but he doesn't have the power to give me a bond mark; though I know he would if he could.

I need to do my last live for Marielli's Mass. It will give me the remaining amount I need to feel comfortable. That money might be needed for us to start a new life, but I've had this idea in my head for a while now, and I just can't shake it. It doesn't help that I just had to pay the government a huge portion of my earnings; plus, I imagine Cash and Axel aren't struggling either. It's just something I've got to prove to myself; at least, I think that's still my motivation, I'm not even sure anymore.

But when Cash looks at me with complete fucking reverence, I consider changing my mind. *He's willing to risk it all. Why can't I?*

I shake all these thoughts as I rise on my knees. I'm already dripping without him even touching me, and God, do I need his fucking knot. I don't have time to fool around; I need the stretch so fucking bad, I'm nearly gagging for it.

I tease him by grinding up and down on his length, coating him with my wetness.

"You sure know how to fucking torture a man," he huffs.

He holds my hips while staring down at where I'm sliding back and forth on him. His hands leave my hips to tangle in my hair and bring my lips to his.

Cash kisses me with all the confidence in the world, like he knows without a doubt his mark will be on me one day, even if it's not tonight.

Our mouths don't part as I slide my hand between us, my fingers tease his knot, causing a moan to rip from his throat, and I swallow it down. I give us both what we want, notching him at my entrance. I slowly slide down his length an inch before rising back up. I do it over and over again, getting further down his shaft every time.

"Fuck," he mumbles between kisses. He lets me ride him, setting the pace.

His cock is perfect, hitting me in all the right places as I move up and down. Cash can't seem to decide where to put his hands as they move from my hair, to my breasts, and then back to my hips.

"You ride my cock so fucking good," he praises before kissing the side of my neck. His tongue trails patterns on my skin as his teeth graze the tender flesh behind my ear. "One day I'm going to mark you right here while you're taking my knot," he whispers, and it breaks me.

I'm not fully there yet, but I slide all the way down, impaling myself on his thick knot. The pressure is intense and takes Cash off guard as he thrusts up from beneath me.

"Look at you taking all of it. Such a good girl. You want your Alpha to make you come?" he asks.

My nails dig into his shoulders as I nod my head and whine. "Please, Cash. You feel so fucking good."

His one hand cradles the back of my head as he places soft kisses down my throat while fucking me from the bottom. His knot stretches me so fucking good it feels like my hearing and vision are going fuzzy. I just hold on to him, letting him take control, and enjoy him giving me what he knows I need.

My clit rubs against the small patch of curls at the base of his cock, and I shatter. The delicious stretch of his knot and the friction against my clit pushes me over the edge. My body collapses on top of his as he continues driving into me. His fist is so tightly tangled in my hair it makes my orgasm last longer than it ever has before. I rest my head against his shoulder as I repeat his name while shudders wrack my body. I can't help it when I bite down lightly on his neck.

It has the effect I wanted as he ruts into me so hard I nearly scream, gushing around his cock.

"Fuck, Lily."

He shudders and his hold on my hair is near bruising as he fills me with his cum, his knot at its full size inside of me.

He thrusts into me a few more times before he sits fully back, his hands leaving my hair and sliding down my back gently. The juxtaposition of rough and tender with Cash is consuming.

It feels like we're in slow motion as we both come down from our high. It's silent between us as we touch and explore. My fingertips graze across the healed scars on his chest, hating that they're there, but proud that he survived and that he's here with me. He doesn't have to talk about it now, but one day I hope he'll feel comfortable enough to do so.

He shifts slightly, and the feeling of his knot still inside of me makes me moan.

"Sorry, baby," he mumbles, pushing back my side-swept bangs.

"That was amazing," I whisper while touching his face, and that has him smiling at me.

Cash doesn't smile much at others, but around me, he

always seems happy. It's an overwhelming feeling knowing that my presence alone allows him to feel like he can let loose and be happy. It also lightens something in my chest, knowing that his offer to bond me isn't just to help me but because he wants me, he needs me.

I've never been needed before... I'm not sure how to handle it.

"Thank you, Cash," I breathe, resting my head on his shoulder.

His scent is so thick and heavy, it's like a warm blanket for my soul. And I know without a doubt Cash was always meant to become my bonded Alpha. I just need to fully prepare myself.

"Anything for you, Lily," he says against my hair.

He wraps his large arms around me while we wait for his knot to go down. I can tell he's being completely transparent with that statement, that he would truly do anything for me.

I felt a small glimpse of hope when Axel said he would figure out a way for us to be together, but now with Cash's promises as well, I can envision my future with more clarity.

I'm going to finish what I started with Marielli's Mass, and that money will buy my future whether it's here on this compound like I always dreamed of or riding off to the sunset with Cash and Axel. Although it feels like something—someone—is missing, but I don't let myself dwell on that.

CASH IS careful about bringing me home, avoiding any cameras. Axel hasn't come home yet, which is concerning. I desperately hope he didn't do something stupid to get himself in trouble. I know he can take care of himself. He more than proved that the night he rescued me from my horrible date.

"Will you or Axel text me when he's home?" I whisper to Cash.

"Of course. Do you need to climb up the roof again?" Cash asks, seemingly less than pleased that I would do that on my own.

"No, Mom and her pack are shooting pool tonight. They won't be home till late," I reply.

I'm wrapped up in his hoodie, which I stole, and I hate that I'm going to have to hide in my room, but at least I'll be able to sleep with it tonight. He takes a fist full of his massive hoodie and drags me toward him. I grin up at him as he kisses me tenderly on my front porch.

"Later, baby."

"Later," I sigh as our faces part, and I turn, opening the front door.

I'm on cloud nine, just about to do a little wiggle of excitement when a menacing voice cuts through my happiness.

"Jesus fuckin' Christ, Lily," my brother's voice startles me, causing me to jump slightly.

"Leon, what are you doing here?" I ask him.

He laughs and throws back whatever he is drinking. Only the oven light is on, making him appear more menacing than his tone truly portrays.

"More like why are you fuckin' Cash?" he spits out, and I jolt back.

"That's none of your fucking business," I counter.

"You're my baby sister. You'll always be my fuckin' business," he states. His voice is calm. He isn't yelling at me, so at least there's that.

"Cash is who I want. I don't want any of these guys Kurt keeps setting me up with," I reply, trying to not get defensive.

"You should," he replies.

"I should what?"

"You should want those guys, Lily. You need to get out of here," he declares.

"What does that even mean? I'm not a stupid little girl. I know what goes on around here. I know Cash isn't an upstanding citizen, but he's who I want."

"You have no fuckin' idea what goes on here, 'cause if you did, you would get the fuck out of Florida and never turn back," he slurs a few of the words, and I realize he's drunk.

I take a few tentative steps toward him, and he scoffs when he notices that I'm wearing Cash's hoodie.

"Then tell me, Leon. Tell me why I need to stay away? Because I don't think I can," I tell him honestly.

His brown eyes, which are just like mine, are riddled with sadness when he looks at me, and I swear on my life they're watery. I don't remember ever seeing my brother cry, not when he got hit as a child, not when our mom came home with bruises… never.

Leon is the strongest person I know, so to see him like this feels foreign. I'm not even sure if I need to stand my ground and talk about what I'm doing, or find a way to bring him some comfort. I feel guilty, but Leon has always been the one comforting me in times of distress, not the other way around.

"I can't," he chokes out. His left-hand grabs the bottle of whiskey, and he pours himself another glass. "You fuckin' stink," he spits out, and I roll my eyes.

I remind myself to try and be compassionate. This isn't my brother; this sad, hopeless man that's been before me over the last few weeks isn't him. I sit down next to him, reaching out and grabbing his hand in mine. He accepts my affection, and I sigh with relief.

"I hate seeing you like this. I'm here for you, always."

He squeezes my hand, sighing heavily. "I know, Lily. That's why you need to leave. If Cash is who you want, then jump on the back of his bike and get as far as you fuckin' can from this place," he warns somberly.

"What about you?"

He laughs sardonically. "There's nowhere else for me."

"What if I feel the same way?"

He lets go of my hand to run his fingers through his hair. "You think I don't want you here? Lily, I love you more than I love fuckin' anyone. The idea of you leavin' breaks my fuckin' heart. But I love you so much that I'd rather you leave, be happy, and get to live a full life than for me to be selfish with you."

"I couldn't leave you and Mom behind," I protest.

"Lily," he sighs out my name and takes another drink. "I know you don't remember much from when we were kids, but do you remember that time we got to go to that park with all the tire swings?"

"Yeah," I reply, wondering what this has to do with anything.

"We made a plan on how we were going to escape, just you and me?" I nod my head at him and he continues. "We didn't take Mom into consideration because we knew there's no way she would leave. No matter how bad that pack treated her, even though they didn't bond her, she was too weak to leave. You're not weak, Lily, you're stronger than you think. You could escape this life, and have more, like we always dreamed of."

My eyes water and I wipe away a fat tear. Leon never brings up our childhoods, and the fact that he's doing so now hits me right in the chest.

"Then tell me straight up, why do I need to leave? If you give me a good reason... I'll do it," I beg him.

I'm being honest, I've already run the scenario of having to leave in my head. It's not what I want–I want to be here, be a part of the club—but if it comes down to the club or the men I want to be with, I'm going to choose them. I just wish I knew what Leon was so afraid of. I want to help him, and I don't know if I can do that if I leave.

He groans, taking another shot and standing up. I have to look up at him when he steps closer to me and squeezes my shoulder. "Isn't seein' me like this enough? I love you, Lily. I pray this isn't the last time I see you, but I sure as fuck hope that you get the hell out of here," he whispers.

I stand up and wrap my arms around his waist, squeezing him tight. His scent is a warm comfort, even though I'm wrapped in Cash's.

"You would tell me if you were in trouble, right?" I ask against his chest. "Do you need money?"

He laughs sardonically and shakes his head, his arms surrounding me, returning the hug.

"I don't need money, I just need to know you're going to be okay."

"Couldn't you leave too? Shouldn't we all go then, if things are so bad?" I ask, wondering specifically why I'm the only one who needs to get the hell out of dodge.

"I'm in for life," he sighs, resigned.

My brows furrow, he just said Cash could up and leave, why can't he? My brother kisses the top of my head and hugs me one more time.

"Just promise me you'll think about it? I'll help you get out if you need it," he promises.

He pulls away from our hug, and I try to tug him back toward me; there's more to discuss, so much I don't understand.

"Leon," I sigh his name as he starts to walk away.

"Night, Lily," he says over his shoulder as he opens the back door and leaves the house.

I notice that he doesn't walk to the clubhouse, but turns toward the sweet house. I'm not sure how to take everything he said, but I know one thing for sure, I need that money even if it's used for running away from everything I love and know. Although I'm going to need more than my brother's drunken words for me to abandon everything I'm trying so hard to keep. I've got to have some sort of hope that I can make this work, that I can make Kurt and everyone else see reason.

But Leon's words ring through my head all night, the fear in his voice, his pleas for me to get out. I don't take his threat lightly, but I just can't wrap my head around what could be so sinister that he doesn't want me here. Everything over the past few weeks is running together in my head; the dates, what's been said about Kurt, how Kurt has been acting.

I lie awake in my bed, combing through our conversation over and over again, knowing that my brother is probably right, and it makes my chest ache. I'm tossing and turning until my phone buzzes on my nightstand.

AXEL

Night, baby.

Glad to see you didn't get in any trouble.

Me? In trouble? Never. Why are you still up?

Just a lot on my mind.

Should I sneak into your room?

I smile, wanting to say yes, but I know my mom and her pack will be home soon.

Maybe another night.

Night.

Night.

I cuddle with Cash's hoodie and struggle with what I should do next, but now that I know Axel is safely home, I'm able to get some sleep.

TWENTY-ONE
BIRTHDAY GIRL

LILY

TODAY IS the day that I've been dreading for weeks—I'm finally twenty-one. I'm not sure why I expected to wake up feeling like a completely different person, but I don't; I feel the same. And no matter how normal I feel, I know what's looming around the corner; I shove it deep down. If I dwell too long about the future or my upcoming heat, I go into a spiral.

I've been replaying so many conversations in my head. Axel's confessions, Cash's promises, Tate's denials, and my brother's fears. They all point me in one direction… Marielli's Mass. I'm giving myself today to enjoy my birthday but tomorrow's it. I'm biting the bullet and masturbating live, and what comes after is yet to be seen, but I've been preparing myself.

All I've wanted is to be a part of the club and stay close to my family, but the reality is… that just might not happen.

There's a light knock on the door as I'm trying to zip up the back of my pink dress. "Come in," I say loud enough for them to hear.

The door clicks open and then shuts. I turn around to see my mom smiling with watery eyes at me.

She shakes her head, wiping away tears. "Shit, I told myself I wasn't going to cry," she chides herself before coming up behind me and helping me with my dress. "You look beautiful, honey."

"Thanks, Mom."

She squeezes my shoulders as we both look at our shared reflections in the mirror. "I never imagined this, you know? The chance to watch you and Leon grow up," she whispers as she touches my hair and looks at me like I'm the center of her world. "I'm so proud of you."

"Why? I haven't done anything special," I state.

"You couldn't be more wrong. You have your own business, everyone here loves you, and you're so confident and strong. I couldn't have asked for a better daughter if I tried."

"Stop or you're going to make me cry, too."

"We can't have the birthday girl crying, now can we?" my mom chastises, wrapping her arms around me and squeezing me tightly. It's sweet until she starts to softly cry.

"Mom, what's wrong?" I turn around in her arms and she cups my face, forcing a smile onto hers.

"Nothing. One day, when you have a child, you're going to hold that little baby in your arms and fall so madly in love. Then in a blink of an eye, they'll be all grown up and you won't know where all the time went," she says while holding back more tears. Her thumbs rub my face, and she just looks at me for a few moments. "You saved my life, you know?" she whispers.

"Mom," I sigh, wrapping my hands around her wrists.

"I know you were little and you don't remember much, but without you and Leon I wouldn't be here. God, I'm so fucking happy I'm here to see this," she tells me.

I wrap my arms around her small frame, and we hold each other for a moment. I try to picture a life where I can't see my mom every day. My mom isn't perfect, far from it, but she's still my mom. She did the best she could with the circumstances she was dealt, and I'm not sure I can ask much more of her. If I leave with Cash and Axel, would I ever be able to come back?

"You'd love me no matter what?" I ask her.

"No matter what," she repeats confidently.

"We should head down," I tell her. She pulls back and nods.

"I only came here to give you your gift anyway," she admits, pulling out a small locket from her pocket.

It's old, and I vaguely remember seeing it around her neck a few times. She pops the top, and it's a picture of the three of us —my mom, Leon, and me—smiling when we first moved here. My chest aches over what the necklace represents—home. I hold it in my hands tightly. I take a few moments, but I can't spit the words out.

I remember this day vividly, it was the first day that I truly slept through the night, and I didn't have to wake Leon up after a nightmare. I feel a crushing guilt, wondering if my brother has ever or will ever have a good night's sleep. Part of me wants to confide in my mom and tell her what Leon said, but something holds me back. Instead, I wrap my arms around her again and give a mumbled thank you against her hair.

"Okay, today is supposed to be a celebration. Let's head outside," she redirects, and I nod my head as she cups my face and kisses my forehead softly.

I wear the necklace around my neck with pride as I walk to the center of the square, where most of the club is waiting to sing me Happy Birthday. I, of course, do a headcount and notice that both Axel and Cash are there, but Tate is clearly missing. It makes my heart ache, but I shove that feeling deep down.

I can't have a missing spot in my heart that belongs to Tate… I just can't.

The synchronized singing starts and my cheeks heat under the attention of so many people as I stare at the twenty-one candles before me.

I close my eyes, envisioning my wish as I inhale a deep breath and blow all the air out in a harsh whoosh, trying to get all the candles to flicker out. Hoping that out of all my birthday wishes, this is the one that finally comes true.

WHILE I'VE HAD a sip of alcohol here and there in the past, nothing compares to how I feel right now. My body feels a little tingly, and everything just feels pretty fucking awesome. That might also be because the party moved into the clubhouse, and I love being in here. It's not that the clubhouse is anything special—it's honestly, slightly unsanitary and a bit of a shithole —but it's my family's shithole, and I love it here.

"You want to dance, sugar?" Atlas asks me from my side.

He might have been cute when he first rolled up to the compound, but now when I look at him I feel nothing. If anything he kind of creeps me out.

"Sorry, she's mine for the night," Shelby interrupts and grabs my hand to drag me to the dance floor.

"Thanks for the save," I tell her and she laughs.

"Please, if anything I was doing him a favor. If your guys caught him flirting he might be dead in a ditch by the end of the night. Plus, Kim said his pecker is, like, super small," she says, and I laugh loudly.

"Well, I'm glad I avoided that."

Shelby holds my hips as I throw my hands in the air and dance. All the guys grumbled when I threw on Lady Gaga, but I see a few of them swaying or tapping their feet to the beat.

"I have a birthday present for you," she leans down to whisper in my ear.

"Oh, yeah?"

"Best thing is… it's free." She grins, and I wonder what this wild Beta has in store for me.

"Where or what is it?"

"Well, I'm inadvertently part of it. I'm the distraction."

I blink at her, wondering if I'm stupid or if I'm just drunk and not following. Shelby just smiles wider as she grabs my hand.

"I'm taking Lily to the bathroom," she announces, embarrassingly.

"Shelby!" I hiss her name, tugging at her hold on my hand.
She's much stronger than me though and drags me along to the
ladies' room. "I don't have to pee."

"Oh, yeah, you do." She tosses the door open and pushes me
in first. I turn around to look at her, but all I'm met with is a
closed door.

"What the fuck, Shelby?" I shout it loud enough that I know
she can hear it through the door.

"You mind lockin' the door, darlin'?" His voice is a cool
balm over my overheated body, and I smile to myself as I reach
down and lock the door before spinning around.

Axel looks fucking delicious in a white t-shirt, his cut, and
black pants. I don't know if it's the alcohol or the way my body
craves Axel, but I'm feeling confident.

"You're my birthday present?" I tease.

He confidently steps towards me, one hand gripping my hip
as the other presses against the door for balance. I look up at
him, biting my lip.

He leans down to whisper against the side of my face. His
breath smells like liquor as he speaks. "If you'll have me,
birthday girl."

"What did you have in mind?" my voice hitches as I ask the
question. I press my thighs together, but his palm moves from
my hip to cup my pussy.

"We don't have a lot of time, and as much as I'd love to fuck
you so good you don't remember how to speak, I want to take
my time with you," he states assuredly.

"Okay," I breathe out.

He clasps my hips, making me gasp as he picks me up and
places me on top of the small ceramic sink. His hands don't
leave me as he leans in and kisses me like it's been years since
our last kiss. I moan into his mouth as his hands grip me harder
while he hitches my dress up and tugs down the waistband of

my panties. I feel the material hang loosely on my left foot, and I kick them away.

The back of my head hits the mirror lightly, making me laugh, but I don't part from the kiss. How could I, when I can feel Axel smiling against my lips? When he breaks the kiss, my first reaction is to pout, but his words end that train of thought.

"Birthday girl's choice: Do you want my fingers or my mouth?"

"Mouth," I answer immediately. He pulls back, smirking at me.

I watch in awe as this man falls to his knees before me. He doesn't give a shit that we're in a bathroom, or that his entire club is just a hallway away. I brace myself by holding onto the sink with one hand as Axel grips my hips and pulls me to the edge. I can't help but tangle my hand in his soft blond hair as he kisses up my thigh. His lips are soft, and there's just enough stubble on his face to make me shiver with each press of his skin.

Each touch is reverent, and I can't help but feel wholly loved and cherished. Maybe it's the ferocity in his eyes, but I never want Axel to look at me any other way than he is right now. His blue eyes don't leave mine as he licks and sucks on the flesh, leaving a trail of saliva behind until he gets to my pussy. I thought maybe with the way he was teasing, he would start off soft and gentle, but he doesn't. His lips wrap around my clit and he sucks. The yelp that leaves me is loud and indecent.

Axel doesn't tell me to be quiet, and I suppose the music is loud enough that I don't need to be. Something about that turns me on even more. The fear of getting caught, of someone hearing, and that this is happening in the clubhouse I'm barred from most times, makes everything ten times hotter.

Axel slides two fingers inside of me as he continues to lick and suck my clit. He goes down on me in a way that lets me know he's enjoying himself, that he gets pleasure from bringing me to the edge of release. There's a nagging feeling of guilt in my brain that I haven't gotten him off yet, but I shove it down and just enjoy this moment.

My grip tightens in his hair, and he moans into my pussy.

Maybe it's the alcohol, the forbiddenness of it all, or maybe Axel is just amazing at eating pussy, but I come way too soon. My thighs tighten around his head as I shatter, mumbling out praise and thanks for how good he's making me feel. His tongue and fingers don't stop, and I know his hand is going to be covered in my release.

I'm trembling and barely keeping myself up on the sink as I clench around his fingers. It nearly feels like too much, and I tug on his hair, attempting to pull him away, but he resists.

"Axel," I whisper out his name. He just moans against my oversensitive clit making me shiver. "Axel, stop."

He pulls back, my slick glistening on his chin.

"Come here," I tell him.

He stands up, stepping between my legs as I bring his mouth to mine to enjoy the taste of myself on his tongue.

"Fuck," he mumbles against my lips. I bring my hands down and unbuckle his belt. He tries to pull away but I don't let him. "Baby, we don't have time."

I just tug on his pants harder and slide my hand into his boxers, pulling his cock out. He kisses me hard as I slide my hand down to my dripping center and gather wetness on my palm. I use my slick as lubrication as I wrap my hand around his length.

He pauses our kiss to press our foreheads together so he can look down at where I'm jerking him off.

"Are you going to come on my pussy?" I ask him, making him shiver.

"God damn, I love you, woman," he practically curses. I pause, and he looks up at me. He doesn't look embarrassed, ashamed, or like he even plans on explaining himself.

"I love you, too," I whisper.

The alcohol definitely helps me admit it, but I've known it

for a while now. I've loved Axel from afar when he felt untouchable, but now that I've seen how we are together, I know I love him.

His lips crash into mine, and I continue stroking him.

"You're mine, Lily Rose."

"Yours," I whisper between kisses. "Mark what's yours," I tell him as I pick up my speed, my thumb rubbing the tip of his cock with each stroke.

I angle the head near my exposed pussy. He pulls away from our kiss to look down and watch where we're nearly meeting, but I watch his face.

His eyes nearly roll into the back of his head and his hands dig into my thighs as he comes. White spurts of his warm cum land on my thighs and pussy lips.

He takes a moment to look at where he's marked me while he catches his breath. There's a calm silence that floats between us. There are no regrets about what we've done. In fact, he swipes through the mess with his fingers and pushes it slowly inside of my pussy with rapt attention. I love the possessiveness of the action, but I'm also thankful as fuck that I'm on birth control. Now all we have to do is figure out how we're going to get out of here undetected.

He gathers a massive wad of paper towels and wets them to clean me up, but I know he'll be dripping out of me the rest of the night. *Why do I love that thought so much?* His touch is loving, and I can't help it when my eyes well up with tears.

"Hey… hey. Baby, what's wrong? Shit, I shouldn't have surprised you with this," he chastises himself.

I grab his cut and pull him towards me, shaking my head. "It's not that. It's just… I love you."

"I know, you told me," he teases with a smirk.

I shake my head. "I know. But Axel… in a few days we're either running away or I'm bonding with Cash," I confess, having made up my mind.

He blinks at me and nods. "I have another plan, too. Do you think you could sneak away tomorrow?"

I squint at him but shake my head. Tomorrow's the day I'm finally going live, securing my future.

"Maybe the day after?" I respond. He doesn't look pleased but nods his head anyway in agreement.

"Do you have access to your birth certificate?" he asks, while still cleaning me.

"I do."

"Good." He kisses the side of my head and leaves it at that, not giving me any other indications of his plans.

He uses dry paper towels next and goes to the corner to grab a backpack. Axel hands me a fresh pair of deodorizing panties, as well as deodorizing spray. I use his shoulders to get myself stable on the ground, tugging on the panties and spraying heavily.

Once I'm done, he pats down my hair and rubs his thumb along my lips. "Two days then. Happy birthday, Omega," he murmurs, kissing me one last time before climbing out the window.

I'm smiling like a madwoman when I unlock the door, and Shelby nearly falls onto the bathroom floor. She grins at me when I smack her arm.

"Were you listening?"

"Yes, holy fuck. That was *hot*. Good present, huh?" she taunts, and I shake my head at her with a smile.

"Fantastic present. Is my scent too strong?" I ask her, and she leans down, taking a whiff.

"I'd say it's somewhere between getting the best head of your life and unpredictable arousal," she jokes. I poke her side, and she laughs.

"You're the worst."

"I'm the best. Now let's go dance… birthday girl." I want to push her again but don't as she drags me back to the dance floor.

I look around, feeling anxious like someone will look at me and know the debauchery I was just a part of. Maybe it's the booze flowing, but no one seems to notice, except for Cash.

I can't help but smile at him as he smirks while shaking his head at me.

The music blares and I realize this is the best birthday I've ever had. All the people I love are singing, dancing, and being drunken idiots. Giving this up might kill me, but it might be my only option. I just hope it doesn't come down to that.

TWENTY-TWO
I SHOULD STOP
TATE

I FEEL like a piece of shit for missing Lily's birthday party.

I'm a grown-ass man and I couldn't pull it together for a few hours to be around her. If I'm being completely honest with myself, it's not just about being around her. It's about being near *him*.

The groan that leaves me is pathetic and self-deprecating as I grab the water on my nightstand, guzzling it down all in one go. While I might not have been at the party, I did my fair share of drinking with myself last night. It was truly pitiful, me alone in my ten-by-twelve foot room drinkin' while I heard everyone else in the club having the time of their fuckin' lives.

I should have left as soon as I got here. I should have known I couldn't have stayed a part of this club with my father at the helm. Now I've dug myself a hole so fuckin' deep, I'm not sure I'll be able to crawl my way out of this one.

I know too much; I feel too much, and truly, I just want this burden of knowledge off my chest. If I didn't have Cash and Axel to confide in, I'm pretty sure I would have slunk away in the middle of the night. Even though I trust them, and truly view them as my brothers, I still haven't told them everything I know.

The weight of this club is fuckin' crushing me. But even if most of them are blind or ignorant to what's happening right under their noses, I can't help but feel like I'm the only one who can fix it. I sound like a pompous asshole, but it's true. The preservation of this club is on my shoulders, and I've made the decision to make it my burden. I could have left so many times and I didn't. I hate to admit that Lily is part of that, but rectifying what I know is going on here has become my biggest driving factor.

I grab my phone, wanting a moment of relief. Just one fuckin' second where I'm not thinking about how to fix the club or how badly I want to fuck my stepsister. My thumbs automatically work together to pull up my favorite porn site and multiple pop-ups catch my attention.

They all boast how you can receive five free minutes to watch live Omega cam girls. After the five minutes is up, you can either pay to stay or you're booted from the chat. I click on the first one, and as soon as I hear her over dramatic moans; I click out and go to the next one.

This girl's face is out of the frame, but she's wearing a white lace bra and thong set as she parts her legs. Her hands are shaky as she toys with the bra straps, pushing them down her shoulders. Her tits are small and perfect, and she shyly rubs her own nipples with her thumbs.

I lick my lips and pull my cock out. Her small actions are enough to get me hard as I stroke myself as she performs her slow seduction. My time is winding down, and I click the corner button to send the woman fifty dollars.

"Thank you," she whispers, and a full-body shiver wracks my body when she speaks. Her voice is soft and light, but there's a quality to it that seems familiar.

I send her another fifty and watch as her hands drag down to her cunt, where there is already a clear wet patch soaked into the white lace. You can see the outline of her pussy lips, and I groan to myself as my thoughts drift to Lily. I just know she'd have a pretty pussy just like this Omega.

The cam girl slides the wet underwear to the side and gives us a clear view of her cute cunt. Her slick creates a bright sheen against her fingers and thighs as she leisurely touches herself. One of her hands stays on her breast while the other slowly dips in and out of her. The noises of her pleasure are soft and fry something in my brain.

I can't see the comments coming in, but she does, and she speaks.

"Once we hit my goal, I'll use a toy," she rasps, and my head tilts, really assessing the voice on the other side of the camera.

It's then that I really look at the Omega touching herself… the sun-kissed skin, the long dark hair I can see flowing behind her, but what really fuckin' does me in is the motherfucking patch quilt that's getting covered with her slick. I spent a whole week above that quilt.

I'm not sure what I'm really upset about right now, that other people are watching this, or how badly I want what I'm seeing. I push it all to the side as unhinged anger takes over me.

I don't think before I tuck my dick away and close the browser. I'm out the door quicker than I realize, my feet moving on their own taking me to my father's house. I don't even give a fuck if he's home; I open the door like I still live there and take the stairs two at a time to Lily's room.

When my hand grips the handle, and twists, I find it's locked. I don't fuck around with knocking, and instead, I simply ram the door with my shoulder, forcing it open. She yelps and attempts to cover herself. I blink rapidly a few times at her setup. The massive ring light at the end of her bed is like a spotlight on her body, and I growl.

She grabs her quilt in an attempt to cover herself as I take a few quick strides and grab her phone. I'm not thinking rationally as I throw the fuckin' thing as hard as I can against the wall. Lily gasps and looks at me with wide brown eyes as I approach her with a finger in her face.

"What the fuck are you doin', Lily?"

She blinks at me owlishly for a few minutes before she drops the quilt and crosses her arms across her chest.

"None of your fuckin' business," she retorts, as she glares at me.

"I'd say you putting your pussy on the internet for everyone to see is my fuckin' business."

Her eyes narrow at me, and she spreads her legs. My eyes have no choice but to look at her wet cunt as her small hand trails through her wetness.

"You said you can't, Tate. So no, this…" she pauses, rubbing her clit in slow circles and moaning lightly before finishing her sentence. "This is none of your business."

I lick my lips and watch her, my anger turning into arousal as a desperate need to show her who she belongs to fills my veins. I try to shake these thoughts out of my head; I try to reason with myself. But I fuckin' lose it as her scent overwhelms me.

My cock is hard again, and all I want to do is touch, taste, and punish her for thinking she isn't mine to take care of. I've told her repeatedly there's nothing between us, but we both know those were fuckin' lies.

When my knee hits the mattress, causing her to shift, she gasps but doesn't stop touching her wet, pink cunt.

She inhales deeply, and I can tell as soon as my scent hits her because she circles her clit more frantically.

Her chest rises and falls as she speaks. "You had no right to come in here like that, and you broke my phone," she tries to scold me, but it comes out breathless and needy.

"I know," I reply dryly.

My brain is completely shutting down as her scent chokes me. The proximity of her wet pussy makes my mouth water. I should get up and walk away. Her phone is broken, so I'm sure she won't be able to do some dumb shit like this again.

"Then why are you still here?" she whispers, her fingers never stop moving.

My hand moves on its own accord, grabbing her wrist softly. She moans at the touch but doesn't stop the movements of her hand. I exhale and close my eyes for a moment as I feel the tendons in her wrist flex as she fucks herself.

We're quiet for a few moments. The only noises are our breathing and the delicious wet sounds her fingers make as she touches herself.

"Tate," she rasps out my name, making me shiver.

I drop my forehead to press it against hers, and her breath fans across my face. My grip lightens on her wrist as two of my fingers cover her own as she fucks herself.

"I should stop," I whisper, and she shakes her head as she picks up speed.

My fingers are so close to touching her, giving me what I want. I know I'm fuckin' sick for wanting it. What's worse is I'm near the edge of not giving a single fuck. I wish this was just some sexual tension, that I could just fuck her and be done with it. But it's not. I want Lily in a way I never thought would be possible for someone like me.

I was rationalizing it, because she's an Omega and it's my natural instinct to care for her, but I know it's more than that now. I want her to be mine; I want to hold her, care for her, fuckin' love her. It's deplorable. There are so many other fucked-up things going on for this to be my biggest priority.

But when I look at her seductive eyes and the way she's biting her lip, there's no denying it. I want her, even though I shouldn't. Not just because she's my stepsister, but because I'd be a fuckin' bastard if I let myself have her.

As she writhes beneath me, all I can think about is how, at this moment, I don't give a fuck. I already clocked my soul a one-way ticket to Hell. I might as well have everything I want on my way down there.

"Right there," she moans as if I'm doing anything.

I want to slide my fingers and touch. I want to move down the bed and eat her out, or pull my dick out and fuck her into this mattress. But I'm frozen; I need to put Lily's life ahead of mine, being with me will cause her to lose everything.

Sure, Kurt will be pissed, might even try to kill Axel and Cash, but I'm sure Lily could convince him to let them live. But if she was with me… she'd truly lose everything.

"Lily," I whisper her name as I try to pull away, but she shakes her head, the softest moan escaping her pretty parted lips.

"Alpha," she whines as she trembles through her release. I close my eyes, relishing the sound, knowin' that it will be the only time she ever calls me that.

Shame and regret washes over me. I should have left already. I shouldn't have let myself have this. Now, I'll not only long for the woman I can't have but now I know how fuckin' perfect she is when she comes.

She comes down from the high of her orgasm and blinks at me, her eyes watering even though I haven't spoken.

"I've gotta go," I say softly, trying to hide my own hurt even if hers is easy to read on her face.

"Tate, don't go, please." I stall for a moment, and her slick-covered hand wraps around my wrist. "Please don't run from me. I wanted this too. I want… you."

"God dammit, Lily," I sigh, pulling away and standing up from the bed. I adjust my hard cock and groan. "I can't be the reason you don't have a family."

I have to turn away so I don't look at her face, cave in, and give her everything we both want.

"Tate," she calls my name, but I'm out the door and heading downstairs before she can say anything else. I briefly hear her rustling around her room, but I don't look back as I head through the square. I need to shower and take a ride to clear my fuckin' head.

What the fuck was I thinkin'? I should have never gotten involved. I keep letting myself get these small tastes of her and then wind up fuckin' it all up. My selfishness is causing more hurt than anything, and I fuckin' hate myself for it.

I'm so lost in my thoughts that I don't notice my father walking past me. I would have just kept walking if he didn't grab my cut and throw me against a picnic table.

"Where the fuck have you been?" he seethes, his nostrils flaring wide.

"Get the fuck off of me," I growl back at him, shoving him away.

"What did you do to her?" he shouts, shoving me roughly and making my ass hit the top of the picnic table.

"Fuck off." I dust myself off and go to walk away when he grabs me by my hair and yanks me back.

"Fuckin' knew I shouldn't have let your worthless ass back in this club. Where is she?" He's yelling behind me, and I elbow him in the stomach to make him release my hair before spinning around to shove him backward. "I'm gonna fuckin' kill you."

"Good, fuckin' do it," I yell in his face.

He grabs my cut as I grab his; it's a back-and-forth of us shoving each other over this sandy patch of grass.

My father is the first one to throw a punch. His fist connects with my eye twice before I can get a shot in against his kidney. He winces, but the old man doesn't give up.

There's a feminine scream, and Lily goes to grab my father's shoulder, but he shoves her away, pushing her to the ground. She winces but dusts herself off before yelling, "Kurt, let go of him. He didn't do anything!"

"He's walkin' around my fuckin' club smellin' like he just fucked his fuckin' stepsister. You tryin' to tell me that's fuckin' nothin'?" he roars in her face.

"He didn't do anything. *We* didn't do anything," she argues, trying to calm him down.

"Like Hell, you didn't do anything. I gave you a fuckin' place to live, treated you like my own and this is how you repay me? You're lowerin' yourself to some sort of club slut, and with him nonetheless," he snarls, causing Lily's eyes well with tears.

"We didn't do anything," she repeats,

"You think I'm fuckin' stupid, Lily? Get your fuckin' ass back in the house now. I gave you some freedom, but consider that shit gone. The first pack that wants to bond, that's your fuckin' lot now," he declares while still holding on to my cut.

I shove him and take a step back. "You can't force her to do shit," I bellow. The old man surprises me by hitting me in the face again, sending me straight to my ass.

He points down at me. "Pack your shit up and get the fuck out of my club." He turns to Lily and points to her. "Get your ass back in the fuckin' house."

"Good ol' dad, huh? Just never listenin' to what your kids want," I snark as I wipe away blood from my lip.

My dad laughs sardonically as he turns to me. "You're not my fuckin' kid and you never were."

I sarcastically laugh again, my tongue involuntarily swiping away another drop of blood. "You shouldn't do what he says, darlin'. You want the fuck out of here, I'll take you out of here myself," I tell her. Her gaze lingers on Kurt for a moment before moving over to me. It's like she's waging a war in her mind over the man she thought my father was and who he truly is. I can say I've gone through the same war myself.

"You're nobody's fuckin' darlin' and you never will be. You're an Omega who needs to do what she's fuckin' told," Kurt seethes at Lily. I watch her face fall, and I can see it in her eyes; the moment she realizes the man she thought was her father was all just an act.

I don't know how to explain that this moment changes everything for me, but it fuckin' does. There's fire in her sad eyes, one that wasn't there before. The main reason I left this alone was because I didn't want to make her choose. He might not be my father anymore, but he was hers. But the way she's looking at him now… that sentiment is gone.

"I told your ungrateful ass to get back in the fuckin' house," he snarls, grabbin' her arm and nearly dragging her into the house. The look Lily gives me over her shoulder is heartbreaking, and for a short moment, I consider the unthinkable. But after a few moments, I dust myself off and make my way back to the clubhouse.

I pack my shit up, but I have no intention of leaving this place or Lily behind. Everything has changed, and I'm all in now, no turning back or changing my mind.

It's time to pluck the old weeds that are choking the club and start anew, even if I die tryin'.

TWENTY-THREE
WAR

AXEL

I'M LYING IN BED, WISHIN' that Lily was here with me or that she would've let me take her away today. But luckily my self-pity withers away when my phone vibrates with a message from her.

LILY

> Your plan… we need to do it tonight.

Can you sneak out around 6 am?

> Whatever we have to do.

Did something happen?

> I'll tell you about it tomorrow. Your plan is solid, right?

Extra solid if you're still considering bonding with Cash.

> I am. I'm ready.

I let out a puff of relief. Finally, some recourse to this fucked-up situation we're in. Half of me wants to relay the good news to Cash, but I'll leave that to Lily. There's a light knock on my door, and I sigh. "Come in."

Tate walks in, a purple bruise forming over his eye, and the left side of his lip is busted.

"Tonight, the raid's tonight," he deadpans.

"You look like fuckin' shit," I tell him, and he shrugs his shoulders.

"You in?"

"We'll be back by mornin'?" I ask him.

"Why? You have plans?"

"I do."

"Yeah, we'll be back by fuckin' mornin'. Get Cash and let's fuckin' go."

"You never said who is givin' you this intel," I say, poking at him. Plus, I'm genuinely curious. Do the Wraiths have a rat in their midst?

"We can trust him, that's all you need to know," Tate replies. With the way his face looks and how shitty his tone is, I don't push him any further.

"You're sure that this is what you want, man? Starting shit with the Wraiths can only end a few ways," I remind him.

I'm down for anything to be honest, but sometimes I wonder what Tate isn't telling us. For me it's easy. I want to be with Lily, and since the new guys have gotten here, I've realized that the club needs some major fuckin' changes. It's clear Tate fuckin' hates his dad, but surely there has to be more to his anger than just hating the Prez.

"Yeah, I'm sure. You will be too. Go get fuckin' ready," he directs, and something about his confidence makes me follow his commands. I nod, tossing my cut on my bed and changing into an all-black outfit.

"YOU'RE SURE ABOUT THIS?" Cash asks Tate from the driver's seat. We're parked behind a line of trees and it feels like we're in the middle of nowhere. For whatever reason, Tate had Cash and I stow our bikes in the back of the van. It makes me wonder what the play is.

"Once you see the cargo, you'll understand," Tate states.

"This has nothing to do with your fucked-up face?" Cash jests.

"It does, and it doesn't," Tate replies dryly.

"Such a fuckin' chatterbox tonight. Want to explain the plan? I need to be home before sunrise," I say. Both of them look back at me but don't question it.

"I need you to put the spike strip down," Tate instructs, lookin' at me. "I'll be behind the big tree over there, and I'll take out the driver and anyone else I can see within my scope. Cash will be on standby if anyone comes out of nowhere. My intel says that there will only be one van and likely two to four club members handling the transit."

"You're still just gonna keep us guessin'?" I ask, feeling annoyed that Tate is keeping secrets.

"You trust me?" he asks, glancing at both of us, and I let out a sigh.

"Yeah, I fuckin' guess."

"Let's do the fucking thing then," Cash says, swinging open his door and we all follow suit.

Tate gets his weapon of choice, setting up shop while I get the tire strip ready and Cash backs us both up.

We're waiting in our respective spots for what feels like fuckin' forever. That's until I see the approaching headlights. It's gonna be super fucked up if this isn't them. But I quickly place the spike strip in place and tuck away in some bushes, waiting patiently.

It's so dark out that they don't see the strip, and we get lucky as the van swerves, each tire losing air. There are two quick pops of Tate's gun before the van smacks loudly into a tree. The engine hisses and smoke is funneling wildly out of the hood. Tate's one of the best with his aim. The driver and passenger are dead or at least severely wounded based on how many shots he fired and the vehicle hitting the tree. We're all careful with our movements, weapons drawn as we surround the vehicle.

I'm walking towards the back, ready to open up the back doors, while Tate takes the front and Cash takes the side. There's another pop, and Cash raises his voice so we can hear.

"Took the last one out. There were only three," he announces as he looks in the driver's side window.

Once Tate confirms by feelin' the pulses of the Wraiths he just killed, they both round the vehicle and stand next to me as I open the back door. I'm not sure what I expected, but gettin' fuckin' kicked in the chest, wasn't it. It throws me off kilter, and Cash raises his gun.

"Don't shoot, fuck. They're Omegas," Tate scolds.

The man who just kicked me has his arms raised, ready to fight as he shields the other Omega behind him. She's small, blonde, and curled up in fear. It's the one thing that helps me not kill the asshole.

"Fuck off," the male Omega growls.

He's not a large man, but he isn't tiny by any means either. He's probably a few inches shorter than me and leaner. His hair is dark and shaggy, hanging in his face as he narrows his eyes at me, ready to kill me. It makes me smile warmly, even though my chest aches.

"We're trying to help you, you fuckin' dick," I complain, rubbing my chest.

"How do we know we can trust you? You could be just as bad as these fuckin' assholes?" he replies, and well, he's got me there.

I look over to Tate who shrugs his shoulders, and Cash sighs.

"Listen, we're happy to just let you go. But that won't stop these pricks from finding you again. So you have two choices. We can take you somewhere safe and offer you protection, or you can fuck off to wherever you came from," Cash says, his tone is kind but isn't as sweet like when he talks to Lily, and I know she would appreciate it.

Honestly, I could definitely see Lily being overly possessive of her pack. The thought makes me smile, and I hope we can get this moving faster so I can get back to the compound and whisk her away.

The male Omega looks back to the woman behind him and sighs. "Fine, we'll go with you."

The woman is quiet but agrees with her companion. Cash holds out a hand to help him out of the cab, but the Omega scoffs at it and jumps down, only to help the female Omega get down safely.

"Got a name?" I ask him. He looks down at my chest, and I notice a small smirk on his face.

"I'm Mason, and this is my cousin Quinn."

The small woman tucks into her cousin's side, her dirty blonde hair covering her face. Mason holds her tight and protectively. Besides the Chuck Norris kick to the chest, the way he is taking care of his family adds another point in his favor in my book.

"I'm Axel, that's Tate, and that's Cash," I introduce, hoping to put them at ease.

Mason looks us up and down, and it's like something clicks in his head.

"We're not the only ones they've taken, you planning on doin' somethin' about that shit?" he asks, but he doesn't look at me, he looks at Tate.

"Yeah, we're doin' somethin' about it," he replies, and both Cash and I nod our heads.

I knew the Wraiths were the worst of the worst, but abducting Omegas and doing God knows fuckin' what with them? It makes my stomach sick. Especially as I look down at the small female Omega, I'm not even sure she's of age.

"What now?" I ask, lookin' at Tate.

I still need to get home and move forward with my plans with Lily. Hell, even if I'm not a part of the Dead Palms anymore, I can't leave without this being resolved. When I look over at Tate's hard glare at the Wraiths van it's clear he's thinking the same.

"We take them to the warehouse. I'll be there, layin' low. You two go back to the compound and act like this shit never happened."

"I thought the whole point of this was so the Wraiths knew this was us?" I question.

"Oh, they'll fuckin' know," Tate promises as he shuts the back door of the Wraith's van. His knife is already in his palm as he drags it across the paint of the vehicle. The message is clear, even if it looks like shit.

Carved in very shaky letters is *DPMC*.

"What message are you tryin' to send? That you're gonna fuck 'em at the same time?" Mason asks, and I have to repress a chuckle.

Tate rolls his eyes, and the male Omega holds the woman tighter, pulling them away from the car.

We all look at the mark, and I wonder how bad the retribution is going to be. We just dropped an atomic bomb on the Wraiths. We need to be smart about our next steps, or they could be our last.

We leave the van hissing against the tree. Tate lights a cigarette and only takes two inhales before he tosses it into the hood of the vehicle. It isn't explosive, but it doesn't take long for a fire to start. We don't wait around long, walking back to our vehicle and getting to work with exactly what Tate said the plan was.

Cash and I put the ramp down and get both of our bikes out of the van as Tate directs the Omegas to get in. The plan is clear, this shit never happened, and we have no clue why Tate is MIA. Even if the Prez holds Tate responsible, he can't know that Cash and I are involved, especially not with the plan I have in place.

Cash and I are standing there as Tate drives off, and I look over at the quiet, large Alpha male.

"You know we probably just started a war?"

He nods his head and pulls out his phone; he looks distraught that there are no messages there.

"If this goes south, we're taking Lily and getting the fuck out of here," he states, and I nod my head.

"I don't think we'll have any problems on that front," I comment, not wanting to tell him what Lily had said to me. It's not my place; plus, I have plans of my own. I already know the moment I tell Cash it's time to go, he'll agree with no hesitation. Tate is still up in the air with his intentions, with the club, and with Lily. "What about Tate?"

"He can make his own choices. If Lily wants him, he can come. But I'm not risking her for his sake."

We're on the same page on that front. While I like pushing Tate's buttons, I don't really care if he's a part of this or not. I can tell Lily has feelings for him, but we could work past that. If he's hell-bent on bringing the club to justice, that's fine—I want that too, especially after what we saw tonight. But to Cash and me, Lily is more important. Her safety and happiness come first, being some hell-raising vigilante comes second.

"Let's go home," Cash suggests, putting his helmet on as we ride back to the compound. The ride home is long, and I know I'll only get an hour or two of sleep before I need to pick up Lily, but it was worth it. I can leave this club with a clear conscience, even if it rips out a small piece of my soul. My job is to keep Lily safe and to make sure she never has to worry like the two Omegas we pulled out of the van tonight.

TWENTY-FOUR
SAFE
LILY

I DON'T SLEEP. Instead, I pack. I pack up everything in this fucking room that means something to me.

I was so fucking naïve. Dumb enough to think Kurt had my best interest at heart instead of listening to my brother's warning nights ago.

He told me early on that I was off limits to the club. I should have known I'd never be able to change his mind. No one ever gets to have everything in life, so why did my massive ego think I could possibly have it all? I feel hopeless, hurt, and broken.

This bedroom holds so many memories for me, safe ones. When my mom first brought us here, it was the first time I had my own bedroom and a door with a lock. My mother told Kurt that pink was my favorite color, and he had this place decorated like a pretty princess room before I ever moved in. Even though I didn't feel the same affection towards Dread, he still built me my bench under the window and the bookshelves that now house all my soap supplies. For the first time in my life, I felt like I was whole, like I had a family.

This room once symbolized hope for me, but now, as I look around, all I see are lies. I always thought I knew the real Kurt and the darker parts of him were necessary for him to run the club… but now? Now, I can't help but feel as if the Kurt I see at home is the facade, the lie, or maybe possibly the man he wants to be, but never truly will be.

His words towards Tate and me bounce around my head, and it hurts. Tate hardly fought back. I know that if he really wanted to, he could've taken Kurt down, so why didn't he?

Kurt tossed me into my room and locked the door. Said that the security system was on and not to leave this fuckin' room until they got back. They've had this trip planned for a few weeks now, and I couldn't be more thankful that they're gone. Part of me wonders if my mom has any clue about the way Kurt spoke to me. *Does she know about his dark side? Does Leon?* Is that why he was so adamant about me getting out of here?

My chest aches thinking about Leon, but I know if anyone would break the rules to still have contact with us, it would be him. Axel and Cash leaving the club would have far more consequences than me. You don't just simply leave the Dead Palms.

What if I'm ruining their fucking lives by having us run away?

I shake the thoughts out of my head. They've both expressed their devotion to me over the club… that hasn't changed… hopefully.

Axel has a plan, and so do I. I'll hear him out, but come tomorrow, I'm leaving this place with Cash and Axel in tow. I'm ready to bond with Cash, even though I didn't reach my goal for my nest egg and it's fast. I'd rather spend the rest of my life getting to know Cash as my bonded than to risk being stuck with anyone else.

I laugh at myself as I pack my clothes. I always had this mindset that finding my pack would be this seamlessly romantic thing, that I would know and I would be one-hundred percent sure.

But what I know is I trust Axel, Cash… and Tate.

Tate's words from the spring flashback to me, and I wonder if my defiance is enough to prove to him that I'm willing to explore what we have between us. Even though it's evident, this tension and connection we can't seem to shake has to be the feeling that everyone talks about, right?

Fuck, my head is a mess and my phone screen is cracked to high hell from Tate throwing it against the wall.

I'm not sure what makes me want to call her, but I just need someone who can give me an outside point of view. I don't second guess myself, I just run my fingers over the cracked glass and find her name, at least my phone still works and isn't completely broken from Tate's tantrum.

"Hello?" her sweet voice says over the phone.

"Liv?" my voice cracks.

"Lily, what's wrong?" I sigh in relief when she remembers me and wasn't full of shit when she said I could contact her at any time.

I laugh slightly over the phone and shake my head, trying to find the words. "It feels like everything is going wrong."

"If you need help getting out of there, I can make it happen," she offers confidently.

I smile at her confidence and her loyalty to me, having only met once. I don't really want Liv to solve my problems, or to get her and her pack involved with club drama. I just need someone who understands, someone to ease my nerves.

"What was it like getting your first bond?" I ask her. She sighs over the phone, and I'm confused by her reaction.

"The first time I was bonded... was against my will." My heart breaks for the bubbly, larger-than-life Omega, but I let her speak. "But my true first bonding with an Alpha was with Grayson, and it was one of the most spectacular moments of my life," she sighs dreamily, and I believe her.

"You were sure he was the one?"

"The men in my life before my pack had a real fucking knack for letting me down and never loving me for me.

Grayson protected me more fiercely than my own flesh and blood did. There's always fear there, but when you find someone who makes you feel safe, who would raise hell on earth for you while loving you endlessly... you can't let that go."

"I'm scared," I tell her honestly.

"It's okay to be scared. It's okay to be unsure. Trust your instincts, they won't let you down," she encourages. Her words click for me in a way no one else's has. My instincts know exactly what I have to do. I can't let my fear of failure or hurt impede my happiness. "And Lily, if you need anything, I'm here for you. Besides my pack being richer than God, I do charity work for a foundation that helps Omegas. If you need anything, call me."

"Thanks, Liv."

"Anytime. If it helps, I kind of have a sixth sense about these things. Those guys are meant to be yours. Goodnight, Lily."

"Goodnight," I reply, feeling just a bit lighter. I'm tired of waging this war with myself of what's most important: my family, the club, the guys. I'm the only one who has to live my life, so at this moment, I choose myself.

I don't sleep, just pack up the rest of my life; I know I'll be tired when Axel comes to get me tomorrow, but I can't spend another day living this farce of a life.

IT'S EARLY as hell when my window slides open and Axel steps into my room. He looks around at the piles of trash bags and duffle bags before looking at me.

"Uh, darlin'?" he asks.

"We're leaving."

"I know, for the day, we don't need this much for a trip that's going to take a few hours," he explains, his brows furrowed, and he uses a gentle tone, probably wondering if I'm having an episode of some sort.

"No, we're leaving the compound. Unless you want to stay here… but either way *I'm* leaving." I shove the last bit of my belongings into a duffle bag, and he pulls up his pants so he can get down to my level.

"First off, wherever you go, I go. Second, what the fuck set this off?"

"Kurt. If I stay here, he's going to force me to bond with the next pack who shows interest."

"Like fuckin' hell he is," he snaps back.

"Exactly, so all my shit is packed. You, Cash, and… you and Cash need to get packed. We're leaving tonight," I tell him plainly. "They're all out for the weekend, they should be back in two days. He all but shoved me into my room and told me if I left, he would chain me to the bed and bring suitors to my bedroom. We only have today to get ready and go." I'm sure I sound panicky, but that's only because that's exactly how I fucking feel right now.

I'm leaving my family behind, everything I know, everyone I love, all so that I can live my life on my own terms.

Axel cups my face and as soon as his skin touches mine, I feel like I might break. As brave as I'm being, my heart fucking hurts.

"Baby, I got you. We're getting out of here, no questions asked. But I'd still like to spend the day with you. I hate seein' you like this. Cash can handle packin' all our shit up. I don't have much, anyway."

"I don't know, Axel. We shouldn't waste any time."

"Four hours, that's all I need," he nearly begs me.

"Can we talk to Cash first?" I ask him.

Seeing him and knowing that he's okay with the plan will make everything easier for me.

"Yeah, baby. Let's go see Cash. Then I'll put a smile on your face before everything changes?"

His hair is tied back behind his head, a single dark blond piece falling in front of his face, and I push it back. The small act of affection makes me smile. It's so simple, but I've wanted to do it so many times, yet I'd never been able to.

"Okay," I reply softly.

"Dread and Prez are really gone?"

"Yeah, they've had this pool tournament on the books in Georgia for a while now, but the alarm is set for the doors."

"Alright, window it is, then." He grabs my hand and pulls me up. I destroyed the room with my frantic packing, and it makes me grimace. Axel grabs my chin and places a tender kiss against my lips. "I've got you, always," he promises, and the fist-clenching around my heart loosens its grip.

He helps me out the window and takes me a very odd route to the clubhouse; I suspect, to avoid club cameras. It's so early that no one else is up, we're still desperately trying to be quiet as we tip-toe to Cash's room. His room isn't locked when Axel turns the doorknob and lets me in.

"I'll give you two a few minutes," he says, kissing my hair, and I'm grateful for his understanding.

I climb into Cash's bed and place my hand against his cheek; he wakes slowly, and I'm glad I didn't scare the shit out of him. His eyes blink awake and his hand shoots out to grip my hip. Winnie is sleeping on his other side, and I have to really control myself to not scoop her up for a cuddle right now. I might be slightly jealous that she's gotten so much more time to bond with Cash rather than with me, but hopefully, that's about to change.

"Lily? What are you doing here?" he rasps.

"If I wanted to leave tonight, would you come with me?" I ask sheepishly, fear of his rejection making the words taste like ash.

"Of course, I would. Did something happen?"

I don't want to talk about it, so I just nod my head and rub my thumb over his cheekbone.

"I'm still scared, but I know it's the right thing to do. It's what I need to do. I choose me, and I choose you and Axel," I tell him, not mentioning Tate. I wish I could speak to him too.

"I choose you too," he promises, leaning down and giving me a kiss. "I know you wanted to take things slower, that you weren't ready. Running away doesn't mean we have to bond, I'll wait however long you want," he vows, and the floodgates swing wide fucking open. He wraps me up in his massive arms and tugs me against his large chest. I feel safe in Cash's arms. Safer than I did when I saw that beautiful pink bedroom for the first time. Liv's words ring in my head, and my spine steels itself.

I can do this, with Cash's strength, I can fucking do this.

"I don't want to wait. I think I've romanticized bonding, while at the same time being absolutely terrified of what it would mean... that there would be a possibility I could bond with the wrong person. But when I look at you, when you touch me, I feel cherished and safe. I'm not going to let my self-doubt ruin what I know deep down is the real deal," I whisper. He pulls back so he can cradle my face as he looks at me.

"I'll always put you first and keep you safe, baby girl."

I nuzzle close to him, his scent soothing me as his chest rumbles with a calming purr. It's then that I remember what I truly came here to talk about.

"Axel wants to take me away for a few hours. Do you think you could handle packing up your stuff? Mine's already packed and in my room." He blinks at me, and I'm afraid he's going to say no, that we're stupid to waste time. "If not, it's no big deal. We can get out of here, and Axel and I can do whatever it is he has planned at a later time."

"It's going to take a few hours for me to get things together anyway, and I need to check in with Tate." He looks over my face as he says it, and I wonder what he sees there. Pain, longing for a hurt man I don't understand? Whatever he sees makes him kiss my forehead. "He's not at the compound, and I don't see him coming back anytime soon. If you see him in a similar light as you see me, tell him."

I pull back and look at the large Alpha I can't wait to call mine. I assumed all of them would be extremely possessive and only want their own time with me, but his assuring me about Tate… is selfless and kind. It just proves that I should bond with him and that Cash will always put me first. I'm not sure I deserve his devotion, but I'm going to take it. I deserve good things too.

"I will," I whisper.

"I know you will. You're my brave, strong girl," he compliments, and I blush. I wrap my arms around him tightly. His scent is going to be deliciously embedded in my clothes for the rest of the day, and I wouldn't have it any other way.

"Thank you, Cash," I sigh against his skin, pulling back to kiss his soft lips.

"Go, have your day with Axel. Clear your head. I'll take care of everything here."

"Call us if anything happens?" I ask him, and he nods his head in agreement. We both get up so he can get everything together. He gives me one last warm hug before I leave the room and find Axel smiling at me.

It's shocking to see because I feel like my Beta might have the hardest time sharing me, but as I take his hand in mine and we head towards the garage, I can't help but feel like it's the first day of the rest of my life.

PROMISES OF FOREVER

"ARE you sure we should be leaving right now? We should help Cash get everything together. I should say goodbye to Shelby... my brother," she rambles, and I squeeze her hand.

"It won't take long, and I need to do this. Do you trust me?"

She squeezes my hand back and nods her head. "Yeah, I trust you."

"I'd take the bike, but I don't think either of us slept well last night. So we'll take a fuckin' cage instead," I say, and she shakes her head as I borrow one of the beaters we have in the garage.

Once we're settled, she rests her head against the headrest. I squeeze her thigh and keep my hand planted there. "Take a nap. I'll wake you up when we get there."

She smiles sleepily at me, and it doesn't take her long to pass out. It gives me a sense of worthiness knowing that she feels safe enough to trust me. I'm sure she has some idea of what I have planned, but she's also had a lot on her mind.

It's not long until we're in Dothan. I find a parking spot in the garage and just stare at her for a moment. I like how sweet and carefree she looks when she sleeps. I'm a selfish asshole for making her come here today, but just like she needs assurances, so do I. It's not that I don't trust Cash… or Tate. But I need my own claim on Lily before I abandon my entire life.

"Darlin', we're here," I coo softly, moving her hair from her face. She yawns and blinks at me.

"How long was I out?" she asks.

"About an hour and a half. Come on, we got a few stops to make," I tell her.

She narrows her eyes suspiciously, but grabs her purse and gets out of the car. She's dressed casually, in shorts and a t-shirt. I would have suggested she just wear one of her dresses, but after seeing the state of her room, I didn't want to stress her out anymore.

"Where are we?" she asks as we leave the parking garage and start walking downtown.

"Alabama," I reply quietly, as I drag her down the street.

"Why the fuck are we in Alabama?"

"You'll see. First stop is here," I tell her, opening to the boutique's door, the high-pitched bell dinging with our arrival.

"Welcome in. Can I help y'all with anything?" the woman working behind the counter greets.

"We need somethin' pretty for my girl to wear," I inform her, and the older woman smiles down at Lily.

"Well, that will be easy enough. You're already cute as a button. Anything in particular you're lookin' for?" she asks me.

"Somethin' white, preferably," I tell her, and Lily turns, blinking up at me.

"Axel?"

The woman gives us a cautious look before nodding her head and rummaging through the store to find clothes for Lily to try on.

"If you don't want this, we can just spend the day havin' fun. You can call me a fuckin' selfish prick, but I want a piece of you to myself. I can't bond you, but I can do this with you, just you and me," I plead, feeling all sorts of vulnerable and fucked up. I hate it. "But, if you'll have me, I'd like for you to be my wife," I say softly, squeezing her hand tight.

Her big brown eyes go all watery, and she shakes her head with a smile. "Yeah, Axel. I'll marry you," she replies, and I feel like I'm the king of the world. I lean down and kiss her softly. She sighs against my lips and I know I made the right call. "Did we really need to come to Alabama, though?" she asks, nudging my side with her hip.

"Yeah, you have to wait three days to get married in Florida, not in Alabama," I state.

"Couldn't wait, huh?"

"Nah. I need you to know that I'm all in," I tell her.

It might also be me being fuckin' pathetic and needing to know she's also all in too. I need to know that I won't fall behind when she has Alphas at her beck and call. I know it's shitty to think that, but it's hard not to. Alphas give Lily something she needs physically and mentally most times. I can't help but feel less than in some ways. It's the first time in my life that I've ever harbored some resentment towards my designation.

Deep down I know Lily doesn't feel that way about me, but it's my own insecurities seeping through.

"I'm all in. I've always been all in with you, Axel. I always will be," she promises, and I swear she can read me like a fuckin' book.

"Then let's get you a pretty dress, and get fuckin' hitched," I cheer. The smile that takes over her face is brilliant as she nearly skips away to the dressing rooms to find something suitable to marry my sorry ass.

LILY SEEMS a little disheartened that all we had to do was drop off the notarized paperwork I already filled out. They didn't even require her birth certificate, just an ID. They'll just let anyone get married here, fuckin' apparently. Once our form is turned in, we're legally married, which leaves me with a pretty bride, but no ceremony. And that just won't do.

"That's it?" she asks as the clerk gives us a copy of our information and how we can get a copy of the marriage license.

"The legal part, yeah. I've got somethin' else planned, though. Don't doubt that, wife," I tease with a smirk, and she rolls her eyes at my obnoxious behavior.

"You're going to call me that in front of Cash constantly, aren't you?" she asks.

She doesn't mention Tate, but I know he's a part of the equation too. There's no way he doesn't abandon whatever moral code he had after what we did last night. Part of me feels guilty for setting this shit in motion with the Wraiths and abandoning the club. I just have to believe that Tate wouldn't do that and that he has a larger plan. Either way, Lily comes first, no matter how much I've loved the club and the men in it. A pit sits in my stomach for being a selfish asshole. I make a mental note to speak with Tate and make sure that this doesn't blow up on the whole club. His issue is with the Prez, not all the men I consider my brothers. I try to push all that shit down and focus on the now. We only have a few hours before reality slaps us in the face.

The walk back to the parking garage is short, and I open her car door before getting in the driver's seat. Lily falls asleep again and doesn't even wake up when I stop to get us food, only when I reach the final destination.

"We're here," I whisper.

"Ugh, we're back home?"

"Get up and find out," I encourage. She sits up and blinks at the house and lake.

"Your granddad's lake house?" she asks in a groggy voice.

"Come with me out to the pier?" I ask her, and she agrees easily.

I leave the food in the car for now as I take her hand and

lead her out to the end of the dock. The lake is calm, and the sun is beating down on the both of us.

"I know that goin' to a fuckin' notary and dropin' off paperwork probably isn't what you ever pictured your weddin' lookin' like." She attempts to interrupt me, but I shake my head. "I'd like to say a few things and make you a few promises, if you don't mind," I continue with an arched brow.

"Go ahead then, *husband*," she sasses, and I swear my dick gets hard the second the word leaves her luscious lips.

I think maybe I understand the whole callin' each other Omega and Alpha now, if that's how it feels.

I hold both of her hands and look at her pretty face when I tell her the truest words I've ever spoken. "Lily, I promise to honor you, respect you, and to always love you. I spent so much time thinkin' there was no chance in hell I'd ever be worthy of you—I'm still not sure that I am—but I promise to work every day to be the kind of man you deserve. I know nothin' in either of our lives has come easy, but lovin' you? That's been the easiest fuckin' thing I've ever done." I feel myself getting choked up, and Lily squeezes my hands, her own eyes welling up with tears. But I press on, needing to get everything out that I need to say.

"I need you to know that puttin' you first isn't a sacrifice because you give me everything in return. You've given me a sense of purpose, and for the first time in my life, I see a future truly worth livin'. You're the most beautiful person I've ever met, and I'll spend every second I have on this earth makin' sure you know just how loved and cherished you are." I sniff slightly and look down at my crying bride.

"How am I supposed to follow that?" she jokes, releasing one of my hands and rubbing a tear from her face. She takes my hand back and looks up at me dreamily. "Axel, I promise you a life of adventure, happiness, and promise. You make me feel like the bravest, happiest version of myself, and I wouldn't trade that for the world. I wanted you so bad for the longest time, and you were right, you know? The moment we kissed, it was a done deal for me, too. You make me laugh in a way no one else can, and it doesn't hurt that you're beautiful inside and out." I scoff at that statement, and she gives me a small pout. "I promise to love you so much that one day you'll finally understand how truly special you are. I give you my honesty, trust, and devotion for the rest of our lives. And I can't wait to see where the world takes us."

On her last word, I swoop down and kiss my bride. It might not be a huge ceremony with thousands of dollars worth of flowers and our family and friends might not be here, but I don't think I could have chosen a more perfect way for us to promise ourselves to each other.

Her arms loop around my neck, and I can't help but pick her up and swing her around. She laughs happily into our kiss, and I've never felt more like a man than I do at this moment. I've wielded a weapon, chosen violence more times than I can count, and thought that's what made me a man, being strong. But with Lily in my arms, promising ourselves to each other, this is the real moment I became a man.

"I think we need to consummate the marriage to make this whole thing legit," she says with a laugh, and I can't help but smile. I quickly scoop her under her knees and carry her bridal style to the lake house.

"I can't leave my wife wanting, now can I?" I reply, and she throws back her head, her dark hair trailing behind her. I make a vow to myself to do whatever I can in my ability to make her feel this carefree and happy for the rest of our lives.

I put the code into the front door and carry her over the threshold. My heart is thumping so fuckin' hard in my chest that I think I'm having a heart attack. We're both quiet, just looking at each other as I move her to the primary bedroom. I've been spending some extra time in this room, making it cozy for her. I knew there was a chance we would need somewhere to hide out, and no one in the club knows about this place.

I place her gently on the bed, the soft cream dress she chose fans out around her, along with her hair. My body is supported by my elbows, but I cover her figure all the same. There's just a soft moment of us staring at each other and taking in this moment.

If you would have told me a few years ago, I would be thrilled to be someone's husband, I would have told you that you're full of shit. But now, looking down at the prettiest fuckin' bride there ever was? I feel whole; I feel like I have true value when she looks up at me and cups my cheek.

"Kiss your wife, Axel," she demands. I give her what she wants, leaning down and pressing our lips together. All of our encounters previously have been rushed and based on frantic need, but this moment is akin to a softness I've never experienced before, one that only Lily could give me.

Her hands tangle in my hair as I use one arm to support myself and the other to cradle her chin. She tastes like my fuckin' salvation as her tongue tangles with mine. I'm completely fuckin' gone for this girl and there's no turnin' back. No one can stand between us now. We didn't need to get married for that to be the case, but I needed a connection with her that no one could dispute. I needed to have my own claim on her, and my sweet wife doesn't seem to mind my boorish need to claim her either.

My hand trails from her chin, down the valley of her breasts to push up the hem of her skirt. I rub her already wet pussy from the outside of her panties, and her hips buck up towards my hand, begging for more.

I slide the damp material to the side and groan into her mouth as my fingertips swipe through her wetness.

"Wait," she stops me. My hand stops but doesn't leave her cunt. She licks her lips, tasting the remnants of our kiss, and I shiver. "I haven't been able to see you naked you know, I feel like that's something a wife should get to see," she pants, and I shake my head with a laugh.

Quickly standing up, I remove my pants and toss my shirt over my head. Her gaze travels from my face, down my torso, cataloging each scar and tattoo before she looks down at my hard and waiting cock.

"Your turn, little wife," I taunt her, and she shivers at the term of endearment.

I wonder if it has the same effect as being called an Omega. She tugs the bottom of her dress and the material stretches over her head. She has a simple pair of white panties on and no bra. She lies there obediently waiting for my instructions. I lick a trail from her navel to her right breast, before taking a perky nipple in my mouth. Her chest rises against my mouth, begging for more as I firmly hold her rib cage, loving the feel of her soft skin against my hands.

I take my time with her, listening to all the sweet sounds she makes while I explore her body. Lily does her own exploration. Her hands move from my hair to my shoulders where she kneads the muscles there. I never want to leave this place. I want to spend the rest of my life tangled in sheets with this fuckin' woman.

She pushes her pussy against my erection, and I moan against the skin of her neck. My kisses trail down until my teeth bite down on the waistband of her underwear, I grab her panties and pull them down her toned legs. My tongue swipes her cunt once before I kiss back up her body until I'm cradling the back of her head and kissing her like I need her touch to survive.

"Please, Axel," she whimpers, and I can't refuse her. I grab my cock and slowly push into her warm, needy cunt.

"Fuck, darlin'."

I don't think we can get any closer than we are now. Every ounce of skin that could possibly be touching is. Our heartbeats pound against each other as we share the same breaths. I press our faces together so we can whisper praise and devotion to one another.

"I need you," she moans.

"You have me. Fuck, you feel so fuckin' good. I love hearin' how wet you are for me, little wife," I whisper, and her cunt clenches around my dick, making me moan into her ear.

Her arms wrap around my shoulders and her blunt nails dig into my flesh as I snap my hips against her. Each thrust is greeted with her scent and the gushing of her perfect cunt.

My pelvis grinds against her clit and her back arches against the mattress, pressing us even closer together.

"You gonna come for me? Hm? Makin' a fuckin' mess, aren't you? Come on, darlin', come on my cock," I urge her, picking up my pace and fuckin' her properly.

She shouts as her pussy milks my cock, and I fall over the edge with her. I find more pleasure than I should when I fill her up with my cum. I don't care if she's on birth control or not. I find myself wanting to keep my cock inside of her for as long as possible, and I do. Just lying on top of her as we bask in our consummation. It's the soft quiet I can only find with Lily as we lie there, pressing kisses on one another's flesh and exploring each other's bodies.

I kiss her one last time, knowing we need to move our asses, but then I realize I never gave her the ring.

"Shit," I hiss, and she furrows her brows at me.

I reluctantly pull out of her but enjoy watching a mixture of our release spill from her pussy. I bend down, pull the box out of my pocket, and plop back down on the bed beside her. She watches with rapt attention as I open the box, pull out the ring, and place it on her finger.

"It was my Nan's. If you want somethin' else… I'll get you whatever you want," I tell her.

She looks down at the vintage opal and diamond ring and smiles. "No, this is perfect, everything is perfect," she sighs, and I kiss her one more time, hating that we can't stay in this blissful bubble forever. We have to face the reality of our situation.

TWENTY-SIX
RETRIBUTION

LILY

I STARE DOWN at my shiny ring while Axel drives us back to the compound. It's perfect, and not what I was expecting to happen this evening. Truly, I thought Axel was going to get us new identities or something, but this was so much better.

I sense he needed this more than I did, having some sort of declaration over me. I'm happy that I could give him this peace of mind as we move forward in this new phase of our life, in becoming a pack. It's only fair that Axel gets a piece of me, too. I don't know what it's like to be the only Beta in the pack, and I never want him to feel less than because he's so fucking far from that. He's perfectly made for me, and now he's my husband.

He puts in the code to the front gate and drives through while I duck down, making sure no one sees us in the same car together. I'm so ready to no longer feel like a secret when it comes to my relationship with him and Cash. My stomach is filled with nerves and sadness, but also some underlying excitement.

He's careful while pulling into the garage, knowing that our first order of business is to check in with Cash. We need to see how far he's come along, what he still needs help packing, and hopefully put a plan in place; starting with... deciding exactly where we're headed after everyone is ready. Then the last order of business is saying my goodbyes, which I will make sure to not phrase as goodbyes, but I need to see some of these people one last time before I can move on. I already know Leon supports this decision, but seeing Shelby is going to be hard. I'm not sure how to leave this place without seeing my mom, but part of me knows if I see her, I'll chicken out.

Luckily for us, Cash is in the garage, filling the van with what looks to be most of my shit. I wonder if he went through my window, or if he was able to disarm the security system to the house... that seems like something Cash would be able to do.

Cash gives Axel a shitty look. We were definitely gone longer than the few hours he promised, but the van looks nearly full.

"Y'all set?" Cash asks, coming around and wrapping his arms around me.

"Yeah, we're all set." I show him the ring on my finger, and he looks over, assessing Axel.

"Engaged?" he asks. There isn't shock in his tone, he's asking more so out of curiosity.

"Nah, skipped that step," Axel replies proudly.

"Married?" Cash asks, looking down at me. I bite my lip and nod my head, wondering if maybe he'll be angry or feel hurt. He gave me the option to bond with him, which I declined, but still went off and married Axel. "Congrats, baby girl," he says, surprising me and placing a soft kiss on the top of my head. "I'm all ready to go. Is there anything else you need before we leave?"

"I need to say goodbye to Shelby, my brother, and leave my mom a note," I tell him, hoping that they let me.

Cash nods over at Axel. "Go with her. I'll get the tow dolly hooked up and we'll head out right after. Dread and Prez should be back within the next couple of hours," he warns. I wrap my arms around the large Alpha, giving him a hug before Axel and I make our way to the sweet house.

My biggest hope is that Leon will be here with Shelby, and it will be a two-birds-with-one-stone situation. I can tell Axel is itching to hold my hand, but he's holding back until we're off the compound. We're silent as we make the walk. I feel like I'm too deep in my own thoughts, while Axel looks more on alert, making sure no one suspects anything.

I don't even make it to the sweet house as Shelby walks our way. She's wearing tight workout shorts and a sports bra. Her dirty blonde hair is piled in a bun on the top of her head, and her cheeks are flushed as she approaches us.

"Hey you two," she greets with a smile, and I do my best to return it. "Where y'all headed?"

"Have you seen my brother?" I ask her, not knowing how to answer the question.

"Not since a few nights ago. Why? What's up?"

I exhale and hold out my left hand. Shelby gasps and nearly drags me toward her chest to get a better look at the ring. Axel has given us a wide berth to speak, and I'm grateful for it.

"No fucking way. You married him?" she gushes, her mouth open wide in shock.

"I sure did."

Shelby grins. "Good. Fuck following the rules. What are you gonna do now? Tell dear old dad?" she asks, and her smile fades away as she reads my expression. "You're leaving, aren't you?" she questions sadly.

I nod my head and wrap my arms around her; she smells like sweat and home, and I'm going to miss her so fucking much.

"Hey," she interrupts. "This isn't goodbye, okay? You have my number. I don't care how these assholes deal with club business, but we aren't patched in. We'll stay in touch."

I swallow and nod, hoping that's the case, but I can't risk Axel and Cash's safety like that. The club will see them leaving as breaking the pledge they made when they patched in. You don't leave the Dead Palms alive.

"Yeah, Shelby, we'll stay in touch. If you see my brother before I do, can you have him call me?"

She nods her head again and hugs me when the screeching of tires startles us. At first, I think it's Cash pulling the van around. It's the same nondescript black van he was packing before, but there's no hitch with his and Axel's bikes on it.

"Fuck!" Axel shouts. "Get into the fuckin' house now!" he barks at us, his feet eating up the distance as he runs in our direction. Shelby and I are fast, but not fast enough. The back door slides open and gunshots are fired.

I watch in devastating horror as one of them connects with Axel. I'm not sure where it hits him, but it's enough to send his body flat on the dirt.

There's screaming, such loud screaming. I want it to stop, but I don't know where the source is coming from. It's not until a man grabs me by the hair that I realize they're my screams.

"Get the fuck off of me!" Shelby spits.

She's fighting, kicking, swinging her arms, and even attempting to bite one of the unfamiliar men.

Yet, I'm frozen.

My body and mind fail me, shutting down as I let myself get taken away. The last image I see before they throw a hood over my head is Axel leaning on his elbow, aiming his gun at the tires of the vehicle.

They're rough with me, shoving me into the van, my cheek hitting the seat before I'm manhandled to sit upright. There are no seatbelts, just two men bracketing me on each side. The van smells stale and unfamiliar, and I swallow thickly as the realization of what's happening to me sets in.

The slam of the van door is jarring. Shelby's muffled struggling is the only thing I can hear. The men are grunting in frustration, and all I wish is that I had some of the fire she did.

Why can't I fight? Why can't I say anything? What the fuck is wrong with me?

The loud pop of gunfire is clear, but the van doesn't stop moving. My body sways between two large bodies that hold my upper arms firmly.

"They're gonna fucking kill you," Shelby seethes.

She's so fucking brave while I'm hopeless. There are no sounds of motorcycles or vehicles following us and every second that passes feels like an eternity. Doom sits heavy in my stomach as I wonder what exactly is going to happen to us.

"Not before I'm done with you," one man growls at Shelby, making me swallow thickly with panic.

It's pathetic, *I'm* pathetic. I didn't even fight, didn't even say a word. I just let myself get fucking taken, and now I might never see Axel, Cash… or Tate ever again.

There are a few bumps on the drive, and Shelby is still kicking up a fuss until one guy has enough.

"Inject her, for fuck's sake," he groans. Shelby is cursing and moving, but slowly the van goes silent as her fight dies off.

They wouldn't kill her, right? It has to be a sedative. Either way, I don't want to find out firsthand. One of us has to stay aware and have an understanding of what we're dealing with. Listening to others' conversations and gathering information has always been a skill of mine. I might not be strong enough to put up a fight, but I have to do something. If Shelby and I have a chance in hell of getting out of this, I need to stay quiet and be strong.

My heartbeat thumps so loudly in my ears that I'm convinced my heart is going to explode, and it only gets worse as the man to my left leans down to speak to me. Even with the hood on, I can scent him. He's clearly an Alpha.

"You've been such a good girl. Stay that way and I won't have to inject you too," he warns threateningly. I swallow thickly, but I don't move a single muscle. "I fucking love when they're meek little things," he comments, and I feel the wetness of tears trailing down my face.

I control my sobs, holding them inside. I can't let them hear me cry or let them see how fucking scared I am. *What did they inject Shelby with? Is she going to be okay? Is Axel?*

Everything has been moving at warp speed, and I try my hardest to calm myself so I can recall the last moment I saw him, trying to remember where he was shot. I try so fucking hard to concentrate, but I can't. All I can focus on is my current situation. The man on the right places his palm on my thigh, making my entire body tense automatically.

"Aw, come on, don't be like that, darlin'. We can have so much fun like I wanted to before," his voice sounds vaguely familiar, but I can't put my finger on it.

I remain silent, not daring to speak, cry, or beg.

There's only one thing that makes sense with the wording he just used. They're Wraiths.

We're going to die… or worse.

"If anyone is going to get to sample the goods, it's me, you fuckin' prick," the man on my left spits to the other.

"Your mama never teach you to share, Reg?" I try to place the name, but I can't. Definitely not a Dead Palms member, but I already knew that.

"I can share just fuckin' fine. But you always rough 'em up too much before it's my turn. I like it when their face is still pretty."

I swallow back the bile that rises in my throat.

I think I'd rather die than let them do what they're insinuating to me. No… I *know* I'd rather die. Memories I don't remember being real flash behind my eyes, and I quickly shut them down, locking them away in a tiny box that I stash in the dark corner of my brain. I don't want to remember anything about our time with the Wraiths, I just want to go home.

Instead, I focus on my breathing and looking for any way out of this. Cash will come looking for us eventually and find

Axel on the ground. Others would have heard the gunshots. An enemy came onto our compound, shot a member, and kidnapped two family members of the club. I take some solace in knowing there are people who care, who will want me home safely.

The only question is if they do find me, what will be left?

TWENTY-SEVEN

KILL SWITCH

CASH

I COULD CONSIDER one gunshot on this compound being a fluke, one of my drunk brothers being a dumbass, and shooting a beer bottle. But the multiple cracks that pop off in the distance have my hackles rising and my body lurching into action.

I'm not carrying, considering I'm in the body shop packing up all our shit. I'm quick, locking Winnie up in the office as I grab the weapons I have stored in the bottom drawer. Two pistols, two tactical knives, and a can of tear gas.

I'm moving as quickly as my feet will take me as I make my way through the square. Tires screech wildly and dust whips behind the vehicle as it hightails fast as fuck out of the compound. It's far away, but I raise my weapon and attempt to take out a tire. They're driving so erratically and fast that I don't stand a chance.

Other club members are now filing outside, strapped and ready for a fight when I see Axel on the ground—alone—clutching his arm with a smear of blood on his forehead.

I'm standing above him in a heartbeat, glaring down at him.

"Where is she?"

"They fuckin' took her. We've gotta go, now," he groans.

Blood trails down his arm as he applies pressure to where he got shot. "Fuck!" he screams as he stands, his footing wobbly as Doc approaches us and starts assessing his injury.

"What the fuck was that?" Doc asks in his thick Irish brogue.

"Fuckin' Wraiths. They took Lily. Fix my shit up quickly. We've gotta fuckin' go," Axel demands, panic, and urgency laced in his tone.

I'm trying not to do the same, to not let the switch that lives inside of me flip; the one I have no control over when someone touches what matters to me. I breathe heavily, a deep inhale, and a slow exhale.

I can't let this rage take over. We have to be smart about this.

But when I look at the blond motherfucker who lost our girl, I want to kill him. If he didn't take her out today, we would have already been out of here. She would have been safe. But I know Lily wouldn't blame him, and if I kill him, she'd never forgive me.

Axel looks at me with complete terror written on his face. "We've got to go get her, now!" he seethes.

"We need a fucking plan," I growl back at him, the analytical side of me taking charge. The worst thing we could do is rush into their club with no plan. That will get us all fucking killed.

Mickey is standing there, looking dumbfounded over the fact that Lily is missing. I turn to face him. "You. With me," I tell him. He nods his head and follows me to the body shop, and while we walk, I get Tate on the phone.

"What?" he groans on the other end.

"Wraiths took Lily and one of the sweet butts," I inform him quickly. Suddenly, the grogginess in his voice disappears, and I can hear him getting dressed.

"How long ago?"

"Just a few minutes ago. We need to be smart about this," I point out, and he curses on the other side of the phone. I'm sitting at my desk, Mickey behind my shoulders as I pull up footage from the cameras I've placed throughout the compound. "I'm looking through the footage now," I tell Tate on the other line.

"I'm packing up weapons; We'll get her back," Tate reassures, though there's panic clearly laced in his voice.

I watch the footage showing the altercation with Axel, how he went down, and how these pricks grabbed the girls. My heart sinks as I watch Lily scream and then freeze with terror, while the other woman fights back.

I rub my chest as an ache rips through me. It feels like I might throw up.

"How did they get in?" Mickey asks from behind me. I almost forgot he was here.

I don't respond, but I pull up the camera that covers the front gate, and I watch in horror as I see them input the code, the gates opening for them. Mickey and I are silent as Tate growls over the phone.

"What is it?" he asks.

"Someone in the club gave them the code," I answer with disbelief.

"Who in the fuck would let the Wraiths in?" Mickey wonders with absolute hatred in his voice.

"Tate?" I question.

"This fuckin' ends now. Get as many members as you can pull together—only those we can trust—and meet me at the gas station on Hines Street. I'll bring a van with as much artillery as I can scrounge from the warehouse. Everyone needs to be armed. We get Lily out of there and take out every single piece of shit who stands in our way."

"How do I know who to trust?" I ask Tate. Clearly, there's a fucking rat in our midst.

"None of the old guys, newly patched and younger members only," Tate replies.

"What about your informant?" I ask, not caring that Mickey is hearing details he shouldn't know. Finding Lily is the priority. If I have to kill him after, I will.

"I'm callin' him now," Tate replies.

"How do we know he didn't let these fuckers in?" I ask. The last thing we need is to give more information to the cunt who gave up our club.

"He didn't. I'd bet my life on it… Lily's life on it," he reiterates, and I guess I'll have to just take him at his word, because I have little else to go off of. "Now, get off the fuckin' phone and do what I told you so we can get Lily back," he barks before hanging up.

If we don't find Lily soon, I may kill everyone in this fucking club.

I'M able to gather six guys quickly to meet Tate so we can come up with a plan. On bikes, it's Atlas, Ink, Mickey, and Maverick. Doc and Axel follow in the SUV, seeing as there's no fucking way Axel could ride with the state of his arm. Doc said he got extremely lucky with a through and through that didn't hit any major arteries.

The ride to the gas station is tense, and the only thing running through my head are the worst-case scenarios. *What if they hurt her, abuse her, or God fucking forbid the unthinkable?*

Guilt seeps deep within my stomach, and I can't help but wonder if this is the retaliation for the raid the other night. *But how would they be able to get into the compound? Or even know to target Lily?*

The more I get lost in my head, the more questions I have. Everyone knows the story of Teresa being saved from the Wraiths and brought to the compound with Lily and her brother Ambien. How would another club just allow that? And why would we keep peace with this club for over ten years?

I've gone along with what Tate has said. I know he knows more than he's been telling us, and right about now, I'm ready to strangle his secrets out of him. If his keeping secrets is the reason Lily was taken… I take a deep breath.

I can't let the switch flip.

Not yet.

Lily's safety is the priority. I chant that over and over in my head. *Keep your shit together for Lily.*

We pull up at the gas station and wait for Tate to get here, but I can't help feeling like every second we waste is another second that Lily is in severe danger. I don't smoke, but when Mickey hands me a cigarette, I take it. The cool nicotine helps the shaking of my hands as we wait.

I picture the pain I'm going to cause any motherfucker who even lays a finger on her. I'll make it as painful as fucking possible, ripping them limb by limb, and forcing them to watch as I take down every single one of their club members.

There is no innocent Wraith in my mind.

They all deserve to fucking die, and I'll gladly do it with my bare-fucking-hands.

I toss the cigarette away and consider taking over everything, saying fuck it when it comes to waiting for Tate to pull up when suddenly the black van squeals into the parking lot.

He's barely parked before the driver's side door flings open, and he's rounding the vehicle to show us the arsenal he brought.

"We're ready when the time comes," he states, addressing the gathered members of the club.

"What do you mean when the fucking time comes? We need to go now," I argue.

"We can't go in right now."

I grab Tate by the cut and get in his face. "Fuck you, we're going in now."

He shoves at me, but I don't move. "You're gonna wanna get your fuckin' hands off of me, brother," he warns calmly.

"You don't fucking get it. I need her back now," I bark.

The dark trauma of my past creeping up, of being too late to save someone I loved. I can't fail again. *I fucking can't.*

"I want her back just as bad as you fuckin' do. But we can't do that at this very moment. There aren't enough of us. The Wraiths have three major commercial properties, and right now I don't know which one she's at. Until we know which building and what we're up against, we need to wait."

"This is all your fucking fault," I seethe at him. "If we didn't intercept that fucking cargo, she'd still be here. In fact, she'd be so safe and fucking far away from your bullshit, we would have been better off." I'm nearly screaming and all the other guys look so confused with what's happening right now. I don't give a shit about airing our dirty laundry.

"If it's anyone's fuckin' fault, it's mine. She was with me when they took her," Axel admits, placing himself in the middle of Tate and me. "I want Lily back more than I need to fuckin' breathe. You two assholes fightin' isn't goin' to get her back. So what's the fuckin' plan?"

Tate glares at me, but readjusts his cut as he circles us up to go over the plan. It's flimsy at best and requires the trust of a third party that Tate won't identify.

Every fiber of my being is telling me to storm their closest club-house and kill everyone on site. I get a grip on myself and decide to follow the program. One slip-up could have them moving Lily to another location, and then we'll never be able to find her again.

PHASE one of the plan is stationing at least two of us near each property so that we have eyes and ears on each building before we act. I'm with Mickey at their main clubhouse. Bikes are lined up in front of the large building, and it's decorated heavily with Wraith tags on the outside.

Mickey and I stand a good distance away, tucked behind some foliage as we watch and wait.

"We'll get her back," Mickey reassures softly.

"You get ahold of her brother?" I ask him.

"Not yet. He's been on a run in Athens for a few days. Plus, he's been avoiding my calls for some time now…" he trails off. I don't give a shit about his relationship drama, so I leave it alone.

The rest of the club has been radio silent. We don't know who to trust, and Tate stands firm on not telling the Prez or anyone who's been patched in for more than five years. I'm not sure if his paranoia is warranted or not, but we can't afford anyone fucking this up.

Two Wraiths are laughing as they bump into each other. *Drunk before five, classy.*

"Take your cut off," I mumble to Mickey, who follows my instruction.

We toss them on our bikes as we casually make our way over to the two guys. They're apprehensive of us, but not completely put off. Having a club as big as theirs comes with the issue of not knowing every club member personally.

"Any good pussy tonight?" I ask with a head nod towards the clubhouse.

"Just the typical club sluts," the one with long, greasy, black hair says. The other guy laughs like the joke is absolutely hilarious.

"You'd think they'd throw an Omega our way every now and then. I mean, we work hard, we deserve it," the older one with the graying goatee supplies.

"No kiddin'. How long has it been?" I respond, thickening my accent.

"Months, Prez has gotten fuckin' greedy," Grease-ball replies.

"Maybe we should take one," Mickey chimes in, and I'm

glad the moron didn't just stand there looking like a fucking idiot.

"Yeah, right. He keeps that place locked up tighter than a nun's cunt," Gray goatee dismisses. It's clear this one knows more information, so I see how much I can get out of him.

"Where is he holdin' them nowadays?" I ask.

He squints his eyes and looks over at me and Mickey again. When he gazes down at Mickey's hand, seeing the DPMC signet ring, I know we're fucked.

Without a second thought, I take out my pistol and quickly fire three shots. The first is right between the older man's eyes. His death is quick, and his body thuds against the ground with a satisfying thud.

I shoot the other man in both the thigh and the shoulder. He falls to the ground, wincing in pain, and I smile as I get down to my haunches. I press a thumb firmly into the wound in his thigh, causing him to scream out in pain.

"Tell me where he keeps them, and I'll end this quickly."

"Fuck you. I ain't tellin' you shit," he groans, and I dig my finger deeper into his thigh.

"My patience is pretty fucking thin. You get one more chance. Where does he keep them?"

He coughs and sputters.

"Fuck you," he grunts.

As a man of my word, I remove my thumb from his gunshot wound and take everything else off of him. His wallet, gun, and cell phone are all in my possession.

I nod my head to Mickey. "Go get the bikes."

He doesn't gape or seem surprised at my show of violence. He's quick to roll my bike over to where I'm standing in the woods. I take out the long piece of nylon rope, tying a secure knot on the triple tree of my bike while Mickey goes and gets his own bike.

"What are you doin'?" the man sputters, blood now seeping

out of his mouth. He doesn't have long, but I plan on dragging this out a little longer.

"I warned you. Unless you're having a change of heart?" I say calmly as I loop the nylon around his underarms, tying it tightly enough that he can still breathe, but it's going nowhere. Once Mickey is back with his bike, I grab another piece of rope, securing it around both of his ankles. Both of our bikes face in opposite directions. "Mickey, you wanna start her up?" I ask as he starts his engine, and my plan becomes clear.

"We're going to rip you the fuck apart," I explain with a smile as I walk towards my bike, starting the engine.

"Please," he begs. I can't control the menacing smile that spreads across my face.

"I mean, I told you I would only give you two chances, and you said no. If I gave you another that would make me a liar." I have to nearly shout to be heard over the purring engine.

"I'll tell you where they're at," he rasps out.

"Should we believe him, Mickey?" I ask him. He shrugs his shoulders and looks down at the poor unfortunate soul.

"Probably not. He's most likely lying, and I kinda want to see how this whole medieval shit works out," Mickey comments, and I smirk at him.

"Where?" I growl behind me, revving the engine, letting him know I mean business.

"The… the home in Buckwood," he sputters.

"See, how hard was that?" I ask him. "Let's end this then," I say, pointing my gun at him. "Mickey, how do we know he's not lying?" I ask, toying with the man, neither of us leaving our bikes.

"We don't," he replies.

"True. Only one way to find out." I rev the engine again as the man I have tied to the bike sobs.

"I'm not lying," he wails.

"Neither was I," I reply as both Mickey and I start driving in opposite directions.

I watch the entire thing, the way his body stretches and contorts. It doesn't rip him in half, but it does the job intended as I watch the life leave his eyes. I take comfort in knowing without a shadow of a doubt that he suffered.

The kill switch deep-rooted in me has been flipped, and I'll destroy anyone who comes between me and my Omega.

TWENTY-EIGHT
RESISTANCE

LILY

THE HOOD STAYS over my head as the van parks, and I'm dragged forcefully around by two Alphas on each side of me. I keep quiet; I even try to make my breathing more even, anything that won't call attention to myself. I don't hear Shelby, so I assume they are carrying her. I just hope they take us to the same place.

The idea of us being separated is crippling, and it makes my breathing pick up.

No. Stay calm. Don't let them see you panic.

Their hands are like manacles around my upper arms, and I want to wince at the treatment. I'm not a completely fragile person, but it's the malicious intent wafting off of them that makes the pain ten times worse.

It's relatively silent as they march us through a series of doors and hallways. I couldn't tell you where we are. We could have been in the van for a half hour or multiple hours. What I do note is that I don't think we're at a clubhouse. My feet sink into carpeted floors as they walk me to wherever they're taking me. Clubhouses would never have carpet. The knowledge makes my stomach drop.

They're taking us somewhere that won't be easy for the

Dead Palms to find. Maybe that's part of their plan. Keep me as far away from my saviors as possible. It's what any villain would do, right?

But then the silence stops and what I hear only makes the situation more dire. There's more than one person crying. One of them seems closer than the other, and my mind races with what they could be crying about.

Based on what the men in the van said about what they wanted to do to me, it doesn't take long to imagine the horrors that happen in a place like this. I don't even have to physically see anything to know that. This building oozes trepidation just from the sounds and smells alone.

The scents are overwhelming and putrid because they're so mixed. It's a barrage of different designations, and it's sour. It's not the scent of arousal, but dread.

A doorknob clicks, and my hood is removed from my head. My hair sticks to the material before falling flat against my face. The scent is ten times worse without the hood on, and I wrinkle my nose in distaste. It takes a few minutes for me to blink and get my bearings, and when I finally get a look at my two captors I see the scythe tattoos on their necks. It confirms what I already know: they're Wraiths.

They shove me into the small room that's probably ten feet by eight feet. The only things in the room are a bucket and a worn mattress on the floor with two blankets that look like they were dug out of the trash.

"Welcome home, princess," the man with the deeper voice sneers: *Reg.*

There's one card I have in my back pocket. One that might not even be valuable. I don't know if the man is dead or alive, or if he even gives a single fuck about me. "My dad, Hammer, can I see him?"

Reg laughs so hard he has to clutch his stomach. "Hammer died a long time ago. Jesus."

He and the other guy continue to laugh like what I said is

the most hilarious thing in the world, and I just blink at them. *How did I not know he was dead?*

"What about Rex?" I ask, the one man in my mother's pack who was kind to me, who actually loved my mother, at least it seemed that way.

"Damn, girl. You really don't know any of your own history. Don't worry. We're here to teach you."

Nothing about what he's saying makes sense, my mom's face is physical evidence of how the Wraiths treated her. Why wouldn't she tell me my biological father and her pack were dead? Wouldn't she be happy to tell me this? It would have put me at ease as a child knowing they were gone. As happy as I was to be a part of the Dead Palms, there was always this fear that the Wraiths would come back and demand that we go home. I guess they are now, just not in the way I thought.

I take a few steps back until my back hits the wall. The wall is sticky and smells like tobacco. Another man with a black eye comes in carrying a limp Shelby. The hood still covers her face as he drops her roughly onto the mattress.

Reg throws two bottles of water and a sleeve of crackers into the room. His hand is on the knob, looking like he's going to leave, but he pauses. His gaze watches the men trail down the hallway before he looks back at me. I'm on my knees, removing Shelby's hood and pushing back her hair.

"You're Wraith's property now. The sooner you get that through you and your little friend's head the easier this will be on you." He slams the door shut behind him, and I finally let myself really cry.

Tears rain down my face as I finally get a solid look at Shelby, which only makes me cry harder. She has a bruise forming on her jaw, a busted lip, and her eyebrow is split open.

"Fuck, Shelby. I'm so sorry," I whisper as I pet her hair and cry.

There's a muffling of someone else crying through the walls, and it breaks any spirit I might have still had buried deep inside me.

Shelby doesn't wake up, and I finally note the small window behind me. I have to claw against the frame to lift myself up to get a good look. When I do... every single ounce of hope that I had dies.

We're in a suburb.

We're where I grew up. My heart sinks, small memories flooding to me. The one bedroom my mother, Leon, and I shared. School lessons in that same room, nights where my mother was taken away and returned beaten to hell. My brain protects me from digging too deep into what happened here. But it all feels so fucking hopeless at this point.

I spent so much time making sure I didn't end up like my mom, that I wouldn't end up with a pack that would hurt me, that I missed the big picture. I was never as fucking safe as I thought I was with the Dead Palms. The sinking feeling that history is going to repeat itself haunts me as I step away from the window, my fate becoming clearer with every second that ticks by.

They're never going to find me. I'm going to die here, just like my mom was supposed to.

I CRY for what feels like hours, just petting Shelby's head. I think it's for my own comfort, not hers.

But eventually, she stirs with a groan. Her hand automatically cups her now purple and green-tinted chin.

"Fuck," she grumbles as she sits up on the mattress, her back flat against the wall. Her chin tilts up toward the ceiling, and she exhales dramatically.

"Shelby, I'm so sorry." She doesn't look at me, just stares at the ceiling, taking in our current situation.

"It's not your fault. We just need to figure out how the fuck we're getting out of here," she responds confidently as she looks around the room.

"We're in a normal house in the middle of the suburbs, Shelby. They aren't going to find us. There's no way out."

"I'm not counting on them finding us," she dismisses, standing with a wince and favoring her left leg. Shelby is taller than me and has no issue looking out the window. The window can't be but a foot wide and tall. There's no escaping that way.

"You don't understand. My mom was kept here for a decade," I confess, lowering my voice.

Shelby has a scowl on her face as she gets down onto her haunches and points at me. "You're not your mother, and I sure as fuck am not going to spend the rest of my life here. I need you to get it together." My head just shakes, making Shelby growl in frustration. She grabs my left hand, forcing me to look at the engagement ring I've only worn for today. "You want to see him again?" I nod my head. "Then stop acting like this is the end of our lives, get your shit together and fucking fight, Lily," she practically yells at me.

The door immediately flings open. It's Reg and the other guy from the van—I don't know his name.

"Was wonderin' when your mouthy-ass was gonna wake up," nameless says.

Shelby doesn't say anything, just crosses her arms over her chest and glares at the men.

Reg smirks and takes three strides to get into her space. He grabs her jaw roughly, causing her to wince but she doesn't give anything else away. I'm sure it has to hurt with how bruised her face is. "Listen here, girl. You're a Beta. A dime a fuckin' dozen, you hear me? You're lucky you're pretty or we would have just dumped you on the way here. Fall in line, or else," he seethes.

Shelby literally spits in his face. "Fuck you."

Reg grabs her arm above the elbow and at the wrist. I watch in absolute terror as he breaks her arm. The snap is loud, and the scream that rips out of Shelby is horrific and brain-shattering. Reg steps away, and Shelby spits at him again.

God, does she wanna die? As much as I admire her, I need her to stop, or she'll get herself killed. We need to stick together and figure out a plan; if we get separated I'm not sure we would stand a chance.

Reg takes another step towards her, and the other man puts a hand on his shoulder.

"Back up, man."

"Fine, you deal with this fucking mess, Tex."

I search my brain for a Tex but don't come up with anything. They both acted like they knew me in the van, but seeing their faces, there's no recollection on my end.

Tex pulls out a knife and holds it in front of Shelby's face. She doesn't break or falter, she just glares. Part of me wishes I was as strong as her, but she's also covered in bruises and has a broken arm, so I'm not sure if she has the right idea.

"Maybe it's not her we need to hurt," he suggests before turning his gaze to me. I back up as far away as I can until I'm cornered. He grabs my chin but turns to speak to Shelby. "From now on, when you act out, she's the one who pays the price."

He takes the tip of his knife and places it against my cheekbone. I'm gripping the covers for dear life as Shelby finally speaks up.

"Wait! No. Don't hurt her. I won't cause any more problems." Her voice is panicked for the first time since we got here, and I swallow thickly. I feel like I might throw up from fear as he applies more pressure against my skin, just enough to make me wince.

"Lessons need to be learned," he tsks as the blade digs into my flesh, and he tugs downward on my face. I scream while he does it, but he doesn't stop for Shelby's pleading or my pain-riddled cries.

Once he's done, he tucks his knife away and grabs my chin. Blood pools over his knuckles as he holds me. "Such a shame, really," he sneers, glaring at my face for a moment before both of them leave the room. My tears sting as they flow into the wound.

A scarred face, just like my mother.

A scar that I'll wear on my skin forever to remember this moment. It feels like failure. My naïve ego thought I could have it all, the club I loved and the pack I wanted. I was so fucking wrong.

I wonder now if Kurt and my brother knew something was brewing with the Wraiths and everything they did was all out of love. If I had just gone with their plans, I could have found nice enough Alphas and lived my life out peacefully.

A drop of blood mars my opal wedding ring, and it seems so symbolic of my life right now. How much I don't want to be in this situation, but I can't regret my decisions. I can't regret wanting to feel truly loved and wanting to stay in my home.

Even if it's been completely taken away from me in a matter of moments.

"Lily, I'm so sorry," Shelby sniffs, grabbing the blanket and blotting my face with her good arm.

When I look up at her face, I don't know if it's the guilt or pain flooding me, but it's the first moment I feel the fight pump through my bloodstream.

"We're getting the fuck out of here, Shelby," I whisper, and she nods her head.

I don't care if it's in a body bag or barely in pieces. I will not live in this hellhole.

TWENTY-NINE

DARK KNIGHT
LILY

THEY TAKE Shelby from the room—separating us—and all I can do is wait and breathe. I wouldn't consider myself a religious person, but maybe in these moments when everything in the universe is out of control, you can't help but pray to something beyond what we know.

I pray they aren't doing what I think they are and that my friend will come back to me whole. Shelby is smart, and maybe they're taking her somewhere that will give her an idea as to how we can escape. I wouldn't blame her if she could get out. I'd want her to take the chance. Maybe if she got out, she could get help from the guys, which would lead to me getting out, too.

Time is relative when there are no clocks and each minute feels like an hour. I just lie on the mattress and wait for her to come back.

If they're separating us for good… I don't think I'll survive.

There's a tear in the mattress, and I focus on that, unraveling each thread gently while I wait, hoping for the best.

"Hello?" the voice comes softly through the wall on my right.

"Hi," I say quietly back.

I'm pretty sure someone sits out in the hallway to monitor us. Even though I don't know how many of 'us' there really are.

"Don't dri…" she says, but trails off. I can barely hear her voice through the wall.

"What?" I ask.

But as soon as the words leave my mouth, Shelby comes stumbling back into the room, another bruise forming on her left eye, but at least her arm is in a sling.

Shelby huddles into the corner of the room, staring at the wall, saying nothing. Reg places a tray holding two sandwiches, applesauce, and two glasses of juice on the floor.

"Eat up," he commands before slamming the door on us again.

I'm on my feet faster than I can think, feeling dizzy as I do, but I push through as I approach Shelby. She winces when I touch her arm, but she doesn't pull away.

"What did they do to you?"

"Nothing. Just eat. We need to keep up our strength. The infirmary is our way out," she reveals. I look at her with too much tenderness, and she snaps at me. "I'm fucking fine. Now eat while I think," she orders.

I don't question her. If she doesn't want to talk about it, she doesn't have to. Her clothes look just as put together as they did before she left. So I take a deep breath, filling myself with hope, before eating my sandwich, which is dry as hell. I wash it down with the juice they provided.

Shelby taps her thigh with her good arm and sits down across from me to eat her own food and drink.

"This place must be around four thousand square feet. There are six bedrooms on this level alone," she whispers. "They keep a guard in the hallway. The walls are thin, so we need to be quiet."

I nod at her, one of her eyes nearly closed from where she was hit.

"It would need to be at just the right time. There must be a few guys who live here and a revolving door of them, who they station at this house."

"What do they want with us?"

Shelby gives me a stern look but shakes her head. "I think they're selling most of the girls. Some are for personal pleasure," she states plainly. There's no room for sugar coating with the situation we're in.

I gulp and wrap my arm around myself.

"If we ever find ourselves alone with one of them, we need to be smart, Lily."

She says it like it's inevitable and that our escape may take some time. The dry sandwich in my stomach threatens to come back up, but I swallow it down.

"If we can just get a phone off of one of them, that would be everything. Especially if we could just send a text and delete it after. I hate to say it, but I think you had the right idea. No more putting up fights, the more docile and calm we are, the more likely they are to lower their guards. If either of us has a chance at a phone or to get out, we take it."

"Okay," I sigh, wanting to die, but the small sliver of hope she's giving me is enough to keep me going. My stomach recoils, though, and I grab my waist at the pain.

"You okay?"

"Yeah, I'll be fine."

There are no lights in the small room, just the window in the corner signifying the time of day. The sun is going down, and Shelby and I decide to lie on the bed. I'm not sure how either of us will get any sleep tonight, but we can't let ourselves fall apart.

We only have each other in this depressing room and in this situation. I take some solace in that; I hate that I put Shelby in this situation, but at least I'm not alone. I'm pretty sure I would have crumbled in on myself by now if it weren't for her strength.

Another cramp hits me suddenly, and I groan. The pain is so

sharp and intense that my vision almost goes out. It reminds me of the last period I had, but worse.

"Lily?"

"Something's wrong," I grumble as Shelby touches my forehead.

"You're burning up. When did this start?"

"I don't know. Fuck it hurts," I whine.

And despite everything, that fact I'm terrified and in pain… I perfume. It doesn't hold the thick warmness it usually does, but it's potent nonetheless.

"Shit, Lily."

Neither of us has to say it. If we talk about it, that would make it real. Shelby shifts so that her body curls behind mine, her bad arm resting on top of me as she gives me the slightest bit of comfort.

She's not mine.

She's not the Beta I want right now.

This wasn't supposed to happen this way, none of it was. I should be on the road with Axel and Cash right now, starting our new lives. I hoped maybe Tate would join us too, but now it doesn't matter.

I'm trapped here, and the idea of what's going to happen to me makes me sob. My first heat is going to be taken away from me, and the worst part, my body won't care. All it will want is the relief and for the pain to go away. But my head and my heart? If there was a way to kill myself in this small room, I think I would.

The thought is dark, and it's the first time in my life I've ever felt this way. It's only a matter of time before they come barreling through that door and take a piece of my soul, one that I can never get back.

Shelby tries to make soft noises of reassurance in my ear, but we both know I'm fucked.

Even if we get out of here, I don't know if I'll survive this. I've survived a lot as a child, my mind hiding away dark truths

I never wanted to face. But this? Them using me in this state… I won't ever be the same.

There's a soft thud in the hallway that makes both Shelby and I startle. She holds me closer to her chest. "It's okay, shhh. It'll be okay."

It won't.

Her lies don't comfort either of us as the doorknob turns. Shelby and I both act like we're asleep, but it doesn't matter as a male hand touches me.

Yet, I don't revolt from the touch. His scent is so familiar, and it's jarring when I turn in Shelby's arms.

There stands my brother… wearing a Wraith's cut.

I go to open my mouth, but Leon puts a finger over his lips. When I glance over at Shelby, she looks just as confused as me. *Are the guys here? Did they take out some members and put on their cuts to blend in?*

Leon's eyes widen as he scents me, but they get even wider when he takes in Shelby's injuries.

"We have to be quiet. You do as I say," he commands both of us. I have so many questions, but right now, all that matters is that we get the fuck out of this place.

Leon holds his weapon up as Shelby and I follow him. I look at all the locked rows of doors, and I tug on his shirt. He gives me the most pissed-off look ever, but I can't keep quiet. Not on this.

"What about the others?"

"I can only get you two out right now. That has to be enough," he urges.

Has everyone in this house not been taken out? The man, Tex, sits in the hallway, but he doesn't look dead; he just looks asleep. I've never in my life had the urge to kill someone, but a part of me wants to take Leon's gun and shoot this man in the head.

Shelby tugs me back to reality as another cramp rolls

through me. I place a hand over my mouth as I whimper. Shelby rubs my back as my brother looks at me.

"They gave her something. She's going into heat," Shelby whispers to my brother.

"Fuck. We've got to be quick. Go down the stairs, to the left, and out of the infirmary. You'll have to drive with Lily on the back," his voice is soft, but I take in every word and tilt my head.

"It's just you?" Shelby questions him for me.

I'm also wondering why he's going to stay here, why wouldn't he be coming with us? I need him. I tug on his cut, fisting it in my hand. The leather is comforting.

"I'll explain everything later, baby. I promise," Leon pleads with Shelby, cupping her face. He looks at the damage there, and I swear my brother almost cries. "No more bullshit after this. I'll keep you safe. Both of you are safe," he declares, looking over at me. He places a kiss on the side of Shelby's head and then mine before we proceed down the hallway.

Leon is here… on his own… with a Wraiths cut on. All the drunken self-loathing nights he's had and self-deprecating he's been doing slowly gets pieced together in my mind. *What the fuck has my brother done?*

Now is not the time or place to ask. We've already spoken more than we should.

Our footsteps are soft on the beige carpet as we make our way down the hall. Leon takes the steps first and we follow, trying to be as light on our feet as possible. It has to be relatively late, seeing as all the lights are off and how few noises there are in the house. Only the mundane sounds of a clock ticking, the air conditioning running, and the gentle hum of some sort of appliance fill the space.

We pass through the kitchen first. Shelby wisely grabs a knife, and I wish I would have thought of that. She wields it in her uninjured hand. I know she won't hesitate to stab the fuck out of someone if they try to stop our escape.

Leon guides us down another hallway, and there's a loud snore, which makes us all pause our movements for a moment. We're stark still in the hallway, but my heartbeat drums loudly in my ears.

The snoring continues in a rhythmic tone, and we continue our path down the hallway. "Fuck," Leon mumbles as he goes to turn the doorknob to the infirmary. He looks to Shelby first. With her arm, there's no way she can hold a gun. Instead, he hands it to me, and I take a deep breath as I grip the cold metal. I hold it steady as he pulls out a ring of keys and unlocks the door. It clicks loudly, making me wince. He pushes the door in, looking around.

Shelby enters first, then me, and last, Leon. He shuts the door softly behind us and locks it. I'm about to return his gun as a shot is fired off. Shelby is right next to me, and I watch in devastation as she clutches the side of her face, falling to the floor.

My heart thunders, and as badly as I want to crash to the floor and console her, I don't. It's like my instincts know everything I need to do right now. I need to get the fuck out of here and to my pack.

Every single person who stands in my way has to die.

I have to fight.

Instead of leading with fear, I raise my gun. My hands are as steady as they've ever been, and I shoot. I hit Reg right in the stomach, and he collapses to the ground, dropping his gun. It slides across the floor. He's gurgling and writhing as I finally turn and face Shelby.

"Where were you hit? Are you alright?" I ask. She pulls her hand away from her face, and I sigh in relief at the fact that it was just a graze.

That is until I look behind her...

My brother lies on the floor, gasping for breath as he holds his chest. I don't even think about how the gunshots would have woken everyone in the house up, or that this will all be for naught as they drag us back to our rooms.

All I think about is Leon, my protector, bleeding out on the floor.

Shelby sobs, crawling over to my brother, putting pressure on his chest as she stares into his big brown eyes that are laced with a fear I've never seen before.

"I'm sorry, I..." he coughs, and a small trail of blood slides out of the corner of his mouth.

My hands are on him immediately. Shelby is already putting pressure on his chest, and I feel useless.

"Shh, it's okay. Where's your phone? I'll call for help," Shelby pleads.

"Should we take his shirt off, what can we do?" I ask Shelby, but she doesn't answer, just looks down at Leon.

His hands are covered in blood, but his palm cups her her face. "I love you, baby, always know that," he rasps before turning to face me. Shelby presses her face against his chest as she sobs in his arms. His blood mars her pretty blonde hair as she holds on to him like the pressure of her head will stop the wound.

"We didn't even get a chance," Shelby sobs out, and mine follow hers.

My brother looks back at me, his brown eyes which mirror mine are hooded, and all I want to do is protect him for once. He's spent his entire life looking out for me, making sure I was taken care of. I want to be able to do the same for him. He deserves to have someone protect him for a change.

"I'm so fuckin' sorry, Lily. I didn't..." He coughs again, and I want him to stop talking as much as I want all the time in the world left with him. "...want any of this to happen," he whispers as tears flow down the side of his face. I wipe them away, my own tears dripping down my cheeks as I try to hold onto my mental control of this moment. My body has different plans, and my vision keeps going hazy, but I shuffle around the floor until I find a wad of gauze in a drawer.

I slide back and touch Shelby's head, getting her to move. She gasps but moves for a moment. Shelby and I work together to fill the wound in his chest.

The gauze does nothing.

As soon as we shove it in, it's soaked in blood and useless.

"Leon, I need you. You can't go," I sob, continuing to push more gauze into the wound. "Don't leave me, I need you!" I nearly shout. Not even caring who hears me. *What's the fucking point of making it out of here alive if Leon doesn't.*

He just made Shelby his ol' lady; they are perfect for each other. She brought the smile back to his face, even though he was clearly going through some serious shit.

Everything fucking hurts as I watch as my brother's breathing becomes rattled and shallow. I know that there's nothing Shelby and I can do. Unless someone gets here fast.

"What else can we do?" I ask Shelby. For the first time, she's devoid of words, just shakes her head and holds my brother.

He opens his mouth to speak again, and I shush him, my own tears splattering against his skin. With how hard he had to try to speak last time… I can't have him pushing himself any further than he already has.

"Just breathe, Leon," I tell him.

Shelby digs around his pocket and finds his phone. I'm not sure who she's calling, but it goes unanswered. It's the moment she completely falls apart; she gently falls back on his chest, trying to use her body weight to stop the bleeding.

Gunshots are going off in the house, but I ignore them. Nothing matters in a world without Leon in it.

There's so much blood, and I don't know what to do. "What do I do, Leon? You always know what to do," I plead with him, but his eyes begin to shut.

I use my thumb to rub his face. Shelby's sobs are muffled

against his clothes as she holds onto him for dear life like sheer power of will could keep him alive.

"We didn't have enough time. Please, Leon. Please stay with me," Shelby begs on a choked sob. I want to beg him to fight, to stay with both of us, but I know these are his final breaths.

He says nothing to her, just holds her hand. He blinks up at me one last time as I watch his chest stop rising and falling.

His hand goes limp in Shelby's.

He's gone.

I don't know what he did, why he was here. I don't even really care if he was a rat. He spent the last moments of his life trying to free Shelby and me, just like he spent all his waking moments taking care of me. I close his eyes as I cradle his face in my hands and mourn.

I mourn my brother, the life I was supposed to have, the very essence of who I wanted to be.

Every part of me feels dead.

Leon was supposed to marry Shelby; hell, maybe build a pack with her and give me a football team of nieces and nephews. Leon was supposed to live a full, happy life. But in a single moment, his life ended, and it feels like it's all my fault.

All I feel is pain. Every part of my body aches, and I do the only thing I can at this moment. I lay all the way down and rest, my brother's blood pooling next to me as I lie in a fetal position on the floor.

Part of me recognizes the Wraith I shot isn't dead. I can still hear his bitching and raspy breaths, but I just don't care. I want him to suffer, but I also feel too weak to be the one to do anything about it.

I want to cease to exist. No one should ever have to deal with this kind of pain; it's deep-rooted in every nerve ending in my body and soul. There's still ricocheting gunshots and yelling coming from inside the house, but I ignore it.

Maybe someone will kill me too.

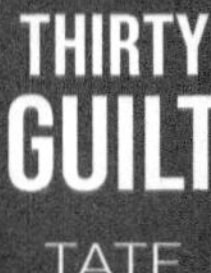

THIRTY
GUILT

TATE

I GLARE at Cash as we all wait patiently throughout this neighborhood. I told him I would find the location, but I guess that wasn't good enough for him. Now that two Wraiths are missing, I'm sure the house is under more security than usual.

"I'm not apologizing for shit. As soon as we get in there, I'm killing every single one of these motherfuckers I come across."

"You just gave away our advantage."

"Fuck off, Tate. They took my girl; they knew we were coming for them. You're the one we should be pissed off at." He points his finger at me and stands tall. "Maybe if you didn't keep so many fucking secrets, Lily wouldn't have been taken. Maybe if we didn't blindly follow you into that raid, I'd have her in my arms right-fucking-now. If there's a single scratch on her, know that's on you, and that you shouldn't forgive yourself," he spits.

And I feel it. I let myself feel every ounce of his hatred. It's valid, but I don't know that Lily would feel the same way.

"As soon as he gets them out, we can go in," I reply sharply.

I'm not goin' to argue with him, and now is not the time to go into all the twisted family history and lies I've been holdin' in or how they've been tearin' away at my fuckin' soul.

"You sure we shouldn't get more of the club involved?" Atlas questions.

"Someone from our own club let them into our compound, until we figure out who the rat is, no," Cash spits back at him. "Unless you're the fucking rat?" He gets in the man's face, and Axel steps between them, acting like a peacemaker.

"Enough with this shit, It's been ten minutes. Should we go in?" Axel asks quietly, his own guilt eating him alive. We've all played our parts in what happened and neither of us deserves any reassurances. None of us want that. We just need Lily home safe.

"He's goin' to call me as soon as they make it out," I reply.

Cash growls under his breath, and Axel just nods.

Atlas grumbles, but soon we're all in motion as a gunshot blasts through the house, with a second pop following not long after.

"Fuck the plan; let's go," Cash demands, and I agree with him completely. All of us, Cash, Axel, Mickey, Maverick, Atlas, Ink, and Doc, go in guns loaded and ready to kill everyone onsite. Cash uses brute force to knock the door down, and it's absolute mayhem from there.

We split into two groups, half of us using the couch in the living room for safety while the other uses the powder room for protection, popping out to shoot when they can.

Ink takes a hit to the thigh, and we place him gently behind the brown sofa. Doc quickly makes a tourniquet and stops the blood flow before picking up his weapon to fire again.

I count about six Wraiths; we're evenly matched until Cash throws a fuckin' can of tear gas into the kitchen. It's the advantage we need as we leave Ink armed behind the couch and run straight into the mayhem.

We kill indiscriminately. There are no survivors, no need to question anyone, just complete annihilation of everyone in this fuckin' house. A man grabs Axel and grips the wound in his arm, making him cry out as they fight hand-to-hand. My aim is steady as I shoot the Wraith, and his body collapses to the ground.

Axel gives me a nod of appreciation and picks up his weapon. When I look over at Cash, he has a Wraith by the throat, asking them where Lily is. The man points upstairs and Cash shoves the barrel of his Glock into the man's mouth before firing. Brain matter splatters the white cabinets before his body falls to the floor. Doc shoots one more Wraith, and it seems like this floor is clear. I nod to the stairs, and the men follow. Cash quickly overtakes me on the steps.

There's a man hunched over in the hallway, but he's not dead. I speak too soon as Cash walks up and pops him right in the head without even flinching. We go to open the doors, but they're all locked.

Cash and Doc struggle to knock down one door. There are two women in the room, but neither are Lily. They shriek and back into a corner, clearly wanting nothing to do with us. We need to find keys and get the fuck out of here.

"Lily?" Axel asks.

"Shelby?" Doc calls out her name.

No answer.

"We need to check back downstairs," I state. "Doc, stay up here and make sure the girls stay safe," I instruct. He nods his head and holds his weapon like he's ready to kill anyone onsite. Maybe we were wrong about the gunshots, and he got them out. Either way, I need to make sure.

Cash, Axel, and Mickey follow me down the hallways. We have to step over bodies left and right. We check three rooms down here, which are empty. When we get to the last one, I swear I hear sobbing through the wood.

"Move," Cash growls.

He shoulders the door with little effort and what greets us behind the closed door is an absolute nightmare.

Leon lies dead on the floor, Shelby crying on top of him,

holding his lifeless hand while Lily lies there in the fetal position, blinking wildly.

Axel turns his head and wretches as Mickey falls to his knees, looking down at Leon. He doesn't say anything, just stares at his lifeless body. A part of my soul fractures at the sight in front of me. So many people loved Leon, yet he didn't think he had any other choice besides what he did? I'm not sure what Mickey and Axel think of his cut, they were his two closest brothers in the club.

His death weighs so heavily on my shoulders, I feel like it's going to crush me fuckin' whole.

He came to me and I could have helped him sooner, but I didn't because of this vendetta. I feel like his blood is on my hands; I feel like everything is on my hands, and there's no way to wash them clean.

Cash blinks down at Lily, but it's not with the usual softness he usually reserves for her. It's rage. He walks over to the Wraith, who is gasping for breath in the other part of the room, and swiftly shoots him in the head.

"I'm going to make sure that the house is clear," Cash announces, unable to look at Lily again.

I want to reason with him, calm him down, and get Lily in his arms. He's so good with her when she's upset. But he's on a mission and until he completes it, he'll only have tunnel vision.

Axel stands in the corner, clutching his stomach, his eyes watering as he mourns one of his longest friends and watches the crumpled woman in front of us.

She doesn't even seem alert, almost like she's in a daze.

I swallow the bile down and get on my knees next to her.

"Lily, darlin'. I gotta get you out of here," I whisper softly to her.

She doesn't respond. A pained whimper leaves her, and it garners the attention of everyone in the room. I push her hair out of her face and hold back a gasp over the cut I see there. Dry blood is caked on her face, and I make a mental note to clean it up while doing whatever I can to prevent scarring.

Shelby lifts her head from Leon's chest to look at me. She's been beat to high fucking hell, and I can't tell if the blood on her face is her own or Leon's. "They gave her something," she croaks.

"Lily, what's wrong? What do you need?"

She doesn't answer, just coils in on herself.

"You need to get her out of here. And all the girls," Shelby urges, while tears trail down her face. Mickey rubs a hand through Leon's hair, and Shelby tracks the motion, both of us noting the tender touch before she's looking back at me. "We need to hurry," she warns, and I nod, thinking about the best course of action.

I look over at Axel, who still looks sick and guilty. I know I need to keep my shit together. Between Cash's murderous rampage and Axel's festering guilt, someone has to protect Lily.

"I need medical attention, so do some of the other girls. But I'm sure they don't trust Alphas," Shelby says, her fingers tracing the patch on Leon's cut. "He wasn't a fuckin' rat," she declares with a sob, and I nod my head. My arm involuntarily reaches out to touch her arm.

"I'm going to make them pay, I promise. I need you to help get these girls out of here safely, and then I'm going to take Lily somewhere safe," I tell her, and she nods, touching Leon one more time.

Mickey stays silent, staring down at Leon's body before following her.

Axel wipes his face and looks down at Lily. "I've got to get my shit together." He sniffs back a sob as he braces his hands on his knees. "I'll text you the address to the lake house. Take Lily there. No one knows about it. I'll help get the other Omegas out of here and calm Cash down. As soon as we can, we'll meet you there. It's not gonna be long before the fuckin' cops get here."

"But she's goin' into heat," I counter.

"And?"

"We should take her to a hospital," I argue.

"You're not takin' my fuckin' wife to a hospital."

"Your what?" I snap, shocked.

"You fuckin' heard me. Now I need a fuckin' minute so I can be what she needs. You know, a lot of this falls on your shoulders, fair or not. She needs you to be the strong one right now. Go to the fuckin' lake house, and we'll handle clean up here."

He bends over, holding back a gag as he digs through Leon's pockets. He takes out a massive ring that must belong to the house and the keys to his bike.

"Take his bike. You know she'll want to keep it," he suggests. He looks down at Lily and kisses the side of her face. "They're all dead, and we're going to get these girls safe. I'll be with you soon," he chokes on the word *soon* but kisses her again as he takes the keys upstairs. He tugs at his hair and wipes his face before he jogs through the house to help the guys get this mess cleaned up.

I scoop her limp body up in my arms and take her outside. Leon's bike is waiting right by the door. He was so fuckin' close, it has me choking back my own set of fresh tears. Despite how I loathe every part of who I am right now, I've got to hold it together for Lily.

Fuckin' Lily. I sigh to myself, thinking about her pain and everything she's been through. She deserves so much more than this, than for me to be the one caring for her right now.

But I have to put that aside. My only focus is Lily, everything else, all my plans, everything that needs to come to light is on the back burner.

My sole focus is keeping Lily alive and trying to ease her pain. It's hard, but I'm able to maneuver her onto the back of the bike. She doesn't hold herself up, so I keep one arm on her as I take the front seat.

Like second nature, she places her feet on the pegs, but I

have to grab her arms and use one hand to hold her against me. I hate not havin' a helmet for her, but what-the-fuck-ever.

My phone dings, and I pull it out.

AXEL

76839 Sperry Drive. Code 8953. We're taking all the Omegas to the warehouse. Thirteen in total.

Meet me at the house as soon as possible.

As soon as I can find Cash.

Great, just fuckin' awesome. I knew Cash had another side to him. He's always so logical and holds it together. But right now, he can't see beyond his rage. Which is great for the work that needs to be done, but right now Lily needs us more.

"Hold on, darlin'. I've got you. You're going to be okay," I murmur to her as I start the engine. She grips my cut and holds onto me tightly; it's the first movement that gives me relief, that she's down there somewhere.

I need to get her back. I've already wasted so much time trying to fix everything for everyone else.

Right now? Lily's my only focus. The club can fuckin' fall for all I care.

THIRTY-ONE

JUST SURVIVE

LILY

"HOLD ON, DARLIN'. I've got you. You're going to be okay," Tate murmurs, and I know it's a lie.

I'll never be alright again.

My mind and body are on completely different pages, but I mentally will this aching need to go away.

I can't… I can't go through this right now… not when….

A fresh wave of sobs flows through me and Tate grips my wrist for dear life, like I might fall off the bike, or purposely fling myself off. The night is cooler than usual, and I shiver.

I'm still wearing the dress I got married in. It's no longer white. There are splotches of blood, a mixture of mine, Shelby's, and Leon's. Not to mention the specks of dirt and filth from being in that house.

It feels symbolic in a way; the hope that I had when I put this dress on, to the complete devastation ripping through me now.

Leon's brown eyes in his final moments keep flashing behind my closed eyelids, and I don't know what to do. He was so scared, but he stayed strong for Shelby and me. Even in his last moments, he was protecting me, and I hate how that feels.

No one ever protected Leon and that reality stings. He and

Shelby could have been endgame, their relationship was just starting to flourish. It was the first time I truly saw him happy and neither of them got to keep it. The idea of having my own glimpse of happiness or even the gratification of my heat fulfilled seems… wrong.

Tate isn't taking me back to the compound. I know that much. Is someone going back to tell my mom?

My poor fucking mom, hasn't she suffered enough?

I've known patched members who have died because of the nature of the club… I just never thought it would be Leon or the men I love the most.

I was a fucking fool.

I thought I understood club politics, thought that I knew what was going on. I didn't know shit, and I'm not sure if I can ever go back to being the fearless girl I once was.

Tate's scent is the only thing keeping me grounded right now. And the fact that I know he, Cash, Axel, and Shelby are alive. That has to be enough to keep me going.

Just survive.

Leon loved me, and I know he wouldn't want me to just roll over and give up. He wouldn't want me to stop living because he isn't here. Yet, the guilt of his death weighs so heavily on me. I think it might crush me whole.

"We're almost there. You're doing so good. You're being so brave," Tate praises while we're at a stop sign.

I hate that his words comfort me. I hate that I get to receive comfort when we just left absolute devastation in our wake.

He doesn't loosen his grip on my wrist as he rides, and I use the contact as an anchor. His flesh wrapping around mine is the only thing I focus on, nothing else. His skin against mine feels perfect. *How have I gone without his touch like this for so long?*

I find myself scooting as close as I possibly can to Tate, rubbing myself all over him and mingling our scents as the night's wind funnels around us. One of my hands leaves his waist, and he nearly crashes as he snatches it back. I just really wanted to touch his windblown hair.

I shake the thoughts out of my head.

No. No. No.

This can't be happening right now. I can't go into heat. I need to feel this; I need to grieve and make sure that Shelby is okay, that all the other Omegas they found in that house are safe and whole.

Giving into my selfish Omega needs right now just can't fucking happen.

I need to resist.

I just need to survive.

Tate can take me to the lake house, he can provide me with food, water, and… that's it. I don't deserve to have my heat satisfied.

This can be the pain I endure.

The idea of hurting somehow brings me comfort. It's like my suffering will wash away the sins that plague me.

It's not what Leon would have wanted, but something about the karmic justice of it all will make me feel better.

If I had been the one to open the door, or if I hadn't spent the day with Axel, maybe none of this would have happened. It all feels like some fucked up butterfly effect, and I hate it. I can play what-ifs for the rest of my life, but the cold reality of every-thing that happened won't change.

Maybe it was impossible to stop all of this, but what is possible is making things right—justice.

Which I can't do anything about until my body hands over all my faculties. Right now, every nerve ending is on fucking fire. I switch from wanting Tate to pull over and fuck me on the side of the road to having him toss me in a ditch so I can cry into the cold, damp ground. The juxtaposition of my emotions is complicated and gives me whiplash.

I focus again on where Tate holds onto me, and I try to not find the fact he's been driving with one hand ridiculously hot.

The feeling fades away fast when I realize whose bike we're riding.

I press my forehead against Tate's back and scrunch my eyes together as tightly as I can.

Adrenaline is fading away and is quickly replaced with need and exhaustion. I fucking hope exhaustion weighs out first. I haven't slept in nearly forty-eight hours, and I wonder if my lack of sleep is partly why I can't think straight.

I shake my head against his back. No, it definitely has to do with the trauma and the way my body is begging for relief.

His tires hit gravel and the bike's speed slows as he pulls up to the lake house. It's quiet here, with just the songs of cicadas and frogs. It's soothing in a way. I love this house, but part of me doesn't want to walk through those doors.

I know what I need to do.

Lock myself away and survive this heat. Once it's done, then I'll be able to think straight. I'll be able to do something besides being fucking useless.

Tate taps my thigh, but I don't budge for a solid minute.

"You can get off the bike on your own or I'll move you, Lily," he says in a low tone. It makes my flesh pebble, and I try to hold back the effect that his voice, scent, and touch have on me. I don't deserve the decadence that is him, not now.

Against my better judgment, I get off the bike and wrap my arms around myself as Tate does the same.

He looks at me like I'm a wounded animal, and I detest the feeling. I look away as he attempts to reach for my arm.

"Don't touch me," I hiss at him.

He puts his hands up in surrender. "Okay, let's just get you inside and cleaned up."

I keep my distance from him but follow him up the solar-panel-lit path. He puts in Axel's code and opens the door, giving me a wide berth to enter the home. I don't let him speak or attempt to console me. I immediately go to the primary suite, lock the door, and begin to undress.

There's a light tap on the door, and I sigh.

"Go away."

"Lily, you can't be left alone."

"I'm not going to fucking kill myself; I'm going to take a shower," I reply and wait a moment until I'm greeted with silence.

I turn the shower to scalding, and my skin abhors it. Every inch of me is recoiling at the sensation, but my mind welcomes it as I sit on the tile shower floor and let the water pour over me. Dirt and blood circles down the drain, and I just watch.

Tears don't fall from my eyes, but my mind goes slightly blank.

I just stare at the tiny cyclone of water disappearing down the drain. It's comforting but I don't know why. I get more vigorous about cleaning under my nails before I wash my face.

I wince as I touch the fresh, forgotten cut. My finger doesn't move even though it hurts.

Sometimes scars are reminders of what you survived, and other times they symbolize what you haven't. Only time will tell which this scar will be for me, but I don't loathe it the way I thought I would when he cut my face.

I'm not worried about my vanity at this point, far from it.

As I work to clean the rest of my body, I can't help but knead my breasts a little, the small touch bringing me immense pleasure. I go to slide my hand to my pussy, but stop myself.

No.

The only way I'm going to get through this heat is by not starting it at all. I have to push through. That means no touching myself or seeking comfort from others.

I can bear the storm.

With a dull ache in my stomach and a desperate need deep in my core, I cut off the water and exit the shower.

The towel feels like fucking sandpaper on my skin, but I dry off with it nonetheless.

Thankfully, the drawers are filled with Axel's clothes. I

throw on a pair of his boxers and a large t-shirt before I sit on the bed.

Four walls surround me, but they somehow feel like they're boxing me in. A cramp rips through my side, and I find myself whimpering, lying down as I curl into myself around the pain.

I can do this; I can get through this.

Pain is nothing in the grand scheme of things. I just need to survive.

There's no fucking way I can go through my heat, to get fucked within an inch of my life after everything I just went through.

My body has other thoughts in mind as my lower stomach clenches so hard my vision goes black for a few moments. There's a loud bang on the door, and I muffle my cries of pain into the pillow.

Tate doesn't knock the door down, but he manages to unlock the simple household knob.

I squeeze my eyes shut tightly so I don't have to see his face. But when his hand cups my cheek, the side with the cut, I break.

Tears fall down my face with silent sobs.

Tate doesn't speak right away, but he lies in bed with me. I don't tell him not to touch me, because I think if he stopped I might cry harder.

"I can't do this right now," I tell him between sobs.

"I know. I know, darlin'," he consoles me.

"It's wrong."

"I know," he repeats, pushing my still-damp hair from my face. "But if you don't, you might really fuckin' hurt yourself. I'm not sure what to say to make this better."

"He's gone, Tate," I remind him. His intense gaze meets mine as he cups both sides of my face, looking down at me.

"I don't want to force you to do this, but if I have to, I will. I'll just wait till you can't take it anymore. But please, baby. Please let me help you, what can I do?" he begs. His own eyes well up with emotion, and there's nothing but pure, honest devotion written on his face. Something I've been wanting to see. I hate that the first time I see it is at this moment.

"They need to pay," I tell him. I've never been a vengeful person. But right now if someone gave me a fuse, I'm pretty sure I would light it and kill every single Wraith without an ounce of remorse.

"If I promise you revenge, that I plan on taking the Wraiths from the fuckin' top, would you let go?" he asks.

"I... I don't know how I can. He didn't deserve this."

"He really fuckin' didn't. Let me take care of you, Lily. I promise when your heat's over I'll tell you whatever you want to know. Or keep you from whatever you don't want to know. If you want me to handle all of this and keep you blissfully unaware, I'll do it. But I can't sit on the other side of that door and listen to you cry in pain. I can't fuckin' do it."

"You'll tell me everything?" I ask, wanting confirmation.

"Everything. I'm not holdin' back anymore when it comes to you."

"You'll make them hurt?"

I don't know if I'm feeling bloodthirsty because of the pain or because of the hurt they caused me, but I need to know. I need to know that the soft side of Tate I'm seeing now isn't going to be what the Wraiths see. I need the side of him who killed a man for hurting dogs, who stood up to his father for me. I need the man who has no remorse to handle my retribution as much as I need the gentle Alpha in front of me to take this pain away.

"I'll make them suffer for everything they've ever done to you," he vows, affectionately rubbing my cheek without aggravating the scar.

"Then make it go away," I tell him confidently as his lips meet mine.

THIRTY-TWO

NEED

TATE

I'M FINALLY KISSING LILY, and it's under the worst possible fuckin' circumstance I can imagine.

Her lips feel soft and precious beneath mine. It's truly everything I could have ever imagined.

As much as I'm enjoying the kiss, along with the way she smells and the nearly desperate way her hands are clawing at my hair, I can't help but resent this moment.

Our first kiss wasn't because I finally told her how I felt or because I don't give a fuck anymore. It wasn't because she cornered me after a night of partying to tell me she doesn't care what my father thinks and that she'd risk it all to be with me.

No, it's a kiss forced out of desperate physical need that was ripped out of her by my enemy. It's a kiss I demanded of her because I'm not strong enough to sit on the other side of the door and let her suffer for something she didn't do. Something that I have my own guilt over, even though I didn't hold the gun or create the situation.

I haven't felt pain like this in a long fuckin' time, and I hate it. There's a deep fuckin' wound inside of me that's been festering for years, and this kiss rips it wide open. I'm not sure I'll survive the damage left behind.

Nothin' has ever felt this good while hurtin' so fuckin' much.

Lily wipes the tear that embarrassingly falls from my face, but she doesn't speak. I'm thankful she's the only one here to see this moment of weakness. I haven't cried since I was a child, and maybe it's because it's the last time I ever truly let myself feel something, but looking down at Lily, it's like I'm feeling every fuckin' emotion I've kept bottled up for nearly two decades. Her own tears long dried up as her basic Omega nature comes to the forefront. She's nearly panting with need and yet, she's still trying to comfort me.

I don't deserve her. I'm not fuckin' deluded enough to think that. But I've wanted her. Ever since that first night I came back to that godforsaken compound, my want for her has only grown.

I've been tip-toeing around this attraction and desire in an attempt to save her. I'm a fuckin' fool. My staying away has only caused her more pain. I should have known she needed more protection. I should have been the one protecting her from *him*.

I try to push away my thoughts of Leon and what I could have done for him too, because if I think too hard about it, I'll break down.

Lily can't have a weak Alpha right now. She needs me to be strong enough for the both of us.

"Alpha," she breathes, it's a mix between a plea and a beg.

"What do you need, darlin'?"

"You."

She's not gentle as she fists my hair and pulls my face back down to hers. I'm the only one in the house with her. Hell, I could very well be the only Alpha to service her heat if Cash doesn't reign in whatever fuckin' monster the Wraiths unleashed from within him.

My chest aches as images of the night flash behind my eyelids, but I have to shove it deep down. I have to push down this feeling of guilt, anger, and inferiority so I can be there for her.

I promised her retribution, and I meant every single fuckin' word of that vow. What I didn't get to promise her is everything else.

Everything I should have said before.

I should have told her that nothing between us was ever a mistake, that I want her, that I'll protect her.

She doesn't know how I feel as I cradle the back of her head and open my mouth to hers; she doesn't know that this moment means fuckin' everything to me, and I've never felt this way in my entire life.

I'm just a motherless boy raised by a man who loathed my existence, who was never meant to have big dreams.

And I truly didn't, I never had high expectations of myself or what my life would be, but as Lily's scent wraps around me and I swallow down all these dark emotions that I can't bear to face right now, the reality of everything hits me. She's the larger-than-life thing I could be a part of. The club can be my legacy. Once I burn it to the ashes, it can rise again like a phoenix.

I can become a better man because it's what Lily deserves. She loves the club, she never wanted to leave, and now I can make it a place worth living for.

"I'm goin' to take care of you," I promise her wholeheartedly. She hums at my words, either not understanding the depth, or not caring.

Thank fuck she gave me her consent before I touched her or I don't know what I'd do. I know I threatened her, and I meant it. Eventually, her heat would be so bad she'd be begging me for relief, but I didn't want my first time with her to be tainted with that memory.

At least I know she wants this. *She wants me.*

I hope she still does once she knows everything. If she doesn't, I'll understand and let her live her life. But I'll live the rest of my life knowing I lost the best thing that ever happened to me.

If this heat is all I get, I'm going to make it the best I can under the circumstances. The room isn't anything special, it's not the nest she deserves, but we'll make do with what we have.

My hand travels from her jaw over the tops of her breasts to her peaked nipples under the worn cotton shirt, and I graze my thumb over each bud. Her back arches, her body clearly over-sensitive with her heat starting and whatever accelerant those cunts gave her.

My anger must be written on my face as she uses her thumb to smooth out the wrinkle of skin on my forehead.

"Sorry, darlin'. Nothin' you did. You're perfect," I tell her, worried about how much of her rational mind is at the forefront and how anything I say or do could cause her distress.

She clearly likes my praise as she grabs my hand and slides it down the plaid boxers she's wearing. It's reminiscent of the night I stormed into her room to stop her from showing everyone online her sweet cunt… only this time, it's my fingers touching her.

I think I might pass out as she glides my fingers over the slick dripping down her pussy.

Her scent is so thick that my knot is already swelling inside of my pants, my body nearly commanding me to jump on top of her and rut the fuck out of her until she's round with my baby.

I hold my breath for a moment, trying to collect myself.

I don't know if she's on birth control or not. *Fuck.*

I'll need to have Axel pick up some morning-after pills or some shit, because there's no way we're getting through this heat without someone coming inside of her. I certainly don't have a condom on me or the self-control to look around this house for one.

"You need to be full, don't you, baby?" I ask her as I slide two fingers inside of her wet, warm center. We both moan as I move inside of her.

"It's goin' to feel so good with my cock deep inside of you."

"Yes," she agrees with a nod, her slick-covered hand going to the hem of her shirt to tug it over her head.

Her breasts are perky and round, just perfect, and I can't help but to lean down to take a nipple into my mouth, sucking as I continue to finger her. My hand is covered in wetness, and I find myself wanting to cover myself in it, soaking up her scent and marking me as hers.

It's like a compulsion: I can't stop, pulling my fingers out of her pussy causes her to whine as I suck my fingers in my mouth and trail them down my chin.

I need her scent on me, fuckin' everywhere.

An irritated noise leaves her, but as I rip off my shirt and wipe her slick over my skin, she preens.

Lily tugs her bottom lip into her mouth as she watches me. It's her first time seeing me shirtless, and I'm marking myself up with her scent. Her pupils blow wide with lust as I stand from the bed, taking the rest of my clothes off of me.

She takes the hint, rolling those hideous boxers off her perfectly toned thighs as I climb back on top of the covers.

I need more.

I need her scent embedded into my fuckin' pores so that when she decides she doesn't want me after this is over, I'll still carry a piece of her with me.

With serious effort, I don't instantly line my cock up with her entrance and rut her like every fiber of my being wants to. Instead, it's my well-muscled stomach that gets pressed against her center as I give her breasts more of my attention, allowing her slick to coat my abdomen.

She thrusts her hips against my skin, begging for more friction.

"Please," she whines. "It hurts."

The words break me. I never want to see Lily in pain, not for the rest of my life.

I slide down, parting her legs wider as I taste her completely. I'm fuckin' greedy with the way I drink her down, lavishing her clit with my tongue and sucking the small bundle of nerves with a vigor I can only describe as needy anguish.

She tastes like her coconut scent with a hint of musk, and I can't get enough. One of her hands tangles in my hair while the other covers her face. Her hips thrust against my mouth, and I double my efforts, needing her to come, needing her to finish in my mouth.

I'm like a starving man and she's my last sip of water. I need every single last drop of what she can give me.

My lips wrap around her clit again as my fingers curl inside of her, stroking the tender flesh inside of her pussy.

She breaks beautifully, pushing me against her core as she drenches my face, and I drink her down.

She could drown me and I'd fuckin' thank her.

Her thighs tremble, but a wretched whine rips through her. My tongue isn't enough. We both know that. Part of me feels guilty for not giving her what she wanted right away, but with me covered in her scent, I finally feel ready to give her anything she wants.

"You need my knot, sweet Omega?" I ask her. She truly is fuckin' sweet. Her taste, her beauty, her fuckin' soul… which will never be the same. I shove the dark thought away and refocus my attention on her.

She tugs me by the hair, and I smirk, wiping my chin on my forearm. She tracks the motion with satisfaction. There's no doubt she can still scent me, but I've been clearly marked as hers.

I'm so fuckin' hers. I can't believe I ever thought otherwise.

I slide a hand over her tender, wet pussy, and she pouts, thinking I'm not going to give her what she wants. I shake my head at her, covering my cock and knot in her slick, which pleases her.

My chest rumbles with a purr—every ounce of me craves her approval—and her scent thickens in the room.

I line the tip of my length with her entrance and slide all the way to the base of my knot. My body falls forward as I use my forearms to support my weight and cradle her head. While I badly wish that this moment was soft and delicate for our first time, our bodies have other plans. This is only proven as Lily bucks up from underneath me, forcing my knot inside of her.

We both moan at the sensation.

Her cunt grips me tightly, and I can't help but do what I wanted to in the first place; I rut her. My hips snap fast and hard, our flesh making a wet, slapping sound with each thrust of my hips.

"Fuck, you feel so fuckin' good," I tell her. She grabs my hair, forcing my mouth to her neck, where I kiss and suck the delicate flesh. I want to bite her so fuckin' bad.

I need it.

I try to pull away from her throat, but she's surprisingly strong, holding me there. My body nearly has a mind of its own as I fuck her relentlessly. She only lets me pull away to speak to her, so that's what I do.

"You love being so fuckin' full, don't you? God, I'm goin' to fill you up. Put my fuckin' baby inside of you and make you mine forever," I promise.

"Alpha," she whimpers, her cunt pulsatin' around my cock and knot as I fuck her.

"That's right, *I'm* your fuckin' Alpha."

Her slick drips down my thighs and her nails dig into my back as she reaches her peak. Her back arches as she grips my hair even harder, forcing my lips against the column of her throat.

My mouth widens, the tips of my teeth drag along her flesh

as the door squeaks open. Whoever dared to interrupt me and my Omega is going to fuckin' die.

I need to claim her, mark her as mine so no one else can take her; so no one else can hurt her.

God, she smells so fuckin' perfect with my scent all over her. My knot is nearly at the largest size, and I'm about to come when another hand grips my hair, pulling me away from her throat.

I come with a groan. "Fuck," I hiss as I buck into her pussy, fillin' her with my cum.

"What in the fuck do you think you were about to do?" I hear Axel's voice as I look down at Lily's perfectly unblemished throat. The asshole's hand is still gripping my hair like a fuckin' vice as I continue spilling inside of her.

My heart beats rapidly in my chest as my sanity comes back to me. My knot has us completely locked together as she pouts up at Axel. Her big brown eyes are fuckin' pissed, and I can't help the rumble of pride that she wanted my mark, or that she's mad at her *husband* for ruinin' our special moment.

THIRTY-THREE
MARKED

AXEL

I HOLD Tate's head back as Lily glares at me. Her pupils are so wide I'm not even sure where her irises start. It's hard to look at her like this when she isn't fully herself, especially after all the horrific shit that just happened.

"Don't give me that look. I'm not lettin' this happen until you're lucid."

"Go away," she groans at me, and I swear to fuckin' God my heart sinks.

"What?" I ask her.

"Let go of my fuckin' hair," Tate snarls.

I nearly forgot he was balls-deep in my wife for a second. I don't let go of his hair, and the fucker growls at me.

"Let me talk to her. You just stopped me from bondin' with her. I know it was the right thing to do, but she doesn't know that right now. It's not personal."

It sure felt fuckin personal.

It feels like Lily is mad at me for not being able to get my shit together and be the man she needed right away. I... I don't have an excuse for how I reacted. I just saw one of my oldest friends dead and my girl nearly comatose. I just needed a second to pull myself together.

"Let go," Tate repeats, and I release him with some force, making him groan. Lily's eyes meet his, and she cups his face.

It feels like a betrayal if I'm being honest, and I hate myself for thinking it. I knew all along she needed Alphas; I worried that it would be like this, that I would be at the bottom of the totem pole when it happened. It's like all my worst fears are coming to life as I watch all her attention focused on Tate.

"He's your husband, your pack," Tate states reassuringly, and I'm glad the fucker at least admits what I am to her.

Lily looks over me and her nostrils flare until her nose scrunches in disgust. I look down at myself; I am completely fuckin' filthy. Not to mention I've been helping to get the other Omegas out of that hellhole and to the warehouse.

"Go shower and change. I think she can smell the other Omegas on you or somethin'," Tate instructs me. When he says the words *other Omegas*, she tugs on his hair, and he groans again. "What the fuck is with grabbin' my hair?"

"She's a jealous one," I say with a sigh, I drop my bag on the floor and follow his directions to take a shower. Even if my ego is hurt, hopefully, he's right, and it's just my scent irritating her. I'm half-naked and on my way to the shower when Tate calls out behind me.

"Where's Cash?"

I sigh again as I grab onto the door handle and reply with the truth. "I don't know." He wasn't around when we were getting the Omegas to the warehouse. I texted him multiple times, but he hasn't responded. I sent him the address to the house; hopefully, he can pull his shit together enough to be here for Lily.

The shower feels nice as the hot water hits all of my tense muscles. I take a moment for myself while I'm in here. This is the last time I get to be sad for a while. I've got to hold it together for Lily.

I mourn my friend, who had drifted away from me, and

now I know why. My mind still can't grapple with the thought of him being a rat, but he sure as fuck had a Wraith's cut on.

He was Tate's inside man, and as much as I want to grill him about what he knows, now is not the time. Our priority has to be helping Lily through this, and then we'll deal with everything that comes after.

Just thinking about the after makes me sick to my stomach, and I have to swallow it down. My gold band glimmers around my ring finger, and I use it to center myself. Lily is the center of my world, she's all that matters right now.

I towel dry my hair and wipe down my body before wrapping it around my waist. My hand is on the knob, and I'm scared shitless she's going to tell me to go away when I go back into the bedroom. It wasn't the nest I wanted for her, but it'll have to do. After this, she can have whatever the fuck she wants.

Tate's left the room, leaving Lily resting on her side atop the mattress. She's a mess, and I think about cleaning her up but decide against it. I really don't want her glaring at me again. Instead, I crawl into the bed with her, feeling cautious and all sorts of fuckin' insecure. I *hate* it.

Tate has put a bandage on her face where they cut her, and I can't help but touch the skin next to the band-aid. Her eyes blink open, and I feel like they're staring at my fuckin' soul for a minute until she sighs in contentment.

"Thank fuck, you know who I am?" I urge her.

She doesn't give me any indication of what she's thinking. She just grabs my towel and opens it before climbing on top of me.

She's a goddamn mess, her slick and Tate's cum sticking to her thighs as she straddles me. But I knew this was part of it. When you marry an Omega, you do your fuckin' research.

I know she isn't going to be the same sweet Lily she usually is. I mean, she'll always be like that to me, but going into heat can change a lot about an Omega's personality. Her body is making all sorts of demands of her, and all she can do is follow her instincts.

Not that it's hard to give Lily everything she wants, it's just more crucial right now. So, if I find myself covered in Tate's jizz; it's something I just got to live with. In fact, I'll probably need to wrap my head around getting used to seeing a lot more parts of Tate than I ever imagined.

"What do you need, baby?" I ask her. She doesn't answer, just slides her wet pussy up and down my cock which is pressed against my stomach. "I'll seriously never get used to how fuckin' wet you get."

She hums but doesn't reply or stop moving all over me. It's only then I see it for the marking that it is. I belong to her, and she wants me to know it. I came in here smelling like a mix of scents she doesn't approve of, but now I'm only going to smell like her, and I guess like Tate.

I think back to all the videos I've watched. "That's right, this room smells like your pack, such a good Omega," I praise her.

She likes that, leaning down to finally kiss me.

I feel like I can fuckin' breathe again. I thought I lost her, thought it was all my fault, that I'd never get to hold her again.

Her hand presses down on my wounded arm, causing me to wince. She pulls away and assesses me. Realizing that I'm fine, she goes back to kissing me while avoiding my gunshot wound.

It's going to be an adjustment to her not speakin' so much, but I know this isn't forever. *It's temporary.*

I just need to be whatever she needs right now.

"I need to be inside of you. Show me how good you can be for me," I tease her between kisses like it's a challenge.

She leans forward enough so she can fist my cock, notching the head at her entrance before slowly sliding down my shaft. Lily presses her hands against my chest, making an effort to not touch my bandaged arm.

She's so wet that it's dripped all over my thighs and balls. With every bounce, there's a smacking noise from how tacky her thighs are with slick. The sound shouldn't be as fuckin' hot as it is. I grip her hips tightly as she uses me, taking what she needs from me. She can have every piece of me that's left to give.

Any piece of me that's good belongs to her.

A small whine leaves her, and I know she needs more. Her heat just started, and really the only thing that's going to get her there is a knot.

My backpack is too far away, and there's no way I can pull out of her right now. She'd probably have a complete meltdown, anyway. Instead, when she lifts, I grab the base of my cock, wrapping my fingers tight around my length and creating a knot with my fist.

She slides back down, pushing me deep inside of her with a satisfied moan. Her pussy grips around my fist, and I won't lie. It feels like she's crushing my goddamn hand, but it's worth it. She gasps at the coolness of my club rings inside of her, and it makes me shudder.

The sensations are nearly too much. With my hand wrapped so tightly around my cock, I'm about to explode, but I need to get her there first.

"You like my club rings inside of you? Don't you, my pretty wife? Make a mess all over them. Come on, baby, give it to me," I nearly beg her.

Her pouty lips part on a moan, and her pussy clenches around my fist and cock so tight I'm worried she might break me. But she doesn't as she shakes and pulsates on top of me. I finally give in, and cum inside of her. I'm grateful for the release, but when she continues riding me I think I might fuckin' die.

"Baby," I plead with her, but she doesn't stop. My toes curl and my back arches with over-sensitivity but she just keeps going. The noises she rips out of me are pathetic and needy as I think of a way to make her stop without causing a meltdown.

"Come here, let me clean you up," I somehow rasp out.

She mulls the thought over, her hooded eyes meeting mine. Whatever she sees there must bring her some reason as she lifts up off my fist and cock. I inhale and choke back the pain radiating throughout my fist as I stretch my fingers out before grabbing her hips and bringing her pussy to my mouth.

There's no time to care about tasting myself or how much slick covers my face. All I can think about is how desperately I need to make her feel good, how I need to take away every ounce of pain she's in.

One of her hands grabs the headboard while the other holds my still-damp hair while she rides my face, taking what she wants.

Lily isn't gentle or forgiving in the way she takes what she wants from me. Her hips glide back and forth over my mouth, placing my tongue in just the right spot. I do as I promise, cleaning her up and giving her everything she needs.

She puts some weight on my shoulder, but I push through it. I need to prove that I can be what she needs during her heat.

She's merciless as she grinds on my face until I'm hitting just the right spot, and she shatters on top of me. She just sits there for a moment, and I grab her hips, flipping her onto the bed next to me. She nuzzles up to my chest now that I smell like only her.

"You did so good, baby, such a good Omega," I praise her.

She hums as her eyes close. I don't need to imagine how tired she must be; I know because I feel the same way. The combination of no sleep the day before, along with everything that went down really wore us out.

As much as I want to stay awake and watch over her, I can't help but succumb to the sleep my body so desperately needs.

I'M NOT sure what time I wake up, but it's to Lily moaning in my ear as Tate fucks her from behind. Neither of them pays attention to me as I get up to go to the bathroom to take a piss. I'm groggy, hungry, and didn't get enough rest. And I know that I won't anytime soon.

I blink away the tiredness in my eyes and taking care of business when a dog bumps into my shin scaring the fuck out of me. It's only then I notice the shower running.

I pet the dog and glance over at the naked man in the shower, blood flowing down his skin into the drain. Someone was fuckin' busy.

"Hey," I say to Cash, and he nods his head in reply. I don't know when or how he got here, but I'm thankful. There's no way Tate and I could have gotten through this alone, and I know it would've broken Lily's heart if he didn't show up.

THIRTY-FOUR
GOOD OMEGA

LILY

THEY NEED *to understand who they belong to*, repeats in my head over and over as the sad Alpha grips my hips and fucks me from behind.

I need my Beta.

He's so sweet and precious. He belongs to me, and when I find those Omegas who scented him, I'll kill them.

The thought is dark, but I can't shake it.

There is a gaping void in the center of my chest. I need my quiet Alpha; the one who takes the best care of me.

Where is he?

Does he not want me anymore?

Have I upset him?

Am I too damaged for him now?

He promised me a bond mark, and I crave it. I'm doing everything I can to make the sad Alpha behind me give me what I want. And what I want is his teeth as deep inside of me while his knot is doing the same, marking me as his and taking what he wants.

No matter how much I beg and plead, he doesn't give me what I want.

I fucking hate it.

"It's okay. You're such a good Omega," he coos behind me. The words are a soothing balm over the rejection, but it's not enough.

Nothing less of a bond mark will do.

The shining ring on my finger glistens as I fist the sheets, and I smile, knowing my Beta gave this to me as his own way of claiming me. His teeth might not be able to mark me in the same way as an Alpha's can, but he's proven his loyalty.

My sad Alpha's knot is deep inside of me, and it feels perfect, but I want more. I want them all covering me in their scents and telling me how perfect I am and that without me, their lives mean nothing.

I greedily need to be at the center of their world.

Something dark and wrong pushes against my mind, but I shove it away. All I can care about is being with my pack, making them all claim me in an irrevocable, undeniable way that my body is demanding.

I want their scents, their cum, their love. I want everything.

A noise to the left of me breaks my daydream, and when I see my quiet Alpha, the last to join us, a part of me calms. A needy whine rips through me. I need him so badly.

Where has he been?

"I'm sorry, baby girl. I'm here now," he reassures softly, climbing onto the bed and sitting in front of me. His body is huge, and I love it. It's like he was built to protect me.

His beautifully dark skin is marred with new scars, and it makes me murderous.

Who dared to touch what belongs to me?

"It's okay. I'm okay. What do you need? I'll give you whatever you want."

I want to scream at him to bond me, but the words don't spill from my lips, just a desperate, needy moan does.

My pussy is filled with my sad Alpha's knot, but I need the one in front of me too. His cock is already hard and dripping from the tip.

I love that my scent alone can do that to him.

I greedily lap at the head. He tastes like *mine* as I swallow him down.

He doesn't smell like me enough, though.

And even though I love his vetiver and lavender scent... he needs to smell like me. There needs to be no doubt that he's taken, that all of them are mine, and they can't take them away from me.

Where is my Beta?

I need all of them.

They should be worshiping me, loving me, begging me to let them bond with me.

"What do you need, baby girl?" the quiet Alpha in front of me asks while he cradles my jaw with his large hand.

I need everything but I can't express it with words, just my body. My head bobs as I suck him down, tasting him. It's hard to focus with all the sensations, but I know I'm doing a good job.

The sad Alpha's knot is tight inside of me, and he groans with each one of my movements. I feel powerful having that effect on him.

I made him fold and give in to me. I never want to stop.

Both of my Alpha's hands are on me, making me feel light-headed with a sleepy sort of daze, but I can't stop. I need them to fill me up, and continue giving me what I need. They make the ache go away.

My Beta comes up next to me, rubbing my back, and I arch against his touch.

They're all touching me, and I feel like I'm in fucking heaven.

Now I just need someone to fucking bite me so I feel whole.

It's hard to focus, and my quiet Alpha takes pity on me, fucking into my mouth. He's usually so gentle, but right now I don't want gentle.

It's like no touch is enough.

I could crawl into their skin, and it wouldn't be enough.

My sad Alpha's knot releases me and then my quiet Alpha's length pops out of my mouth before I shift onto his lap, begging to be knotted again.

Will this ache ever go away?

He cradles my face as he fucks me, denying me his knot, and I'm so close to snapping, to demanding that they give me what I want.

"I'm sorry, Lily. I'm here now. I'm so, so sorry," he whispers. I don't know what he's talking about, but if he doesn't give me what I want soon, he will be sorry.

Luckily for the both of us, he does just that, giving me his knot and stretching me perfectly, causing the ache to pause for a small, precious moment.

My mind feels jumbled, but his arms wrap tightly around me, helping to center my thoughts.

My pussy grips him, holding him tight inside of me as I break and fall apart in his arms until glorious sleep takes me again.

THIRTY-FIVE

JEALOUSY
CASH

I'M STILL KNOTTED inside Lily. As soon as she came, she passed out in my arms. Fuck, it feels good having her back in my grasp.

"Where the fuck have you been?" Tate whisper-hisses.

He wouldn't get it, neither of them would. I know they care about Lily and her brother, but this felt like a repeat of my previous failures. Something I don't want to talk to them about. The only person I'll be delving into my sordid history with is her.

"I killed three more Wraiths, snuck into the compound, and brought back the van with all our shit in it, and the goddamn dog," I clarify, pointing my chin at the door where Winnie is crying. She wants in, but there's just no way I can have her sitting in the corner while we all fuck Lily's brains out.

"What's the situation at the warehouse?" Tate asks.

"Thirteen Omegas, not including the two from the raid and all the guys who went with us to get Lily," Axel chimes in. "It's pretty fuckin' crowded," he informs. I can tell he's stressed, and I feel guilty for leaving him to do that on his own, for leaving all of them to do what I had to do.

"Do we have a backup plan if anyone comes snoopin' around the warehouse?" Tate asks.

"Ink's old trailer, but that's gonna be an even tighter squeeze," Axel answers.

"I gave Maverick access to my cameras; he should know if anyone's coming," I tell them. I knew I couldn't just leave them without any protection. "If shit goes south, he'll take them to the trailer until it's safe again."

I should have done more, but I did the best I could with the memories present. When I saw Lily on the floor, next to her brother's dead body, I lost it. Well, I lost it before then but I feel in control now.

"You back to yourself?" Axel asks.

"Yeah, I'm good. I wouldn't miss this." I look over at Tate. Part of me trusts him. I have this whole time. But it's clear his secrets run deeper than I imagined. "We need to clear the fucking air. If we're going to be a pack, no more fucking lies."

Tate nods. There's guilt clearly written on his face.

"I know; no more lies. We need to get through her heat first. After that, all of us, all *four* of us, are goin' to sit down and figure this out. Was anything off at the compound?" he asks me.

"Not that I could tell. I still have the camera feeds active. We could use those to check in on things when all of us aren't there. You know Prez is going to suspect shit," I point out.

Tate shakes his head. "No, he's known well before then." He looks over to Axel. "Tell the guys to not let anyone else go to the compound. We'll bring them here if we have to as a last resort, but no one can go back to the compound, not till my dad is taken care of."

"What are you goin' to do?" Axel asks him.

"I'm goin' to kill my old man," he declares. Neither of us says anything after that. I hold Lily tighter in my arms, each of the other men touching her in some way too. "I'm going to run into town, get some more food, and probably pick up some Plan B or shit," Tate grumbles.

"You need to make sure none of her scent is on you if you're going out. Plus, she's on the pill. Just have the food delivered," Axel suggests.

"Can we trust someone to do that?" Tate asks. Axel rolls his eyes.

"I don't think the Instacart driver is going to know that we just uprooted our club, committed murder, and are hoarding our Omega here durin' her forced heat," he chastises Tate like he's fucking stupid. The Alpha must be exhausted because he doesn't clap back; instead, he just nods his head at Axel's idea. "I'll handle it, you go do a perimeter check," he directs Tate.

"And take the dog out too," I call out.

Tate throws his head back, groaning, but nods, knowing the Beta is right and that we need to keep up on security.

Lily was kidnapped, taken off our own fucking compound with little resistance, and who knows who the snakes are within the club itself?

I hold Lily in my arms, unable to sleep, but finding a small bit of comfort in the fact that she's safe and warm in my grasp.

Even when my knot goes down, I keep my cock inside of her warm pussy, not daring to move her even an inch. I need as much of her skin against mine as possible.

Eventually, she stirs on my lap, and my chest aches, knowing how fucking tired she must be. Her skin is feverish and sweaty as she looks up at me. Her pretty brown eyes are half-lidded as she touches my face, making sure I'm really here.

Her fingertips graze over my body, checking for new wounds. She merely grazes over the scars that have been there for over a decade. Her touch is soft and gentle, that is... until she gets to the female name buried in lotus flowers tattooed on the back of my forearm. She stares at it for a long minute, her eyes blinking rapidly.

"Lily, let me explain," I try to reason with her, but she's off my lap in a flash.

She paces the room completely naked, and I stand up to trail after her. I'm behind her, and I go to reach for her as she spins and pushes against my chest. She doesn't move me, which frustrates her even more, and she starts to smack at my chest.

When she doesn't get the reaction she wants, she opens the bedroom window, and I'm immediately terrified about what she might do next. Thankfully, she doesn't jump out or do something crazy, but she does start ripping the bedding off and tossing it outside.

"Lily, baby girl, give me a second and let me explain," I say calmly to her.

"No!" she shouts in my face, finally finding her words.

She grabs my boots off the floor and tosses them one by one out the window in an extremely dramatic fashion before doing the same to my clothes.

I'm out of my depths seeing her like this, and I'm surprised by the reaction. I've had the tattoo for years, but I guess she didn't see it the night we were together.

"Ugh!" she screams in frustration as she attempts to pick up the mattress topper.

It's too heavy and eventually, she gives up. Instead, she grabs the lamp on the bedside table, which actually has an audible crash when it meets the ground outside.

"What the fuck is going on in there?" Tate shouts from outside, doing his security rounds.

"Lily, it's not what you think. Can we talk?" I ask her again.

Exhaustion is thick in every fiber of my being, and I'm not sure how to reason with her. I'm sure it's a mix of jealousy, being overtired, and everything that's happened in the last few days. I can't bring myself to be demanding of her, though.

Axel storms into the room and looks around at the mess with wide eyes.

"The fuck happened here?"

I show him my arm and say, "She saw this and freaked out."

"Well, yeah. You're gonna have to burn it off or somethin'," Axel suggests, and I stare at him like he's an idiot.

"It's my sister's name, you fucking moron."

"Then tell her that," he argues, trying to approach Lily.

"I've been trying," I reply dramatically.

"Use your Alpha bark, you dumbass," he shouts back at me as Lily tosses one of his shoes out of the open window.

The idea of using it on her right now feels deplorable, but I can't have her thinking I've betrayed her or letting her continue to spiral like this.

"Come here now, Omega," I bark at her. She drops the cup of water she was about to throw and Axel curses at the mess. She obediently listens to the order, but I can tell she's pissed about it. When she's in front of me, I cup her face and look deep into her eyes. "It's my sister's name. It's a memorial tattoo. I wouldn't tattoo anyone else's name on my body besides yours," I promise her.

She looks down at my arm, still pouting.

"I can cover it up. Would that make things better?" I ask her. She bites her lip, and her gaze seems unsteady as she finally nods her head in agreement. "Okay, I'm going to cover this up. Axel, why don't you get her in the shower? I'll clean up this fucking mess," I tell him.

Lily looks pissed about the shower, but I'm too tired for this shit. So, I use my bark on her again. "Go shower with Axel, now," I command her.

She narrows her eyes at me but does as she's told.

Fuck, this is so much harder than I thought it would be.

I DON'T THINK anything could bring people closer together than the absolute debauchery that has happened in this small bedroom. After this is all over, we're building her the nest of her dreams, because these close quarters are bullshit.

Lily is extremely needy, which I didn't expect. She

demands all of us be present as much as possible. It's been nearly impossible for any of us to sleep, and I wonder how much more we can all take, but it doesn't stop it from feeling so fucking good.

I'm underneath her, rutting into her tight, needy pussy, while Axel fucks her ass. None of us even knows if she's done that before; I highly doubt she's had two at once. But she all but shoved him back there, demanding to be as full of her pack as possible.

Tate stands on the bed, feeding his cock down her throat, making our Omega hum with approval.

"Good, Omega. Look at you taking your pack. You're so full, aren't you, darlin'?" Tate encourages, and she mumbles around his cock.

Axel and I work in tandem, fucking in and out of her tight holes. No matter how fucking tired I might be, this is everything. I never thought I would be one to share, thinking I'd have to suck it up during a heat. But it's so hot watching her take all of us, and seeing how much she loves it.

She wants to be used by her pack; she wants us to make her feel good, and we do that by all taking her at once.

"Does that feel good, baby girl? God, your pussy is so tight," I groan, which is true normally, but the pressure of Axel's cock also inside of her makes it even more tantalizing.

I've been good. I haven't bonded with her, despite wanting to do so every fucking second since I've gotten here.

The vein over her throat pulsates as she takes the both of us —my resolve wanes. It's not going to last much longer.

Axel finishes first, and I can feel his cum leak out of her as it drips down to where she and I are connected. She clearly does too because she pops off of Tate's cock and turns around to take his mouth in hers, rewarding him for giving her what she wanted. I'm holding back. I know she needs my knot inside of her, but I can't help wanting her to myself.

"You love taking your pack at once, don't you?" Axel taunts.

She licks her lips as Tate fists his cock and pushes the head back into her parted lips.

"How'd we get so fuckin' lucky? Look how perfect you look wrapped around my cock," Tate praises, making her suck him down like her life depends on it.

His hips shudder as he comes down her throat. A small amount is left on the corner of her mouth, which he pushes in with his thumb before kissing her dutifully.

They both make sure to touch her and praise her before each of them takes a much-needed break to eat or clean themselves up.

That leaves us alone for the first time since her tantrum a few days ago.

"You need my knot, sweetheart, don't you?" I ask her.

She cups my jaw roughly, bending forward. I place my lips on her neck, kissing her soft skin, knowing I'm not leaving this fucking bed without leaving my mark on her this time.

"Such a needy, wet, Omega. And all for me? I'm going to give you what you want. I'll always give you what you want."

I need to be connected with her in a way that no one can take from us; I need to know that she's safe or how she's feeling at all times.

"You remember what I promised you? You still want my mark?" I ask her.

She moans, and a shiver rolls up my spine as she responds with a raspy, "Yes!"

She's been nearly non-verbal her entire heat. But right now, we both know what we want.

"You're going to be so good for me, taking my knot and my mark, aren't you?" I ask against her neck, breathing in her sweet scent.

I need this more than I need to breathe, and I push inside of her, my knot stretching her cunt as she takes me. She moans into my ear as I settle into her and rut into her from below. The anticipation is what sends us both over the edge as my knot reaches its largest size and her pussy milks me through her orgasm.

My mouth parts, taking her flesh into my mouth as I bite down, marking her as mine.

She screams in pleasure as I bond us. Lily's fingers dig into the back of my head, firmly holding my mouth to her throat.

The combination of our release and the bond mark connecting us is monumental, in a way I can't even describe. It's like nothing in my life ever meant as much as this moment does.

I can feel her love, contentment, and relief flow down through the bond connection.

She needed this just as badly as I did. I wrap my arms around her back, holding her warm body against mine.

"So good. You feel how much I love you through the bond?" I question, not caring if it's the first time I've said those words to her or the fact that it's the first time I said them to someone who wasn't my family. Lily already knows, she feels it. "You're so perfect, thank you."

She nuzzles her face against my neck, scent marking me and herself, making me feel whole.

Lily has single-handedly pieced me back together into the man I knew I could be.

THIRTY-SIX
LUCID

LILY

THE BOND SINKS deep within me, and I feel a huge weight fall off my shoulders. I'm not completely back to myself.

I still have this burning need for more.

This sense of newly found security helps tone down this errant need that never seems completely satisfied.

My quiet Alpha's scent is thick and fresh all around me, and I can *feel* him. His protectiveness and eagerness to please me flow through our newly created connection. He kisses the bite mark along my neck, and I shiver.

Reality is slowly coming back to me, as tears well in my eyes. I'm not ready to have these horrible feelings slam back into me. It's easier to let my instincts guide me.

I want to stay in heat forever. I'd just live in this bed and never leave, never have to feel real-life problems.

He cups my cheeks, encouraging me to look into his deep brown eyes.

He's so perfect and big, ready to protect me. He's also just so fucking handsome, with his beautiful dark skin and the black and gray tattoos that cover it. When that thought flits across my mind, I look down at his forearm which is covered with a bandaid.

Good.

I'll need to mark him with my name next.

"Hey, sweetheart. You with me?" he asks, and I shake my head in disagreement.

I don't want to go back to the world fucking me at every turn. I just want to stay cocooned in this bed and to be continuously cherished by these men. It's easier this way.

"Take your time. We're not going anywhere," he promises.

His knot is still locked deep inside of me, and I shift on his lap, making him groan. The door to my left clicking open catches my attention, where my sad Alpha and Beta walk in.

The sad Alpha's mouth drops, and he points at us. "I know he doesn't have any hair to grab, but are you going to yell at him too?" he asks my Beta.

"No, they talked about this beforehand. You did not," my Beta chastises him plainly.

I'm still pissed that he stopped me from bonding with my sad Alpha, so I just narrow my eyes at him.

"Oh, don't give me that shit. Once you're back to you, you'll be thanking me."

I don't know about that. I also don't want to go back to being *me*.

Being me means facing everything that's happened. Being me means I don't have a home to go back to. Being me means Leon isn't here anymore.

The thought is like a cold slap to the face from reality, and my mind is no longer foggy with want. I'm me again, sadly.

Cash wipes the tears from my face as the satisfaction from the obscene amount of fucking and my newly formed bond ebbs away from me.

"I've got you, let it out, baby girl," Cash reassures, and I do.

It's embarrassing, me falling apart with his knot still inside of me. Axel and Tate stare at us from the doorway as I completely crumble against Cash's shoulder. Every part of my body hurts, and I'm so fucking tired I'm not sure how I'm still able to think.

"It all really happened, didn't it?" I ask between sobs.

Cash's sadness for me flows between us, and I can just sense how much he wishes he could make this all go away. I wish I could too.

"It did," Cash confirms, allowing me to just cry in his arms.

Axel and Tate grab a clean blanket and wrap it around my shoulders as each of them places a hand somewhere on my body. I feel selfish, making this all about me. Axel lost a friend, and Tate lost a stepbrother. I'm not the only one who is experiencing loss, not by a long shot.

"Is Shelby okay?" I ask.

"Doc is takin' care of her," Tate tells me while he kneads the back of my neck.

"And all the other Omegas?"

"They're safe. We didn't... we didn't lose anyone else," Axel confesses.

I'm grateful he doesn't say my brother's name. I'm not sure I'm ready to hear it yet. I'm sure as hell not ready to talk about what our plan is, or what exactly went down a few days ago.

"It's late. Why don't you get some sleep and we can all talk in the mornin'? Do you want anything to eat first?" Tate asks.

At that exact moment my stomach chooses to growl so loud that it echoes throughout the room. It would be comical if I weren't so upset.

"Thank God, you've hardly eaten," Axel comments.

He gets up, kissing my hair before going to the kitchen while I sit here with my two Alphas. Well, my Alpha and my stepbrother. I still don't know where Tate and I stand.

He obviously cares for me, being there for me throughout my heat, and I consider him mine. But I don't know what his true intentions are; I just remember him promising me vengeance, there wasn't time to discuss anything else.

Sure, maybe he tried to bond with me, but that has more to

do with his Alpha nature demanding it versus him truly wanting it.

Now's not the time to try and figure it out either.

There's already a deep-seeded guilt filling my stomach over bonding with Cash. *Why should I be able to bond with someone when Leon never got the chance?*

"Hey, no thinking like that. We're bonded, you married Axel, those are permanent things. I won't let you feel guilty over that shit for even a second, you understand me?" Cash reprimands gently.

Easier said than done. I don't reply, because I don't want to be a liar.

Axel comes in, just as Cash's knot deflates, releasing me. The amount of fluids that flow from me is mortifying, and I quickly wrap myself in the blanket, sitting on the edge of the bed. I feel lightheaded. If someone poked me, I might just fall over completely.

Axel holds a bowl of just some simple broth, bringing the spoon up to my mouth. I know I should feed myself, but I genuinely feel too weak to do so. So I let him care for me. My stomach clenches as I take small sips. Each one of them seems more than relieved over the fact that I'm eating, and it makes me wonder how much trouble I gave them during my heat.

Ugh, my first heat.

It's not like I was expecting to remember much, but everything feels fuzzy. Maybe it's better that I don't remember, if I'm being honest.

My eyes are practically closing on their own accord as I finish up the bowl of soup. Axel places the bowl on the side table and picks me up bridal style. Tate takes off the sheets and replaces them with fresh ones while Cash grabs a warm washcloth.

I know what we just did was beyond intimate, but when Tate places me on the bed and Cash cleans me reverently with a washcloth... it somehow feels even more so. There's no time to feel embarrassed, at least, not anymore. Cash wraps me up, getting ready to lie in bed with him, and I soak in his warmth, even though a part of me misses the messy sheets.

Axel comes to lie on the other side of me as I watch Tate walk out the door, and I wish I had the courage to ask him to stay.

MY HEAD IS THROBBING, and I have to wipe drool off of my cheek when I finally wake up. I have no concept of what day or time it is. All I know is I'm completely alone. There are noises outside of the door, letting me know the guys are still in the house, so I relax a little.

Part of me doesn't want to get out of this bed. This defiled bed could suck me up whole and I think I might be okay with it.

Getting out of this bed means going back to real life. But before I can do that I need to find my fight. I need to pull myself together so that I can be useful, and help take down the people who put Leon in this position. The horrible men that hurt me, Shelby, and all of those other Omegas need to pay.

I know Leon's killer is dead; I helped make sure of that. But every single man with a scythe tattoo needs to suffer.

There's so much I don't know; so much shit that must have been going down while I was in heat. My nosy nature and need for vengeance is what has me crawling out of the bed, heading for the shower.

From my head to my calves, my body aches. It's a mixture of the rough treatment from the Wraiths and the adoring treatment from my pack... well, that's mostly accurate. Axel and Cash for sure are pack... Tate is still in the air.

I'm too weak to stand and shower, so I just grab my prod-ucts and sit on the floor as I wash myself. It's clear I didn't shower much during my heat. It makes me cringe, especially when I wash my hair and have to detangle some caked-together strands.

How attractive.

My skin prunes as I sit there, not wanting to leave the warm oasis that is this shower. My eyes are closed, just letting the water hit me when a deep voice startles me.

"You done, darlin'?" Axel questions.

His arms are pressed against the vanity as he stands there, fully dressed in a white shirt, his cut, and dark pants. I sigh, looking at his fingers. He still wears his dead palms rings, but his new wedding band is truly what sticks out.

I've got to hold it together, if not for myself, then for him—for them. They can't focus if they're worried about me having a complete fucking meltdown.

I'll have a breakdown when it's appropriate, I decide.

"Yeah, I'm done."

He reaches into the shower, turning off the water before grabbing a towel and holding it out for me. It smells like Tate; I'm guessing not much laundry had gotten done during my heat, and I don't hate it.

I was in the hot shower for too long and now my vision is slightly hazy. Axel takes mercy on me by picking me up and placing me on the vanity.

He uses another towel to dry my hair before using a brush to get out the last few knots. I'm shocked when he tugs a pair of my own panties and shorts up my legs.

"Where did you get these?"

"Cash brought the van with our shit here," he answers.

"Oh, he's been back to the compound? Did he bring Winnie?"

Axel sighs and nods his head. "Just that first night, your stuff and the dog are here. A lot of shit's been happenin'."

"What's been going on? Is everyone okay?"

"Let's get you dressed and then talk about it with the others."

"My mom… does my mom know?" I choke down a sob.

Have your breakdown when it's more convenient, I remind myself.

"I'm not sure. I know she's safe, though."

I appreciate his honesty, and that he isn't sugarcoating things for me. He pulls a t-shirt over my head, and I poke my arms through it.

"Let's go to the kitchen, you need to eat and drink more."

I nod, and Axel holds out his arm. I use him for support as we head to the kitchen. Tate is making something on the stove, while Cash is completely immersed in his laptop. Winnie is happily perched on his lap, and as much as I want to shower her with love, I don't have the energy.

I sit down across from him, and Axel immediately puts a Gatorade in front of me. I nearly down the whole bottle in one go, and he places a glass of water next to it. I'm not going to be the one to start the conversation because I know the least of what's going on. So I just sit there as Tate puts a pile of pancakes and bacon in front of me.

Each bite seems to make me feel stronger and more aware. No one speaks until I'm finished, pushing my plate away from me, not able to take another bite.

Three pairs of eyes stare at me, and I wonder who is going to start speaking first. It's Tate who shocks me.

He runs his hands through his hair before placing his elbows on the table and grabbing his head.

"I'm not really sure where to fuckin' start, if I'm being honest, and we really don't have time to get into every detail," he begins, his voice soft.

"We need to know how much you *want* to know, Lily? Do you want us to take care of this? To keep you out of it and just assure you everything is going to be fine, or do you want to be all in with this? Before you make your decision you need to know it's probably worse than you imagined," Cash calmly asks me. He's seen me panic about club business before, but he also knows I can pull my shit together.

"I think we're past keeping me in the dark. I'm all in," I inform them.

My leg shakes under the table as I wait for them to tell me everything I need to know, and it's far more sinister than I ever could have imagined.

THIRTY-SEVEN

HARD TRUTHS

TATE

I WANNA SPILL my guts to her, to tell her everything, almost as much as I want to keep these dark secrets tucked away forever.

I'm about to open my mouth, ready to give her the Cliffs-Notes version of the whole sordid story, but then Axel's phone rings.

When he picks it up, I know it has to be one of the guys at the warehouse.

"Hello?" Axel answers. He just listens for a few minutes, rubbing his forehead like it will somehow help him think faster. "Fuck. Talk to Tate," he barks, handing me the phone.

"Shit, they're packing up to leave," Cash states, looking over at the monitor where I see my father, Smiley, Davidson, Pipes, and Boomerang getting on their bikes to leave. I'm shocked that Dread isn't with them.

I draw my attention back to the phone as Mickey frantically talks over the line. "Blaze called me. Prez said he was doing a run to the warehouse. What do we do?" he asks me. We moved them from the warehouse to Ink's old trailer, but when shit got too crowded and the warehouse had been searched by my dad, they brought them back to the warehouse.

I feel guilty that I've been giving orders over the phone to the guys while my place was here with Lily. But now, it's time to step up. These are the moments I need to not only prove myself to the club, but to Lily and her chosen pack as well.

"Is it possible to get everyone out in one sweep?" I ask Mickey.

"Yeah, we have the one van and we can toss some of the Omegas who are in better shape on the back of bikes, but where the fuck do we go? We can't go back to that fuckin' trailer again," he argues, and I get it. That's a lot of people to fit into a small area, and who knows if someone we can't trust knows about the location.

I look over at Axel, knowing that this place has meaning to him, but we're fuckin' desperate. He gives me a firm head nod, and I take it for what it is.

"I'll send you the address. It'll do for now."

"I don't like it, Tate. We've listened and stuck it out here like you said, but we're ready to go home. Are you really ready to give us the whole fuckin' truth or what?"

"Just get to the lake house and I'll tell you everything. Don't let my father see you on the road. Do you understand?"

"He's the Prez, man," Mickey refutes.

I know Mickey is feeling lost. Everyone in the club knew he had an on-again-off-again thing with Leon, but I can't let him fuck this up. Everyone at the warehouse knew we had a rat at the club, someone had to of let the Wraiths in to take Lily and Shelby. Maybe it's the only reason they've done a good job of keeping their mouths shut, but they're getting restless. I need to make sure that they don't slip up and put themselves and those Omegas in danger.

"He's also the same man who allowed Lily and Shelby to be taken from the compound. Get your asses out of the warehouse now. Do you understand?" I order Mickey, but the whole time I talk to him over the phone, I'm staring at Lily across the table.

I watch her eyes water as the bomb I just dropped lands on her.

"There's no way," Mickey tries to argue over the phone.

"Get to the lake house and I'll explain everything. Don't let them see you," I tell him again before hanging up the phone.

Lily crosses her arms and stares at me, her mind reeling over the information, and I just wait for her to speak.

"Kurt... Kurt, let them into the compound?" she whispers.

"He's the whole reason all those Omegas were held captive, why all the other Dead Palms chapters have failed, and why your brother was wearin' a fuckin' Wraiths cut," I inform her, trying like hell to keep my voice even.

"But he loves the Dead Palms... he wouldn't do this to me... to my mom," she tries to reason.

I rub at my worn knuckles as I watch her rub the bond mark against her neck, clearly finding some comfort there. There's a feeling of jealousy and regret that crashes into me as I watch her. My mark should be on her too, but I know I haven't earned it.

"How do you know?" she questions me.

"Mostly Leon, but I've been piecing shit together," I confess, knowing the only way to work through this with her is by being completely honest.

Lily swallows, and it's almost like I can see the wheels turning as she looks around.

"Leon had been drinking a lot. He wouldn't tell me much. Why would he tell *you* anything?"

"He didn't mean to, if I'm being honest. As soon as I came back to Tallahassee, somethin' didn't sit right. I knew that my dad wasn't a good man. Hell, I guess none of us are, but I never expected it to go this deep."

"I don't understand..." Lily holds herself tightly, trying to make sense of the small pieces of information I've given her.

Cash looks over at me, giving me a look that says I need to spit it all... now. I groan, but she needs to know specifics, just as much as I know the club will need proof. Little do they know my proof is sitting inside that warehouse with them right now.

"Fuck, I really don't know where to start," I grumble.

Lily blinks at me and looks down at her nails. "Kurt didn't rescue us from the Wraiths did he?" she asks, her voice sounding so timid it cracks my heart in two.

"No, they took you. I'm not sure how many Wraiths my dad and the old crew took out back then, but they took out their entire club structure, which included your mom's pack. Don't get me wrong, I'm sure my father was the lesser of two evils in that situation, but it wasn't a rescue. It was him takin' what he wanted."

Lily wipes a tear off her face and nods for me to continue.

"My mom had died a few years before that, and they really wanted another Omega. Your mom's scent called to them, not to mention she looks a hell of a lot like my mother, and you and Leon… I think y'all represented startin' over for my dad. I really can't be sure, to be honest. But when they overthrew the Wraiths' Prez and top dogs, they decided to take your mother and you two with them."

"He always treated me like a daughter, though," she tries to reason, and I nod at her.

"He doesn't like people he can't control, and I think that's why when you defied him about findin' the pack of your choice it pissed him off. Or maybe he truly thinks you and Teresa are more important than these other Omegas he's treatin' like animals. I don't know if he has the capability to really love anyone."

"My mom?" she asks.

"I don't know, darlin'," I answer her honestly, and she looks away for a second.

"You really think I made him mad enough to sell me to the Wraiths?" she chokes on the words.

I groan, looking over at Axel, who throws an arm over her shoulder and helps me explain.

"Darlin', Kurt didn't sell you to the Wraiths. He *is* the Wraiths."

"What?" she gasps, spinnin' to face Axel.

"I didn't want to believe it either, but… fuck. Just show her," Axel says, lookin' at me.

I sigh, and pull out my phone, clicking play on the voicemail I have saved. I put it on speaker and as soon as Leon's voice plays, tears fall down Lily's face.

He's clearly drunk as his voice comes over the phone. This was well after he told me everything, it's the night my dad had him patch into the Wraiths.

"I can't do this anymore, Tate. I can't do this to the guys at the compound. I didn't want *this*. I didn't fuckin' *want* this, man. You've got to watch your back. He's goin' to take out whoever isn't loyal one by one. The ones he trusts he's planning on bringin' over to the Wraiths. You've got to promise me you'll get Lily out of there. I didn't have any other choice. I've got to keep Shelby safe now. He said if I did what he wanted, he'd let me bring her with me. It's fuckin' bad here man, I don't know what to do." The voicemail cuts off, and Lily replays it three more times.

"But why? Why would Kurt do this? Why would he be playing both clubs?"

"He's only playin' one club, darlin'," I reiterate, and she blinks at me.

"The Wraiths know he's the Prez of the Dead Palms?"

"More than fuckin' know it. I always thought the ceasefire between the clubs made no fuckin' sense, but I was too young to understand, and then, as soon as I could, I left Tallahassee. I put this place so fuckin' far behind me I just never thought about it till I came back," I admit to her.

"Then slowly, each chapter kept getting busted, or blown to pieces," Cash interjects.

"But *why*?" Lily asks, still trying to wrap her mind around the man who raised her like his own, being an absolute piece of shit.

"Money," Axel replies. "The amount of money he gets traffickin' Omegas and doin' the deals the Dead Palms aren't willin' to do is obscene."

"He did all of this for money?" she asks sounding exhausted.

"It's a big part of it, but truly I think it's because of the power. He wants control over everything and everybody. I'm not sure he even knows when enough is enough," I explain.

"Kurt is why my brother is dead? He's the reason Shelby was beat to shit. Why I started my heat early?"

Sadness is written all over her face, and the look she's giving me right now is going to haunt me forever.

"I'm not sure how much he orchestrated or how much was his guys not following orders. But I think he did it to keep Leon in line, and possibly hurt the both of us after that night he thought we were together," I admit softly.

Guilt is one deep-cuttin' motherfucker.

"You still plan to keep the promise you made me before I started my heat?" she asks, a blush creeping over her face when she mentions her heat.

Her warm brown eyes are filled with tears, but there's determination behind them too. She won't just let him get away with this.

"You know what you're askin'?" I want to confirm.

"Just… just don't hurt my mom," she pleads.

"We don't know what she knows, but we never would have hurt her."

"There's no way she could have known about Leon or Kurt taking me, there's no way," she argues adamantly, and I believe her.

I hope for all our sakes that's the truth. Teresa knowing about all of this shit might just be the thing that breaks Lily completely.

"For the record, we think your mom is innocent. My dad offered her a better life, and she took it. She's never been one to question much," I point out.

"So what's next?"

"We kill my father and take the club back," I declare.

She doesn't break, just nods her head. I know horrible things are on the horizon. Although I can't help but feeling just a sliver of hope that we might all make it through this.

THIRTY-EIGHT

CALM BEFORE THE STORM

THE LAKE HOUSE quickly becomes crowded with Omegas I've never met before and members of the Dead Palms who look completely defeated.

I don't really like that all of these Omega scents are coating the inside of this house, but I'm shoving that feeling down.

Now is not the time to start throwing shit out of a window and having a fit. I cringe when that pleasant little flashback hits me. But I still have the mental reminder to figure out whose fucking name is branded on my bond.

I shake my head as Mickey walks in. He looks like complete shit.

He's big, nearly as big as Cash, but he doesn't hold the same overwhelming Alpha presence he usually does. His beard looks worse for wear and there are deep purple bags under his brown eyes.

I don't think as I approach him and wrap my arms around him. He stiffens but eventually returns the hug.

"I'm so sorry, Mick," I sigh softly.

"I am too," he replies sadly.

Picturing him and my brother together didn't make much sense. Two big-ass dudes with larger-than-life personalities. But as I pull away from the hug and look into Mickey's watery eyes, I see it. He really loved Leon, even if my brother didn't completely feel the same way.

"You holdin' up okay?" he asks as I pull away, wrapping my arms around myself.

I shrug, asking, "You?"

"I'm glad I've had somethin' to keep me busy," he answers while looking around the house.

Clearly, some of the Omegas are still frightened, but no doubt more so about the Wraiths coming back to get them instead of their current situation.

"Thanks for helping them get out."

"It was the right thing to do."

"Do you know where Shelby is?" I ask him.

"Fuck if I know," he replies, all the softness leaving his face as he walks away from me.

I exhale and chastise myself. Clearly, there's a sore spot there, and I make a mental note not to bring it up again.

I feel Cash through the bond before I feel him wrapping his arms around me. "We're having a club meeting and making some plans. We'll be back in a bit," he states.

There's an annoying prickle in my stomach that doesn't like the idea of them being away from me, but I nod regardless.

"We won't be long," he repeats, nodding towards the kitchen window. "Shelby's out on the dock."

"I'm going to go check on her."

"Stay close, understand?" is his response.

I nod, and Cash kisses the side of my head before he leaves towards the front yard with the rest of the club. The Omegas in the room seem to calm down as soon as they all leave, and I guess I don't blame them.

While I know for certain none of those men would hurt an Omega, they all just left a horrific situation. It's hard to differentiate who are the bad guys and who are the good guys. I mean, I knew the club wasn't wholly good, but fuck, I never thought things would be this bad. I'm still trying to wrap my mind around the fact I lived under the same roof as a monster. I'm not sure that guilt will ever go away. Especially as I look at all the devastated faces around me. He put these Omegas through hell.

There's one Omega who looks completely unphased, however. The only male Omega in the group. He stands in the corner with his arms crossed as he seems to watch over the women. He looks over at me, but nothing on his face reads as hostile; it's like he is keeping a mental note of everyone who comes and goes from the house.

I break his stare as I open the back door and head down to the dock. The warm outdoor air is welcoming compared to the overwhelming scents from inside the lake house.

Shelby is sitting with her back to me as her feet dangle over the side. I hope she doesn't hate me or tell me to fuck off as soon as she sees it's me.

I take a deep breath, sliding off my shoes, and sitting down right beside her.

She doesn't look over at me, and my stomach pinches.

"I can't look at you right now," she says softly.

"Shelby… I'm so fucking sorry," I reply, and try to hold back tears.

Her uninjured arm reaches out as she places a hand on my thigh. Her other one is tied up into a sling, and her poor face is still covered in yellowing and purple bruises.

"I'm not mad at you. It's just if I look at you I'll see *him*, and I can't handle that right now," she admits.

I swallow, and I can understand what she's trying to get across. Leon and I looked so much alike, and I'm just a reminder of everything that's happened. I wonder if she'll ever be able to look at me.

"You know about what Kurt made him do?" I ask her, wondering what she's been told.

"Doc told me," she replies with a sigh. "I knew something was off. I knew he was gone too much. I knew he was drinking way more than he should. But it just felt like when we were together I could make his worries disappear, so I never pushed him. I just wanted to be the person who could bring him peace."

"This isn't on you."

"It's not on you either," she shoots back, still not looking at me.

"It feels like it is."

Shelby turns her head and stares at me, her sad blue eyes meeting mine. She doesn't cry, but it looks like she wants to.

"It's not your fucking fault, and he would be so angry hearing you say that. *You* didn't kidnap all those Omegas inside. *You* didn't make him join the Wraiths. *You* didn't take us away from our home. *You* didn't break my arm. And *you* sure as fuck didn't kickstart your heat during the worst moment of your life. So *you* will not hold the weight of a horrible man's decisions on your shoulders, do you understand me?"

I swallow thickly, holding back my own tears.

"I understand."

She whips her head back toward the lake, no longer able to look at me as she sighs.

"They won't let me help," she scoffs.

"What? The club?" I ask, wondering why she would ever think they'd let her.

I might be bonded to Cash, married to Axel, and brought into the fold of some club business, but I'm not a true member... and I never will be.

"Yeah, I want to gut that motherfucker and his disgusting club," she seethes.

I don't bring up that she has a broken arm, a swollen-to-hell face, and that she wouldn't be able to do much.

"I think all you can do is keep yourself safe and try to move on," I tell her, trying to take my own advice.

"It just doesn't feel like enough. I feel like I should be doing more."

"I know," I reply, resting my head on her shoulder. I let out a sigh of relief when her head rests against my own.

Shelby doesn't hold me responsible for what happened, so I shouldn't either. But that's always easier said than done.

We sit in silence, watching the lake ripple softly. Right now, there's nothing else to be said between us. We both have a tremendous amount of healing to do, but I don't think either of us can do that until the Wraiths are completely destroyed.

"I DON'T LIKE THIS," I tell Axel as he holds my face, explaining bits and pieces of the plan to me.

"I know. I don't either, but this is our chance," he urges me to understand.

"You stay here with the others; Ink is going to stay behind too," Cash states, and I look over to Ink, who has his leg propped up.

"I'll make sure your mom is safe," Tate promises.

"What about Dread?" I ask, my heart aching for my mother.

Not only did she lose a son, but she's about to find out what a lowlife, piece-of-shit Alpha she's been living with for a decade.

Tate looks at me softly, his hand gently gripping my chin, tilting my face to look up at him. "I can't make any promises when it comes to him. Anyone who has defected against the Palms has to go."

I swallow and nod.

"Stay safe, and we'll be back soon," Tate promises.

He shocks me by leaning forward and placing a chaste kiss against my lips. He doesn't say anything else as he glances at me one last time before leaving the house.

Axel and Cash take their time touching me and reassuring me that they will come back. I can feel the eyes of all the other

Omegas on me as they shower me with affection, and I feel more than uncomfortable.

Mickey, Doc, Atlas, and Maverick all leave with my guys, and a sense of terror fills me. What they're about to do, there's a chance that one of them won't come back.

Shelby still hasn't entered the house, so I go to sit next to Ink.

He's one of the quieter members of the club, but he's always been kind to me. There's a small blonde Omega sitting next to him. They aren't touching, but I swear she's sitting next to him for comfort.

"I'm sorry about Ambien," he says.

It feels weird hearing my brother's road name, but it actually brings a small smile to my face, thinking about it.

"I'm sorry you got shot trying to get us out," I respond.

"Oh, this little thing. It's no big deal," he says, pointing to the lower part of his leg that is wrapped up.

The Omega next to him makes a sound of distress, and Ink looks over at her. I'm not sure what look he's conveying, but she turns away and starts quietly speaking to the male Omega I noticed earlier.

"What's going to happen to all of them?" I ask Ink, looking around the room.

"More than half have homes to go back to," he replies.

"The other half?"

"Guess it all depends on how tonight goes," he sighs solemnly.

My stomach drops just thinking about what my pack is going to do in order to keep me safe and to restore the club I thought I loved so much.

It's hard to grasp the lies I grew up on. How can the man who paid for my ballet lessons and bought me the supplies for my soap shop be the same one who has been kidnapping and selling Omegas? The same man who reverently kisses the burn marks on my mother's face? Who brought me heating pads and medicine during my period?

It's almost like Kurt is a coin, two sides that are completely different but somehow are one and the same. There's always been an edge of danger around him, but I would have never expected this.

He was not only flipping members of the Dead Palms that he trusted over to the Wraiths, but he was simultaneously taking out anyone he saw as a threat.

His selfishness destroyed all those other chapters, and it's why he wanted Tate gone so badly.

There was no way Tate would have ever gone along with joining the Wraiths. I thought I could've said the same about Leon, but he thought of Kurt as a father just as much as I did.

He didn't have a choice.

At least, that's what I keep reasoning with myself. Leon was scared and couldn't figure a way out, so he gave in to what Kurt wanted. He trusted the man who took us in, loved our mother, and gave us a life worth living.

I don't know what his plans were with me. Was he just trying to scare me and Leon into submission? Or was he genuinely going to sell me?

The words from that second horrible date ring through my head. It feels like a lifetime ago, but I clearly remember the guy saying I wasn't worth the price Kurt was asking for.

I think Tate was right, Kurt doesn't truly love anyone.

My hand touches the cut on my face, and I scoff at myself. I fought so fucking hard not to end up like my mother did with the Wraiths; I was coddled into a false sense of security under his roof.

But as I soak in the feeling of my bond with Cash and look down at my wedding ring, I know that I didn't choose incorrectly. I might have a scar to remind me of the devastation I went through, but I chose right.

As much as I love my mother, I'll never be like her.

The pack I chose is not only committed but their devotion and moral compass are things I can live with.

I just hope to God that they all come back safe and sound and that I actually get a chance to live the life I always dreamed of… with them.

THIRTY-NINE

THE PLAN

AXEL

THE PLAN IS loose as shit, and I hate it. All we truly needed to get the guys to open their eyes was Leon's voicemail, the paper trail from the fallout of the other chapters, and the confirmation from a few of the Omegas after showing them the Prez's picture, whom they immediately recognized.

It disgusted everyone that the man we followed could do this. If he could hurt his own children, his own chapters, what's to say he wouldn't hurt them?

Everyone is ready for battle, especially Cash. The look on his face is menacing and I understand why he didn't tell Lily everything he did that night we got her back. We left that little tidbit out when we spoke to Lily on Cash's request. Considering what he did to those poor motherfuckers, it makes sense. There's a side of himself that he wants to protect Lily from, and I respect that. She can keep thinking he's the sweet, quiet one, even if he is the most demented of the three of us.

We're bonded by our club and the need to protect it. Even if it means protecting it from the man who gave it to us in the first place, gave us somewhere to belong. No one fuckin' hurts my girl and gets away with it. It's probably fucked up that it's my main motivator, but I don't give a shit.

I hate that we're leaving Lily behind, that the odds are against us, and that we even have to do this shit.

But it has to be done.

Not only to give Lily peace but for all of us. This club has been our home and salvation for most of our adult lives, and we've all just found out that it's built on a fuckin' lie.

Part of me thinks Kurt liked the feeling he got from being in charge of both clubs. With the Wraiths he has money and power, but with the Dead Palms, he has devotion and a true sense of family. The greedy motherfucker wanted his cake and to eat it too, not giving a shit about who he hurt along the way.

The two clubs aren't the same, and I'm assuming the power got to him; that he finally had enough of his double life. Or maybe the Wraiths were putting pressure on him, I don't know. But I imagine we're gonna find out soon.

None of it matters, not really. All that matters is he took my fuckin' girl. I want to throw up when I think about all the possibilities of what he intended to do with her. Was he truly going to sell her? Or did he do all of this to teach his stepchildren a lesson; the lesson that they need to fall in line or he will make them fall?

He's got to go, along with the Wraiths and anyone in the Dead Palms who betrayed the brotherhood.

Our plan is to take Kurt out first, to cut the head of the snake before dealing with the rest. The Wraiths have more members, but with Kurt no longer at the helm, there will be a mad scramble for structure before they can retaliate.

Cleaning up shop is easier said than done.

Kurt's not a fuckin' moron. He had to know about the warehouse. Though we left no survivors, he has to suspect it was us. There's a reason he searched the warehouse first, and why he went back today.

The main advantage we have over them is Cash's cameras. I'm so thankful for that paranoid fuck. Even if I don't like that he's bonded with Lily in a way I can't.

At least she's *my* wife. Neither of them can take that away from me.

"He's goin' to be on high alert," Tate points out, leaning over Cash's shoulder as we watch the Prez and his chosen men roll back up to the club.

"We need to take him out first," Cash states. "Once he's out, we'll see who tucks their tail between their legs in shame and who had no clue. You know the guys who are unaware will be shocked by his death and the others won't."

"Do we know who else might be on our side?" Tate asks.

"Blaze, Heath, Jay, Torn, and all the new patch overs," Mickey answers confidently.

I nod my head in agreement and so does Doc.

"All the old guys, they seem in on it," I state.

"Are we showing no mercy?" Cash asks, but the question is very much geared towards Tate.

"There's no fuckin' mercy for traitors," Tate replies, and there's a rumbling of solidarity between all of us.

"How many of us has he called?" I ask, knowing I've had five missed calls from the Prez.

Maverick and Doc are the only ones he's called, and collectively we decide that they'll be our distraction.

"We need a reason for them to trust you being on the compound. Lower his guard down, the last thing we need is him calling the Wraiths for backup again," Tate says.

"Why hasn't he already done that?" Mickey asks.

"And show the Wraiths he can't control the club he built? There were no witnesses at their stash house. Kurt might suspect, but he doesn't have proof. If the Wraiths catch a whiff of this weakness, they'll eat him alive. Seven dead and all his Omegas gone? He wouldn't survive it; there would be a mutiny," Tate replies, and we nod.

"Who are we pinnin' it on?" I reply.

"The Outlaws?" Cash shrugs.

"Works for me. You ready?" Tate asks, lookin' at Maverick and Doc.

"Fuck, just do it. Don't break my fuckin' nose," Maverick grumbles.

Tate decks him in the face, and I follow suit. It feels fuckin' wrong beating the shit out of a brother like this, but it needs to be believable. Cash and Mickey wail on Doc, leaving enough physical evidence to appease our plan.

"Fuckin' hell," Doc complains when Mickey hits him in the jaw. He pushes the large Alpha away. "That's fuckin' enough, mate," he spits.

His eyebrow and lip are bleeding, and Tate nods with agreement.

There's a round of sorrys from all of us, but Doc and Maverick take it in stride.

"Alright, you bag of dicks, what's the fuckin' story?" Doc asks.

Tate smiles, and it grows even more sinister as we go over the plan.

WE'RE SITTING ON OUR FUCKIN' hands for what feels like forever. Cash's cameras give us a good view as Maverick and Doc pull up to the gates, their code still working, which is a relief.

Kurt has his gun drawn as they pull up to the clubhouse, but as soon as he realizes who it is, he lowers his weapon.

There's no sound, but we know the story they're telling; that Shelby and Lily were taken, and they went after them. But as soon as they did, the Outlaws intercepted them as payback for us blowing up their warehouse.

Prez's fury is palpable through the camera feed as he scratches his beard and looks at the state of Maverick and Doc.

Supposedly, Cash and I are fuckin' dead in this so-called story, which is just rude. Tate is left completely out of it since he's supposed to be shunned. Mickey, Atlas, and Ink are being held as leverage as are all the Omegas.

The carnage left at the stash house is being completely pinned on the Outlaws, and it's just a waiting game to see if he'll buy it.

Maverick and Doc weren't close to Tate at all, and we're all bettin' on the Prez takin' that into account when we chose them to go back to the compound.

There's a scurry of men going into the clubhouse and others getting their bikes ready.

"I think this is gonna work," Tate comments, an exhale of relief escaping him.

"As long as the other guys are on our side," I chime in, and Tate grunts in agreement.

If we're going to direct the club where we want them, we're going to need help, especially getting the Prez alone.

"As long as we're right with who's on our side, this should work," Cash agrees.

We watch as the Prez storms into his house; he stays in there for a few minutes before leaving… alone.

Tate lets out a sigh of relief, but I know we're both not looking forward to what we have to do next.

We all know the exact promises we made to our Omega, and they were loose at best.

It takes some time for the club to pack up and head out. We all know where they're going and we have time. The plan is in place; Maverick and Doc will be keeping tabs and letting us know where everyone is.

Mickey, Atlas, and Cash are following the club while Tate and I handle this next step. Neither of us looking forward to this shit.

"You sure you don't need me there?" Cash asks Tate.

"We'll handle it," Tate replies.

Part of me wonders if the reason he doesn't want Cash there is that he's worried he would snap and make a hasty decision. I'm wondering if Tate shouldn't be there for the same reason. Dread is more of a father to him than the Prez ever was. Is this a choice he can follow through with?

"Let us know when you've got 'em," Tate orders Cash.

Cash smacks Tate's shoulder before smacking mine. We're all wearing Dead Palms cuts, we're taking our club back tonight just as much as we're exacting revenge.

"Let's go," Tate declares.

WE HAVE to climb the fence, which is a complete motherfucker, but we can't afford to be seen on the cameras or set off any alarms by entering our code.

The only people left on the compound are a few sweet butts, Dread, and Teresa. Everyone else is on the road, headed right where we want them.

We go around the back way, climbing the roof and going through Lily's bedroom window. Apparently, I'm not the only one who's snuck in here a few times before. We're as quiet as we can be, but it's hard with how much of a mess her room is. Shit's still thrown everywhere from her packing up her shit.

We both have our guns drawn as we go down the stairs.

I was expecting to have to pull Dread and Teresa from their bedroom, but they both sit together at the worn dining table. Teresa holds Dread's hand on top of the wood and Dread has his own weapon in the other hand in a relaxed position on the table.

"Son, take a seat," Dread says.

Tate looks over at me in confusion, and I just shrug, pulling out a chair across the pair. Teresa looks sad, but not she-just-lost-her-son level of sad.

Fuck.

"Do you know why we're here?" Tate asks him.

"I'm not stoppin' you, son, he needs to be taken out," Dread responds calmly. Teresa whips her head to look at her bonded Alpha.

"What?" she asks in shock.

Thank God, she didn't fuckin' know… well, at least not the most sordid parts.

"Did you know?" Tate asks.

"Which part?" Dread asks, and I can tell Tate wants to punch him in the fuckin' face.

Tate looks over at Teresa, and she looks back at him with pleading eyes.

"Did you know he took Lily and Shelby?" Tate clarifies.

"What?" Teresa squeaks before Dread can answer.

"He said he had nothin' to do with that," Dread answers.

"What about Leon?" Tate questions.

"What about Leon? Is he okay?" Teresa asks.

"Fuck," Tate and I both say under our breath as we look over at Dread. It's clear he doesn't know about Leon.

"What *do* you know then, Dread?" Tate asks.

Tate stands, taking away Dread's weapon, which the older Alpha allows. Tate presses the cold metal against the older man's temple and holds it there.

"What you tell me next will be the deciding factor if you die here and now, or if I let you leave here with your Omega," Tate warns.

"I know he's been workin' with the Wraiths, tradin' in dirty shit. I know he's been laundering money, and that he's takin' out other chapters," Dread states honestly.

"Why didn't you do anything?" I ask while Tate keeps the gun pressed against his head.

Teresa looks around the room in shock, but she doesn't speak.

"He's in my fuckin' pack; he's my Prez. I couldn't be the one to do it," Dread replies calmly.

Teresa is clearly dumbfounded, her mind reeling as she looks over at her Alpha.

"Dread, where are my children?" she asks.

"I don't know, baby," he answers, ignoring the weapon against his head.

"You're not lyin' to me?" Tate asks, shoving the tip of the gun harder against his skin.

"No, where are they?" Dread asks.

Tate doesn't drop the gun, but his head tilts back as he looks at the ceiling for a second.

"Pack up your shit. You two need to leave and never come back. If you come back here, Dread, I'll fuckin' kill you, you hear me?" Tate growls and I can tell it's hard for him to get out. "Take Teresa and get the fuck out of here. Retire."

"Come on, T," Dread urges, standing up and attempting to pull Teresa up.

Her watery eyes look up to Tate, not getting up out of her seat.

"What did Kurt do to my kids?" she asks, tears flowing down her cheeks now. I feel bad for the woman, but part of me feels like she should have done a better job as a mother protecting her kids.

"Lily is safe; Cash, Axel, and I are goin' to take care of her. I need some time, but I'll let you see her eventually. You can talk on the phone, but you can't stay here, not if you want to be with Dread," Tate tells her.

Teresa looks over at her Alpha and back at us.

"Where's Leon?"

The look Tate gives her tells her everything she needs to know. Her hands cover her face as she breaks out into sobs. Dread wraps his arms around her, looking at Tate with complete shock.

"I don't know if you're lyin' or playin' me for a fuckin' fool,

Dread. But I'm lettin' you live because you raised me more than my own father did, and I can't take away both of Teresa's Alphas. So if you're gonna go, go now," Tate commands calmly.

Dread gets on his knees before his Omega, completely understanding that the poor woman not only just lost a son, but is going to be feeling the horrific pain of one of her bonds dying as well.

"Baby, I got to get you out of here," he urges her to move.

The woman is distraught, and who wouldn't be? But she pulls herself together for a moment, even though her breaths come out unevenly.

"You'll let me see her?" she questions hopefully.

"When it's safe," Tate responds.

"Kurt did this to my children?" she asks like she needs confirmation of what a piece of shit her Alpha is.

"He did," Tate states.

"Then make it hurt," Teresa whispers, getting up with her Alpha and walkin' away. Something about those words resonates with Tate, and he takes a deep breath as they start to walk away.

"One more thing, Dread," Tate calls out, making the man turn with his Omega in his arms. "Call him and tell him Teresa needs him, you'll meet him at the warehouse."

It's the final test, Tate needs validation that he's making the right decision. Dread nods, pulling out his phone; it goes to voicemail, and he sends a text as well. He holds it out, showing Tate the message.

"I never wanted this shit to happen, kid," Dread says.

"Just go," Tate dismisses them.

Teresa walks away with her bonded, and I hope Lily understands her choice.

A part of me feels sick that she is choosing to go with Dread and not stay for Lily, but how could she? She was bonded to the man who attempted to destroy this club, even if she's an Omega. That wouldn't stand up well with the club. Teresa might be naïve to what was going on in her own house, but she isn't stupid.

"You did the right thing," I tell him, and I mean it whole-heartedly.

"Hope so," he replies.

"You did; Lily will understand."

"I can only fuckin' hope. Let's get on the road," Tate sighs.

My heart practically pounds out of my fuckin' chest the entire ride. We haven't received any concerning messages, but part of me knows this isn't going to be fuckin' easy.

FORTY
EXECUTIONER

I'M nervous as Axel and I ride towards the warehouse, and I don't know if I did the right thing letting Dread go, but I just couldn't do that to Lily or Teresa. I know what I have to do when it comes to my father, and even if my palms are sweating and it feels like I might throw up, my conscience is clear on that front.

Teresa already lost a son and is losing a bonded Alpha, I couldn't take Dread away from her too—at least that's what I'm telling myself. I don't think I could have killed Dread. Maybe if he knew about my father deliberately takin' Lily, but after what he said… I just couldn't.

I shake my head, focusing on the road and the brutal task ahead of me.

The club is being diverted to Panama City, while my father should be held up at the warehouse.

I pull out my phone as it buzzes. It's a text from Cash.

He lets me know that they have my father tied up, but they're worried about the rest of the club becoming suspicious. I have the same fuckin' worry. All it takes is them turning around and coming back to the warehouse for us to have a full-on civil war on our hands.

I know I'll have to kill men I've known my whole life, but I still haven't wrapped my head around it all. I have to be the one to take my father out; it has to be me who sets this wayward club straight.

If I don't handle this now, Lily won't be safe and this club will fall.

I'm not sure how I went from a nomad to being completely devoted to this club, but I am.

Maybe it's because this is where Lily wants to be, or maybe as his son I have to absolve the club of his sins, no matter if the cost is my soul.

My heart rages in my chest as we pull up to the warehouse. The two bikes out front are my dad's and Doc's. Cash probably hid his bike 'round back so my father wouldn't suspect anything.

Now that it's about to go down, there's a sinking feeling in my gut that won't fuck off. Can I really go through with this? Can I really put my own fuckin' father down?

I haven't thought about my mother in years; it was easier to forget her. But of course, now is when her memory comes out to haunt me. I know she would hate the man I've become, but I think she would've hated my father more.

I don't know how my father conned two beautiful Omegas into his web of evil, but there's a part of me that worries I'm doin' the same thing to Lily. I swallow that shit down quick.

Don't be a fuckin' pussy.

"You need a second, man?" Axel asks me as we hop off our bikes, just staring at the warehouse. "You don't have to be the one to do it," he offers.

"Yeah, I do."

"We've got your back," he reminds me.

"Let's just get this over with before anyone comes lookin' for him."

I take a deep breath and swallow the bile rising up my throat when I open the door to see that they've strapped my father to a chair, his lip bleeding. He spits blood out onto the table and gives me a shit-eating grin.

He laughs, throwing his head back before looking back at me.

"Who would've thought the first time I was ever proud of you would be the moment you wanted to kill me," he taunts calmly.

It's almost like he thinks he's going to get out of this.

"Gotta say, tellin' me somethin' was wrong with Teresa and to turn back was smart. I felt her sadness and anxiety down the bond. You got Dread to flip on me, huh?" my father accuses. This time there's malice clearly threaded throughout his voice.

"All I told her was the truth about the man she bonded with," I state.

He laughs again. "You don't know shit, boy."

"I know you got her son killed and staged her daughter's kidnapping."

I'm not sure if I expect him to lie, or try to cover his ass, but he doesn't bother.

"Being the President of a club presents you with some hard choices. It's my job to make a decision. I didn't want them to be weak the way you are."

He's trying to goad me, but I can't let him get to me.

"For which club?" Cash spits out next to me.

"So he speaks," my father retorts, rolling his eyes at Cash. My father looks back at me before continuing with his little speech. "Leon needed to grow the fuck up, understand the price of being my son. You wouldn't know anything about that, now would you?"

"No, I really fuckin' wouldn't. Why do you hate me so much?" I ask.

I shouldn't care, I really shouldn't fuckin' care what a walking dead man thinks about me, but I just have to know.

"You're the reason I became what I am. If your mother hadn't been out, droppin' you off at your friend's house she never would have gotten picked up by the Wraiths. Do you know what they did to her? And it's all your fuckin' fault. When she died, every good piece of me went with her. How could I ever love the reason my *true* Omega died? You made me lose my soul by fuckin' existin'," he sneers.

His vengeance towards the Wraiths makes more sense now, why he went after them and took their Omega as penance. But his greed and ego are what drove him to become what he hated so much.

I keep my face straight, not letting his words hit their intended target, even though they do. I'm also glad Teresa never had to hear him say this shit, either.

"You're not even gonna try to plead for your life?" I ask.

He laughs again, his teeth coated in blood from where he got hit in the face.

"You think I don't have contingencies in place? That I didn't think it was fuckin' odd Maverick and Doc showed up and suddenly half of my problems were dead? You're either arrogant or a fuckin' fool."

I take a step toward him where he sits at the worn, wooden dining table. I lift my gun towards his head and my palm fuckin' shakes.

"You can't do it; you don't fuckin' have it in you. You kill me and the whole club falls apart. The Wraiths want their Omegas back and want retribution for the men you took out. No matter how you look at this, you're a dead man," he rants, twisting the situation around.

The confidence that radiates out of him is astounding considering I have a gun aimed at his head, and he's tied up in a chair.

"You really wanna be the reason both of your parents are dead?" he taunts.

"I just want you to know that Teresa and Lily hate you. That everyone in the club will know the real man you are." I lean forward so only he can hear me. "I'm gonna burn down every vile fuckin' thing you built. No one will mourn you, no one will remember you, every piece of you is goin' to be removed from history. I hope you rot in fuckin' hell."

I pull back, and he opens his mouth to speak, but I steady my hand, pulling the trigger. The gunshot is near deafening, and the breath I was holding expels from my chest as I look at his brain matter that's now splattered along the table.

I heave a few deep breaths as I look down at him, the man who gave me life, who raised me in the club culture. The man that never loved anything but himself and destroyed every fuckin' thing he touched, including me.

I'm not sure what takes over me. I know he's dead, but I shoot him two more times in the chest for good measure. An agonized scream rips out of me as I put my gun away and look over his body.

I never wanted this, I never wanted to be this man, but he made me this way, and I don't know if there's any coming back from this.

A hand grips my shoulder, and I jolt from the touch. Cash's deep voice has me relaxing and releasing some tension.

"You did what you had to do. That's a sign of a true leader if I ever saw one. Don't let anything he said get to you. They were the words of a dying traitor. Stay focused and remember what we're fighting for," he encourages, and I nod.

"Fuck," Axel groans as we all collectively hear the rumbling of engines in the distance.

"Shite," Doc hisses, looking down at his phone. "They know somethings up."

"Do you think Dread warned them?" Axel grunts, anger lacing his words as we all draw our weapons.

Luckily, we're stashed away in a warehouse filled to the brim with illegal weapons.

"No, someone else had to have flipped," I shout back, needing that to be the case. If I let Dread go and he fuckin' did this to us, I'd never forgive myself.

I stand by the window, peeking out of the brown shitty curtain as I watch the rest of the club approach. It's everyone… including Atlas… who should not be with the club right now. He's supposed to be waiting in the van with Mickey.

"It's fuckin' Atlas," I announce to the guys.

"He knows where the fuckin' lake house is," Cash growls in a warning tone.

Before I can even respond, he's out the back door, and I curse under my breath as I watch the rest of the club get off their bikes. I'm not sure what he's told them, but it can't be everything.

Guys I know for a fact are on our side are still standing beside the rest of the club. If they knew everything Maverick and the others would be dead already.

Atlas points at the house and speaks, but as soon as his mouth opens, a bullet flies right through his head, killing him instantly.

"Fuck!" I shout.

As soon as Atlas' body hits the ground, everything turns into utter mayhem. Bullets fly towards the house. The window next to me shatters, and I shield my face from the flying glass as I do my best to aim at the men I know are our enemy.

It's a blessing that we have guys on the other side as they take out some of the older members. They don't even expect it. Maverick, by himself, takes out Smiley and Boomerang. There are members of the club that look completely fuckin' confused as to what's happening, and I make a note of their faces, in case they survive this.

There might not be much of a club to lead after all is said and done.

I aim, hitting Pipes in the center of his chest, and watch him fall. The gunfire seems to finally come to a pause, the men no longer shooting are on my side, as far as I know. We're going to need some serious fuckin' vetting if we're going to continue to be a club.

Part of me thinks we should cut our losses and toss our patches into a bonfire. But as I look around at the bloodshed and trauma that has happened here, there's no fuckin' way this is all for nothing.

Still, I draw my weapon as I go outside. Fuck, this is a mess. Between my father inside and the bodies riddled over the dusty front lawn, the cleanup is going to be extravagant.

Doc and Axel follow me as we take a headcount of who's left and who's dead.

It's then we hear grunting coming from behind us, all of us spin to watch as Cash and Sasquatch go at it, hand to hand. They're the only two Alphas in the club who are matched in size. And with the way they're brawling, there's no clear shot to take Sasquatch out. I thought he was on our side.

What the fuck is happening?

We watch in horror as Sasquatch takes a knife out of his belt and he impales it into Cash's face, sending him to the ground.

Axel is quicker than me as he takes the risky shot, shooting Sasquatch in his abdomen. He collapses next to Cash's body as we run over. Both of them are still breathing, until Axel shoots Sasquatch in the head, ending his life.

Cash moans and writhes on the ground, his head gushing blood in a way I've never seen anyone survive. Axel and I stare down in shock at the man our Omega bonded.

"What the fuck do we do?" Axel shouts.

Doc comes running over next, thank fuckin' God he's here. "Get me some fuckin' clean towels now!" he shouts.

A few of the guys spring into action as Doc looks down at Cash.

"Fuckin' head wounds are the worst. I won't be able to tell how bad it is until I can get it to stop bleeding and see how deep it is. We need to get him to a hospital immediately."

Maverick comes running over with some clean towels and Doc applies pressure.

"Call Mickey, have him bring the van; we'll use it for clean up later," I tell him. Thankful as fuck that the warehouse is in the middle of bum-fuck nowhere.

Maverick is immediately on the phone calling Mickey, and I hope he'll be fast enough to get here in time.

My breaths are heavy as I place my hands on my knees and vomit on the ground. I use the back of my hand to wipe my mouth as I pull my shit together. I can't look at Cash right now, I just fuckin' can't.

Instead, I turn around while Maverick, Axel, and Doc help him.

"What's the body count?" I pant out in demand to Heath.

"Seven dead. Atlas, Smiley, Davidson, Pipes, Boomerang, Sasquatch, and Hugh," he rattles off.

Hugh was on our side, but as far as numbers are concerned, it could have been so much fuckin' worse. Cash might be added to that count, though, and I don't know if Lily will survive it.

"Don't lift your fuckin' hand, hear me," Doc yells at someone, but I don't turn around to see who.

I only let out a sigh of relief when Mickey drives like a bat out of hell towards us. We had him and the van stashed with the sole purpose of helping us dispose of my father's body, but shit just got so much more complicated. Atlas was supposed to be with him, and as much as I want to trust Mickey, I'm not sure if I can yet.

"Holy fuck," he grunts as he backs the van up, getting as close to Cash as possible.

I finally have to turn and deal with the matter at hand as it takes nearly all of us to lift the weight of him into the van. He moans, and I take that as a good sign while we get his body precariously situated in the back. Axel is the one holding the towel against his head as he glares down at his pack mate.

"You better not fuckin' die, it'll kill her," he grumbles.

I feel like I'm going to have a fuckin' heart attack, but I keep it together as Mickey drives recklessly to the hospital. We left the other guys behind to start sorting through the shit at the warehouse.

This is my worst nightmare.

"You stay with him. We're all covered in blood and shit. We can't take the cops on right now," Doc tells Axel.

"Everyone, take your cuts off," I order them.

I hold the towel against Cash's head while Axel removes his cut. Doc takes a switchblade out and cuts Cash's cut off from the shoulder seams.

"Fuck, he's lost so much fuckin' blood," Axel comments.

"I don't think it's deep. Head wounds are cunts," Doc says.

Mickey pulls up to the emergency bay, and we get out of the van while medical staff bring out a gurney.

It feels so fuckin' wrong leaving him there with Axel. But it has to be done. We can't all stay. There's clean up, there are Omegas who need to get home, and Lily waiting on us.

The weight of the world is on my shoulders, and I don't know if I'll fuckin' survive its crushing weight.

FORTY-ONE
FRACTURED BONDS

I HATE FEELING USELESS, so instead of sitting on the couch and going into a complete spiral about my guys, I decide to cook dinner.

I've never cooked this much pasta in my life, but it's the only thing we had enough of to feed this many people.

"Do you need help?" a soft voice asks me.

"Sure," I smile back at her. It's the quiet blonde that was next to Ink earlier. "I'm Lily."

"Quinn," she says her name shyly.

"Do you want to do the garlic bread?" I ask her. She just nods, some of her hair covering her face as she gets to work. She's easily the smallest woman here, and she seems on the frail side.

Ink and the broody male Omega stare at her all while she helps me with dinner, and my nosy-ass wants to know why.

"What's the deal with the male Omega?" I ask her quietly.

"He's my stupid fucking cousin," she says back in a whisper. "He shouldn't be here," she adds with irritation laced in her voice.

"None of you should be here," I correct her, and it's clear that she doesn't understand the context as her eyes widen. "No, what I mean is that none of you should have been taken in the first place. No one deserves what they were doing to Omegas."

Her posture relaxes as she nods her head.

I'm browning the meat when I feel it.

Pain, anguish, and fear race through the bond. I drop the spoon and fall to the floor, clutching my head.

"What's wrong?" Quinn shrieks, but she doesn't touch me.

"Fuck," I hear Ink hiss from the other room.

He isn't able to get around easily, needing to grab his crutches first. He's on his way over to me, but my vision is going black. What is happening with Cash right now?

I can't lose him.

Haven't I lost enough already?

I hear voices around me, but it just feels like I'm underwater, nothing makes sense. Cash is in so much pain and is fading quickly, our bond nearly hanging on by a thread.

Cash is supposed to be the strong one, the one that holds everything together with his quiet, reassuring presence. I need him to be okay, I can't—I won't—be able to go on without him.

My heart races in my chest, feeling like it's cracking, and it's the final blow before I shatter, breaking into a million tiny shards.

A firm hand grabs my jaw, and I blink at the man holding my face so roughly. It's the male Omega, Quinn's cousin.

"I need you to pull your shit together. I can't have you on the back of a bike if you're losin' it," he spits.

"Fuck, cut her a break," Ink snarls.

The Omega doesn't let go of my face, but Ink is on his crutches looking down at me.

"I can't ride with my leg, and shit is fucked up right now. None of the guys can come and get you. Mason can drive you to the hospital," he explains.

"What?" I ask.

They both ignore me as they have their own conversation.

"You sure you know how to ride?" Ink asks the male

Omega, whose hand I shove away from my face.

"Yes, I can ride. We either sedate her, or I take her to the hospital. Which is it?"

God, this Omega is an asshole.

But if he's going to take me to Cash, I can't say anything.

"You realize who her pack is?" Ink reiterates to Mason.

"Oh, yeah, we're well fuckin' acquainted. Are we goin' or what?" he snarks.

"You better not fuck up my bike or drive recklessly with Lily," Ink chastises Mason.

If my chest wasn't aching and every fiber of me wasn't sick with worry, I'd appreciate his care for me.

I need Cash.

My heart sinks over the fact that I can't feel Axel or Tate. *What if they're hurt too?* That thought has me hyperventilating.

"I can't fuckin' take her like this," Mason repeats, waving his hand at me. His cousin glares at him and smacks his chest.

"Mason, you're being a fucking dick."

Ink has to hold onto the counter as he gets down on the floor to look at me. "It's Cash, Tate and Axel are safe. But Cash is in the hospital; he's still alive," Ink says soothingly. "Just breathe, okay?"

He goes through the motions with me, coaxing me to breathe in through my nose and out of my mouth. Once I'm finally able to breathe evenly, I stand up, using the counter for support, and look at Mason.

"No bullshit on the back of the bike or I'll bring you right back here," he threatens.

I just nod because I really need a ride to the hospital. Once I get there, I might punch him in the face, though.

"I'll be right back. You call me if anything happens," Mason says to Quinn, and she rolls her eyes at him.

I follow Mason out of the house, and as much as I hate getting on the back of someone's bike who isn't my pack, I do. I grip his shirt tightly so that I don't have to touch any of his skin.

The drive to the hospital is agony, and the realization that I'm feeling nothing at all through the bond with Cash makes me want to die.

I LEAVE a pissed-off Mason behind me as I storm into the emergency room lobby. I'm frantic as I head to the reception desk, but a blood-covered Axel cuts off my trajectory. He grabs me by the arms, and I stare into his dazed blue eyes.

He doesn't speak and neither do I as I look at the amount of blood covering his white shirt.

Axel holds me in his arms as I collapse to the floor.

"Hey… they wouldn't let me back. Lily, look at me," he urges as I just sit haphazardly on the floor. "Lily." He shakes me slightly, and I look back up at him. "He's gonna be okay, he's drugged up, but he's gonna be okay," he reassures.

"He's okay?" I parrot, and Axel nods his head.

"Lucky bastard doesn't even need surgery. The knife got him good, but he only has a small skull fracture. He needed a blood transfusion, and a fuck-ton of stitches, but he's gonna be okay," he promises while rubbing his hands up and down my arms.

"Where's Tate?" I ask.

"He's dealin' with clean up. Prick doesn't have a single scratch on 'em."

"I need to see Cash."

"Come on, you're his bonded. They'll let you back," Axel says, helping me on my feet.

Mason finally comes into the waiting room, glaring at everyone as he searches for us. Axel takes me under his arm and approaches him.

"After we get shit cleaned up, we can all go back to the

compound. Can you figure out which Omegas have a place to go home to and which don't?" Axel asks him.

Mason looks at him, and then at me. "What about the Wraiths?"

"Trackin' down Omegas isn't gonna be their biggest concern right now," Axel replies cryptically.

"What's the plan for Omegas who don't have a place to go?" Mason asks, he phrases it like he isn't an Omega himself.

"We've got a club to fuckin' rebuild. Anyone who wants to stay and help can stay. I can't say that things are safe or that everything is gonna be fine, but it's a roof over their head and a promise that no one in the Dead Palms will lay a hand on them," Axel vows.

If I wasn't so worried about Cash, I'd melt at his words, but my anxiety is turned up to level ten, and I need to make sure he's okay.

Mason doesn't reply verbally to Axel but gives him a pat on the shoulder before walking away.

"I don't like him very much," I say to Axel, who just laughs.

"Me either. Fucker kicked me in the chest when we met."

"I like him even less. Can I please go see Cash now?"

"Yeah, let's go," he agrees.

He places a soft kiss on my forehead as he talks with the receptionist. She's leery at first because we haven't legally submitted forms as a bonded pack. My being married to Axel apparently doesn't mean shit, but when Axel shows the woman the bite on my neck, she finally relents. The only caveat is that I can't bring Axel back with me.

"I'll be right here waitin' for you, okay?" I take a deep breath as he cups my face. "You're my strong, brave girl."

It's the push I needed. Cash needs me to be the strong one right now. He's been the one I could always rely on when my life was going to shit, and now he needs the same from me.

I can do this.

The woman takes me to Cash's room. When we walk in, I notice he has a massive bandage on his head and is hooked up to a few different machines. At least he seems to be peacefully asleep, there's no tension written across his face, and that's a relief.

"He got really lucky, if the knife was just a few inches to the right, it would have been a different outcome," she states.

Thanks a lot for putting those thoughts in my head, you fucking bitch. I must glare at her, because she slowly retreats, leaving me with my poor, broken Alpha.

I should pull up a chair and hold his hand, but I can't help myself. I need to be as close to him as I can be. I need to feel him. I'm super cautious as I crawl into his bed, making sure I don't interfere with any of the wires or put any weight on him, just my hand over his chest.

"You're not allowed to scare me like this," I tell him, knowing he won't respond.

"I can't lose any of you. It would break me."

I stroke a line up and down his toned chest. I know he won't be waking up anytime soon, but just feeling the warmth of his skin and hearing the tone of his heart monitor puts me at ease.

"I don't think I can take much more. Life isn't supposed to be this fucking hard," I complain to him.

There's still so much I don't know about what went down with the club, but right now my focus is solely on Cash.

I rub the underside of his jaw softly. The bandage covers half of his head, and I can only imagine that the stitches cross over his tattoo.

"It's okay, just another scar showing you survived," I tell him softly.

I wish the rest of my pack was here, but at least I know they're okay; Axel is in the lobby, and Tate is safe. It's not the most ideal, but it's something I can hang on to and ease my fears.

I fall asleep next to my Alpha's healing body, hoping that I'll wake up to a better set of circumstances.

MY HEAD'S THROBBING, and there's an annoying, low beeping noise in the background. My eyelids feel heavy and scratchy as I blink them open.

The bright fluorescent lights above have me slamming them shut again, but I can feel my Omega next to me, holding my hand. It's a relief that has me wanting to open my eyes to make sure she's real, while taking deep, even inhales of her scent.

"He's awake," she cheers softly.

I'm thankful it's not too loud. My head pounds viciously, and the only reason I'm staying awake is because she's here. I smack my dry lips together and the weight on the bed shifts. There's a clanking of ice cubes before a straw is placed between my lips.

"You need to drink," she says.

I hate her taking care of me like this. It should be the other way around. I should be the one supporting her right now. She's been through so much, and I know she needs to feel more settled after her heat.

She needs me, and I'm wearing a fucking hospital gown— it's mortifying. The itchy material rubs against my skin as I try to blink my eyes open again.

"There you are," Lily beams, her warm eyes meeting mine.

I feel her relief through the bond. There's still the sour taste of worry, but she's relatively happy at this moment, as much as someone in this position can be.

"Good job not dyin' on us, asshole," Axel sasses, my heavily lidded eyes finding him standing behind Lily.

"Don't even joke about that," Lily scolds him.

"Sorry, darlin'."

I clear my throat and before I am able to speak, Lily is shoving the straw back into my mouth again. I take a few more sips to appease her, and she places the large water cup on the side table.

"What happened?" I rasp out.

My memories are foggy. I remember Tate killing his father and taking down Atlas, but the rest is a blur.

Axel rubs the back of his neck and looks down at Lily.

"Yeah, what happened?" she parrots, crossing her arms over her chest and glaring at Axel.

He's wearing a fresh outfit, but Lily is wearing the same clothes from when we left the lake house. I don't like it. I should be taking better care of her.

"Sasquatch got the upper hand on you, but luckily, his aim was shit. Nearly scalped your bald head, but you got lucky. I don't even know how many stitches they put in that massive head of yours, but besides that, you only have a small skull fracture," he explains.

"You'll have some pain for a while, some headaches, but the doctor says it should heal on its own. They're letting you come home tomorrow."

"Okay," I reply.

Even though I want to ask where *home* is? Are we going back to the compound? Are we staying at the lake house?

"We're going back to the compound," Axel says, answering the question I didn't verbally ask. "We're settin' the Omegas up in the Prez's old house for now. Lily will stay with us at the clubhouse."

I don't miss Lily's grimace when he mentions her stepfather. I'm still not sure what she knows, so I keep my mouth shut. I lick my lips, and she brings the straw to my mouth again.

"Baby girl, I'm fine."

"You're not fine. You don't know how scared I was. So you're going to shut up, drink your water, and let me take care of you. I want to. It's something to keep my mind on," she chastises me.

"Okay," I reply as she shoves the straw back into my mouth.

"Lily and I are gonna go get the dog and the van with our shit. We'll come back in the mornin' to bring your sorry-ass home."

"Give her big-ass head a kiss for me," I tell Lily.

"I will," she promises, leaning down to kiss my cheek.

It's probably a mixture of the head injury and the complete lack of sleep over the past week, but as soon as they leave, I fall right back to sleep.

I'M SETTLED in my old room in the clubhouse, petting Winnie between my legs, just waiting for Lily to come back and spend time with me. I hate feeling useless like I do right now.

But I'm definitely not the only one. Axel's arm is still sore, although he's fine. Ink and Blaze are both healing from gunshot wounds, and the club is now down nine members—ten if you include Dread being shunned.

The club is anemic, and my greatest fear is being indisposed if shit goes south. The door clicks open, and Winnie's head pops up, both of us hoping it's Lily, but it's just Tate.

There are deep, dark purple bags under his eyes. He looks like shit as he walks in and sits in the chair in the corner.

"How you feelin'?" he asks.

"Better. My head still hurts like a motherfucker, but I'll live. Everything cleaned up?" I ask.

"We dropped the bodies off at the Wraiths' clubhouse and Mickey set it on fire," he informs me in a disinterested voice.

"I thought the plan was to make it look like this shit never happened?" I ask him.

When we originally hashed everything out, we were going to take the bodies and bury them in the swamp.

"Got outvoted," is all he says, and I smirk. Smiling hurts my fucking face.

"You're really doing this?" I ask him.

"Yeah, and we're doin' it the right way. No more dictatorship, no more secrets. A real fuckin' brotherhood, the way it should've always been."

"And the Wraiths?"

"Think Mickey killed a few more in the fire. Their numbers are low and they're scramblin' after we took my father out. We're keeping the gates locked and stayin' put for now."

"Wouldn't they want to attack while we're down?"

"They're also fucked. Between the guys we took out at the stash house, the Dead Palms traitors, your personal kill count, and the clubhouse, they're not lookin' so hot," he sums up.

"We can't let our guard down," I tell him.

"If you and Axel wanted to take her and leave, I'd understand," he says.

I'd roll my eyes, but it would hurt too much.

"Get the fuck over yourself, Tate," I grind out.

His head jolts up as he looks at me. There isn't much fire left behind his eyes. He's exhausted. We all are.

"She never wanted to leave here. She loves the club, and fuck, maybe if you stop feeling so sorry for yourself, you could let her love you, too."

He scrubs his face with his hand, but says nothing. Not that I expected him to. I know Lily wants him, and after everything we've been through since we came here, I already consider him my pack. But it's their place to sort their shit out, not mine.

The doorknob twists, and this time it's Lily who walks into my room. Winnie perks up immediately at her presence.

"Tate," she says his name calmly, like he's a wounded animal, and he looks up at her. She makes a frustrated noise as she goes to approach him, but he stands up from his chair.

He doesn't look at her while he speaks. "Do either of you need anything?"

"Tate," she sighs.

"I'm goin' to go get some sleep. Let me know if you need me," he rushes out, not looking at either of us as he leaves my room.

My room is simple and small, but it's not ideal for our situation or the place I truly want to be. Lily deserves a large comfy house, with a nest and a place for her hobbies. But she agreed with Tate's decision to house the Omegas in her old home. I don't think either of them wants to live there—the history cuts too deep.

"Come here," I tell her softly.

She sighs in frustration over Tate but is careful as she climbs into the bed to lie next to me and pet Winnie.

"He's under a lot of stress. Give it time," I tell her.

"I just want to talk to him, but he runs away every time I walk into a room."

I sigh and lean over to kiss her hair. She smells like her sweet coconut scent, and I take comfort in knowing she's safe and here with me.

"It's not my place, but he's got the club in his hands now. He's clearly who we're going to vote for as the next president. And I think he just has a lot of guilt over… everything," I say.

I worry about saying too much to Lily and causing her more emotional distress, but she doesn't say anything, instead, she traces my tattoos with her fingertips.

"Can you tell me about this one?" she asks, her finger

landing on the lotus tattoo with the name Leilani in small cursive in the middle.

I'm not sure if her interest is vested in jealousy, or just wanting to know more about me. Either way, I knew the conversation was going to happen, eventually.

"It's a memorial tattoo. For my sister," I confess.

Her hand stops moving on the tattoo, and her brows furrow for a second.

"I thought you said she found a pack and everything settled down for her?"

"I lied. I didn't know what to say. The wrong people took her, and I couldn't protect her. Trying to find her is how I got most of my scars, but it wasn't enough. Losing Leilani was the reason I joined the Dead Palms down in Miami. I was lost for a really long time and blamed myself for what happened to her."

"I'm so sorry, Cash," she whispers.

There isn't much else to say. I'm not about to dig up the horrific history of what happened. It's too painful, and I'm appreciative that Lily seems to get that. If anyone understands me to my core, it's her.

"I think when you were taken, it brought up a lot of memories of that time. I'm not proud of the way I handled things, and I won't tell you everything I did to get back to you. But I *had* to get you back. I couldn't let history repeat itself."

She snuggles closer to me, and it feels like both of us just get it. We've both lost a sibling in a horrific way. It's hard to explain the kind of grief it leaves behind.

"I'm sorry for throwing a fit about it during my heat," she grimaces.

"You didn't know, and I kind of liked how jealous you got," I reply, trying to keep the tone light.

It's clear she's not ready to talk about her brother, and I won't push her. Just like she doesn't push me for any more details. We can read each other better now that we're bonded, and I'm grateful for it.

"I can't promise I won't throw a fit about it in the future. If I'm in my right mind like now, I'm fine. But during my heat, I seem to be very possessive."

"I'll just cover it up when you're in heat. And maybe we'll make sure there are no breakables when we build your new nest.

"You're so good to me," she sighs dreamily, her dog resting her head on Lily's hand.

"That's my job. You're my girl."

She snuggles closer to me, and my door opens again. I'm going to fucking kill someone if I can't get more alone time with Lily. Of course, it's Axel, having a house wouldn't stop the needy Beta from sneaking into my room. He couldn't stay away, and I don't blame him.

At least he's quiet as he comes to lie next to Lily on the other side of the bed—that's way too fucking small for three people.

"I think tomorrow I'll go check in on the other Omegas and see if they need anything," she muses out loud.

I worry about her taking care of everyone else besides herself, but keeping herself busy is what's helping her heal right now. I found staying busy with the club was what brought me peace when my sister died. Lily has to place her focus on helping in order to cope. I'm happy her vice isn't harmful, at least.

"How many wound up staying?" I ask.

"Quinn and her cousin, Mason," she says his name in an irritated tone. "The twins, Hannah and Maggie, and Ellie. The rest had families to go home to," she says the last part sadly, and I'm not sure how to make this better for her.

"We're a family now," Axel interrupts, tossing an arm over her hip.

"We are," I agree with him.

"I know we are. It still hurts though," Lily says.

"You know she had to leave. There was no way she could stay here and be happy. There was no way people wouldn't look at her differently," Axel points out, talking about Lily's mother.

He doesn't bring up her stepfathers or Leon; though, I think it's understood she's lost more than any of us throughout this ordeal.

"I know, I just want to talk to her," she mumbles with a sniffle.

"I'll talk to Tate tomorrow, okay?" Axel offers.

"Thank you."

We're so fucking whipped, and neither of us even cares. I take this moment to relax and not worry about all the bad shit that could happen. Right now, we're safe. My Omega is in my arms, my dog is on my lap, and my girl's husband is somehow the voice of reason.

I think we're going to be okay.

I FINALLY GOT SOME SLEEP, but it was in bits and pieces. Nightmares plagued me every time I closed my eyes. The nightmares are a mix of my own memories and different outcomes. Like what would have happened if I didn't get to Lily in time? The other vision that haunts me is seeing my father's dead body over and over again.

It's the price I had to pay for this life, and I just have to fuckin' deal with it.

Some sleep is better than none, and everyone is in a place where we can finally hold church.

My hands are flat on the worn table, and it holds a different meaning for me now as I look down at it. I want to burn it and start new. This wood feels like it's steeped with lies and betrayal; it's not the way I want to start this club.

Mickey, Maverick, and Doc walk in, and I tell each of them to grab a corner of the table.

"Uh, why?" Maverick asks, taking a corner anyway.

With us all being large Alphas, we're able to lift it, carrying it through the double doors and out toward the fire pit.

"We're goin' to cut it up and burn it," I respond, turning away from them and walking back to the empty meeting space.

The room seems so much larger without the table there, and I take a seat.

The three Alphas follow suit, all of them giving each other looks like I'm fuckin' crazy. The rest of the club files in, and I hate it when Ink hobbles in on crutches, Blaze has his arm in a sling, and Cash has a huge wad of gauze taped to his head.

There are sixteen of us now. A few months ago, twenty-six of us sat around this table and room. Even though I'm filled with anger, I'm also filled with a sense of loss. There never should have been that many lives taken, and it's all because of my father's selfishness.

"Where's the fuckin' table?" Axel asks.

"We're burnin' it. We're startin' new. No more unilateral bullshit, no more secrets. This is supposed to be a fuckin' brotherhood," I proclaim, standing up and looking at the men around me, hoping to fuck I can trust each and every one of them.

"This club was diseased. My father was the infection, and I handled it by takin' him out. I know it's a heavy responsibility, and I can understand if you don't want the son of a traitor at your helm, but I promise to do right by you and bring this club back to its former glory if I'm voted in as your next Prez."

Heath stands up. He's one of the guys who's been around for a few years, and I wondered where he stood. He was with us at the warehouse, one of the men who didn't seem to know what was going on, but he nods his head.

"All in favor of Tate being the new president," he calls out, and I'm shocked when every hand in that motherfucking room goes up.

It thaws a piece of my cold dead heart, knowing that they want me here and they don't hate me.

"We're gonna set this club up right. No one sole pack runs this shit. We might have our own packs outside of the club, but I consider us all a giant pack of our own."

There's an overwhelming sense of agreement as we figure

out everyone's new place in the club. Certain guys are interested in titles while others just want to stay plain ol' members. It doesn't take us long to figure out the standing, and I'm grateful for it.

Heath is taking the notes for the meeting, and he stands up to read off the list.

"President, Tate. VP, Doc. Myself as Secretary. Cash as Treasurer. Sergeant in Arms is Mickey. Road Captain is Maverick, and Tank is our Enforcer. Is this agreeable to the club?" he asks.

A rumble of pride runs through my chest. Sure, my father took most club business to a vote, but to vote against him was to vote against your own wellbeing. This feels like a real fuckin' club.

We go around in a circle, everyone nodding their heads, and our club is finally unified.

"First order of business is the Omegas," I state.

"And the sweet butts," Doc says.

"Right, both of them. If there's anyone here who can't keep their fuckin' hands to themselves, we can handle that now. If one of them wants to join your bed, fine, but there will be no tolerance for disrespect."

"Here, here," ricochets throughout the room.

"The Omegas will stay at the main house. I'll be buildin' a home for Cash's pack if they want one. The old homes are up for grabs and will go based on pack priority. Single guys stay in the clubhouse. All in favor?"

Every hand is raised, and I let out a sigh of relief.

"We need to talk about our plans against the Wraiths," Mickey chimes in. I nod, giving him the floor as the new Sergeant of Arms. "There is no truce after what they did, only annihilation. As much as I want to take them all out one by one, we need to rebuild first. We have more to lose now when it comes to our compound. Too many members are currently injured, but we need a plan in place, just in case."

He explained that Atlas went to smoke a cigarette and abandoned him alone on the hill; he had no idea that the man was going to rat on us. For now, I have no choice but to believe him. His actions spoke louder than his words, but I will be keeping my eye on him.

"We can't afford to go on the offensive, but I agree," I reply.

"It's only a matter of time before the feds get involved. The body count is too fuckin' high right now," Doc chimes in.

"What? We're gonna just let them act first?" Tank asks. His deep voice is startling, cause you hardly ever hear it.

"We need to get our house in order and figure out their plan before they have a chance to act," Axel says.

It shouldn't feel this significant having every member adding to the conversation, but it does. I feel like I've finally done something right.

"No one acts alone when it comes to the Wraiths. We're gonna get our revenge, but it needs to be at the discretion of the entire club, understood?" I say and there's agreement throughout.

"We're going to need to expand some of our businesses to deal with the loss of income that Kurt's activities were bringing in," Cash brings up, and Blaze nods from the corner.

"I'm working on expanding our grow house situation, and there might be an opportunity to grow opium," Blaze states.

"Opium?" Mickey asks apprehensively.

"If we want the big money, that's where it is. Unless Doc can get more guns in from his supplier?"

"They're already sending over as much as they fuckin' can with them being international shipments," Doc replies, seeming frustrated.

Blaze wins the vote, ten to six.

"I'm going to need help getting set up," Blaze says. "Is there a possibility some of the Omegas can help?"

"No," Ink interjects quickly.

"It should be up to them, don't you think? We're housin'

them, offerin' them protection. If they want additional cash, they can help Blaze," Mickey reasons.

"Not the opium—weed only," Ink responds sternly.

Ink wins the vote, and a few of the guys offer their assistance to help with the grow house along with anyone else on the compound who would like to earn their keep.

"Old members' bikes are in the shop. I'll be workin' on gettin' them fixed up and sold," Axel says, adding his contribution.

"I'll work on gettin' a new table, and I think that's all... unless anyone else needs the floor," I state.

All the surrounding men look at me like I'm not a complete bastard, and there's a glimmer of hope building inside of me. I'll be able to make a difference and right the wrongs of my father.

I don't have a gavel, and I plan on burning my father's along with the table. I stand and leave, my club at my back. The future in front of us won't be easy, but it feels fuckin' bright.

I'M TAKING an axe to this piece of shit table when the male Omega—fuck, I can't remember his name—approaches me.

"I can make you a new table," he announces.

"You know woodworkin'?" I pant, wiping the sweat off my forehead and placing the axe down.

"Yeah, I know how to ride too," he says, looking at me like I'm not picking up what he's throwing down.

"Okay," I reply.

"I want to prospect for the club," he deadpans.

Fuck.

"I'll bring it up at the next meetin'."

"You will? Really?"

"I said I would. Now, what do you need for the table?" I ask.

His face is expressionless as he tilts his head toward me, trying to get a read on me.

"I'll make you a list. When's the next meetin'?"

"Not sure," I answer honestly, picking up the axe and going hard on the table.

I don't know how I feel about an Omega joining the club. It's never been done before. I want to be a different president than my father was, but I don't know if this is something I can do. What if he's too much of a distraction on the road?

I don't know why the Omega wants to join, but all I can do is bring it up to the club. The weight of everything isn't on my fuckin' shoulders. Sure, I'm the president and I need to lead, but we're a club, we need to make decisions together.

The man walks away as I continue chopping away at the wood. My muscles protest each time the axe hits the wood, but the strain feels good.

Not too long after, I sense *her* walking toward me before her scent and sweet voice hit me.

"Tate?"

"Lily," I counter calmly, no longer chopping the wood.

She's too close, and I wouldn't ever want to put her in danger. I think I've done far enough of that.

"Can you look at me?" she asks softly.

I sigh, but take off my sunglasses and look at her. The scar on her cheek is healing nicely, her dark hair is in a bun and she's wearing shorts and a plain t-shirt.

Why does she have to be so fuckin' cute?

"Have you been sleeping?"

"Yeah, I've been sleepin'," I lie.

"I think the clubhouse is too crowded. I think we're going to move into Smiley's old place for now," she says.

"Okay," I reply. It's a good idea.

It will be a relief not to have her sweet smell up in the clubhouse all the time.

"I'd like for you to come with us," she states.

Her brown eyes plead with mine, and I don't want to tell her no, but I don't know how I can say yes, either. I want her, undoubtedly; I know I don't deserve her, but that's not the issue. I've hurt her so deeply, and I'm not sure I can forgive myself for that. The guilt of Leon's death, and her mother's banishment, weighs heavily on me, heavier than killing my father does.

"I don't know, Lily."

"Will you think about it? It would be a comfort to me to have you there, even if we don't share a room."

She's fuckin' killing me.

"How can I say no to that?" I ask her.

"You can't," she says with a smile.

"Okay."

"Okay," she sighs before walking away.

SMILEY'S HOUSE is so dated. Luckily, he was clean. Though I would have preferred that he was a decent fuckin' man. I moved all my shit into one of the spare rooms. This house only has three bedrooms and one and a half bathrooms, so it's still a tight fit. Lily deserves better, and I'm working on it.

Part of me still wants Cash and Axel to run away with her. If she's not here, I won't have to worry about her so much.

I knew if she stayed, she'd make me fold. I'm already in love with her, but I know when I bond with her I'll never have a single day of peace for the rest of my life.

I guess it's no different from the anxiety I have over her now, but I know it will be intensified if we're bonded. Axel was right to stop me from biting her, during her heat.

I wonder if I'll ever stop hating myself so fuckin' much.

As much as I try to sleep every time I shut my eyes, my

worst fears flash behind my eyelids. Maybe I need to talk to Blaze about taking something to help me sleep.

My door creaks open, and her soft feet pad across the floor before she crawls into my bed wordlessly.

She wraps her small arm around me, and it's quiet for a moment.

My body stills, but her scent cocoons me. She isn't trying to be sexual, just offering me comfort when I don't deserve it.

"It's okay, baby, I got you," she whispers my own words back to me. It's at this moment I realize that I've already lost this internal battle with myself, and I fall asleep without the nightmares haunting me.

FORTY-FOUR

INVISIBLE SCARS

LILY

I WAS WORRIED that when I woke up Tate wouldn't be here, but shockingly, he is. At some point in the night, we switched positions. Tate's now behind me, his leg in between mine, and his arm is a heavy weight around my waist.

His scent is soothing as he breathes evenly behind me. I should get up and start my day, but there's no way that I'm getting up when he's sleeping so well.

We need to talk, and I'm running through different conversation scenarios in my head when he wakes up. His hand flexes on my waist before he takes it away, as well as his leg. I'm quick to spin around in the bed and face him. His hair is an adorable mess as he blinks away the sleep in his eyes.

"Morning," I say first.

"Mornin'. What time is it?"

"Ten."

"I slept till fuckin' ten? Hell," he grumbles, and it looks like he's about to get up. No, we need to have this conversation now. I tug on his arm and pull him back down to the bed.

"We need to talk," I tell him sternly. I'm not letting him run away anymore, or fucking stew in self-pity.

I need him, and he needs to step up.

"Okay," he concedes, lying back down on his side, staring at me.

All the scenarios I ran through my head earlier fly out the window as I look at him. *What was it I wanted to say?*

"You want me?" I ask him, keeping it simple.

"Yes."

"But you don't think you deserve me?" I ask him.

That's the biggest read I've been able to get off of him.

"I don't think. I *know* I don't fuckin' deserve you, Lily," he admits softly, and I can tell he genuinely believes that.

"Then why did you kiss me before you left the lake house?"

"Because I thought it would be the last time I'd ever see you," he replies, and I have to swallow down a whimper. I don't like the idea of him talking about not coming back to me.

"But you're attracted to me. You have feelings for me?"

"It doesn't matter, Lily. How can you want to be with someone like me? I sent your mother away. I didn't do more to help your brother. I killed my own fuckin' father. I'm not a good man, and I never will be."

"You think I'm going into this with rose-colored glasses? You think I don't know who you are? I know exactly who the three of you are, and I love you all, regardless. I don't blame you for any of those things, and no one else does either. I need you to be a part of my pack or you'll be hurting me," I tell him.

Am I being manipulative? Probably. But I honestly don't care, because it's the truth. If Tate walks away from this, it'll shatter me.

"I can read between the lines of the things you three don't tell me. I know you're dangerous men, but I also know that none of you would ever hurt me," I plead with him, my hand gripping his wrist.

"What if I'm just like him?" he replies.

"Like who? Your father?"

"He ran this club into the fuckin' ground, Lily. You lived under the same roof as him for a decade and you didn't know.

How do you know I won't turn out to be just fuckin' like him?" he asks. His eyes grow glossy, but he doesn't cry.

I cup his face, and he leans into my touch. His beard is thicker than usual, but it's soft against my palm.

"Because your father never asked those questions. He never worried about his morality or who he hurt. You care, Tate. Your heart is so fucking big and you don't even realize it. Please let me in," I plead.

Now my own eyes are welling with tears.

His hands come up to cup my face, and we just stare at each other for a moment before he speaks again.

"I want you. I've wanted you for a long time, but I'm fuckin' scared, Lily."

"So am I. Be there for me, and I'll always be there for you. I love you, Tate," I tell him softly.

His eyes close, and he takes a deep inhale as he presses his forehead against mine.

"I love you too, so much," he admits, pressing a soft kiss against my skin.

The touch makes me shiver, and I sigh with the sense of relief that fills me. I know all our issues aren't resolved, but this feels like a step in the right direction.

I tilt my chin in his hold and his lips meet mine. The movement is tentative; I'm scared of spooking him. But when his lips touch mine, it feels so right. It feels like the pieces are clicking together and a part of my heart is healing.

I don't know why, but as he kisses me, I cry.

He doesn't stop kissing me softly, but his thumbs wipe away my tears while he continues.

"I never want to hurt you again, Lily Rose," he murmurs when he breaks away from the kiss.

"So don't," I reply, knowing he would never do anything to truly hurt me.

He presses his forehead against mine again, just stroking my cheeks as my tears fade away.

"I have your mom's new number… if you want to call her," he offers, pushing my messy hair behind my ears.

I blink at him and try not to cry again.

"I'd like that."

This small moment means everything to me, and I know we need more time together, more *genuine* time together.

Tate must be having the same realization as me because he asks, "Can I have you to myself tonight?"

I can't help but grin and nod enthusiastically.

"Good, why don't you have Doc take another look at this today too," he says, gliding his thumb just underneath my scar, but not touching it.

"Axel needs to have his wound checked, anyway. We'll go together."

"How is your *husband* going to feel about havin' to share you with someone else?" He uses the word husband as a swear, but I look past it.

"I think we've gone well past the point of sharing, haven't we?" I ask, and his cheeks heat an adorable shade of pink. I kiss his flushed face as I get out of the bed.

He's up on his elbows as I lean in for another kiss.

"I'll see you tonight," he says.

"Tonight."

I make my way to the shower, the weight on my shoulders feeling a little less heavy, but it's still there. There's still so much I haven't let myself feel, and I feel guilty over it.

How can I want to forget everything that happened while also wanting to hold certain memories close to my heart? It's a truly hopeless feeling.

Being safe, having my pack, and the club the way it is truly eases some of the discomfort. I know Leon would have been so proud of what Tate is doing here; I just have to hold on to that and try to live my life in a way he would be proud of, too.

"I REALLY DON'T KNOW why I need to see Doc," Axel complains as I tug on his hand while we walk to the clubhouse.

"Well, I want him to look at my scar and no one has looked at your arm. You got shot," I remind him.

"It wasn't even that bad. I'm fine."

I roll my eyes at him and pull the Omega / wife card.

"I'm your wife, and it would make me feel more settled if you went and saw him," I tell him.

"You're a fuckin' menace. You know I can't say no to that."

"Exactly, now quit your bitching. Let's go."

He lets me tug him along the dirt road as we walk through the clubhouse and go to the back room, which is set up as Doc's infirmary.

He gives me a polite smile and pats the table for me to sit down.

"What's going on, love?" he asks.

"Don't call her love," Axel growls behind me.

"Can we have some privacy?" I ask, turning back to look at Axel.

He narrows his eyes at me and then at Doc, but leaves the room.

"Touchy one, your Beta," Doc teases.

I shrug and wring my hands together.

"Is there something you wanted to talk about? Are you hurting somewhere besides your face?" he asks. His touch is soft as he looks at my scar with approval.

"I know I can't really leave the compound right now, and that I have a pack and everything. But I don't want to unload all this grief onto them," I confess.

I know Doc was a doctor in the Defence Forces, but he feels like the only one I can ask. When you're around a bunch of bikers, mental health isn't at the forefront of everyone's mind.

"I have a friend. They can do everything virtually," he says, pulling out a card and handing it to me.

"You had that ready to go, just like that?"

"Tried to give Shelby one," Doc says with a shrug.

"And what did she say?"

"To fuck off and for my ginger-ass to get the hell out of her business," he sighs.

"That sounds like her. Maybe I can talk to her."

"Don't think she's up for much talking these days," he says, and I swear he seems sad about it.

"Did you know my brother well?" I ask him.

Doc was one of the new patch overs. I'm not sure how much time he spent with Leon.

"No, not well. He wasn't around much. But it seems like everyone loved him and is devastated about what happened. I am sorry for your loss, love," he replies sweetly, looking at my face one more time. "Everything with your scar is looking well. Just give it time and it will barely be there."

Even if it goes away completely, I will always know it's there.

Sometimes scars are invisible and this will be one I'll carry with me forever.

I hold up the card before stuffing it in my pocket. "Thanks again for this, and hopefully Shelby will come around," I say, hoping that someone will get through to her.

"Aye, I hope she does too," he responds. "Now send in that towheaded fuck. I've hardly even looked at his arm."

I nod and drag Axel to sit in front of Doc. He doesn't seem worried about the way his arm is healing and gives him a clean bill of health.

"You happy now?" he grumbles.

"Extremely," I reply smugly, as I take his hand in mine.

He leads the way and I get nervous as he walks us to my old house. He skirts around the side until we're at my—our—tree.

I climb up to my perch and he follows me till we're snuggly

on the same branch, his arm over my shoulder as he holds me close.

"How are you doin'?" he asks softly.

"I don't know," I reply.

"I'm always here, you know that? You know I cared about him, too. It's been a lot, and it's okay for you to be sad. You don't have to pretend around me."

I rest my head against his chest, hearing his heartbeat and taking a deep breath.

"Part of me is so pissed at him, you know? I had money. I could have gotten him—both of us—out of here. He should have asked for help a long time ago."

"We'll come back to the money part later," he notes before pushing me to continue.

I grimace. *Shit.* I guess Axel is the only one who doesn't have an inkling about what I was doing online. But I was kind of hoping to just take that snippet of my life to the grave. Marielli's Mass feels like a lifetime ago in the grand scheme of things.

"I don't think he felt like he could, not until the patch overs came here. Even then, he didn't really want to tell Tate. We didn't know what was goin' on in our own fuckin' club. He was doin' what any man would do to keep the people he loved safe. And he did that, he got you out. Who knows what would have happened if he wasn't there? All this guilt lies on Kurt, no one else. He didn't suffer enough for the pain he caused, but we're here. We get to live.

"I know it's fucked up to say this in the wake of everything. But I'm so fuckin' happy, Lily. I never thought I'd have somethin' like this, someone like you." He pauses to kiss my forehead before he continues to speak. "I don't know how to explain the way the club feels right now, but it feels like there's finally hope. It's not just existin' in this life hopin' I don't die. I have somethin' to live for, truly fuckin' live for, and I wouldn't trade it for nothin'."

"It feels wrong to let myself be happy, you know?" I ask.

"Leon would be pissed off to hear you say that shit, you know that? Your mom too," he reminds.

I swallow thickly.

"Did she look okay when you saw her?"

"She was devastated, and for what it's worth, I don't think she wanted to leave but knew she had to," he promises me while rubbing my arm.

"Tate gave me her number. I think I'm ready to call her."

"Do you want me to stay, or go?" he asks, and I lean in closer to him.

"Stay, I always want you to stay," I confess.

I take out my phone, along with the little piece of paper with the number on it, and dial. My heart rate is through the roof as it rings a few times before my mom's voice filters through the line.

There are a lot of tears at first, both of us just letting the emotion out of hearing each other's voices again and grieving over what we lost. She lost a son and a partner. I can't imagine how she's feeling going through all this.

I love my mom—truly, I do—but I think her leaving was for the best. I'm not sure I'd be able to move forward and want to heal myself if she was here.

Once we're both calm enough to finally talk, I'm the one to break the silence.

"You're safe?" I ask her.

"I'm safe, are you?"

"Yes, we've gone on lockdown on the compound while we figure things out."

"Lily… if I would've known—"

"There's no point in talking about the what-ifs," I interrupt her, not wanting to shoulder the weight of her guilt on top of my own.

"You're right. They're taking care of you, like they promised?"

"Yeah, they're taking care of me."

"I'm sorry I didn't stay," she apologizes, and there's a long pause over the phone.

"It was for the best," I finally tell her, even though I feel bad saying it.

"Everyone needed a fresh start. I hope I get to see you soon," she says softly.

"As soon as we can make it work, where did you end up, anyway?"

"Texas," she replies. "It's different here. It's weird, just going out and doing things where no one knows who you are."

I hope my mom finds peace and can live a life where she's actually free. I realize now Alphas have manipulated her whole life, and she did the best she could. I don't think she was truly built for this life, and now she gets to actually live.

We're not the same, and I take some solace in that.

"Love you, Mom," I tell her softly.

"I love you too. I'm proud of you. Don't be a stranger," she says before we hang up.

I lean into Axel's touch; he doesn't say anything as he holds me and we just enjoy each other's company.

There's a point in your life when you realize that your parents are real people, who have gone through their own shit, and that they're flawed. It's a hard reality of life, but I hope that even though things will never be the same, that I can still have some sort of relationship with her. We'll never live under the same roof again, but I have hope that we'll have something, even if it's just simple phone conversations while I sit in a tree.

FORTY-FIVE

FUCKIN' PERFECT

TATE

I'D BE A FUCKIN' liar if I said I wasn't nervous.

I knew if Cash and Axel chose to stay on the compound with Lily, I'd give her whatever she wants, even if I don't think it's the right choice. I'll probably go to my grave thinking she could do better than me and knowing I'll love her more than she'll ever love me, but that's something I'll have to live with.

She said she needed me to be happy, so I've gotta work through all my bullshit to make that happen.

She's adamant that she knows what she's getting into and that she believes in me. Maybe her believing in me will need to be enough for the both of us right now.

I'm waiting for her in the middle of the square by the massive fuckin' bonfire I have going. That table went up in flames beautifully. It feels like a cleanse, and I wonder what else I need to get rid of in this fuckin' place to make it feel like my father was never here.

I guess it's wishful thinking that I'll ever be able to achieve that. He was here, and I suppose it's important to remember a tarnished history just as much as it is to remember the good parts.

Axel surprises me by coming and sitting next to me.

"She had to see Cash first. I'm not crashin' your date, don't worry," he teases.

"Okay."

"Hell of a fire," he comments as the flames dance in front of our faces.

"Yeah, it really is. I'm glad it's gone. I'm glad *he's* gone."

"Me too. For what it's worth, I think you're doin' a good job. I gotta imagine there's a lot goin' on for you, but being there for her is just as important," he scolds me softly.

I wish I didn't need the kick in the ass, but I do. I've gotta get over all this bullshit and hateful rhetoric I have in my head.

"I know."

"You're a fuckin' brick wall, man," he says with a laugh.

"I'm workin' on it," I promise, and I mean it.

I'm tired of keeping secrets and telling half-truths. I know I'll have to be completely honest with Lily. If she wants to bond with me, I won't have a choice in the matter, anyway.

I pull a beer from the cooler and hand it over to him. The top fizzes slightly when he opens it, and he quickly downs a quarter of it.

We spend a few moments just sitting in silence and looking at the fire. Maybe being in a pack with this asshole won't be as bad as I thought.

That thought quickly leaves me as soon as Lily walks around the fire and Axel starts acting like a complete asshole.

"Got a spot for you right here," Axel calls out, tapping his thigh.

"I thought you said you weren't here to crash my date," I glare over at him.

"That's right, totally forgot," he jokes as he stands up, kissing Lily on the side of her head before going off on his merry-fuckin'-way.

That Beta is going to drive me fuckin' crazy. But I can't deny he's as annoying as he is loyal.

"You sure you wanna stay married to him?" I ask Lily as she takes his seat.

"Very sure. Maybe we should take his last name as our pack name?" she taunts with a smirk.

I narrow my eyes at her, and she just starts laughing her ass off.

"You should see your face."

"I think we should come up with our own pack name," I tell her honestly.

I don't think any of us have true ties to the family names we carry. I certainly don't like the idea of carrying on my father's; Axel never talks about his family and neither does Cash. The idea of starting fresh, just like the club soothes something inside of me.

"I'd like that. We need to come up with something strong," she muses, thinking out loud.

"Stone," I throw out, looking over at her, and she scrunches her nose. "Valor?" I try, and she tilts her head.

"I like it. We'll have to talk to Axel and Cash about it. You came up with that pretty quick."

"I guess it's all the road name shit."

"How'd you get your road name? I mean, Cash is great with finances and Axel works on bikes, so those made sense. I always wondered about yours."

Fuck. Awesome, what a great way to start this date.

I take a sip of my beer, realizing I didn't offer her the drink I brought her. I pull out this overly feminine-looking pink glass bottle, taking the lid off, and handing it to her. She takes a sip and makes a noise of delight that goes straight to my dick.

Giving her food or drink provides me an amount of pleasure I didn't expect, and I make a note to do it as often as possible.

"Oh, that's sweet. I like this one," she comments. "Back to my question."

"You ever been to Carrabelle?" I ask her, and she shakes her head. "There's a state park there called Tate's Hell State Forest.

It's the place where I killed my first man on my father's behalf... it's also the same day I left Tallahassee for good," I admit.

When I look over at her, she doesn't look disgusted or scared. She just seems intrigued and maybe a little gleeful that I answered honestly.

"You didn't want to?" she questions.

"There are a lot of kills that I don't feel regrets about, but that one definitely hurt. My father gave me the road name, and it stuck. When I look back at it, I think he knew I would loathe the name, and that's why he gave it to me. It's a reminder that he was above me, that I followed what he told me to do. I think that was the worst of it all. I killed that man specifically because my dad told me to, no other reason. That was the last day I ever let him control me."

"Do you want me to call you Thomas?" she asks softly, and I shake my head.

"Nah, the name grew on me. It's who I am now. But I'm not proud of the origins."

She's quiet for a moment as she watches the fire and takes a heavy swig of her drink. It looks like she's contemplating something until she makes a noise in the back of her throat and stands. I assume she's going to leave me sitting here like a fuckin' asshat, but she shocks me by coming to stand right in front of me, before promptly sitting herself on my lap.

I shift and clear my throat.

"Don't get all shy on me now. I do remember some parts of my heat," she states.

"Oh, yeah?"

"Yeah, I remember you couldn't seem to get enough of my scent," she teases, and I can't help it as I lean over and get a whiff of her sweet coconut-smelling self.

"I wish we could have had more time before," I admit.

"Me too," she sighs. "But when it comes to the things we did during my heat, I don't regret anything. Well... maybe I regret throwing shit out the window." She snuggles closer to my chest. "I wouldn't have changed who was there or what happened in that room, though. You were there when I needed you, and I know you always will be."

She shifts on my lap, and I groan.

"Do you still have your room in the clubhouse?" she asks.

"Yeah, why?"

"I think we should go back there."

"Couldn't we just go back to the house?" I question, wondering why the fuck she wants to go to my old room at the clubhouse?

"I've kind of always had this fantasy," she confesses shyly while shifting on my lap.

"Of the clubhouse?"

She shrugs, and I pull her closer to me, making her perfume, which in turn makes my dick harden.

Is she really ready for this? Am I a prick if I sleep with her right now? She reads me like a fuckin' book.

"I want to feel good. I want *you* to make me feel good. Sitting around here moping and hating life isn't going to fix anything."

"Are you sure it's not too soon?" I ask, needing confirmation that I'm not going to make shit worse.

"I'm allowed to be sad and still enjoy my life. Feeling guilty or denying myself isn't going to change anything. "

"How'd you get so wise?" I ask her with a smirk.

I'm honestly just glad she's not spiraling or falling into a pit of guilt and self-loathing. Which seems to be happening to Shelby. Doc's told me he has it covered, but I'm not sure he can handle it. I wonder if Lily would have had the same fate if she didn't have us; I feel sick over the thought.

"Doc gave me a number to a friend of his. We talked through some things. I think I'll continue talking to her now and then," she says shyly like I'd judge her for getting help and it pisses me off.

I grip her chin and force her to look at me.

"Never feel embarrassed for takin' care of yourself. I'm glad you're talkin' to someone."

She smiles at me. "There he is," she beams. "Take me back to the clubhouse, Mr. President," she demands with a giggle. I shake my head at her, grabbing her by the waist and tossing her over my shoulder. She laughs and squirms as I carry her to the clubhouse.

"The guys are gonna want to fuckin' kill me," I joke.

"I'll try to be quiet." I smack her ass playfully, making her laugh more.

Fuck, I love hearing her laugh. It makes me smile, and I wonder when was the last time I ever felt this light.

"Don't you dare," I order her. Her perfume fills my nostrils, and I groan in response.

I open the front door to the club, which leads to the main bar area, causing multiple heads to turn our way. I make note of the fact that some Omegas feel comfortable enough to spend time here, and it eases something further in my chest. I'm making this club a safe place. I'm not my father.

"Put me down," Lily hisses, her head upside down as she tries to smack my ass.

"Don't mind us," I say, as I start walking down the hall.

"Oh, hell. I'm gettin' the fuck outta here," I hear one of the guys complain.

They can fuck off for all I care. Lily wanted this, and I'm gonna give her what she wants. It's not like I haven't heard them fuckin' more often than not.

"I didn't think this through," Lily bitches. "They're all going to know what we're doing in your room.

"They better hear it too," I tell her, and she pinches my thigh, making me jump.

"Oh, you're gonna pay for that one," I warn her as I get my door open, locking it behind me. I'm gentle as I toss her onto my bed. She bounces as she looks up at me with wide eyes and dilated pupils.

She clears her throat and looks away for a second, the sight making my heart sink. Maybe she's changed her mind, and she's not ready.

"If it feels right to bond during… you have my permission," she whispers.

"What?" I reel back, shell shocked.

"I don't want to pressure you or anything. But for me, it's inevitable, and I don't see any reason to wait. So if it feels right for you, I want you to know you have my permission, that it's not some lust-filled—"

I tangle my hands in her hair and crash my lips against hers, stopping her from giving me any more of her pretty words.

She wants me to bond with her.

She's giving me consent now because she knows I wouldn't do it in the heat of the moment. I'm not sure there's ever been anyone in my life that understood me the way that Lily does.

Fuck, I want to be everything she deserves.

I'm soft with her because I don't know what she really likes. I know what Lily in heat likes, but this is us navigating what we like together. I don't want to scare her off or be too intense from the get-go. I can do sweet and gentle. It's what she deserves.

The kisses I pepper on her jawline and neck are nearly feather-soft. She groans and tugs on my hair roughly, making me moan in pleasure.

Fuck, I love when she pulls on my hair.

"I don't want to be treated like glass."

"I just don't want to do nothin' you don't like."

She grips my cut roughly, tugging me flush against her body.

"If I wanted gentle, I wouldn't be here, Tate. Fuck me the way you fantasized and felt guilty for," she demands.

My cock presses tightly against my pants at her words, and my hand instinctively goes to her throat.

"Lily, darlin', you have no fuckin' clue what you're askin' for."

My thumb rubs against her pulse point, feeling her heart race as her lust-filled eyes meet mine.

"I know exactly what I'm asking for. The question is, are you going to give it to me?"

This woman was put on this planet to fuckin' destroy me.

"You're sure?" I question again.

She gives me a look of irritation before her face softens. "I've never been more sure of anything. Treat me like I'm *yours*," she commands.

"Because you are mine, isn't that right?" I ask her, my hand trailing from her throat to her jaw before my thumb grazes her bottom lip.

She opens her soft warm lips, and I push my thumb inside of her mouth. Her lips wrap around me, and she sucks my thumb deeply into her mouth while she holds eye contact with me.

My thoughts run wild with all the things I want to do with her. Being with her during her heat was rough, wet, and more than enjoyable. But Lily wasn't totally there. Her pheromones were running the show. I want her to want me in this way because she–the woman–not the Omega needs it.

"Are you goin' to be a good girl and do what I tell you to?"

She nods her head with my thumb still in her mouth before I tug it out with a pop. I smear the saliva that's on the tip against her bottom lip.

"Please, Tate," she begs.

"Please, what? What does my girl want?"

"Touch me," she whimpers, and I press my clothed cock against her open legs.

"I am touchin' you, Darlin'."

"Less clothes," she pants. Her tone is impatient, and now I know I'm gonna make her wait for it.

I leave all my clothes on while I unbutton her shorts and tug them off her thighs. She doesn't wait for me as she rips off her shirt, exposing her perfect, braless chest. She's eager as she starts to roll down her thong. I grab the stretchy material and pull it the rest of the way down her legs.

"Now you," she says, her gorgeous naked body hitting my bed. She's lying on her back, her body resting on her elbows as she spreads her thighs and shows me her wet, needy cunt.

"Mmm. Not yet," I deny her.

She licks her lips, but doesn't sass me back. I'm almost devastated when she listens to me; I kind of wanted to show her what happens when she's being a brat.

"Do you know how fuckin' perfect you are?" I ask as I crawl on top of her, my knees sinking into the soft mattress.

Her legs widen as she makes room for me, her pussy pressing against my pants making a wet spot.

I kiss along her throat, avoiding the side that has Cash's mark. I lick her sweet flesh and suck the skin between my lips. Her hips thrust against me as I smile against the column of her throat and place kisses against her jaw. She squirms under me, and her small hands go for my belt.

I grip her wrist hard, not enough to leave a mark or hurt, but hard enough that she knows I'm displeased.

"I said not yet, if you can't listen, I'll have to tie these pretty little hands up," I warn, kissing her wrist before letting them go.

Her eyes grow wide as I say it, but I can tell she isn't completely opposed to the idea.

"I'm gonna take my sweet fuckin' time with you, darlin'. Do you know how many times I fucked my own fist thinkin' about havin' you this way?" I ask, leaning down to kiss her chest, ignoring her nipples completely.

She's getting frustrated, tugging at my hair and making me moan from the feel of her nails raking against my scalp.

"Please, Tate. Please touch me."

I lean forward and take a nipple in my mouth, biting the flesh enough to make her startle with a gasp.

"I am touchin' you. If you want something from me, you're gonna have to be specific."

"I want you to go down on me," she replies confidently.

I smile up at her, and her fingers massage my head as I slowly make my way down her body, leaving a trail of kisses in my wake.

When I'm by her sweet pussy, it takes everything in me to not just lap her up and give her what she wants. But I think I've become addicted to hearing how much Lily wants me, I need her to really beg for it. Maybe there's a sick part of me that thinks if I hear her say it enough, I'll actually believe it.

I'm slow, kissing her pelvis, her hip, and thighs.

I keep pressing my lips up and down her strong yet soft thighs. The side of my face will touch her pussy lips, but I don't bring my mouth there.

She grows impatient, trying to direct my mouth where she wants me.

I graze my teeth against the inside of her thigh, causing the softest moan to slip between her lips and her whole body to shiver.

"Please, Tate. I need it. I want you so fucking bad," she whines.

"How bad?" I ask.

I'm a fuckin' prick, and I don't even care.

"You've made a mess of me and you haven't even touched me yet. I need you," she whines, her eyes pleading with me to finally give her some relief.

I give in. My mouth meets her pussy, and I groan with need and satisfaction as I drink her down. Lily's scent and taste will never get old.

I think I fuckin' need it to live.

It's like no matter how much of her taste hits my tongue, I can't get enough. I shift my body so that I can press my tongue deep inside of her while my thumb rubs circles against her clit.

Her warm wetness trails down my chin as I consume her.

Lily's scent is thick in the room, and my dick is excruciatingly hard in my pants. But God, do I want to see her fall over the edge of ecstasy before I give her my cock, making her scream while she takes my knot.

I lick up her entrance and bring my mouth's attention back to her clit. When I look up at her face her head is thrown back in pleasure. One of her arms is tossed over her face, while the other is still deeply entangled in my hair.

My lips wrap around her clit, and I suck hard.

"Fuck. Tate, I'm gonna come," she moans.

I keep the same pressure and wait as she breaks apart. Her thighs nearly crush my face as she trembles and holds my head against her pussy.

Her release fills my mouth, and all I can think is that nothing has ever tasted sweeter.

FORTY-SIX

FUCKIN' FINALLY

TATE PULLS his body up between my legs. He nearly has me ready to come again as he uses his forearm to wipe off the slick from his chin. I can't help but revel in the fact that he's covered in me, that he *smells* like me.

God, do I want him to claim me as his in every other way.

He didn't say it's what he wanted, but I know as soon as he knots me, I'll be begging for it. If he doesn't bond with me, I'll be hurt, but I'll understand if he isn't ready. I have to take what he gives me, and right now, he's giving me everything he can.

The way he looks at me as he climbs up my body, though it has me about ninety-eight percent sure he's going to give in.

I need his bond desperately like I need air to breathe, to be able to live. I just know when my pack is complete I'll have a settled sense of peace. I'll feel more secure. I'll be able to get through anything with all three of them linked to me.

"You did so good," he praises in a soft voice, kissing my throat before bringing his lips to mine.

He tastes like me, and I love it.

It's official, any chance I get I'm scent-marking the hell out of Tate. I want his mark on me, and I want to constantly mark him up with my scent. Maybe I'll also make him get a tattoo… I should actually make them all get tattoos—matching ones, of course.

The thought has me perfuming and making a low growl escape Tate.

"Get on your hands and knees and present that sweet little pussy for your Alpha," he rumbles against my ear.

I think I die from his tone and the rough way he helps flip me on the bed. With my stomach flat against the mattress, I do as he says, pushing my ass up into the air for him.

This position feels so exposing, raw, and dirty.

I fucking love it.

"Such a good girl for me," he groans, and I swear I can hear his wide smile as he says it.

The clank of his belt buckle and zipper have me keening with want, and the thought of him fucking me with his cut on makes me wetter.

It's what I always wanted, what I always dreamed about. A rough biker who's only sweet for me but treats me like his property at the same time.

Next time I'll need him to record it so I can watch it again and again… and again.

His large hands knead my ass cheeks, causing a needy whimper to fall from me. He lets out a dark chuckle and fuck, it has a rush of want flowing through me. I can feel my slick dripping down my thighs in anticipation.

I desperately need to feel his rough, demanding hands on my body, for him to shove his large cock deep inside of me and give me his knot. But the sadistic bastard just keeps grazing his fingertips along my skin touching me everywhere he can, but not in the way I crave. I feel some hope as he climbs behind me, his hard length pressing against the crack of my ass cheeks, but he doesn't push inside.

His hands stroke up and down my back before one of his hands slides down the back of my neck and grips my hair roughly, pushing my face harder into the mattress.

"Good?" he tests.

"Yes, more. Please, Tate."

He squeezes one ass cheek before fisting himself and slowly sliding the head of his length inside of me. He doesn't press in deep, only giving me a few inches. His hand is relentless in my hair, so I finally give in and start to beg.

"I want your knot. No, I *need* your knot."

"That's not a nice way to ask," he tsks with a smack to the underside of my left cheek.

I think I nearly come on the spot, my pussy clenching around what little of his length he's giving me. I could definitely get down with more of that. He smacks my ass again, and my back arches, my body involuntarily begging him to fuck me before my mouth does.

"Please. Please, give me your knot. I need it." I'm pathetic as I plead with him, but I don't even care.

Tate tugs on my hair hard as he roughly thrusts inside of me, giving me every single inch of him all at once.

I can't help the near scream that rips out of me from the delicious stretch. The pain mixed with the immense amount of pleasure is going to send me over the edge far too quickly.

I consider begging him for his knot again, but he already seems so full of himself, so I don't give him the satisfaction.

"Fuck, I'll never get tired of this pussy," he states with a growl in his voice.

Tate keeps my head pressed to the mattress, and I fist the sheets as he takes what he wants. He's rough with me, although I can't help but think it feels more like worship. The way he's fucking me and holding me like I'm the only thing that matters in his world is consuming, and I'm not sure I'll ever get enough. With each thrust, more of our combined arousal drips from my core until it's coating my thighs, and you can hear the sticky wetness of my pussy as our flesh meets.

How can I be so full of him but still want so much more? I

want him to knot me roughly and sink his teeth into my neck, claiming me as brutally as he is now. No, I fucking need it.

His hand smacks my ass once more before he wraps it around my middle as he tugs me by my hair so that my back is pressed against his front. The leather of his cut is cool against my heated skin, making me shiver. Tate doesn't stop thrusting inside of me as he holds me up and his mouth presses against my neck.

"This is what you want, darlin'? You want my knot deep inside of you and my mark on your fuckin' neck?"

"Please, Alpha." It comes out as a whimper, and he pushes his knot into me, making my knees buckle.

His hand leaves my hair so he can wrap both of his arms around me and rut me from behind. I use his muscular arms for purchase, likely digging my nails into his flesh as he slides a hand down my torso to play with my clit.

"Gonna mark you as mine, Lily Rose," he says softly.

Those words break me, and I come apart completely. My vision goes hazy as my pussy grips his length and his knot fills me entirely. The stretch is just the right amount of overwhelming as he moans in my ear before dropping his head against my neck, gliding his lips over the spot he's chosen for his mark.

He's gentle as his teeth sink into me, branding me as his. My orgasm continues to rip through me as our connection forms and I feel him, truly feel him.

I can't help the tears that spill out over my face from the overstimulation and happiness. I can finally feel Tate, and it feels like I'm finally home.

I'm where I've always wanted to be, and it's in his arms.

Tate kisses the mark reverently as we both breathe heavily, our heartbeats thumping in sync while we hold one another. He moves slow as he shifts us onto the bed so we're lying on our sides. It's not an easy feat to do while knotted together, and he may have groaned in discomfort on the way down.

He grabs a worn patch quilt blanket and tosses it over me.

"You're still dressed," I note with a laugh.

He shrugs behind me but holds me tighter. "Seemed like you liked it. I think you got off on me wearin' my cut while we fucked."

He's not wrong.

"We're bonded," I breathe out in a whisper.

He nuzzles my neck, the feeling of contentment flowing through the bond, and I'm not sure Tate has ever had that feeling in his life.

"Yeah, we really are. Thank you," he says softly.

It's as if words can't fully express what we're feeling, but the bond between us does. We lie there in silence, just basking in the afterglow of our bonding.

Even when Tate's knot releases us, he stays inside of me for a while; I find it more comforting than I should.

Tate is the one that breaks the silence. "We should shower," he whispers, and I nod.

My back aches slightly when I get up, but I'm distracted when Tate takes my hand in his as he walks us to his attached bathroom. I'm so fucking lucky he has a room with a bathroom. The idea of using the communal bathroom in the hallway of the club makes me want to curl up and die.

Tate finally undresses, and I get to see every lovely inch of him. He has the Dead Palms signa tattooed on his back, and a few tattoos scattered over his chest. I can't help it when my fingertips graze every single one.

As soon as the water is warm, we file into the shower, and I wrap my arms around him. I can't help but feel like bonding with Tate has somehow healed a part of my heart, and I refuse to let myself feel guilty about the way I chose to heal myself.

"IF YOU DON'T QUIT BABYING me, I'll take you over my fucking knee," Cash complains as I try to help him take his shirt off.

"You have a skull fracture and like eight million stitches in your head!" I shout back, and he winces, making me feel guilty. "Sorry," I whisper.

"No, I'm sorry. I fucking hate feeling like this."

"As soon as your head is better, I'll let you boss me around all you want. I promise," I counter sweetly.

"Stitches come out in five days anyway," he grumbles like he's trying to talk himself down.

I straddle his lap where he lies on the mattress. He hates being stuck in bed, but the amount of headaches and general tiredness forced us to keep him confined in this room.

"You'll be back up, scowling at everyone but me, in no time."

His large hands grip my hips, and he squeezes. He finally seems semi-settled, obviously still pissed about being in this bed, but he doesn't seem on edge like he did when he first came home. We both know there are still threats out there, and who knows if we can ever truly let our guard down, but there have to be some peaceful moments in between all of life's chaos.

As I look at his handsome face, I can't help smiling at him. I can sense that he feels loved and taken care of through our bond, and that's all I ever wanted.

"I like seeing you smile again, baby girl," he says quietly.

I feel shy at that moment, but I nod my head. I've been working through the guilt, and maybe part of me is still in denial about everything that happened, but I know I've got to live. If not for my sake, for my pack's, and for Leon's.

"I'm working on it," I promise him.

"What are you up to today?" he asks. I know he doesn't want to be left alone in this room again.

Tate and Axel are doing club shit that I don't want to know

about, so staying with Cash seems like the perfect way to spend the day to me.

"Well, you see... I have this Alpha." I grind on his hips a bit and smirk. "Poor thing is bedridden and being a total nightmare about it. So I thought I'd keep him company all day."

"Is that so?"

Winnie chooses that moment to whine and use her nose to nudge Cash's hand off of me, begging for pets.

"I'm really pissed she likes you more than me," I whine with a pout as he pets the dog that was supposed to be mine.

He gives me a small grin as he keeps one hand on me while the other pets the dog.

"Once we get the new house built, if you want to get her a friend, we can," he suggests.

"I think it's only fair. This time when we get a dog, I will only let her around me and none of you for weeks, so she imprints on me. This isn't fair," I grumble as I give in and pet her too. She accepts my touch, loves it even, but the little brat doesn't look at me the way she looks at Cash.

"I should take her out, and then we can spend the day together in bed."

"Fine," Cash agrees.

"Come on, girl," I say to her, clicking my tongue.

She looks to Cash for orders, and I want to roll my eyes. He gives her a tilt of his head, and the dog follows me outside. The compound is entirely fenced in and Winnie is friendly, so I don't bother with a leash while I let her sniff, stretch her legs, and do her business.

I'm flipping my sunglasses off the top of my head due to the bright-ass sun when I see Shelby for the first time since we left the lake house.

She's walking to the sweet house, and I follow after her, shouting her name. She doesn't turn until I finally grab her arm and tug at it, forcing her to spin around. She stumbles nearly losing her balance, and there are dark circles under her eyes.

She looks like she has been out all night with the state of her clothes and the stench of beer wafting off of her.

She's absolutely drunk… and it's not even noon.

"Are you okay?"

"No. I'm not like *you*. I don't have the perfect little pack that'll help me forget all this horrible shit that fucking happened," she spits.

She might as well have slapped me in the face. It would have hurt less.

"Fuck, I didn't mean that. Just leave me alone, Lily," she growls, trying to tug her arm away from me.

"I'm worried about you," I say softly, doing my best not to take her words to heart.

"I don't need anyone else on this stupid fucking compound worrying about me. I'm fine. I'm dealing with it. I'd be better off if everyone just stopped bothering me all the time. I don't want to talk about it, I don't want to think about it. Just…" she sighs and shakes her head, her tone going softer as she speaks. "Just leave me alone for a little while, okay?"

"Shelby," I sigh out her name, not knowing what to say.

I know that I can't leave her alone. She's clearly not okay. We went through a lot together and while I have three people to lean on; she has no one.

Her big blue eyes are welling with tears, and she shakes her head. "No, I don't want to do this right now."

I ignore her words as I wrap my arms around her and hold her tight. She sobs drunkenly against my shoulder, her cast between us and her other arm hanging limp. Eventually, she wraps her uninjured arm around me and hugs me back.

"I'm always here for you, okay?"

"Okay," she hiccups.

Winnie comes between us, and Shelby gets on her knees to pet the dog. Winnie licks up her tear-streaked face, and I watch the tension rolls out of her a little.

"Do you want to watch her for a few hours?"

"Really?" she asks, and I nod my head.

"I'll pick her up at three."

"Yeah, I think I'd like that."

If Shelby can't talk to people about her feelings, maybe she'll do it with a dog. It seems like something that might work for her. It also gives me a reason to check on Shelby in a few hours when I pick Winnie up.

She calls Winnie's name and my dog obediently follows her to the sweet house.

I'm about to walk back to the house when Maverick stops me, waving me down with a huge basket in his hand.

"What's that?" I ask.

It's already partially open, but it's far too feminine-looking to belong to one of the guys.

"It's a gift for you, sorry it's all fucked up. We had to look through it for safety reasons," he apologizes with a grimace.

"Thanks for bringing it," I say, going to grab the basket.

"Nah, I'll walk it to your place," he replies.

I give him a soft smile, and he trails behind me to the house.

"So, Cora stuck around?" I ask. The Beta and I aren't as close as Shelby and me, but I like her all the same.

"Yeah, hopin' to fuck she doesn't change her mind."

"She won't," I tell him honestly.

If she was going to leave, she would have already done it by now.

I open the front door, and Maverick follows me down the hall to the main bedroom where Cash is lying down.

He places it on the dresser, and Cash gives him an odd look.

"Alright then, feel better, man. See ya later," Maverick says, clearly wanting to get the hell out of here.

FORTY-SEVEN

LUCKY

CASH

LILY IS the only reason I haven't lost my mind. If it weren't for her giving me shit left and right, I know I'd be up off of this bed and pushing myself past my limits.

I have to remind myself constantly that we're no longer in immediate danger, that we're safe inside of the compound. But I know this ceasefire won't last forever. Eventually, the Wraiths will act... or we will. There's no way both clubs can be left standing, too much blood has been shed for that to happen.

Lily comes back into the room without the dog on her heels and instead has Maverick following her holding a big fucking basket.

"Shelby is going to watch Winnie for a few hours," she explains without me having to even ask.

I wait until Maverick leaves before I respond back.

"Are you sure that's a good idea?"

I've heard from Tate just how unwell Shelby is doing, and I don't know if leaving our dog with her is the best plan.

"I don't think Shelby knows how to really express herself around people. Maybe she'll be able to let out some of her feelings with Winnie. Plus, that means I get you all to myself."

"Are you jealous of the dog?" I tease her with a smirk.

"No, I'm not jealous of the dog."

"It seems like you're jealous," I counter, liking her posessiveness far more than I should.

"Fine. Sue me for wanting you all to myself."

"You know I like it. What's with the basket?"

She pulls out a pale pink letter and smiles as she reads it.

"It's a gift from Liv, the Omega who came with her pack to get the rest of the dogs."

"I didn't know you two kept in touch," I reply.

"We text every now and then, and I have a standing invitation to their swanky-ass mansion in Connecticut," she says with a waggle of her eyebrows.

"What does the card say?"

"Congratulations on finding your pack. I knew they were yours the moment I saw them. Wishing you the best, Liv," she reads, turning the card over and looking at the back before rummaging through the basket. "Mmm, truffles," she hums in delight, grabbing two of them before popping one in her mouth and holding the other out in her hand.

She climbs onto the bed and takes the same position as before by straddling me, my hands automatically going to her waist. She pops the truffle into my mouth, probably in an attempt to silence me while she speaks.

"I haven't asked you how you feel now that I've bonded with Tate. I know you were expecting it and you don't have any issues with him, but I just worry that I should have given you more warning before it happened. It wasn't fair of me to bond with him while you're hurt, and I'm sorry—"

I have to swallow the truffle quicker than I want to in order to stop her rambling.

"Hey, look at me," I interrupt her, tipping her chin up and forcing her gaze to mine. "Did I wake up from a nap with my cock hard? Yeah, I definitely did," I start, and she grins at me. "But you did nothing wrong. I can feel how whole it makes you through the bond, and it makes me happy. I only want to see you happy, baby girl, nothing else matters."

I mean every word, and I know she can feel the sincerity through the bond. I knew Tate was going to join this pack, it was only a matter of time. Since he's bonded her, I feel how much lighter her emotions are, and I couldn't have asked for anything more.

Her perfume fills the room, and I have to swallow thickly as she shifts on my lap.

"How bad does your head hurt?" she asks, her hands softly rubbing against my neck and shoulders.

"Not too bad," I lie.

I know if I tried to bend over or do too much moving, I'd be dealing with an excruciating migraine. But I don't need her fussing over me. She needs to know I'm still the Alpha she bonded with.

"Good enough for some kissing?"

"I always feel up for that," I promise her.

She leans forward gently, making sure she doesn't touch or bump my wound as her lips press against mine. My hands squeeze her soft flesh as I press her against my hardening cock.

Thank fuck I'm not hurt enough for it to affect my sex drive. Though, I'd think it would be impossible for anything to make me not want Lily in the most carnal way. She's my everything, and I'm not afraid to admit it.

Before I came and patched over to this club, I didn't know what direction I wanted my life to go in, but I swear I found it in her. I'll never say it out loud, but every single fucked-up thing that's happened since I've gotten here was worth it, as long as I get to have her.

Lily's hands clasp my neck as she kisses me. I feel her love for me float down our connection. She pours it all into the kiss, showing me just how much she needs me and wants me.

I never truly knew how badly I liked feeling needed until her, until this club.

Lily comes first, but actually making a difference in this club is a close second. I'm not sure if it's because I may have finally found a place worth calling home, or if it's because the club matters so much to Lily. But does the reason really matter?

Lily feels small in my arms as she shifts her body weight, making me groan.

"Okay?" she asks, pulling away from our kiss.

"More than okay," I tell her, snaking my hands under the hem of her dress and pushing down on her ass cheeks to grind her pussy harder against me.

There are barely any clothes between us since I'm only wearing my underwear and she's wearing one of those sweet little dresses I like so much. My fingers graze the dampness of the thin layers between us, and I can't deny how much I fucking need her in this moment.

It's worth my head feeling like someone is taking a hammer to it if I get to be inside of her again.

I remove my hand from her plump ass and attempt to slide it into the front of her panties when she stops me. She smirks as she cups my cheek.

"Let me take care of you," she offers, sliding down my body to grab the waistband of my boxers.

"Fuck," I hiss as she tugs the material down my thighs.

She lightly drags her teeth against one of my legs.

"You know, I've been wondering where I'd want you to get my name tattooed on your skin," she starts, taking in all the tattoos that cover my legs. "But there's hardly any room left," she pouts.

"We'll find somewhere," I promise her.

If she wants me to get a tattoo on my fucking face, I will. *Her name on my forehead sounds nice.*

She smiles, knowing she got what she wanted as she opens her mouth and swipes the head of my cock with the tip of her tongue. In this position, I can't see her pretty face as she sucks me down, so I slowly shift my body so that I'm lying flat on the bed, just a soft pillow behind my head so that I can watch her as she takes me.

She moves so that she's nearly on her stomach between my legs, glancing up at me every now and then while she tortures me with her mouth.

Her hand grips me at my knot while the other one jerks my shaft. Her pillowy lips wrap around the head as she sucks the top few inches.

"I'm not going to last long with you doing that, baby girl," I warn her.

A flash of desire falls over her face, and I can tell she likes the idea of having that kind of power over me.

"You look so fucking pretty with my cock in your mouth. How much can you take?" I ask her.

With determination, she slides me deeper into her mouth before withdrawing. She hums, relaxing her throat, taking more of me with each go, and I almost lose it with each bob of her head.

She gags slightly. When she hits a certain spot, her saliva drips down my length and over her fist, but she keeps going.

"So perfect, look at you," I praise her.

The words of encouragement spur her on as she takes me as deep as she can, her lips touching my knot.

My hand tangles in her hair as I keep her there for a short moment and enjoy the warmth of her mouth covering me.

She pulls up, taking a deep breath. A chain of spit connects her bottom lip to my dick, and I groan at the sight.

Her tongue swipes out, licking the slit of my cock, and it breaks me. As soon as she suctions her lips back around me, I lose all control.

I fill her mouth with my cum, and she takes every drop. Her eyes hold mine as she drinks me down.

Her self-satisfaction flows down the bond, and I know she feels my relief and pleasure.

The little minx licks me from knot to tip after I've finished, and I can't help but moan at the overstimulation as she continues to play.

My cock is softening, but she slides up and straddles me.

"See, being taken care of isn't so bad," she taunts.

"No, you can do that whenever you want."

Her wet panties rub against my abdomen, and I make a silent vow to not leave this bed until I see her fall apart, too.

"I need to see you come, sweetheart. What do you want?"

"We can't risk anything with your head," she scolds.

"I don't need to move much to get you off."

"Prove it," she challenges with a conspiratorial smile.

I shift her body so that she's now straddling my thigh, her knees holding the brunt of her weight.

"Rub that sweet little pussy on me until you come," I tell her.

"I need to take my underwear off," she says, attempting to get up.

Instead, I grab the side of her thin panties and rip the seam at her hip.

"Hey," she complains.

"I'll get you more, and then I'll rip those, too. Now do what I said."

She tries to act affronted, but she does what she's told. Her slick soaked pussy slides along my thigh as her sweet perfume fills the small bedroom.

"I'll never get enough of your scent. You smell so good."

I grab her dress and bunch it around her hips so I can watch her pussy glide against my skin.

"That's it. You're going to come all over me, aren't you? My jealous little Omega likes marking me up with her scent, doesn't she?"

"Yes," she whispers back.

One of her hands reaches out to press against my chest, balancing herself so she can ride me harder. I know with each pass of her clit on my muscular thigh, she's getting closer to the edge of ecstasy.

"Come here," I direct her so that I can kiss her and she's at a better angle to ride me.

She moans softly against my lips as I squeeze her ass, helping her shift up and down my thigh.

"I need you to coat my leg with that sweet pussy. You're going to be a good girl and come for me, aren't you?" I ask as her neck tilts, and I kiss my bond mark on her throat.

The left side of her neck is mine, and I suck and lick at the marking that signifies our bond.

"Such a good Omega for me. You drive me fucking crazy," I growl out.

Her grip on my shoulder tightens as her hips rut back and forth. Some of her movements become stilted, and I take over, pressing my leg harder against her cunt.

"Make a mess of me, baby girl."

My words seem to be her breaking point because she moans in my ear, and I feel a gush of her wetness pooling on my leg.

"That's it. So good," I praise her as she breathes heavily in my ear.

We just lie like that for a long moment, her still on top of my thigh as I rub small circles on her back.

"Mmm," she sighs dreamily, climbing off of me and resting her head on my shoulder. "What do we do with the rest of the day?"

"Just give me ten more minutes," I joke, making her laugh.

Her body is so tightly pressed against mine, and I still can't get enough. I lean down and kiss the top of her head.

"As soon as I'm better and shit isn't so messy, I want to take you somewhere," I tell her.

"Where?"

"Anywhere. You said you wanted a life of adventure. I never forgot that. I'm not keeping you cooped up in this place. That's no fucking way to live."

"I don't mind it for now. I know it's necessary, but you're right."

Her fingertips trace the scars on my skin while we lie together, and I feel so content I nearly forget about the stitches in my head for a short moment.

"Where would you want to go?"

"There's so many places; New Orleans, Austin, California, Montana, maybe Myrtle Beach," she lists.

"Myrtle Beach is a hellhole," I reply.

"A hellhole I haven't gotten to see for myself."

She pokes my side, and I immediately buck away from her touch, making her laugh.

"Then it's settled. As soon as it's safe, we'll take a trip."

"All of us?" she questions.

"All of us. As much as I want you all to myself, I get it. You don't have to worry about sharing with me, Lily. I'm not as jealous as you," I tease, and she pokes me again.

"Take that back," she growls, and the little shit pokes me so hard it's a mix between tickling and torture.

"Okay, I take it back. I'm the more jealous one, but I accept them. You need all three of us, and what you need will always be the most important thing to me."

"How did I get so lucky?" she sighs wistfully, nuzzling closer to me.

"I ask myself the same thing every day."

I already knew I loved Lily, but now I know for certain there isn't a single life in which I could live on without her.

FORTY-EIGHT
OUR DARLIN'
LILY

EACH DAY THAT PASSES, life gets easier. It doesn't hurt that the change between before and now can be seen all around me. The change throughout the compound is palpable, and I welcome it.

I wish Leon were here to see it; I know he'd be proud.

The hurt and pain of his loss isn't something that just goes away, but there are moments where I'm able to live in the present, and I'm grateful for it. Usually when one of my pack mates has me wrapped up in their arms and my full attention is on them… it's like the pain goes away, and I welcome the momentary delusion wholeheartedly.

On the other hand, there are just as many moments where I'm alone or too lost in my thoughts that I can't escape the reality of him not being here.

It's during one of those moments where I'm contemplating what could have been while sitting in my tree when Axel comes walking by with something behind his back.

"What do you have?" I ask him with narrowed eyes, happy for a distraction.

"Can you come down?" he asks softly.

I climb down and stand in front of him. He looks so handsome today, and I can't help but tuck a loose strand of hair behind his ear.

He seems like he's on edge, and it has me concerned as I try to peek behind his back.

"What is it?"

"Leon's ashes," he whispers, pulling the simple black urn from behind his back and presenting it to me.

There's a lump in my throat as I stare at it. I had assumed they left him at that stash house.

"You… you all went and got him?"

He was wearing a Wraith's cut, so I had figured they all thought he was a traitor and would've… just left him there.

"I know it's not a full funeral like he deserves, but it's the best we could do," he shrugs.

"No, Axel… this, this is everything."

I'm so over crying, but I can't help it as I throw myself at him for a hug. His arms surround me in warmth as he holds me close.

"Thank you," I mumble against his chest.

"I'd do anything for you, darlin'," he promises, and I know he means it.

He hands me the urn, and we walk back to the house. I think about what Leon would have wanted me to do with these, but he was young, and we never talked about the possibility of him dying or what the aftermath would look like. I know immediately that my mom should have a piece of him. I also wonder if Shelby having a piece of him would help or hurt with what she's going through.

For now, I'll hold on to him, but I know I'll figure out a way to keep Leon's memory alive and honor his life in any way that I can.

"Do you want to stay home, or do you want to go to the party at the clubhouse?" Axel asks as I put the urn in a curio cabinet in the living room.

"What's the party for?" I ask.

"Being alive and shit, I guess?" he shrugs, and I laugh.

"Is Cash going?" I ask.

"Nah, he still can't drink, and he said it would be too loud."

"We can go for a little while," I offer.

I take another glance back at the urn, and I'm filled with so much love and tenderness. Having Leon's ashes here, having some sort of closure to everything that happened, settles something in me. I take Axel's hand, and we head over to the clubhouse.

"YOU KNOW, husband. I think you're gonna get lucky tonight," I slur as I sit on Axel's lap.

He throws his head back and laughs before plastering my neck and jaw with kisses. Tate and Cash both actively avoid touching each other's bond marks, but Axel doesn't seem to give a shit as he kisses every inch of me.

"You're hoggin' her," Tate complains from the seat next to me.

I lean back, but there are far too many of those pretty pink drinks in my system. Axel holds my back, and Tate cradles the back of my head, steadying me as he presses a kiss against my lips.

"Which one of you is going to dance with me?" I ask.

Tate's cheeks heat, and Axel laughs.

"You gonna complain about how I'm hoggin' her now, asshole?"

"No," Tate mutters, kissing me one more time before Axel pulls me up and tugs me to the dance floor.

Almost everyone is here, and the air feels so light and fun. I mean, I only have my birthday party to compare it to, and there's still an undercurrent of stress, but nothing like it was before.

All the Omegas except the twins, Hannah and Maggie, are here. They seem the most resistant to accepting the life we are offering, but they chose to stay nonetheless.

Ellie is in the middle of the dance floor, eating up attention from a few of the guys, while Quinn and Mason sit in a corner together.

Shelby is noticeably absent and my heart sinks. The other beta girls are here, though. Cora is all over Maverick, and Kim is pouring drinks.

"Hey, no stress. Dance with your husband," Axel encourages, pulling me out of my thoughts.

I smile up at him as he holds me through a slower song, and I press my cheek against his cut. We slowly sway to the music, and it hits me that this is all I ever wanted.

My home, my pack, and this family of a club.

It's not perfect, but it's mine.

I perk up when I see Shelby walk into the clubhouse. She seems shy as she walks through the space, heading for the bar. She doesn't speak to me, so I let her be.

One day it won't be so tense between us, but until then I'll take it at her pace.

The music changes to a faster song, and I grin as we switch up the way we're dancing, singing along to the song as I sway my hips. Axel's hands are all over me, and he is for sure getting lucky tonight.

Well, he gets lucky most nights. But tonight he can have me all to himself if he wants. It's stupid when I think of it. Out of everyone in my pack, if someone was going to decide to up and hoard me from the others, it would be Axel.

The music fades out, and Tate holds up his drink, the rest of the club following suit.

"To the Dead Palms, and the start of a true brotherhood," he says, raising his glass higher.

There are cheers throughout the room as everyone drinks,

and I grin over at my Alpha. He smirks, but sits back down in his seat.

The music doesn't start back up right away, and shouting draws everyone's attention to the faceoff happening between Mickey and Shelby.

Mickey is comically larger than Shelby, and I've missed most of the conversation, but I grimace when he points his finger in her face and sneers out his next words.

"Maybe he'd still be fuckin' alive if he didn't go back for your slutty ass," Mickey shouts at her. My jaw drops, but it's not from his words.

It's the way that Shelby pulls back her good arm and punches him right in the fucking face. I swear I can hear the crunch of his nose or her hand—I'm not sure which—but the sound makes me wince along with some of the other guys in the club.

Mickey grabs his face as blood gushes from his nose, and Shelby grimaces as she shakes out her hand.

"Oh, fuckin' hell. Really, love. Didn't I just patch up your other fuckin' arm? Let's go," Doc urges, dragging Shelby away.

"What about my face?" Mickey complains as they walk away.

Shelby holds up her hand with a cast and gives him the finger.

"Go fuck yourself, Mickey. Next time, it will be your small, pathetic dick I punch!"

Mickey goes to follow her, but Tate grabs him by the arm and ushers him to another room in the clubhouse.

"I hope she's okay," I say to Axel.

"She's a fighter. She'll figure her shit out," he promises.

The music starts to play again, and it's like the altercation never happened as everyone resumes their dancing and enjoyment of the night.

I consume two more pink drinks, feeling so light and airy as

I sway to the music. Axel looks down at me like I'm his every-thing, and maybe I am.

"You're ours forever, darlin'," he says with a smile.

I grin, biting my lip, and nod, feeling completely loved and cherished at this moment.

"Let's get out of here, it's too loud," Axel suggests.

He takes my hand in his, and we walk outside. The table Tate rage-chopped has significantly held the reserves for wood any time we wanted to have a fire pit, just like the current blaze holding up in the middle of the square.

It's just us, and I sit on his lap when we sit down. The night is dark and the stars are bright as I look up. I feel at peace, and part of me feels like Leon is smiling down on us right now.

Yet, having my Alphas here would be the thing that made this night absolutely perfect.

As if I summoned him through the bond, Cash comes strolling out to the fire with Winnie on her leash.

"There you are," I greet them with a grin.

He leans forward and kisses my cheek with the scar, and the sweet attention makes me feel loved; I feel seen.

"How was the party?" Cash asks, scooting his chair closer to us. Winnie sits in between his legs, paying us no attention.

"Fun, minus the part where Mickey and Shelby got in a screaming match, and she punched him in the nose," I tell him, reaching out and holding his hand in my lap.

Neither of the men seem to have an issue with being around each other, and I'm grateful for that. It has to be a mix of wanting me happy and being in the same club. Whatever it is, I'm glad that they can work together and be civil. Not that there isn't jealousy, but for the most part we work well as a newly found pack, and I'm excited to see what our future looks like.

"Did he deserve it?" Cash asks.

"Definitely fuckin' sounded like it. If he would have spoken to Lily like that he'd have more than a broken nose," Axel responds.

"Someone would have to have a death wish to mess with our girl," Cash comments, and I smirk, shaking my head.

I love the possessiveness they have for me, might even crave it.

I consider calling Tate and asking him to come to the bonfire, but I don't have to because he strolls out of the clubhouse with a lit cigarette between his lips. He looks so fucking good, and I think I need a repeat of what we did in the clubhouse the other night.

"Fuck, darlin'," Axel murmurs, no doubt my scent is perfuming more than I'd like right now. *Stupid Omega pheromones, always giving me away.*

I squirm in his lap. "I can't help it that everyone in my pack is really hot."

"But I'm the hottest. It's okay, you can admit it," Axel counters, and I push his shoulder.

"You're all equally attractive in my eyes," I reply, and I truly mean it. Each of them is handsome and lovely in their own way, and they're each mine.

"I can feel your need down the bond, little Omega," Tate teases, leaning down and placing a kiss on my lips.

"Well, are you three going to do something about it, or are we going to sit by this fire all night?" I ask with a smirk.

"That's it, let's go home then," Axel orders.

Tate takes a step back as Axel scoops me up.

"You don't have to carry me," I chastise, even though I totally want him to carry me.

"I'll carry my bride wherever I please, thank you very much."

"She's also our Omega," Tate reminds Axel impatiently, pointing to Cash and himself.

"Semantics. Y'all better hurry up if you don't want to be locked out of the bedroom," Axel jokes as he runs away with me in his arms. I laugh frantically as I wrap my arms around his neck and look back at the rest of my pack.

My fucking pack.

I'm so in love, and I don't want to ever hide it. The world could change in the blink of an eye, and it's important to hold onto what's important in life. Sometimes the road traveled is painful, but this one was worth it.

I went from being nobody's darlin' to having my dream pack and building the life I always wanted for myself. So I don't plan on wasting a second of this new life I've found.

The road ahead isn't going to be easy. Who knows what tomorrow is going to bring, but I choose to live in this moment with my chosen family, surrounded with love. The Dead Palms' future is unpredictable, but I think we all know it's something worth fighting for.

FORTY-NINE
EPILOGUE

LILY

THE ISSUE with traveling with three bikers is the limited amount of space you have when packing for a trip. Cash was the one who had to bite the bullet and add the pull-along cargo trailer to his bike.

He's pissed about it but doesn't complain as he tows all of our shit, and I ride on the back of Tate's bike.

I make a note to treat Cash extra special when we get to our hotel tonight. Luckily, New Orleans is only a little under six hours away. We've stopped each hour to stretch our legs and for me to switch whose bike I ride on the back of.

I squeeze my arms around Tate and rest my chin on his shoulder. I love riding with each one of them, but Tate is the most touchy-feely when I'm on his bike. I swear it's an aphrodisiac for him, not that we really need much help in that department.

We're nearly in the city and stopped at a stoplight when he rubs on my thighs. I accidentally bump my helmet against his, and he curses.

"Stupid fuckin' helmet," he complains.

Legally, he doesn't have to wear one while we're home, but he does through the states we're riding through. I wish he would wear one all the time, but he's been a pain in the ass about it. Axel at least wears one when I ride with him, but I've caught him more than once not wearing it when he's out with the club.

We pull up to the hotel, the guys parking their bikes before I hop off. Somehow the humidity is even worse here, and it slaps me in the face as I remove my helmet.

Tate removes his helmet as well to reveal his dark hair sticking out in all different directions. I grin as I attempt to smooth it down. Time certainly hasn't changed how attractive I find him; if anything, my attraction has only increased the more memories we make with each other.

He leans down and places a soft kiss against my lips.

It takes my breath away, and I have to hold it together. Hotel sex is for later. We have plans. It's the first time we've been able to get away. It's long overdue, but I don't want to miss a second.

"Let's get checked in," Cash suggests, taking my hand and walking toward the hotel. "Pack Valor," he states to the hostess once we reach the reception desk.

"Yes, I have you booked in one of our pack suites. One double king, is that correct?"

"Yes," Cash confirms and pulls out his ID and credit card, handing it to the woman.

She's professional, and I can tell everyone is grateful for that. The last thing I need to do is start this trip out with a jealous fiasco. We'd planned this trip, not realizing how close to my heat it would be, but we didn't want to reschedule.

That doesn't mean certain nesting behaviors aren't plaguing me. I shove them down, though; we need this trip, and we're planning on being home well before my heat actually starts.

The hostess hands Cash three room cards, and I try to not be offended. Of course, I won't be roaming around without my pack, but damn, I should get my own fucking key card.

"Can we get one more card, please?" Cash asks.

He just gets it. *God, I love him.* If one of my Alphas got a reward for knowing what I needed at all times, he would absolutely be the recipient.

Cash hands me the card, and I hold on to it like it's something precious. I suppose it is. I've never actually stayed at a hotel before. I'm in awe as we walk through the lobby, passing a counter with a sign that states *free cookies.* Axel grabs a handful, handing me one as soon as we get in the elevator.

"Are you excited for dinner?" Axel asks.

"Almost as excited as I am for the ghost tour," I reply.

"We're gonna have a great time," my Beta says with a kiss to my head.

I'm so full of excitement I can hardly contain it as the elevator opens and we make our way down the hall to our suite.

Cash opens the door, and it's gorgeous. I mean, I suppose I don't have anything to compare it to, but the decor is a sharp white and deep purples. The bathroom is massive, but that doesn't compare to the absolute obscenely large bed in the middle of the room.

"Holy shit," I whisper.

Tate grabs me by the waist and flings me onto the mattress, making me giggle wildly. He grins and follows me onto the bed.

I love seeing him smile and how happy I make him. He's not my sad Alpha anymore; he's my strong one. He shoulders the weight of being the head Alpha of our pack and being president of the club with so much grace.

"You better stop lookin' at me like that, darlin', or we won't leave this room," Tate threatens.

"There's no way that can happen. Muffuletta was promised to me, and I'm not touching anyone's penis until one of those sandwiches is in my mouth."

"That's just mean, Lily," Axel groans from where he stands by the window.

I shrug and let myself soak up the luxury that is this giant bed.

"We're going to grab all of our shit so we can change and head out soon," Cash says.

He leans down and kisses my cheek like he won't be back in just a few short minutes. And of course, since he gave me a kiss, Axel follows up with one before they leave. They always kiss my cheek over my scar, though there really isn't much of one anymore. I'm grateful for that, even though I know it's there. It's just nice not to have to see it every time I look in the mirror.

The hotel door clicks, and Tate's hand comes up to cup the back of my neck.

"You like it?"

"I love it. This is great."

"Good, I'm sorry it took so long," he sighs, and I can see guilt rearing its ugly head.

"Hey, none of that. You built me the house of my dreams and created a club worth being proud of. I'm happy, Tate; truly, fucking happy, and you're a huge part of that."

"I know. I just didn't think it would take actual years before we felt like we could get time away from the club," he grumbles.

"Rome wasn't built in a day. You needed time to make sure you built a club you could trust, and you did just that. I'm proud to be your bonded, and we have all the time in the world to travel together."

"You're really happy? Even though we spend most of our time on the compound?" he asks.

"Yes, I'm really, truly happy. Plus, it's not a hardship when I'm actually part of the community, you know? Before, I was tucked away and not a part of the club. My life is full, Tate. This is just a bonus."

"Now that Doc has really stepped up, I want to be able to take you out more," he says.

"I'd love that," I tell him, wiggling closer to him.

Fuck the sandwich. I need to prove how happy I am.

The hotel door clicks open, and Axel quickly drops our stuff onto the ground.

"Oh, are we fuckin' instead of goin' out to eat now?" he asks with a smirk.

"No, we're eating first," I scold playfully, pulling away from Tate.

"I'll eat you first, darlin'," Axel counters with a wink.

I genuinely consider his offer, and he knows it as he smirks back at me.

"No, we're getting food. If we get started now, we won't leave the hotel tonight, and we only have a few days as is," Cash interjects. I smile at him, loving that he's our travel dad.

"Fine, *Dad*, ruin our fun," Axel complains, causing Cash to roll his eyes.

Axel loves calling him that and getting under his skin. While Tate might be the one in charge of the club and making a lot of decisions, Cash keeps us grounded, and we truly need it. Because if Axel and I are alone, I'm definitely susceptible to his impulsive ideas. Like the time he thought it was too hot outside, and we made a giant slip-n-slide on the back hill of the compound. I scraped my knee, and you would have thought I had a mortal wound with the way Tate and Cash reacted. I won't lie, the slide was fun as hell.

All in all our balance is perfect. It's taken time for everyone to find their place in the pack, but we've only gotten closer as time goes on. There are still bouts of jealousy when it comes to my time, but we work on it as a unit, each and every one of us would do anything for one another.

I'm so fucking lucky.

Tate groans and shifts in his pants. "We gotta get the fuck out of here."

"Sorry," I whisper, knowing my emotions are getting all lovey-dovey. Usually, once that starts, the horny thoughts happen next.

I will not think about how good they all look right now, or how badly I want them to all come inside of me one after another while wearing their cuts.

"Christ, Lily. You're not helping," Cash complains.

"Okay, okay. Let me just get changed and we'll go."

I MOAN AROUND THE SANDWICH; it's honestly life-changing. My mates don't seem to agree, as they all glare at me due to the noises I'm making while I eat.

I shrug and take another large mouthful. They can deal with my erotic noises while I eat the best sandwich I've had in my entire life.

We're seated on the outside patio of the restaurant and people are walking up and down the street. A woman is carrying this massive frozen cocktail, and I can't help but to stare.

"I'm going to need one of those before the tour," I announce, pointing to her drink.

"That thing is as big as you," Cash argues.

"Mmm, I think I'm well acquainted with large things by now. I want one."

"I knew you would be like this on vacation," Axel comments with a laugh.

"Like what?" I ask.

I'm un-lady-like as I shove the sandwich in my mouth, but God it's good.

"Like money doesn't exist on vacation," he replies with a laugh, and my cheeks heat.

"Oh, I mean, I don't want—"

"He's fuckin' with you, darlin'. You can have whatever you want," Tate cut me off, and I hide behind my sandwich.

I still make soaps in my free time, but I mostly live off of the guys' income. None of them would let me spend the money I had saved from Marielli's Mass. Cash was adamant that I save it so that I would always have it and never feel stressed. But the truth is, I know I don't need it. I'm just waiting for the next big thing I really want, then I'm going to spend it all.

"Vacation is the time to splurge; plus, the situation at the club is really good," Cash encourages.

He's not wrong, a lot has changed in the last two years, things—people—none of us could have planned for.

"I was just jokin'. Our girl can have whatever she wants, especially on vacation," Axel corrects.

My need to fuck with him after his joke is high as I smirk at him.

"Oh, can I finally go get a professional massage?"

All three of them say no at the same time.

"Even if it's a lady?" I complain.

"I'll work on my form," Axel counters, and I shake my head at him.

The massages he gives me always end up with a happy ending. Not that I'm complaining, but I also am.

I'm completely stuffed by the time we finish our meal, and I almost regret getting the biggest drink I could order, but it was on principle. The take-home plastic container is shaped like a naked woman's body, and I'm obsessed with it.

I hum around the straw as the strawberry pina-colada mix slides down my throat.

"You don't have to drink all of it," Cash points out.

"Do any of you want a sip?" I ask, holding it out.

All three of my pack mates stare at me like I'm crazy. Watching them sip from this massive straw while wearing their big-bad-biker cuts would have made my night.

One of them has a hand on me at all times as we meet up with our tour and learn the history of the French Quarter as well as the speculated hauntings. It might spook me more than I'd like to admit, but this place is definitely fucking haunted.

The great thing about having three massive bikers as your

pack is that absolutely no one fucks with you. We walk through large crowds with a wide berth and not a single soul tries to speak to us.

While Cash is the biggest in the pack, Axel and Tate are also very good at intimidating people. I'm not sure why I like it so much; the idea that these three rough-around-the-edges men become soft for only me makes me feel gooey. I can't help myself, and I just stop every few steps to mark one of them up with my scent. That sentiment goes both ways with our possessiveness over one another.

Axel is buying some Roman Candy that I just had to have as a woman approaches him. Out of all my pack mates, people should know he's taken. He's wearing a wedding ring for Christ's sake.

The woman is about to open her mouth when Tate curses beside me, and I tug him along, going to stand next to Axel.

She acts like I don't exist.

"Is your motorcycle here? I'd love to see you ride," she slurs drunkenly.

I don't care if she's had three naked-lady frozen drinks. You do not talk to a married man like that. Axel goes to speak, but I step in front of him.

"No, it's not."

She looks past me to Axel, like I didn't just speak directly to her.

"I'm in town for two more days. Let me give you my number."

"Bitch, do you wanna d—" Tate covers my mouth and glares down at the woman.

"I think you best be goin' now," Axel dismisses her, hardly even looking at her.

I like that.

"Let's get you back to the room," Tate suggests.

And I nod, because I don't really know how to fight. I am all bark and no bite. Plus, my feet are sore, and I'm so tired of carrying around this giant drink.

Part of me is still angry as we walk back to the hotel, which I really hope is not haunted. No, it seems far too new to be haunted.

"Such a jealous little thing, isn't she?" Axel chuckles, amusement shining in his eyes as he wraps his arms around my waist and we head up the elevator.

"Oh, leave me alone. It's not like any of you wouldn't do the same thing. You're all just so scary-looking that no one would be stupid enough to approach me."

"You're right, baby girl," Cash agrees.

I smile at him, remembering that he deserves a reward for having to be the one to trailer all our shit on this trip.

I lick my lips, and he smiles at me. I love it when Cash smiles, mostly because I'm the only one who ever receives them, and Winnie. I'm really working on not being so jealous of the fucking dog, but sometimes when he praises her for doing a trick, I can't help myself. It's pathetic, I know.

My perfume wafts in the small elevator, and all of my mates go on high alert.

I might be tired, but I'm never too tired to be with my pack.

FIFTY

EPILOGUE

AXEL

I PROBABLY SHOULDN'T GET off on Lily getting pissed off on my behalf, but I'm just a man, after all.

I could have shut that woman down immediately, but Lily threatening her life makes me kinda hard.

I am who I am.

She's perfuming like crazy in the elevator, making both Tate and Cash groan. Since I'm the only one who isn't controlled by my pheromones, I just soak in her scent and grind myself against her backside.

As soon as the elevator opens, we're all spilling out and practically running towards our room. Lily is as fuckin' ravenous as they come, and we've spent a lot of time getting to know each other in ways I didn't particularly imagine.

I could, without a doubt, pick Tate and Cash's dicks out from a dick lineup, and I'm not sure how I feel about that information. All I know is we keep Lily satisfied, and I've really come to love watching her get off, whether it's by me or another member of our pack.

It seems like tonight is going to be no different as the room door opens. She immediately jumps into Cash's arms, and he catches her as she wraps her legs around his waist and seals her mouth over his.

Being in a hinge-pack relationship is always interesting since Lily is our main focus. But she's not shy in her desire or love for each and every one of us. I was always worried that the Alphas would come first and that I'd be left behind. That hasn't been the case at all. Lily has a lot to manage with having three pack members, but we all feel loved and give it back in return.

It doesn't stop me from pushing their buttons at every turn, though.

"That's not fair. Where's my kiss?" I ask, faux pouting.

Cash gives me the finger behind Lily's back as she squirms down out of his arms until she's back on her own two feet.

"What do you want, darlin'?" Tate asks her.

She looks between the three of us and licks her lips.

"I really want you all to come inside of me," she says breathlessly.

The three of us give each other a look... that's a very Omega-in-heat answer. Tate acts like he's pushing her hair back, but he's definitely checking her temperature. He smiles and gives us a quick shake of his head.

Thank fuck.

She should still have a few weeks before her heat, but she's been a little touchier than normal the past few days.

"We'll give you whatever you want, but are you gonna take off those clothes and show us what's ours?" I ask her.

She undresses quickly. There's no slow seduction about it. She wants us to fuck her so that she can pass out, and we can do it all over again tomorrow. And we're all absolutely eager to give her what she wants.

We're all still clothed as she looks around at us in hunger. She gets off on being the only one that's naked while we wear our cuts.

"You want your pack to take care of this aching pussy, little Omega?" Tate asks her.

His hand cups her pussy as she presses her ass against his crotch.

"Yes, please," she responds sweetly.

"Always so needy for your pack. God, I'll never get enough," I tell her, getting to my knees in front of her.

Lily is the only fuckin' person who can bring me to my knees. Tate slides his hands up to her breasts as I lick her sweet cunt.

Tate whispers filthy things into her ear as he holds her up. Her thighs are already shaking from the attention I'm giving her pussy.

"You're gonna make a pretty mess all over your Beta's face, aren't you, darlin'?"

She moans, and I have to hold one of her thighs still so that she doesn't buck away from my mouth.

Lily wraps a hand in my hair and holds Tate's arm for stability, but she looks straight ahead. More than likely, Cash is jerking himself off while he watches.

My tongue circles her clit over and over before I take it in between my lips and suck hard. It causes her to shatter, and she trembles in Tate's arms through her release as her sweet slick fills my mouth.

Her nails dig into my scalp as she moans and writhes between the two of us. I pull back slightly, using her thigh to wipe off my face before giving the tender flesh a soft kiss.

"Come here, sweetheart," Cash purrs from the bed, now completely naked. I stand up, watching as Lily crawls up the bed and straddles her Alpha.

There's no teasing or preamble. She just slides down his cock easily with how wet she is.

Both Tate and I follow suit, removing our clothes, and tossing them somewhere in the room. I stroke myself as I watch Lily ride Cash. God, she's fuckin' beautiful when she's being herself.

Her dark hair flows wildly behind her head, and her small tits bounce with each thrust.

I get onto the massive bed, and Tate does the same. We're bracketing each side of her as she rides Cash. The Alpha grabs her hips and takes over, fucking her from the bottom as she strokes us both at the same time.

Her movements are shaky, but I love it when she touches me. She can do whatever the fuck she wants to me.

She pulls up off of Cash, and he groans from the loss of her. So do I when she releases my cock. She slides down Cash's body, kissing his chest before taking his slick-covered length and putting it down her throat.

I'm faster than Tate as I move behind her, grabbing her ass and lining my cock up with her dripping pussy.

She moans as I slide in, causing her to take Cash deeper. Tate lies down next to Cash and she shifts, taking turns sucking each of them down her throat.

Her slurping sounds, along with the way her slick sticks to my skin, have me thrusting into her roughly. Her ass cheeks smack against my pelvis with each stroke.

"Fuck, baby, I'm not gonna last," I grunt behind her.

She hums around one of the guys' cocks, and I don't bother holding back; we all know what she wants.

I fill her up with my cum as my orgasm rocks through my body. A few labored breaths accentuated by my groan indicates my release and a sweet noise of pleasure leaves her as well.

She slides back up Cash's body and places his length back inside her. It seems like Tate is going to have to be the one to wait tonight. I need to get her off again, though, so I dig through my bag and pull out the lightweight vibrator wand.

As soon as I have the device, I take my original position at her side and hold the wand over her pussy while she fucks Cash. She grabs my wrist to hold the wand steady as Cash fucks her from below. Her slick is everywhere, and the room is saturated with her scent.

Lily moans loudly as she reaches her peak. Her hand drops from my wrist as she rides out the waves of her orgasm.

"Fuck," Cash hisses beneath her. "Gonna fill you up, baby girl."

She moans again as Cash picks up his pace to reach his own release. As soon as he does, Lily lets out a satisfied hum before rolling off of him and laying flat on her stomach between Cash and Tate.

Cash kisses her cheek and heads to the shower, while Tate grabs her hips, placing her ass in the air before fucking her from behind.

"This is what you needed? You want me to knot your pack's cum inside of you? Such a dirty, sweet thing for your pack," he pants as he drives into her.

She takes it beautifully, her pretty face pressed against the soft comforter as Tate uses her body in the rough way that she likes.

"Do you want to come again?" Tate asks her.

"Please," Lily responds quietly.

Tate nods at me, and I slide the toy and my hand under her stomach, holding the vibrator against her clit again. She gasps at the sensitivity but doesn't go to push me away or ask me to stop.

Tate's flesh smacks against her own repeatedly and she keens for it as she pushes her ass further against his pelvis.

"God, you look so fuckin' perfect," I praise her as she shudders.

"Such a good Omega, such a perfect pussy," Tate tells her, both of us never tiring of telling her how spectacular she is to us.

Lily fists the sheets, and I turn up the level of the vibrator. The moan that rips out of her throat is loud and feminine as she breaks apart. Her slick covers the toy and Tate as he presses his knot inside of her, making her orgasm last even longer.

Her thighs shake and her breaths come out in heavy pants. I

take the toy away, her body relaxing slightly as she takes Tate's knot, and he finishes inside of her.

As soon as he does, it's like relief washes over her.

Tate and I share a look, and I know both of us are wondering if we should cut this trip short and head back home. Her nesting behavior is getting worse, and the last thing we need is for her to go into heat when we're nearly six hours away from home.

I push her hair away from her face, rubbing her scalp while Tate massages her lower back.

"You good, darlin'?" I ask her.

"More than good," she sighs with a soft smile.

"As soon as this heathen's knot is out of you, I'll take you in the shower."

Tate rolls his eyes and continues working on the muscles of Lily's back. He leans forward, placing some kisses on her shoulder blades, and she eats up the attention.

Cash gets out of the shower and climbs up on the bed. I swear he passes out in under two minutes. I'm not sure where that man learned how to fall asleep so quickly, but I've been jealous of it during Lily's heats.

There's a wet sound, and Lily hums as Tate pulls out of her, a mixture of all of our cum and her slick drip out of her. I grab Cash's towel and hand it to her as she climbs out of the bed, following me to the shower.

I steal all the moments alone with her as I can. Maybe I'm a greedy asshole, but I don't care. I have no issues sharing with Cash and Tate, especially when it comes to sex, but I also need my private time with Lily.

Since Cash was just in the shower, it barely takes any time for the water to heat. I cradle Lily's body next to mine as I hold her upright in the shower. It's nice to just hold her like this sometimes, the soft sounds of water falling behind us and nothing else.

She pulls back and rests her chin against my sternum. I lean down and place a soft kiss on her lips.

"You feelin' okay?" I ask her, pushing her half-damp hair out of her face.

"Yeah, I feel perfect."

"I think we're all just worried you'll go into heat early."

"If I feel anything that seems off, I promise to let you all know. You know I nest for a long time before my heat," she says, and I nod.

"You're right, we just worry."

"And I love you all for it," she replies.

She kisses the tattoo above my heart, the one with her name. We all surprised her last year when we each sat down with Ink and got a tattoo in honor of her. Mine is a snake wrapped around a lily flower. Cash just straight up got her whole name tattooed as large as he could on a vacant spot on his collarbone. Tate's tattoo is on his ribs, a skeletal hand holding a lily flower.

She's a little obsessed with them, and I can tell her having a claim on us is important to her. I also never take off my wedding ring, and she's the same way.

"Love you forever, darlin'," I whisper to her as I massage her hair.

"I love you too."

She rests her head against my chest, and I hold her. I never thought I'd love someone as much as I love Lily, but I'm grateful for it every single fuckin' day.

FIFTY-ONE
EPILOGUE

CASH

ONE OF THE good things about being able to fall asleep so quickly is that I always wake up early. So does Lily, it feels like mornings are our special time together, and I cherish it more than I think she'll ever know.

She's stuck between Tate and Axel as her eyes slowly pop open. She gives me a soft smile as she untangles herself from her other two mates and climbs out of bed.

"Hey," she says in her sleepy, soft voice.

"Hey."

She comes to stand between my legs where I'm sitting, and I pull her close to me. Lily loves being touched; she loves intimacy, and so do I. I never thought I would be one for public displays of affection, or the type of partner who would constantly be wanting to touch my Omega. But with Lily? I just can't get enough.

"Do you want to go get breakfast?" I ask her, knowing full well these two assholes are going to sleep in for at least another few hours.

"Just let me get dressed," she responds, kissing my cheek and heading to the bathroom.

When she comes out, she's wearing shorts and one of her

Dead Palms t-shirts. The back says *property of Pack Valor*, and it's definitely one of my favorites.

I take her hand, and we leave the hotel room quietly so as not to disturb Tate and Axel. Well, that's on her end. Mine is so that they don't wake up and take away my alone time with her.

The sun is still low in the sky as it rises, and we walk hand in hand down the already busy streets until we come across the cafe I had in mind.

She orders a drink that is more milk and sugar than coffee, and I keep it simple with just a splash of milk and one sugar. We order some beignets and two breakfast sandwiches. We agree to get Tate and Axel sandwiches on our way out and bring them back to the room.

The cafe has large open windows that face out toward the street, and we sit down at one of the empty tables near them. It doesn't take long for our drinks and food to come. I keep one hand over the back of her chair as I slowly drink my coffee.

Lily grabs a beignet and takes a large bite, powdered sugar landing on her nose and cheeks. I look over at her with a smile, and she laughs, blowing the sugar right into my face. Which makes her laugh even harder as she tries to swallow her food.

She covers her mouth with her hand as she tries to pull it together. I shake my head, but I can't help grinning at her.

"You got sugar everywhere." I scowl, and she starts laughing again.

Her eyes are watering as she finally calms herself down and looks at me.

"I guess that's what I get for taking such a big bite."

"Do I have any more sugar on me?" I ask.

She smiles and uses her thumb to wipe the excess sugar off my face and shirt.

"It was really good though. You should have one."

I grab one of the pastries and place it on my plate, appeasing her. Thank God Tate and Axel aren't here. The last thing I need is for them to make fun of me as I try to eat this ridiculous powdered sugar treat.

Lily stares at me, waiting for me to take a bite, so I give in. Picking the piece up with two fingers, I place it in my mouth.

It's actually really fucking good.

Lily's smile is knowing as she watches me eat.

"Really freaking good, isn't it?" she asks.

I wipe my mouth and nod as I continue to chew.

"Right, as always," I say.

"Hmm, what's the saying? Happy wife, happy life?"

"Happy Omega, happy life," I say back to her, and she smirks.

She leans against my shoulder slightly, and I swear her head feels a little warm.

"How you feeling, baby?"

"Good, we have the swamp-boat thing today, and I'm not missing it."

"Of course not," I reply.

But I have a feeling by tonight, we're going to be headed home.

Fuck.

It's taken nearly two years before everything felt safe enough on the compound to leave, and when we finally do, it seems like she might be going into heat early. I wrap my arm around her and squeeze tight. I'll be keeping a watchful eye over her to make sure she's okay. The second I think she might be slipping, we're hauling ass back to Tallahassee.

I SIT in the back of the airboat with Lily, while Axel and Tate sit up front. Both of them bitched about the circumstances. But if I'm sacrificing anyone to get eaten by an alligator on this fucking ride, it's them.

I truly didn't even want to do this, but it was on Lily's list as one of the top things she wanted to do. We all have on headsets with the communication line open. The headset nearly dwarfs Lily's face.

The idea of spending the day in the swamp didn't appeal to me. But it's absolutely worth it as Lily laughs with glee when the boat picks up speed, whipping around the water.

She holds onto my arm as the driver trails through the water. This is why I was adamant about being the one to sit next to her. Meanwhile, Tate and Axel have to hold on to the side bars so they aren't bumping into each other every time the driver makes a sharp turn.

At one point, the driver pulls over to the side, and we see five alligator heads poking out of the water.

"Oh, hell no. It's time to go home," I complain, but Lily just grabs my arm harder and laughs.

The captain goes on about the wildlife, the alligator population in the bayou, and the laws for hunting said alligators.

The captain even throws a few pieces of meat into the water, and I watch in horror as the alligators fight over it.

Someone get me off this fucking boat.

"It's not like they can get you, you're fine," Lily reassures.

"I think this is at the top of the list of the most ridiculous shit I've done for you," I tell her.

She gives me a smirk, knowing I've murdered for her. It just always goes unsaid. It's better that way.

The boat thankfully starts up again and we leave the fuckin' ancient dinosaurs behind us.

The airboat whips and weaves as we continue our journey. Now and then the captain points out wildlife or certain areas. I pretty much tune it all out, ready to get back to civilization. I'd much rather do the cemetery tour than this shit. It's not so much the swamp part, but the fucking animal part. I have no issues with fast vehicles on land or water. But just knowing there are alligators everywhere sets me on edge.

"Who knew alligators were the thing that would take you out, Cash?" Axel teases.

"Maybe I should throw you off," I snap back.

"Then Lily would be sad and never forgive you."

"It's true," Lily says with a shrug.

"It might be worth the risk," I reply.

Tate laughs and grabs Axel's arm, pretending to push him off the side. A small shout leaves him as the rest of us laugh. *Serves him fucking right.*

THE BOAT finally pulls back up to the dock, and we make our way back on land. Though it still doesn't feel safe where we are. That's the thing about alligators being able to live on land and in the water. I don't like it one fucking bit.

Our next stop is some hole in the wall restaurant. Thankfully, they have outdoor seating, and we pick a table as we get our menus.

"You gonna try the alligator balls?" Axel taunts, and I kick him under the table.

"I believe it was you who screamed like a little bitch on the boat ride, not Cash," Tate comments.

"You were trying to push me off, you ass."

"Still, you were the only one who screamed," Tate says.

"We could go again and switch seats. See how Cash does in the lower front row," Axel argues.

"I think one boat ride is enough," Lily interjects, playing mediator as she looks down at her menu. She seems a little out of it as she reads.

"Darlin', you good?" Tate questions.

When she looks up from her menu, she says, "I think... maybe I'm just hungry."

We share a look around the table, and she proceeds to scold us.

"Okay, enough. You all act like I'm a ticking time bomb. If I don't feel right, I'll tell you. Christ."

We're all completely told off as we order our food and eat. As much as this place might seem like a shithole, the food is delicious.

When we're done, Lily seems a little tired. All of us try to act inconspicuously as we monitor her every movement.

"Maybe we can go to the room for a quick nap?" she asks.

"Whatever you want, baby girl," I tell her.

She rides on the back of Axel's bike on the way to the hotel, and she's quiet as we walk up to the room.

As soon as she gets inside, she takes nearly every pillow on the bed to make a soft area for herself. She doesn't even notice what she's doing, and she falls asleep right away.

"Fuck, we're gonna need to pack our shit and get ready to go home," Tate states.

I can tell he feels guilty, a lot of the club decisions ride on his shoulders and that's why we haven't gone on a trip until now.

"She'll be fine. We can make it up to her with another trip," Axel reassures.

"We were supposed to have two more days. Her heat wasn't supposed to start for, like, another two weeks," Tate complains.

"When has anything in our pack gone according to plan?" I ask.

"Fuckin' never. It's bullshit."

He's not wrong. It feels like anytime we plan something, it always gets fucked up. But truly, Lily is safe. We're taking good care of her, and that's all that really matters.

"I'll pack up our shit and get my bike ready," I tell them.

They pack their own stuff up, and I take it all downstairs, getting everything in order. We're all nervous about when she wakes up and how she'll handle the news. None of us want her to feel like we're telling her what to do, even though we are. A lot of times when she's nearing her heat she is the last to know, but all of us have picked up on the telltale signs.

When I make my way back to the room, she's awake and blinking wildly at us. She holds the blanket to her chest and sighs.

"We're going home, aren't we?" she asks.

The disappointment is palpable.

"We gotta get you home and safe, darlin'," Tate says softly.

Lily nods her head in resignation.

"I just wanted more time here with you guys. I guess, I didn't want to face that it was coming," she admits with tears welling in her bright eyes, breaking all our fucking hearts.

"Hey, as soon as we can, we'll go to Myrtle Beach," I offer.

She laughs and wipes a tear from her face. "You said it was a shithole."

"A hellhole. But a hellhole you haven't been to nonetheless," I correct.

"You promise?"

"I promise," I reply.

"We can always come back here, too. It's not a long ride. I told you, we'll be gettin' you out more. But right now, we need to get you safe, and that means going home and getting your pretty ass in your nest," Tate rationalizes.

"Ugh, okay," she sighs.

"She should ride on the back of my bike for a while, we don't want to set her off bein' with one of you," Axel suggests.

I want to roll my eyes, knowing he wants as much time with her as he can steal, but he has a fucking point.

"Fine," I grumble.

"Shit's all packed up. Let's get you home," Axel says.

She looks around the room one more time, and I can tell she's disappointed that our trip is being cut short.

"We'll make it up to you, I promise," I repeat with a kiss to the side of her head.

"I know, at least we got some time here," she sighs, and it's a gut punch. We just got here yesterday.

"Let's get goin' then. Come on, darlin'," Axel says, taking her hand and leading her out of the hotel to his bike.

WE'VE BEEN on the road for nearly four hours, and at least we're in Mississppi, but Axel has us pulling over. We all follow suit and park at the nearest gas station.

"What's up?" Tate asks.

Lily hops off the back of Axel's bike, tossing her helmet and making her dark hair spill over her shoulders before she begins to pace.

"Lily, sweetheart?" I ask her.

"I just… I gotta… can you take the edge off?" she asks me.

The thing is, there's really no taking the edge off when a heat starts. Me giving in now could mean she fully spirals into her heat. But there's also no way she can sit on the back of a bike for another two hours in pain.

I take off my helmet but don't get off my bike.

"Come here," I tell her, and she immediately listens.

Axel and Tate get off their bikes and make a barrier between where I am with Lily and where someone could walk by.

I grab her chin and look at her face. Her pupils are dilated, but she's not fully in heat. Although, it's coming soon.

"I'm going to play with this pretty pussy and then you're gonna get on the back of Tate's bike so we can get you home. You understand?"

She bites her lip and nods her head.

"You know how fucking hot you look right now?" I ask because fuck, she looks good in her riding boots, dark denim jeans, and her Dead Palms shirt.

"Mmm," she replies as I unbutton her shorts.

"Are you sure you want to be covered in slick the rest of the way home?" I ask.

That has her pausing.

"For Christ's sake. I'll dig her out some shorts. Tate is big enough to stop anyone from seein' anyway," Axel says.

"Thank you," she calls over her shoulder to him, giving him a smile.

"You better look at me if you want me to touch your pussy, Omega," I warn, and her gaze snaps to mine. "There's my good girl."

I unzip her jeans, having just enough room to slide my hand down into her shorts. She's soaked as my fingers glide through her drenched pussy lips.

"What do you want, baby girl? Fast?"

She nods her head eagerly, and I don't waste any time, sliding my fingers inside of her while my palm rubs against her clit.

"That's it. Come on, coat my hand in your slick. I want to be smelling you the whole ride home. I'm looking forward to knotting this pussy over and over again," I murmur in her ear.

Her hands grip onto me for purchase and even with her shorts on, the wet sound of my hand on her pussy is obscene.

"Give your Alpha what he wants," I command her.

Her nails dig into my skin as cars drive by and patrons pull up to the gas station. But Tate's glare is enough to have them automatically looking the other way.

She moans as she leans over, her head pressed against my chest as her thighs shake, and she crushes my hand between her strong thighs. I use my other hand to cup the back of her head.

"You did so good; do you feel better?"

"A little, yeah. We really need to get home."

I kiss the side of her face and take out my hand. I wipe her slick off on the denim as Axel slides up behind her to help her out of her drenched panties and shorts before putting on fresh clothes.

"Go and get on Tate's bike. No stopping unless you really need to, okay?"

"Okay," she replies softly.

I give her one last kiss as she walks over to Tate. He puts her helmet on, and they mount his bike.

I just hope we can make it home without an incident or one of us dying from being distracted.

FIFTY-TWO
EPILOGUE

TATE

LILY GRINDS on my back almost the whole fuckin' way home.

It's torture.

But somehow I managed to get us home safely. We're inside of the gates and pulling up to our house. I'm happy we chose to build, not only so Lily and I could escape the house we grew up in, but because it shows I could provide for my pack.

Our home is all the way in a private part of the compound and is surrounded by oak trees.

"I'm gonna go check on Winnie and Tuck and make sure Shelby and her guys are good with keeping them a few more days," Cash says.

I'm sure it won't be a problem. They love having the dogs over. Honestly, they've become the mascots of the compound.

"I'm going to go get one of the guys to do a food run for us," Axel says.

I hop off the bike and Lily tosses her helmet on the ground but doesn't get off.

"Well, it looks like I've got you all to myself, darlin'," I tease her.

A slow smirk takes over her face, and she holds her arms

out. I quickly wrap my arms around her and pick her up, carrying her into the house.

"About time you got to use your new nest, don't you think?" I ask her.

Her nest is on the first floor, in the back of the house. We built it without any windows since a basement was out of the question.

The bed is on the floor, and I place her softly against the light blue sheets she chose.

"Turn on the soft lights," she requests.

I do just that, turning on the warm, white lights that trail along the trim of the ceiling.

She scrunches her nose.

"It doesn't smell like us anymore," she complains.

"You want me to change that for you?" I smirk at her.

While lucid-Lily is a huge fan of having clothed sex with me, heat-Lily wants everyone naked the whole time. So I automatically start undressing and tossing my clothes into the hamper on the left.

She appreciates my body as she looks me up and down before holding her hands in the air. I take the non-verbal cue and remove her shirt and then her bra. I can't help but kiss the soft flesh of her chest as she plops back onto the soft comforter.

Everything screams soft femininity in here, and I hate to admit how much I like it. It's perfect and gentle, just like Lily is.

"You know one of these days I'm gonna convince you to let me get you pregnant during your heat."

"Mmm," she hums.

"I'll time it just right, so I can come inside of you as many times as humanly possible and knot you to make sure it's mine," I trail on.

I don't know why, but her heat always fucking does this to me.

I unbutton her shorts and tug them over her hips along with

her panties. I toss them somewhere in the room and move back up her body. Her perfume fills the room as I cup her face.

"Are you goin' to make me and this room smell like you? Such a good Omega. Mark your Alpha with your scent," I praise her.

I lean down, sucking on her bond mark, and it sends her over the edge.

Her hands tangle in my hair as she presses her lips against mine. She's rough, and her skin is scorching hot.

She whimpers as her abdomen clenches.

"Don't worry, I'm gonna make it go away," I promise.

I push right into her dripping pussy. Her muscles spasm against me, and my willpower shatters immediately as I begin to rut into her.

I need to watch myself fuck her, so I pull back, holding her thigh up as I push back into her.

"You look so perfect wrapped around my cock."

My dick comes out wetter each time I thrust into her, and the room smells like coconut, making me shiver.

Her small hand glides down her body, and she plays with her clit while I fuck her. I almost come on the spot, but I hold it together.

"Fuck, darlin'. You gonna come for me before I give you my knot?"

She pants, nodding her head frantically, her fingers working at a faster pace. Her walls clench around me, and I moan as I continue to drive into her.

I can't hold my knot back any longer, and I push deep inside of her, a shiver tingling down my spine as she takes me. We're locked into place as I continue to fuck her until my hips stutter, and I groan. My grip on her thigh is brutal as I finish inside of her.

She's shaking with her own orgasm beneath me as we both breathe heavily before I lean over on top of her.

Her arms and legs wrap around me, like no amount of skin

touching skin will be enough. I cradle her head in my arms and push her hair away from her face. Her brown eyes are half-lidded and dreamy as I kiss her again.

"God, I love you so fuckin' much," I confess.

She smiles and unconsciously rubs the tattoo on my side, which I had gotten just for her. I pet her hair and kiss her face as we wait for my knot to go down. The guys should be back at any moment. I know it's going to be a long few days. Lily doesn't like it when any of us leave the room. But we put a daybed on the other side of the room so we could try to get more sleep during her heat.

Not that I really care if I get much sleep. Being there for her when she needs us is truly the most important thing.

Cash is the first one to get back. He automatically sheds his clothing and sets them in the corner before joining us on the bed. Lily's fingers trail his collarbone, looking at her tattoo. Her gaze drops to his forearm, where he currently has his memorial tattoo covered up with a large bandaid.

Lily feels a lot of guilt over that when she's not in heat, but Cash is good about covering it when she's in this state. Her first stint of throwing shit out of a window might be the other reason we didn't put any windows in her new nest.

"Hey, baby girl, how are you feeling?" he asks her.

Her pussy clenches around me and my knot, making me groan, and I rest my forehead against her neck.

"That good, huh? I'll give you what you need next," he says.

Axel comes in next, undressing himself like it's heat proto-col, and gets on the bed.

It should be weird how comfortable we've gotten around each other, but it's what a pack does. There are no secrets or clothes between us.

Axel comes to her other side, and she looks so completely fucking happy. I can't help but pepper her face with kisses, enjoying my moment with her and our pack.

I never thought life would ever be as enjoyable as it is now. I didn't know what I thought when I stepped foot back on this compound, but finding my reason to live wasn't what I expected.

This is my club, my pack, and I'm beyond fuckin' blessed.

A Few Months Later

I sit in the sand, feeling uncomfortable as fuck in a bathing suit as I watch Axel chase Lily with a handful of seaweed.

Cash hands me a beer, and I pop the top as both of us watch them.

"It's not as much of a hellhole as I thought," he states.

I laugh and shake my head.

"To be fair, we did see a woman giving a blow job by the dumpsters last night after dinner."

"That's true, and don't forget the amount of shit we've seen on this beach," Cash replies.

We watch as this couple walks by; the man is holding the woman around her waist, making out with her neck while he grinds his junk against her back.

"We don't ever look like that, right?" I ask with a grimace.

"Definitely fucking not, and if we ever do, shoot me in the fucking head," Cash grunts.

Lily comes running back over to our area, and I notice her shoulders getting a little red.

"Come here, darlin'," I tell her, and she ducks under the umbrella. Her cute tits are nearly in my face from the way she's bent over.

I swear I could've killed multiple men for even glancing in her direction. *But that would ruin the vacation.*

"What's up?"

"Your shoulders look a little red."

She sits down in front of me, her hair already in a messy bun as I grab the lotion and start massaging it into her skin. She moans, and the last thing I need is to be getting a hard-on while wearing a fuckin' swimsuit.

Axel takes his seat and grabs a beer from the cooler as we watch the waves crash against the shore, and the... *unique* people around us.

A petite woman in a bikini holding flyers walks up to Cash and is about to hand him the flyer, but Lily bats it away.

"Oh, sorry. My name is Jenn. We have a beach party going on later tonight. I just wanted to invite you all."

"We're good," Lily says.

"I could give you guys my number if you change your mind," Jenn offers.

"We don't have phones," Lily deadpans with a straight face.

"Um, okay. Well, the information is on the flyer if you guys change your mind."

"We won't," Lily snaps.

"Alright then," Jenn tucks the flyers back against her chest and walks away.

Lily scoffs and leans back against my chest.

"Pretty sure she was inviting you too, darlin'," I point out.

"Ick. She kept saying you guys, and she handed the flyer directly to Cash. It doesn't help that you're sauntering all over the beach nearly naked. All your tattoos just glistening in the sun and shit," she sasses, and we all bark out a laugh at the same time.

She tries to get up, but I just squeeze her tighter against me, kissing her all over until she finally gives in and starts laughing with us.

"So, what's the verdict on Myrtle Beach?" I ask.

I don't think we could have asked for a better trip. There have been no issues at home, and it finally felt like we got to relax.

"I'd say it's pretty great. But anywhere with you three would be perfect," she says. "Now, are you two going to get in the water or not?"

"Sharks," is Cash's reply.

"I don't know what's in that water," I retort.

She scoffs and looks over at her Beta. "Axel?"

"Yeah, come on, darlin'."

They head back toward the water and my head tries to wrap around what I did to deserve this life. Sometimes I'll give myself some credit; I worked hard to make the club what it is today, but when it comes to Lily, that's all her.

Without her, we wouldn't have any of this.

She runs out to the water, holding hands with Axel, and it really sinks in that this is my pack forever.

I'm one lucky motherfucker.

ALSO BY SARAH BLUE

Want more Liv and her guys? Check out Omega's Obsession by Sarah Blue

Other works by Sarah Blue

Pucked Up Omegaverse

One Pucked Up Pack

Don't Puck With My Heart

Puck Around & Find Out - Date TBD

Heat Haven Omegaverse

Heat Haven

Omega's Obsession

Protector's Promise

Too Tempting

Heat Haven Holidays

Want to take a walk on the paranormal side?

Charming Your Dad

Charming the Devil

<u>Charming as Hell</u>

The Carlson Brothers - Contemporary Romance

Swallow Your Pride

Forget Your Morals - Coming 2024

ACKNOWLEDGMENTS

Leisha – You really pushed me to keep writing this one and to really bring out my inner theatrics. You've become one of my biggest cheerleaders and I truly can't thank you enough for being there for me through this book.

Nikki – You always help me elevate scenes and push me to make things even better than they are. Thank you for reading the madness as it's written.

Lindsay – Without Lindsay the dog would have gotten forgotten. Thank you for reading as I wrote and for keeping track of Winnie.

Jessica – Editing superwoman, thank you for all that you do and being so amazing with me for this release.

Sandra – Your daily updates with GIFs and images while reading truly bring me so much joy. The cover you created is everything and I'm obsessed with the compound map. I'm not sure how you keep outdoing yourself.

Sam – I'm truly in my angst era and your support truly helps me get better with each book.

Kim – Thank you for your attention to detail and reading this in its last stages and for just being such a supportive person.

Stephanie – Thank you for continuing to be the slickest omega reader I've ever met. You little hyphenating hound.

Kaylah, Ava, Delanie, and Kristen – Thank you for reading through this book and using your experiences to ensure that Cash was a well-rounded and properly depicted character. I can't express how much I appreciate your time and effort.

Kassie - For all the encouragement and love and hoping on this early to double check for any issues.

Val – Thank you for being my PA and any attempts in trying to tame the chaos.

ARC Team – Thank you for sticking with me and your time for not only reading Nobody's Darlin' but for posting your review and sharing content. I wouldn't be here without you.

Jax Teller, Chibs, and Juice – You created the monster and now you have to live with it.

Gemma Teller – Please don't kill me.

ABOUT THE AUTHOR

Sarah Blue writes contemporary sweet omegaverse, erotic, why choose romances. She loves romance in nearly any genre. When she isn't writing you can find her nose buried in a book or lit up from her kindle. She loves the sweeter side of romance and creating interesting characters while adding adventure and spice. Writing strong female characters and male characters willing to show weakness is something that makes her gooey on the inside.

Sarah lives in Maryland with her husband, two sons, and two annoying cats. If she isn't reading or writing she is probably working on a craft project or scrolling on Tik Tok.

www.authorsarahblue.com
@sarahblueauthor on Instagram and TikTok
Sarah Blue's Reader Group on Facebook

www.ingramcontent.com/pod-product-compliance
Lightning Source LLC
Chambersburg PA
CBHW061851310726
48972CB00004B/980